ROOT
CAUSE

ROOT CAUSE

A Novel

STEVEN LAINE

TURNER PUBLISHING COMPANY

Turner Publishing Company
Nashville, Tennessee

www.turnerpublishing.com

Root Cause

This is a work of fiction. All the characters and events portrayed in this book are either products of the author's imagination or are used fictitiously.

Cover design: Maddie Cothren
Book design: Tim Holtz

Library of Congress Cataloging-in-Publication Data
Names: Laine, Steven, 1975- author.
Title: Root cause / by Steven Laine.
Description: Nashville, TN : Turner Publishing Company, 2019 | Description based on print version record and CIP data provided by publisher; resource not viewed.
Identifiers: LCCN 2018022449 (print) | LCCN 2018030506 (ebook) | ISBN 9781684422616 (ebook) | ISBN 9781684422593 (pbk.) | ISBN 9781684422609 (hard cover)
Subjects: | GSAFD: Suspense fiction.
Classification: LCC PR9199.4.L3385 (ebook) | LCC PR9199.4.L3385 R66 2019 (print) | DDC 813/.6–dc23
LC record available at https://lccn.loc.gov/2018022449

9781684422593 Paperback
9781684422609 Hardcover
9781684422616 eBook

Printed in the United States of America
17 18 19 20 10 9 8 7 6 5 4 3 2 1

Sparkling like Champagne and bold like Corvina;
Big thanks to my sister Tor, you're A-Okay.

CHAPTER 1

TUSCANY, ITALY

"Worst winery in Italy: Visited here for the first time but will never go back. Only thing worse than the wine was the winemaker, who was rude and unhelpful. Would not recommend this place to anyone!"

"Bad winery, worse wine: We visited Donatelli Winery over the weekend. We almost drove right by but decided to stop in. I wish we hadn't. The grounds were unkempt, the buildings dilapidated, and the winery is poorly set up for visitors. Chairs anyone? Since we were already there, my husband and I decided to at least try the wines. No surprise that they tasted terrible. We ended up pouring them straight into the spittoon. The water was the only thing worth drinking. Give this one a miss."

"Beautiful view, but not much else: Go here for the beautiful view of the Italian countryside, but don't linger. The grounds, wine, and winemaker are enough to put you off wine forever."

"Not impressed!: The employee who 'took care' of us looked like he hated his life and his job. The service was terrible, and the wines just as bad. We later found out the employee was actually the winemaker. If he doesn't care about this establishment, why should we? With so many great wines to taste in Italy and so many beautiful wineries to visit in this area, why would anyone go here?"

Corvina Guerra set her espresso down and shook her head in disbelief. She read one terrible review of the winery and its wines after another. There were over four hundred online reviews, all of them unfavorable. And those were just the ones written in English. The Spanish and Italian reviews she read were just as damning and even more colorful. She cringed each time she read of another disappointed reviewer's experience. It wasn't hard for her to guess what was wrong with the winery and its wines, but the online reviews told her only one side of the story.

Taking advantage of the free Wi-Fi in the café she had stopped at en route to Donatelli Winery, she finished reading the last of the reviews on her iPad and paid for her coffee.

A ten-minute drive in her rental car along narrow country lanes brought her to the winery of ill repute. Tall, conical trees cast late morning shadows along the route. She pulled in, unsure of what to expect. A quaint Italian villa and a kindly old man were not what she anticipated. The winery owner, Marco Donatelli, was waiting and opened the car door for her. She looked up into a weathered but warm face, etched with wrinkles and a smile that was welcoming and sad at the same time. Thick white hair trimmed short accentuated his receding hairline. He wore faded blue jeans and a beige collared shirt with the sleeves rolled up, revealing tanned forearms. She pegged his age as about the same as her father, who had recently turned sixty.

"*Prego, Signor Donatelli,*" she said after stepping out of the car. "I'm Corvina—we spoke on the phone." She shook his hand and felt the same rough skin she had felt on winemakers' hands around the world. Years of farming and physical toil left a mark. She loosened her scarf—a bright, floral-print silk she had picked up on her last visit to Paris—and took in her surroundings.

"Corvina, thank you for coming. Please, call me Marco. Your father and I have known each other since we were boys. I'm sorry it has taken us this long to meet . . . and under such circumstances," the winery owner said. He seemed to struggle with the last few words.

Her father had called her out of the blue and asked if she could drop by his friend's winery because he was having "quality issues." Despite her hectic schedule as a flying winemaker and the fact that she normally didn't consult out of the purview of her employer, Universal Wines, she was between consultations, so she'd reluctantly agreed.

She followed Marco toward a rustic two-story home. He offered her a seat on a dark-green wrought iron bench. Layers of paint were evident in areas where it was flaking off. The view from the bench was stunning; she looked out onto a sun-drenched vineyard stretching off into the horizon. The obvious lack of pruning among the vines detracted from the view and further signaled to her that all was not right at the winery.

"I read some of the online reviews of your wines and winery. They are not kind," Corvina said.

"That's an understatement," Marco said, and joined her on the bench. "Damn social media. Unfortunately, the problems persist. Despite the best efforts from my winemaker, the reviews haven't improved and my sales continue to plummet."

Corvina held back from commenting that the winemaker seemed to be the *cause* of the problems; he was, therefore, unlikely to contribute a *solution.*

"Well, I'd like to start with touring your facilities. Afterward, we can taste the wines themselves." She glanced over at the winery, eager to begin.

"*Sì, sì,* of course," Marco said, and looked at his watch.

"Is now still a good time?" Corvina asked. It was just past ten in the morning.

"I told Guido to meet us here so we could see the winery together."

"Guido?"

"My *star* winemaker," Marco said. The emphasis on "star" led Corvina to believe Marco was not oblivious to the impact his winemaker was having on the winery.

"Forgive me for saying so, but your star winemaker doesn't seem to be popular with your visitors."

"He's been with us for only three years. He tells me it takes time to make great wines and soon my winery's fortunes will turn around—especially with your help. I think you two will make a good team."

Team? What on earth had her father told him? Before Corvina could react to Marco's statement, a car approached and parked behind Corvina's. A lanky man wearing faded jeans and a plaid collared shirt joined them on the porch. A lit cigarette dangled from the corner of his mouth. His face was narrow with angular features, and his pointed chin was darkly tanned and unshaven.

Corvina and Marco both stood up.

"Guido, this is Corvina. She is the flying winemaker I was telling you about," Marco said.

"*Ciao*," Corvina said. She held out her hand to greet the winemaker.

"Well, you're here. Let's get this over with," Guido said. He shook Corvina's extended hand lightly without looking her in the eye. He turned toward the main building of the winery, took another drag of his cigarette, and then dropped it in the gravel.

Corvina glared at Marco, who smiled weakly in return and then turned and followed his winemaker. Watching the men walk away, she had half a mind to return to her car and fly back to Barcelona.

Guido led her and Marco into the winery. Corvina was shocked by the state of the equipment.

"Is this where you make your wine?" she asked, incredulous. She took in everything the bare, flickering incandescent tube lights struggled to illuminate and marveled at the state of the facilities.

"No, it's where my grandmother makes her preserves," Guido said. "Haven't you seen a winery before? I thought you were a winemaker. Don't you recognize wine-making equipment when you see it?"

"This place is filthy. At a glance I can tell you have no hygiene controls in place, and the equipment is ancient. I wouldn't even let my nonna *in* here, never mind to make wine or preserves," Corvina said. She was used to dealing with defensive winemakers.

"What do you know?" Guido asked.

"I know your oak barrels are overused." She pointed to a row of barrels. "How many times do you use them before replacing them?"

"At least five. I do retoast them each time. I'm not a complete idiot."

"I don't doubt it. So why do you think you're getting such poor reviews on your wines?" Corvina asked. She peered into an empty barrel.

"Most of those reviews are about wines made *before* I got here," Guido stated.

"And what about the negative comments on the wines made *since* you arrived?" she asked. She knew full well most had been written in the past three years.

"I'm still finding my style and the best blend of the grapes. Great wine takes time, you know. How many wines have *you* made?" Guido asked.

The comment hit home, but Corvina ignored his question. She instinctively lifted her scarf to cover her mouth and nose as she ventured farther into the winery. She inspected the equipment, another row of barrels, and the overall facilities. Discarded equipment lay everywhere. The space had not been cleaned for some time, and there were no signs of attempts to keep the winery organized or presentable. She could see why so many poor reviews had been written; there was nothing positive to write about.

"When are you going to replace this equipment?" she asked Marco. "Some of it is decades old," she added, pointing to a row of cement tanks.

"Guido says it doesn't need to be replaced," Marco answered.

Corvina shook her head. "You're both living in denial. The state of this winery is abysmal. No wonder you're not producing quality wines."

"The wines are fine. The online reviews are all bogus. Many are written by our competitors," Guido said.

"Sure. Can you show me where you store your reserves?" Corvina asked.

The winemaker led Corvina to a shed next to the main building and swung open the doors, revealing shelf after shelf holding hundreds of bottles along with barrels stored upright on the floor. A cloud of dust motes, disturbed by the door's opening, swirled through the warm, stale air. Corvina saw no sign of the temperature being regulated to keep the wines cool.

"Why on earth are these wines not stored in a cellar?" Corvina asked.

"It's much easier to get them from here. It's closer," Guido said.

She gave Marco a look and nodded at Guido to close the door.

She could have cried. She would have given anything to have her own winery and make her own wines, and here was an owner who was blind to the condition of his winery and a winemaker who didn't care. What a waste.

"Shall we taste the wines?" Marco said brightly. He clapped his hands as though the tour of the facilities had been an unparalleled success. Corvina followed the men back into the villa, putting her thoughts in order.

"Here are some of our latest wines," Guido said, and pointed to five bottles on Marco's kitchen table. He opened the first bottle and poured them each a generous portion.

Corvina raised her glass to the window to check for clarity and brought it to her nose. She inhaled deeply, swirled the wine in the glass, and tasted. She swished the wine in her mouth to coat every surface and then spat the wine into the sink. It was something she had done thousands of times, and she was able to draw her conclusions quickly.

"This wine is completely unbalanced and astringent," she said without hesitation.

"I think this bottle must be oxidized," Guido said. He set the bottle aside without tasting any of the wine himself.

"How about this one?" Corvina poured a small amount from the second bottle into a clean glass. She smelled the wine, took a taste, and quickly spat it out.

"It tastes very musty, again not balanced, and flabby," she said.

"I think this bottle is corked," Guido said after he tasted a small amount.

"The smell and taste are not of a corked wine. It tastes over-oaked, yet your oak barrels are well used. Are you using oak chips?" She already knew the answer; she had seen bags of them on the ground in the winery.

"What if I am? Lots of winemakers use them," Guido said, and crossed his arms.

"You're using too many. The flavor is overpowering the wine."

"Let's try another," Guido said, and poured each of them a small amount from the third bottle.

"It tastes foxy and has no fruit on the palate nor any finish. I don't think I need to taste any more. When did you pick the grapes?" she asked Guido.

"We harvested in late September," he answered. He tasted the wine himself but didn't remark on it.

"That's too early. It's why your wines are weak, unbalanced, and lacking in flavor," Corvina said.

"Is this true, Guido?" Marco asked.

"She doesn't know what she's talking about. We couldn't harvest any later—I'd already planned my holidays and couldn't change them," Guido said. "Besides, picking the grapes early means the wine they produce will be more delicate."

"I thought you were harvesting too early, but I gave you the benefit of the doubt," Marco said. "I didn't think you would let your personal plans jeopardize the wines."

"Are you going to listen to her or to your winemaker?" Guido challenged Marco.

Marco cringed as though Guido might strike him, and everything immediately became clear to Corvina. The winemaker was just another bully.

Marco tasted the wine once more and frowned. He looked at Corvina and then looked at his feet. He wouldn't make eye contact with Guido.

"Would you give us a minute?" Corvina asked the winemaker.

Guido grimaced and left the kitchen.

"Your winemaker is the problem, Marco," Corvina said when Guido was out of earshot. "He's destroying your business and damaging your reputation. With the quality of grapes you can produce here, there's no reason you can't produce wines as good as, if not better than, your neighbors. I can recommend a few good winemakers who could help you and who may even be looking for a new challenge. But you have to let Guido go."

"What if I give him just another year? Let's see how the wines from this vintage turn out," Marco said, a man hanging on to the last vestiges of hope.

"Stop fooling yourself. Three years of bad reviews—half about the wines and half about the winemaker himself—dwindling stocks and sales, and what do you have to show for it?" Corvina almost felt sorry for the man. But he was the one who had hired the winemaker and had turned a blind eye to the obvious mismanagement of his winery and the poorly made wines.

Guido returned.

"Why are you listening to her? What does she know? A flying winemaker. Wine is made on the ground, not from the air. If you want my resignation, just ask," Guido challenged Marco. He crossed his arms over his chest.

Corvina watched Marco to see how he would respond.

"I want your resignation," Marco said, his gaze fixed on the bottles on the table.

"What did you say?" Guido asked. His arms dropped to his side, and he took a step closer to Marco.

"I want you to leave," Marco said with more conviction in his voice. He looked his troublesome winemaker in the eye. "You are not making good wines, and you're running my winery into the ground."

"You'll be sorry, old man. This place will fold without me!" Guido stabbed a finger at Marco.

"I think you should leave," Corvina said.

Guido glared at Corvina and then stomped out and marched to his car.

She watched him drive away. It was not how she'd pictured her visit unfolding.

"*Grazie, grazie,* Corvina," Marco said once Guido's car was out of sight. He slumped into one of the kitchen chairs and exhaled heavily.

"Don't thank me until you get this place back into shape and start producing decent wines," Corvina said. She briefly entertained the thought of staying on and running the winery herself. How easy it would be to quit her job and stop traveling and be closer to home. She snapped herself out of her reverie when she realized her father had probably orchestrated the visit to lead her to these exact thoughts.

She emptied the open bottles of wine into the sink and rinsed out the glasses. "But you need to get more involved and open your eyes. Never mind the state of the equipment and facilities—look at your vines." Corvina looked out the kitchen window above the sink and pointed at the vines. "*Tutto comincia nel vigneto*—it all begins in the vineyard. Speaking of which, I noticed your vines haven't been pruned for some time. Let's go have a look."

Marco showed her out of the building and into the vineyard, which began just three meters away. When it came to wine, every square centimeter of plantable land was valuable.

Corvina followed Marco between the vines. He stopped halfway down a row and held out some off-colored leaves. "I think some of the vines have been infected with something," Marco said.

Corvina pulled her silk scarf tight and donned a pair of latex gloves—which she carried with her on all her winery visits—before reaching out to examine the leaves. She noted the cluster of vines and leaves around her all had the same dry, undernourished look.

She crouched to inspect the leaves closer to the ground. They looked and felt the same. The grapes, too, looked withered. Something was hampering the vine's growth and ability to flourish. She dug her fingers into the dirt surrounding the base of one of the vines until a long, bare section of rootstock was exposed. She brushed off as much dirt as she could and studied the rootstock and surrounding dirt with great care to confirm her suspicions.

The undernourished-looking vines made her suspect Marco's vines had aphids, but seeing their tiny yellowish-brown bodies writhing in the soil and crawling along the roots left no room for doubt. Without a magnifying glass, she couldn't see them in great detail but knew that most of the one-millimeter-long bugs would be wingless females. She could see small areas of dead tissue along the vine. The tiny bug attacked the vine by biting at the roots. Its saliva caused uncontrolled cell growth, creating knots where bacteria could enter the plant, travel up, and kill the rest of the vine.

"When did you first notice the infestation?" she asked Marco, wiping the dust and dirt from her gloves.

"You think it's an infestation? Not an infection?" Marco asked.

"Definitely an infestation," she replied.

"What do you think it is?"

"It's not what I think it is—it's what I *know* it is." Corvina stood. "Marco, you have aphids. Just look at the decline in canopy vigor around you."

"But I use pesticides, and my vines are grafted. How can I have aphids?" he asked. His voice had risen two full octaves. He looked around the vineyard as if seeking an explanation.

"Not just any aphids, but it looks like some variety of phylloxera." But how was *that* possible? The vineyard was in the heart of Italy, and Marco's vines were grafted, the best means of resisting phylloxera.

Corvina knew well that the only way to stop phylloxera from attacking the vine's roots was to graft the top half of susceptible vines onto American roots. Since the vineyard pest was native to the United States,

American vines were immune to phylloxera, having developed immunity over years of exposure. Vines native to Europe, however, specifically *Vitis vinefera,* like those here, were not immune to phylloxera and could not recover from the insects' bites.

She had to get back to Barcelona as soon as possible to tell her boss. If she was right, Marco had bigger concerns than a bad winemaker—and wineries all over the country might be in jeopardy. "Oh no, oh no, oh no." Marco was shaking his head from side to side. He appeared to be in shock.

"Marco, how old are your oldest and youngest vines?" she asked.

"The oldest are twenty-five years—those are the cabernet sauvignons. The youngest are the pinot grigios. I just planted them last year." Her father's friend looked crestfallen. He covered his forehead with one hand, and his eyes went wide. "What's going to happen to them now?"

"They're going to die. All of them," Corvina said. She removed her gloves by turning them inside out, keeping her hands clean in the process. She wished she could just as easily unsee what she had seen among the roots. Phylloxera was a winemaker's worst nightmare. She stared out over the vineyard and shuddered to think how far the aphid might have already spread.

CHAPTER 2

CROSBIE'S AUCTION HOUSE
BOND STREET
LONDON, ENGLAND

The auction was already under way when Bryan Lawless entered the room.

The wine he had come for hadn't yet gone under the hammer.

He took a seat toward the rear of the room, where he was able to observe those who had arrived earlier without being observed himself. Close to a hundred people—buyers, collectors, and the simply curious—filled the chairs ahead of him facing the front of the room, where an auctioneer stood behind a marble podium.

Bryan's training as a sommelier enabled him to read the room at a glance. This skill was invaluable to selling wine and handling egos. He needed to be able to look at a table full of guests and evaluate the situation in an instant. Who was the host? Who was the host trying to impress? What could the host afford, and how much were they willing to pay? Who could safely be ignored? He discovered early in his career he had a knack for deciphering facial tells and body language. His hyper-observational skill gave him an edge when selling wines and meeting new people.

In the middle of the room he spied a cluster of Emirati, either from Abu Dhabi or Dubai, whispering among themselves. It wasn't unusual to see Emirati at auction, but it was unusual to see them bid for wine.

He also noted the presence of several Chinese bidders, known for their insatiable thirst for expensive reds, as well as aristocrats with Old World money speaking quietly in French and English and nouveau riche dot-com millionaires from the US in casual attire.

Though each occupant of the room was intriguing and worthy of note, it was Crosbie's wine expert—a Master of Wine, or MW—in whom Bryan had an interest. The Master of Wine sat to the side of the auctioneer, overseeing the auction and watching the audience. Bryan recognized three other MWs sitting toward the front of the room.

He knew everything about the Institute of Masters of Wine. Founded in the UK in 1955, the institute included winemakers, importers, buyers, retailers, consultants, journalists, bloggers, sommeliers, and senior executives of the industry.

To become a Master of Wine, each candidate passed an examination testing the depth and breadth of knowledge of the international wine industry to the limit. On average, of the seventy-five candidates who sat for the examination each year, only eight passed.

Bryan knew this because five years ago, when he was only twenty-seven years old, he had been poised to become the youngest Master of Wine—had it not been determined he'd been sleeping with one of the examiners. His indiscretion, of course, cast doubt over the veracity of the tasting element of his examination, leading to his expulsion from the institution with no chance of taking the examination again or ever becoming a Master of Wine.

The institute and many of its members closed their doors to him. In spite of their decision, Bryan went on to become successful in his own right, without the MW designation. He reveled in the opportunity such auctions afforded him—the opportunity to pit himself against certified Masters of Wine.

Finally, the moment arrived to present the wines Bryan had come to see auctioned off in the purest example of grape deification.

Bryan watched as the collection was carefully carted out, crate by crate, and described in great detail. Each lot's provenance was reviewed and given credence to the satisfaction of all—but most importantly, to the satisfaction of Crosbie's chief wine expert.

Over six hundred bottles were featured, representing such famous Bordeaux châteaus as Le Pin, Lafite, Latour, Palmer, d'Yquem, and Cheval Blanc.

Burgundy's wines were also prominent, led by two parcels of Liger-Belair and Raveneau purchased directly from a European estate.

There were half-bottles, magnums, verticals, and cases of six and twelve. The vintages spanned from 1942 to 2005, the latter reputed to be as good as, if not better than, the 1982 vintage.

Bryan had been anxiously waiting for this day. It was rare for such a collection to be put up for auction; however, once in a while, entire private collections were discovered or estates chose to liquidate them, as was the case in this instance.

The auctioneer moved on to the lots. Many of the wines were still in their original château-stamped crates. The top lots were snapped up by the Asian and American buyers. Money appeared to be no object.

Bryan silently watched on as the lots sold quickly and without fuss, fetching handsome prices, many over their original estimates. The speed of the purchases confirmed to him such auctions' attraction to an international audience and the thirst among collectors to purchase wines with well-researched and supported provenance.

Next up were the single bottles. Bryan sat a little straighter. These were always the more interesting sale items, as they tended to appeal to avid fans of a particular producer or vintage and often attracted one-time buyers who were more emotional in their bidding.

The first few bottles sold well and without incident. The process was tedious, but the experienced auctioneer kept the pace moving swiftly.

Bryan had to stop himself from jumping up the moment the wine he had come for was announced—a single bottle of Pétrus, 1982.

"Here we go." He held up his paddle following the first three bids and entered the bidding.

"Fourteen hundred pounds to the man at the back of the room." The auctioneer nodded to Bryan. "Do I hear fourteen hundred fifty?"

The price was driven higher and higher, the excitement in the room rising as the single bottle of Pétrus commanded an ever-increasing amount.

The bottle attracted bids from around the room, from collectors and wine lovers alike. It wasn't long before the pedestrian bidders dropped out and Bryan found himself in a bidding war with a buyer at the front of the room who refused to relent, even as the bottle surpassed the high estimate provided by Crosbie's.

Bryan kept driving the price upward until the other buyer slapped his paddle down in disgust. He turned around and looked at Bryan with contempt. Bryan smiled politely back at him.

"Sold to the gentleman at the back of the room for six thousand pounds." The sound of the gavel closed the bid, and the single bottle was awarded to Bryan. He jumped up as he went to collect his prize as though he'd just won a BAFTA.

Next to the auctioneer, Master of Wine Max Perfetto groaned when he saw Bryan coming up the aisle to take possession of the bottle. Bryan took great satisfaction in seeing the inward collapse of Max's expression. He didn't need to be hyper-observant to guess what Max was thinking. Max's crushed, sallow countenance contrasted starkly with his tailored suit and polished shoes.

Bryan grabbed the bottle from the auctioneer's hands and began inspecting it as a connoisseur would. He lifted it gingerly to the light to see its contents and held it at eye level to read the label.

"Does it meet your satisfaction?" Max asked.

Bryan startled and let the bottle slip from his hands. He was careful to make it look like an accident.

The bottle crashed to the floor and shattered. Its contents spilled onto the marble flooring and adjacent carpet.

The three Masters of Wine at the front of the room gasped in unison.

An otherworldly pause stilled the room. Then, as if by silent command, the three Masters of Wine rushed to the front of the room and plunged their fingers into the carpet. They raised their hands to their noses and mouths, sniffing and tasting the wine off their fingers. It wasn't every day a bottle of Pétrus 1982 was opened, though Bryan would have preferred to open it in the normal fashion.

He reached down and picked up the bottom, unbroken half of the bottle that still held some wine. He held it out to Max, who was standing now and looking at him with unbridled fury.

"Taste it," Bryan insisted.

Bryan could see Max was reluctant to take the broken remains of the bottle in his well-manicured hands. When he finally did, he lifted the wine to his nose to take in its aroma.

Bryan watched as Max put the bottle carefully to his thin lips and tasted the wine. His fine patrician features twisted in confusion, followed by annoyance as he rolled the wine around his mouth as if looking for a particular note but not finding it.

"Not getting that nose of prunes and spices? Any aniseed? Leather on the palate?" Bryan asked.

He could see Max grow more enraged as he continued to taste the wine while glaring at Bryan. Max spat the wine back into the broken bottle. His lips and teeth were stained red. Though the wine no longer occupied the cavity of his mouth, words didn't follow.

"How's that lingering taste of cinnamon and mocha?" Bryan whispered so only the auctioneer and Max could hear.

Bryan felt everyone in the room watching him and Max.

Finally, Max spoke, but his words were whispered in Italian, "*Il vino è contraffatto.*"

Bryan smiled as Max looked out onto the crowd.

"The wine is counterfeit," Max said loud enough for the audience to hear. To Bryan, he looked mystified.

The three Masters of Wine on the floor nodded in agreement.

Many in the audience rose to their feet and began shouting. The room was in an uproar as earlier buyers came to the dreadful conclusion the wine they had just purchased could also be *contraffatto.*

Bryan took the opportunity to carefully pocket the top of the bottle with the cork still inside. It would make a great addition to his collection. He left the auction house the same way he had entered it—empty-handed and smiling. He heard his name being called as soon as he left the building.

"Bryan!" He looked across the street to see a woman with a large black umbrella crossing toward him.

"Oh shit," he muttered under his breath. "Oh, hi, Candy. What brings you to Bond Street?" he said brightly when she reached his side of the street. He stepped close enough to share her umbrella. It was drizzling lightly. Candy was one of the most prominent wine experts in the UK. Born in London, she was a Master of Wine and wrote extensively on wines, with several published books to her credit. She was also the reason Bryan could no longer become a Master of Wine.

"I received a phone call from a colleague who told me someone was about to make a nuisance of themselves at an auction. Was I misinformed?"

He noticed she still styled her straight brown hair the same way, cut short at her neck. Her usual bright-red lipstick—which always made an impression at wine tastings and on the tasting glasses—contrasted sharply with her dark suit and black pumps. She looked as fit as he remembered.

Bryan turned at the sound of the door slamming open behind him.

Max Perfetto burst out the front door of the auction house. The Master of Wine pointed at Bryan. "I'll make you pay for this!"

"Why don't we discuss this somewhere else?" Bryan said to Candy as he grabbed her by the arm and directed her down the street and around a corner, away from the fracas he had created at the auction house.

"What was that all about? What have you done to poor Max?" Candy asked.

"Poor Max? I just saved him from major embarrassment. Some of the bottles he was auctioning were counterfeit."

"And you couldn't have just told him that before the auction started?" Candy asked. He remembered how angry she used to get when they argued.

"It's not *my* job to tell him how to do *his* job."

"Oh, Bryan, grow up. When are you going to stop attacking the institute?"

"Maybe when the institute apologizes for barring me from becoming a Master of Wine. Besides, I'm not attacking the institute."

"No, just all of its members. And why, because they wouldn't let you join the club?"

"Seems like a damn good reason to me," Bryan said. He'd spent thousands of pounds and years of his life studying to become a Master of Wine. "Maybe they'll realize it would be easier for everyone if they just let me join the institute."

"That's never going to happen as long as you keep working on your own as you have been. It's always Bryan against the world with you. Do you even really want to be a Master of Wine?"

"I did."

"Well, maybe if you used your skills for something productive instead of just criticizing everyone else, you'd have a chance to come back."

"Do you mean that?"

"Not everyone in the institute agrees with the decision to bar you for life. But you would need to persuade a few of them to let you back, and that wouldn't be easy." He heard a softening in the tone of her voice.

"Are you saying you would help me?"

"I might, if you could give me something to help your cause. The MWs have a meeting right after Vinexpo Bordeaux, a month from today. The members will need a reason to take you back and need to be convinced you're worthy of the MW title."

“A reason? Like what?”

“I don’t know, but it had better be a good one. After what you just did to Max in there, you’ll be even more loathed. Pull it together, Bryan, or you’ll never get another shot.”

He watched his ex walk away toward Piccadilly, her last words swirling in his head. He absently raised his wine-stained fingers to his nose and smelled the fake Pétrus. Did he really still have a chance to become a Master of Wine?

CHAPTER 3

EL PRAT AIRPORT
BARCELONA, SPAIN

Corvina's flight into Barcelona arrived early, so she decided to have a snack and a glass of champagne at one of the airport's bars while she waited for her boss. It was dinnertime, and she hadn't eaten anything since the biscotti she'd had with her espresso before seeing Marco that morning.

Next to her iPad was a paperback copy of *The Vines of San Lorenzo,* a detailed account of Gaja, the famous Italian winery not far from her own family's winery and vineyards in Piemonte, where her Italian father and Spanish mother now lived. She had been making wines with her father since she was old enough to pick grapes.

Flicking between her correspondence and various websites, she took time to tap out a tasting note on the Bollinger 1996 Champagne she had ordered. Her earlier encounter with Marco and Guido still reeled in her mind, and she needed the distraction.

She held up the glass to study its appearance. The champagne's clarity was good, with a medium intensity and a pale golden hue. Its bead was fine, persistent, and strong, meaning its bubbles were small, frequent, and tightly formed. Overall, it was appealing to the eye.

She set the Riedel flute down and swirled the champagne around the glass and then held it up to her nose. She inhaled deeply. The nose was bright and well defined. The wonderful aroma was clean with a pronounced intensity and had no whiff of any faults. She smelled brazil nut as well as hints of caramel, mushroom, and orange zest, all reined in by a salty minerality.

She inhaled the aroma twice more before tilting the German-made flute to her lips. True to its nose, the robust nutty and caramel flavor filled her senses. The wine's crisp acidity was a delightful juxtaposition to its creamy texture. The vibrant and delicate mousse tickled her palate as she swallowed. The finish was exquisite and lingered in her mouth.

Relishing the taste, she felt more aging would soften its powerful bouquet and add to its rich complexity. It was a superb example of the Bollinger style, and she concluded in her tasting note that the 1996 vintage was fully developed with a lot more years to give.

She took another sip and closed her eyes.

"*¿Cómo es tu vino?*" the bartender asked.

"Delicioso, gracias," Corvina replied. She opened her eyes, somewhat annoyed to have her reveries disturbed but happy to share her delight.

The bartender left her to finish her champagne and returned to his *mise en place* slicing fresh limes.

She saw her boss, Vicente Avila, approaching. She smiled brightly, dropped her book into her purse, closed her iPad, and left sufficient money on the bar to pay for her champagne.

She kissed Vicente on both cheeks in greeting at the bar's entrance.

"How was Tuscany?" Vicente asked. He was wearing a navy-blue tailored suit that struggled to hide his size. He wasn't fat, but he was a big man. A full beard and mustache accompanied by bushy eyebrows completed his bear-like appearance.

"Interesting," she said. She led him to a coffee shop where she could tell him about the aphids she'd found in Marco's vineyard.

"Vicente, it was really phylloxera in the vineyard. But the vines were grafted onto American rootstock. How is that possible?"

"Technically it's not. It's probably just a localized event, or maybe he had a patch of ungrafted vines or the wrong rootstock. Why were you even there?"

"My father asked me to consult for a friend of his. Don't worry, I'm caught up on my work and all my clients are fine. So, what if it's not just a localized event? Other vineyards will be at risk—maybe even already infested," she said. She was well aware that phylloxera had devastated Europe's vineyards once before, largely because its impact had been underestimated. She worried what the aphids' reappearance in Italy signified. Her father's vineyards could be at risk too.

"What do you want to do about it?" Vicente asked.

Corvina sensed he was humoring her.

"I think we should tell Universal Wines so they can warn all of our wineries. We need to step up precautions and monitor vineyards." She spoke quickly and tugged at the ends of her scarf, something she did when she was nervous.

"Corvina, Corvina, slow down," Vicente said as he raised his hands and patted the air in front of him in a patronizing way. "You found one patch of infested vines, and you want to set off every alarm?"

"Vicente," she said, and leaned forward over the small coffee shop table, making it tilt toward her. "I'm not suggesting we sell off our vineyards. But I think we need to highlight this to headquarters in California to make sure the company and the wineries it owns and represents take the threat seriously."

"You're talking about hundreds of vineyards around the world. What would that accomplish? People would either ignore it or panic about it."

"Or they might check out their vineyards to make sure they're not infested and then take preventative action to ensure they don't get infested," Corvina said. Why couldn't he see this?

"At whose expense?" Vicente asked her. He leaned back in his chair.

"The winery owners, of course. We pay for those that belong to us, and independent winery owners we represent pay for themselves."

"Are you listening to yourself?" Vicente asked her.

"I feel like I'm the only person here who is," she said. She leaned back and crossed her arms.

"What do you want me to do?"

"Call James Harvey in California, tell him what I found, and recommend he issue a company-wide communication."

"You want me to bring this directly to the CEO? My boss's boss's boss?" Vicente said, and laughed.

"I think it's the only responsible thing to do," Corvina said.

"Corvina, I'm not going to bring this to the CEO. It's one small incident."

"Can I?"

"What do you mean?"

"Can I bring it to his attention?"

"You mean send him an email about phylloxera in one vineyard?"

"No."

"Okay, good, because for a second I thought you—"

"No, I think it would be better if I told him in person," Corvina interrupted him. "I checked, and there are seats available on a late morning flight. I could be there tomorrow and tell him face-to-face. It will take only a day, and I have no visits scheduled with my customers. Besides, I've never been to the corporate office, so this is a good excuse."

"An excuse, yes—good, I'm not so sure," Vicente said. "Maybe I should ask Sergio to follow up on this," he suggested.

"Sergio? Sergio couldn't tell the difference between an aphid and an acorn," Corvina said. Sergio was her counterpart in the company, and they both reported to Vicente. He had been hired before her and treated her like an underling when in fact they were of equal status. She was clearly the better winemaker, leading to the tension and resentment defining their working relationship. Corvina was thankful their paths rarely crossed.

"I'm not suggesting you work together. I'm suggesting he look into your hunch, and you focus on your customers."

"Seeing phylloxera in the vineyard was a shock, and I'm worried it's already spreading. Sergio isn't as close to this as I am. It was my discovery, so I should follow it through," she said with as much finality as she could muster. She knew her fellow flying winemaker would jump at the chance to take a project away from her and usurp her in any way he could. Ever since she had joined Universal Wines, the man had been a pain in her backside.

"Are you worried about your parents' winery?" Vicente asked.

"Of course I am. It's their whole life," she said. *And mine as well.* She had grown up playing in her family's vineyards and hoped to one day return and take over the winery.

"You know I can't back you up on this, right?"

"Can't or won't?"

"Corvina, take the time you need. You know I always support you. But on this, you're on your own."

Upon returning to her home in the Gràcia district of Barcelona, Corvina slid the handle inside her suitcase and leaned it against the wall, set her shoulder bag down, and removed her scarf. She would unpack and repack in the morning.

For a hopeful moment she expected to see her estranged husband, Luis—slim and well-muscled—leaning casually against the doorjamb leading to the living room. She could picture his unshaven face and calculating eyes. He had a dark complexion, in part due to his Catalonian heritage, but also from his time spent outdoors working as a contractor. Her friends told her he could have been a model. But the man, who hadn't pulled his weight in their relationship, was not at home—nor had he been since they split six months ago. She missed his company, missed his laugh, and especially missed the sex. Better than barolo, she used to tell him. But his cheating drove them apart, and she couldn't find it in her heart or her mind to forgive and forget.

Corvina glanced at the unopened cans of paint in the corner of the kitchen. They were intended for the bathroom. They were also a catalyst for the ongoing arguments they used to have in the kitchen when either of them returned home from work. They argued a lot about her frequent traveling, a factor of her career he'd said he accepted when they first married. Clearly that was no longer the case.

She looked up at the clock on the living room wall with San Francisco written underneath it. Beside it was a clock for Barcelona and one for Rome. The last was for London, where she often found herself for wine-related events and exhibitions. The hands had stopped turning on the London and San Francisco clocks.

She reached into the fridge, where she had left a bottle of 2012 Viña Sol—a popular rosé from Torres, a local winemaker.

She opened the bottle and poured herself a glass and then watched Netflix for an hour.

She called home before going to bed.

"Hi, *Mamma,* it's me. Just wanted to let you know I'm back in Barcelona."

"*Gracias,* dear. Have you and Luis talked recently?" her mom asked in Spanish.

"Not lately. How's *Papà*?" Corvina changed the subject. Luis was still a sensitive topic, and she tried to avoid talking to her parents about him.

"His usual self. He wants to talk to you."

Her father came on the line and said in his native Italian, "Corvina, how's Marco and his winemaker?"

"Marco is fine," she said, switching to Italian herself. "His winemaker is now unemployed. Everyone is better off."

"Good. Any interest in taking on the job yourself?"

"Ha ha. No, Papà. I have a job. Besides, I don't think now would be a good time to take over. I found out his vineyard is infested with aphids."

"Aphids? I knew things were bad at his winery, but not that bad. Good thing his winemaker has left."

"Papà, the aphids have nothing to do with the winemaker," she said.

"So when are you going to come home for good?" her father asked. She heard his voice drop when he asked, like he was trying to be gentle.

"Papà, I've told you—I live in Barcelona now. I have a great job."

"And what about Luis?"

"We haven't spoken for a while. I don't know what's happening."

"I'm sorry, honey. Give it time."

"You're not going to say marriage is like a fine wine, are you?"

"No, but I do miss making wine with you."

"No, you miss telling me how you think wine should be made," Corvina said, and laughed. She didn't want to think or talk about her failed marriage.

"We used to make great wines together. We could still make great wine, father and daughter."

"No, Papà. *You* made wine. I watched." She loved her papà dearly but recalled how he never listened to a thing she said about how she thought they could improve the wine, modernize the winery, or introduce new wine-making practices. It was part of the reason she'd left Italy in the first place.

"Corvina, you're still so young. You have much to learn," he intoned.

"Papà, I'm twenty-eight years old and have learned a lot," she said. She knew he still thought she knew only what *he* had taught her about wine making. She had worked in vineyards all over Europe and consulted for dozens more. "Papà, I have to go now. Say bye to mom for me. *Ti amo,*" she said warmly and hung up the phone.

Desperate for bed, she went to the bathroom. The door Luis had removed to sand down to bare wood was still missing. She had to step over a plastic tarp bunched up in front of the sink to get to the toilet. Tools and pieces of pipe and pipe fittings lay scattered about the floor. The walls were bare where they used to have tiles, and the ceiling was unfinished. She could see into the rafters above.

She went to the kitchen to wash her hands and brush her teeth, since the sink in the bathroom was still not connected.

She switched off the lights on the way to the bedroom and climbed into bed alone. She stared up at the ceiling in the dark and pictured in her mind aphids marching across Europe.

CHAPTER 4

UNIVERSAL WINES CORPORATE HEADQUARTERS
SAN FRANCISCO, CA, UNITED STATES

"What do you mean he's not available?" Corvina asked the stern-looking woman sitting behind the reception desk in the lobby of Universal Wines headquarters. A taxi had taken her straight from the San Francisco International Airport to the office, located an hour outside of the city and surrounded by experimental vineyards. She had one hand clenched on the desk and the other wrapped around the extended handle of her small black rolling suitcase. Not much more than a day had passed since her discovery of the aphids in Tuscany, and she was exhausted.

"I'm sorry, but it looks like Mr. Harvey's calendar is full." The woman behind the desk moved a mouse around and stared at her monitor.

"Please check again. My boss, Vicente Avila from the Barcelona office, made the appointment yesterday. I've just flown from Spain to meet Mr. Harvey."

"I see. Please understand our CEO is a very busy man," the woman said.

"I do understand," Corvina said. She held back from saying something she would later regret. "That's why I made an appointment," she said, and smiled with effort.

The woman moved the mouse around some more. Corvina leaned forward to see the screen, but the angle was too great.

"I see there was an appointment in his calendar, but it was canceled early this morning. It looks like he has an appointment out of town," the receptionist said.

"Is he still here now?" Corvina looked at a pile of mail beside the receptionist. A manila envelope on top bore the CEO's name; it also carried the address of the headquarters and specified the eighth floor.

"He's in a meeting. Why don't I call the chief operating officer, Mr. Harvey's deputy?"

"Sure. While you do that, can you point me to the washroom? I've been in and out of planes and airports for the last twenty hours." The receptionist gave her a sympathetic look and pointed across the lobby.

Corvina found the ladies' room and freshened up as best she could. A large mirror over the sink reflected the hint of bags under her big brown eyes.

She brushed her dark-brown hair and touched up her lipstick and mascara. She adjusted the dark-blue silk Gucci scarf with its classic paisley print she had chosen for the meeting. Its color conveyed strength and power—or at least she hoped it did.

She left and went straight to the elevators. Seated behind the large reception counter and already engaged with another visitor, the receptionist didn't see her. Corvina entered the elevator, stepped to the side to avoid being seen, and pressed the button for the eighth floor. She pressed it again and willed the doors to shut. She expected someone to shout at her from the lobby and a security guard to stop the elevator.

The doors finally closed, and the elevator took her to the eighth floor.

When the doors opened, she stepped out with confidence and turned right. Based on her impression of the building from the outside and the dimensions of the lobby, she knew that more of the building was on her right than her left, and she didn't want to be called out for looking lost.

Corvina walked by a boardroom and glanced inside. There was a meeting in progress. She spotted James Harvey speaking at the head of the table. With his bald head and hawkish features, he was hard to miss. Corvina continued on until she reached the end of the hallway. There she found a small lounge with an empty reception desk and two polished wooden doors leading to what she presumed, and hoped, was the CEO's office. Thankfully no one else was around. She took a seat on a low leather sofa and waited for the meeting to end.

She had to wait only ten minutes before the CEO himself entered the lounge. He was smartly dressed in a dark-gray suit and a bold red tie.

"Mr. Harvey, I really need to speak with you," Corvina said as she stood up. "We had an appointment."

Corvina's sudden appearance seemed to throw the man off guard. Had she chosen the best strategy?

"Yes, I know. I'm sorry about that, but a last-minute meeting came up in Washington that I have to attend," the CEO said, and opened one of the two doors and then stepped into his office.

"I've flown all the way from Barcelona to see you. Can you spare me just a few minutes?" Corvina followed him into the office without waiting for an invitation. He was behind his desk looking through a drawer.

"Why?" The CEO stopped rummaging around his desk long enough to look up at her.

"Well, to make a long story short—"

"Please," he said, and continued going through his desk.

"I discovered phylloxera on grafted rootstock in an Italian vineyard."

"So?" Harvey answered without looking up.

"So it's highly unusual for phylloxera to attack vines with grafted rootstock." Corvina was talking to the top of the man's head as he continued to look through the papers on his desk. She ran the ends of her scarf through her fingers while waiting for him to respond.

"And?" Harvey lifted a folder from under a pile of papers and stuffed it into the side of his laptop carrier.

"And it could be a threat to neighboring vineyards. One of our clients is in the vicinity."

"Listen, Miss . . . ?" He came around the desk.

"Guerra. Corvina Guerra. I work out of the Barcelona office. I'm one of the company's flying winemakers."

"I've always hated that term. Anyway, Miss Guerra, aphids and vines have been in an arms race for millennia. I don't see how this is a disaster in the making."

"It might not be an isolated incident."

"Of course it's not. There's been another case right here in California," Harvey said.

"*¿Que?*" Corvina asked. She was stunned.

"One of our own vineyards reported it last month. But California has had aphids before."

"That's because everyone used the wrong vine clone for grafting, one that wasn't resistant to phylloxera," Corvina said. She had read much of phylloxera's history, both in Europe and in America, on the plane ride to the United States.

"What do you want, Miss Guerra?" Harvey asked. He closed his briefcase and headed for the door to leave his office.

"What if it turns out to be a new form of phylloxera, one that can't be stopped with grafted rootstock?" Corvina asked. She followed the CEO out of the office, closing the door behind her.

"Two infested vineyards doesn't call for a panic."

"I'm not panicking, but I think it's worth investigating further. Don't you?"

"Not really. Right now, I just want to get to the airport on time," he said. He looked at his watch.

"Wouldn't you want to get ahead of this in case it turns out to be something worse than two isolated incidents? To be the man who saw there was a problem before anyone else and led his company out of danger?"

Harvey gave her a strange look. "I ask again—what do you want?"

"I want to investigate these outbreaks. If they turn out to be nothing, then I've only wasted my own time. If there's something more to it, then Universal Wines can take responsibility for highlighting the issue and potentially stopping whatever's happening in those vineyards."

"Something more?" Harvey asked, and stopped walking.

Corvina almost collided into the CEO's back.

"Well, given the rate of infestation I saw in the one vineyard in Tuscany, the aphid must have been introduced months ago. They don't just appear overnight. Someone could be spreading them."

"You mean someone is doing this intentionally?"

"The thought had crossed my mind. Yes, it's possible."

"Do you have any valid reason to believe or, dare I ask, any proof to support that notion?"

"Well, no."

"Being an experienced winemaker, I assume you must be familiar with the extent of the damage phylloxera caused when it last spread across Europe," Harvey said. He started walking again and pressed the down button when they reached the bank of elevators.

"Yes, of course. It almost wiped out Europe's vineyards to the point where the entire industry collapsed. That's why I'm so concerned. We must act now, before it's too late." She followed him into the elevator.

"Do you know how many vineyards we own and how many winemakers we represent globally?" Harvey asked. He pressed the button marked "L."

"Not exactly," Corvina answered. Was he trying to change the subject? She had his time for only another minute.

"Over one hundred seventy-five owned and over five hundred represented," he said. He stepped out of the elevator when it reached the lobby, not waiting for Corvina to exit first.

"Listen, if you really want to pursue this—and I'm not encouraging you—find out what you can by checking out the infested vineyard I mentioned here in California, and then let me know what you discover," he said over his shoulder. "Whatever you do, don't go starting a panic among our wineries or attract any unwanted attention." Harvey turned and walked out of the lobby of the grand building.

Corvina wasn't sure she hadn't wasted her time coming to California on a wild bug chase. Maybe Vicente was right. Maybe she was being impulsive.

A black sedan was waiting for Harvey outside. She stood in the middle of the glass-and-steel atrium and watched him get in and the car drive away.

20:10
THE TENDERLOIN DISTRICT
SAN FRANCISCO, CA, UNITED STATES

"Password?" A woman's eyes peered out, scanning the street through a small panel in the middle of a varnished door. Her gaze settled on Corvina.

"I'm here to meet a friend," Corvina stammered, taken aback. She took her finger off the intercom button and looked around. The Uber driver must have brought her to the wrong address. She double-checked the SMS with the address and confirmed she was at the right intersection: Jones and O'Farrell.

The streets were lined with cars. A U-Haul van and a car out of the 1950s with tail fins stood out, but otherwise there wasn't anything unusual about the neighborhood, aside from its name. Corvina was unsure whether it used to be a meatpacking district or if the Tenderloin moniker referred to a more fleshy trade. She didn't see any women about, working or otherwise. The street was deserted. Not the type of place one would expect a cocktail bar.

She saw two signs protruding from the building on the corner of Jones and O'Farrell Streets. The higher of the two signs promoted Hotel Shawmut and promised "Reasonable Rates." Even more bizarre was the second sign. It read "Anti-Saloon League San Francisco Branch Est. 1920." What on earth did that mean?

"Password?" the woman behind the door asked again.

Corvina checked her phone and realized there was more to the text than the bar's name and address. Her friend had also written "PW Book." When she had first read it, she'd had no idea what it meant.

"Book?" Corvina said to the woman behind the varnished wooden door.

The door opened, and she stepped inside the speakeasy bar Bourbon & Branch.

Her eyes took a few moments to adjust to the light. Once they did, Corvina was amazed. The space had wooden floors throughout, and the walls were adorned with dark-red fleur-de-lis patterned wallpaper. To her right, a long bar of polished wood and a back bar filled with hundreds of spirit bottles anchored the room. Two bartenders were making drinks.

A giant, spiky glass chandelier offered an intriguing focal point as it hung from a tin ceiling two stories high, augmenting the light provided by dozens of candles.

Music played in the background to add atmosphere but not so loud as to drown out the urgent hush of conversation coming from the dozens of patrons at the bar and in booths and at small tables.

Corvina swore she felt a whoosh of air, as if the pressure inside the bar had changed, sealing off the Tenderloin district outside.

"Corvina!" her friend called out from across the room, where she was climbing out of a brown leather-backed booth.

"Rachel!" Corvina exclaimed. The two women hugged, drawing admiring stares from the male patrons and bartenders. "Oh my God—you look fabulous," Corvina said. She stood back and held her friend at arm's length. Rachel still wore her dark-brown hair to her shoulders, and her blue eyes sparkled.

"As do you. And I see you still have impeccable taste in clothes." Rachel reached out to feel the scarf Corvina had picked for the evening. Covered in bold, abstract shapes in primary colors with a black border, it was one of Corvina's favorites. Her father had bought it for her in Florence from Etro, the Italian fashion house, and gave it to her when she returned from her first international trip to make wine in Australia. "How long has it been?" Rachel asked her.

"Too long. You need to get out to Barcelona more often."

Years ago, after a tumultuous time at work, Rachel and her boyfriend, Ed, took a holiday to Barcelona. They had needed to get out of San Francisco and away from the investigation that almost shut down the psychiatric clinic where Rachel worked. During a visit to a vineyard a short distance from the city, Corvina was introduced to Rachel and Ed at a lunch hosted by the winemaker. They got along, and the two women had kept in touch ever since.

"You said you had a meeting this morning. What else have you been up to today?"

"I went jogging down the Embarcadero from the Port of San Francisco all the way up to Fisherman's Wharf and back. Then a power nap to get over the jet lag."

"Where are you staying?" Rachel asked.

"The company put me up at the King George Hotel. But only for one night. I arrived early this morning and leave tomorrow already."

"Wow, rough quarters," Rachel said, and rolled her eyes. "Let's get you a drink. They make the most delicious cocktails here."

"Okay, but I really need to talk about what's happening at work," Corvina said.

"Order. Drink. Talk. In that order." Rachel passed her a menu.

Corvina studied the menu and was impressed at the level of sophistication each libation announced in its ingredients. While her expertise was enology, she appreciated a well-thought-out cocktail list when she saw one. The cocktails used unusual base ingredients, such as Chartreuse, Laphroaig, Rittenhouse Rye, and St. George Absinthe.

"What is this place?" Corvina asked.

"It's a speakeasy, like during Prohibition and in *Boardwalk Empire.*"

"What is a speakeasy?"

"During Prohibition, patrons of this type of establishment would order alcohol in a whisper and *speak easy* so as not to raise suspicion or be overheard," their waiter announced with perfect timing as he came to take their drink order.

"And what is the Anti-Saloon League?" Corvina asked.

"It was an organization that lobbied for prohibiting alcohol production, sale, and consumption in the US. Its triumph was nationwide Prohibition being made part of the Constitution with the passage of the Eighteenth Amendment in 1917. Enforcement began in 1920 through the Volstead Act, named after the man who sponsored the act in congress. Thankfully, reason prevailed when Prohibition was repealed in 1933.

"The JJ Russell Cigar Shop, where you're sitting now, operated during Prohibition. Although the double-entry record books will show not many cigars were sold," the waiter delivered in a well-practiced line.

"Despite its popularity, Russell's was never raided by Prohibition agents due to the elaborate precautions the operators took. A password was required to gain entry to the shop. Once in, only the request for a particular brand of cigar would lead to a trap door in the floor being opened to allow guests into the basement. Here, the city's best bartenders treated guests to Canada's best bootlegged contraband liquor.

"If at any point in the evening you hear the sound of a brass warning bell, you'll be invited to exit the speakeasy via one of five secret exit tunnels."

Corvina saw Rachel smile at the waiter's spiel, clearly having heard it before.

"You ladies look like you're conspirators of some sort, so I would recommend the Cloak and Dagger. It's a deep, sophisticated cocktail made up of Bushmills Black Bush, Dolin Blanc, Sapling Maple Liqueur, cinnamon pear gomme, and rounded off with Old Fashion Aromatic Bitters. It's one of my favorites."

"Sold—we'll take two," Rachel answered.

Though Corvina urgently wanted to speak to Rachel about work, it was nice to be distracted, even if just for a few minutes. She sat back, letting the leather banquette take her weight, and willed herself to relax.

"What brings you to San Francisco?" Rachel finally asked.

Corvina told Rachel about her trip to Italy, the discovery of the aphids in the Tuscan vineyard, the conversation with her boss, her meeting with the CEO that morning, and her subsequent visit to the locally infested vineyard where she found more signs of phylloxera infestation.

"I don't think it's natural," Corvina said.

"Not natural?"

"It's as though someone is behind it and spreading it intentionally," Corvina clarified. "And I feel like I'm the only person who's concerned."

"Why would someone want to destroy a vineyard?" Rachel asked.

"Lots of reasons, I suppose. Maybe they were hurt in some way by the wine industry."

"Oh, like someone's family member was killed by a drunk driver?"

"That seems extreme, but maybe someone depended on the industry and somehow it led to the loss of their livelihood."

"Maybe they were put out of business because of wine, like maybe they ran a microbrewery. There are a lot of them around here."

"That's possible. Maybe it's not to avenge anyone or take revenge but to benefit from."

"Oh, like an insurance scam. Ed could talk your ear off about those. It's how we met," Rachel said.

"I recall you met your husband in a mental institution."

The waiter returned to the table and set down their drinks. He gave Rachel a funny look and then returned to the bar.

"I don't think the location is what matters," Rachel said, and smiled.

"It's a better story than meeting in a hardware store," Corvina said. "And how is Mr. Wonderful?"

"Still wonderful, though his penchant for eighties rock gets a little tiring. At least I got him to trade in his pickup truck. We bought a crossover."

"One step closer to a minivan. Soon you'll be living the American dream as a full-fledged soccer mom," Corvina said.

"So what's your grand plan now?"

"That's the problem—and why I wanted to see you. I finally convinced my company to let me pursue this, but I'm not sure where to go from here except to look for more infested vineyards. I'm not sure how productive that would be on my own though. I need help."

"I hope you're not asking me. I don't know much about wine, I'm afraid, except when it tastes good."

"No, sorry. But I thought you might be able to help me come up with options."

"You need to find someone who knows about wines, obviously. Oooh—and who is tall, dark, and handsome!"

"This isn't a blind date, you freak. I'm serious. And I'm married. I need someone to share my ideas and thoughts with and who is an expert in wine or phylloxera."

"So I'm just a sounding board, am I?" Rachel asked with a smile. She was typing on her phone at the same time.

"Of course not. So aside from being tall, dark, and handsome, what else would my mystery helper need to be?"

"Well, he would need to be flexible in his job so he can travel and have a proven investigation track record."

"Are you in HR or psychiatry?"

"It's a fine line between the two."

"So how am I supposed to find this partner?"

"What about him?" Rachel held her phone up for Corvina to see an image of a good-looking man.

"Bryan Lawless? Who's that?"

"It's who comes up when you Google tall, dark, and handsome wine expert."

"Are you serious?"

"You have anyone else in mind?"

Corvina took another sip of her cocktail and realized that since nobody else came to mind to assist her in her quest, it was the best suggestion she had.

CHAPTER 5

KING GEORGE HOTEL
SAN FRANCISCO, CA, UNITED STATES

"Who is Bryan Lawless?" Corvina asked a fellow flying winemaker based out of Burgundy, one of her counterparts in the company. She and Rachel had wrapped up the evening after their third round of cocktails just shy of midnight; it was late morning in Western Europe.

She scanned the wine list the bartender had given her at the Clock Bar adjacent to the lobby of the King George Hotel and ordered a glass of 2011 Vintners Blend Old Vine Zinfandel from Ravenswood. Though bottled as primitivo in her native Italy, she conceded that zinfandel was *America's* grape. She took every opportunity when Stateside to enjoy its robust, mouthwatering, and spicy wines.

"He's an industry blogger," the voice on the other end of the line emanated from the heart of Burgundy.

"Bryan Lawless is a *blogger*?" Corvina tapped the screen of her iPad, looking for the man's website.

"I've heard he's also a Master of Wine, but not quite."

"What does that mean?" she asked. She scrolled through a list of wine blogs that appeared on her tablet's screen.

"I'm not sure."

"You're not doing a great job selling him. How come I'm the only person who hasn't heard of him?" She found the site and double tapped the screen.

"I don't know. He writes reviews and stuff and articles on the wine trade. His latest piece was titled 'Your Sommelier Is Laughing at You.' A good piece, and a scathing indictment on the trade."

"Okay. I'll call him. Do you have a number I can reach him on?" she asked while looking through the site for a way to contact him. Contact details weren't provided.

Her colleague in Burgundy texted her a phone number with a +44 country code—the United Kingdom.

The bartender came back with a generous pour of the wine she had ordered. Knowing in advance the blend would be around three-quarters zinfandel, with the rest being made up of syrah and petite sirah, she anticipated it to be—like most of Ravenswood's zinfandels—big, bold, and unapologetic.

She wasn't disappointed when she swirled the glass, held it up, and inhaled the aroma of black cherries, raspberries, and blueberries complemented by hints of oak developed over months of aging in French oak barrels. Her first sip was an avalanche of fruit flavors held together by solid tannins and residing in her mouth with a long, fruity finish. The flavor grew in complexity. While the deep-purple grape of Croatian origins would never hold the same allure for her as nebbiolo, her favorite Italian varietal made famous by barolo and barbaresco, she was entranced nonetheless.

Bryan's site had a blog and detailed reviews of thousands of wines. It also featured numerous critiques of restaurant critics, as scathing as many of the critics were of the restaurants they dined in. A section of the website allowed visitors to find wine pairings for any and every dish imaginable. There were also links to numerous scientific articles explaining a program that predicted how wines would taste based on an algorithm Bryan had developed. Corvina liked the section on counterfeit wines and how he had discovered a number of them being sold at auction houses across Europe. He sounded like a good investigator—exactly what she needed.

After an hour of addictive scrolling through the website and a second glass of wine, against her better judgment she called the number she'd been given. It went to a generic voicemail.

She left a brief message saying she would like to meet. Several minutes later, she received a text with a time and place to meet in London at a wine bar on Fleet Street. She tried calling the number back, but it still went to voicemail. She hadn't planned to go to London, but it appeared she now had little choice if she wanted to meet Bryan.

The alternative, of course, was to continue going it alone and trying to solve the mystery by herself. That wasn't appealing, nor did she think it was the best strategy. The complexity of the predicament was beyond anything she'd ever tackled, alone or as part of a team. Corvina realized she would need every available resource at her disposal, no matter how unusual and removed from her comfort zone.

Plus, as much as she loved her job, she often became lonely and melancholy when she traveled for long periods on her own. Downtime away from others had its place, but she found stretches of days at a time without meaningful human contact or conversation was anathema to her.

She brought up a hotel booking site where she could always get good rates at the Hotel 41 in Victoria. It was a discreet boutique property. She reserved a room for the following night.

Having done everything she could from her perch at the bar, Corvina raised the glass in toast to the "godfather of zinfandel," famous for his promise of no wimpy wines.

"Thank you, Joel Peterson," she said.

"What a true zin is meant to be," the bartender agreed.

She savored the wine's lingering finish and thought about the tall, dark, and handsome man she would soon be convincing to help her investigate the spread of phylloxera. Before she could indulge herself in that thought for too long, the magnitude of the task that lay ahead of her took hold in her mind. How long before her parents' vineyard succumbed to phylloxera and to a fate similar to the vineyard she had seen in Tuscany and the one she'd seen just that morning in Napa—rife with phylloxera, and the winemakers none the wiser about its presence until it was too late?

CHAPTER 6

FLEET STREET
LONDON, ENGLAND

Corvina weaved through a crowd of smokers standing in clusters on the paved sidewalk and made her way into the wine bar Bryan Lawless had designated as their rendezvous point.

It was just after eight on a Friday night, and the bar was heaving with young urban professionals. The music was louder than it needed to be and was augmented by all the hard surfaces, forcing patrons to shout at each other across thick wooden tables.

Once inside, Corvina scanned the bar. After a few sweeps, she noticed a man sitting by himself upstairs. He was slim, had short dark hair, and looked at home leaning back in a wooden chair. He wore a white collared shirt with the sleeves rolled up, dark suit trousers, and black leather shoes. The man raised his glass and smiled when she caught his eye, and she noticed he didn't have a wedding ring. Either he thought she was a waitress and he wanted another drink or the lone man was Bryan Lawless.

Corvina pushed her way through the mob in front of the bar and went up the stairs as fast as her heels allowed.

The man's table was empty save for a glass holding a few melting ice cubes, a wedge of lime, and a clear plastic stirrer.

He had arrived early.

"Hi, I'm Corvina."

The man stood and extended his hand. "Bryan." He was taller than she expected. And more handsome. His picture online didn't do him justice. Rachel would be pleased.

She removed her scarf—a cream-colored metallic silk blend with an embossed tribal motif that seemed out of place in the dimly lit bar—and draped it and her bag over the back of a wooden chair and then took a seat. Bryan sat back down and crossed one leg over the other. Not much of a talker, Corvina thought.

She fished a business card out of her clutch and presented it to Bryan. He glanced at it and slipped it inside an inner jacket pocket.

"Sorry, I don't have one of my own. I'm self-employed," he said.

Seated on the upper level of the busy wine bar, she had a good view of the thriving business. It was also quieter there, allowing them to speak at normal volume.

Corvina caught a server's eye. She came over to their table.

"A glass of soave, please," Corvina said, taking in the girl's appearance. She had thinly plucked eyebrows, bleached blonde hair, and three silver studs in each ear. She looked barely old enough to drink herself.

"Sure, and for you, sir? Another gin and tonic?"

"Yes, please. Is the manager working tonight?" Bryan asked.

"He is. Something the matter?" the server asked.

"No. I'd like to meet him, if you wouldn't mind asking for him."

"Sure, let me get him."

"Why do you need to see the manager?" Corvina asked.

"You'll have to excuse me for a few minutes. I'm working right now."

Corvina looked around the bar. Her gaze settled on his empty glass, which the server had neglected to clear. She raised an eyebrow.

"Consider it a demonstration of what I do," Bryan said.

Bryan's G&T and Corvina's glass of wine arrived before the manager did. Corvina enjoyed a taste of the wine. She was curious about what it was Bryan wanted to demonstrate.

"What seems to be the problem?" the manager asked without preamble when he reached their table. He was breathing hard from walking up the switchback set of steps leading to the upper level. Given his considerable girth, that wasn't surprising. Corvina spotted large rings of sweat underscoring the armpits of his blue collared shirt.

"No problem," Bryan replied. Corvina looked on with interest, wondering what she was about to witness.

"Then can I help you with something?" The manager wiped his brow and the top of his shaven head with a cocktail napkin he'd plucked from their table.

"No, as a matter of fact."

"I don't understand—what do you want?"

"I'm here to help *you,*" Bryan said. Okay, maybe a little arrogant, Corvina thought.

"Help me with what?" the manager asked.

"Take a seat. You can watch the show with us."

"What show?" the manager asked. He looked at Corvina, hoping she could explain. She maintained a neutral gaze but was curious as hell.

Bryan gestured once more to the empty chair between them. "I wouldn't want you to miss this."

The manager sat down, shifting his considerable weight into the straight-backed wooden chair. Beads of perspiration lined his brow.

"Now pay attention, and keep an eye on your bars," Bryan said.

The manager still looked confused.

"Your bartender," Bryan said, "the one with the spiky blond hair on the bar downstairs, is underringing almost every sale. Watch him add up the drinks in his head, collect the money, and then put the excess cash into the tip box."

They watched the bartender serve three separate customers. On each occasion, it was obvious a lesser number of drinks was rung in than was ordered. Cash was entered into the till *and* the tip box on each transaction.

"I'm going to fire the bastard!" The manager shifted in his chair to get up.

"Sit down," Bryan commanded. "That's only the tip of the iceberg."

The manager pulled his chair back to the table, bumping it in the process and threatening to knock over Corvina's glass of wine. She pulled it to safety and had another taste.

"How many milliliters are in a standard bottle of wine?" Bryan asked the manager.

"What?" The question caught the manager off guard. "Seven hundred fifty."

"And what is your pour on a regular glass of wine?"

"One hundred fifty."

"How many glasses per bottle?"

"Five."

Bryan turned his attention to the upstairs bar.

"The bartender with the eyebrow piercing is underpouring each glass of wine, stretching each bottle to six glasses instead of five. The cash for every sixth glass goes into the tip box."

"How can you possibly know that?"

"I've been watching her for three straight shifts. Don't worry, I've been keeping my receipts, and they'll all be expensed," Bryan said.

He's been here three nights just observing? Okay, he's patient—a good quality in an investigator, Corvina thought.

"What the—" the manager said.

Corvina stifled a laugh.

Bryan didn't let the man finish his sentence. "Do you know what the price difference is between a champagne bottle sold at retail and a bottle sold at wholesale?"

"What?"

"A lot. Your Taittinger by the glass is not *your* Taittinger—someone is smuggling their own bottles in and selling them. Check your garbage tonight and compare the number of empty bottles to the number of bottles sold. The variance will surprise you."

The manager was still sweating, but no longer from exertion.

"Next. Your Belvedere is in fact Smirnoff. Someone swapped the alcohol and is now pouring Smirnoff out of a Belvedere bottle. I've had it tested. Mixed with juice or a soft drink, no one could tell the difference. You can confirm this by comparing your stock purchases to stock sales.

"Similarly, upsells sold at the table only get given the spirits from the well, as the customers can't see what's being poured. And since they're served with mixers, they can't taste the difference. So when the waiter upsells a guest from Cuervo Gold to, say, Patrón Añejo Tequila, they're still getting the Cuervo but paying for the Patrón. The difference goes into the tip box.

"Your buy-three-glasses, get-the-bottle-free promotion is providing a giant loophole to at least two of your waiters. They're giving the remainder of most unclaimed bottles to their friends or selling the remainder for cash to other customers, in effect selling the same drinks twice—once for you and once for them. Leftover wine sold by the bottle is being resold by the glass. This was what was happening at a famous five-star hotel on Piccadilly not too long ago. It's a well-known scam.

"How long do you keep guest stock for guests if they buy a bottle of spirits and don't finish it by the end of the night?"

"Maximum, one month," the manager answered.

"Then what?"

"We reintroduce it into our stock and sell it or dispose of it."

"That's what you *think* is happening. The guest stock you keep for VIPs isn't being disposed of and is being sold for cash to regulars. Only, the cash is going into your bartenders' tip boxes and not the tills.

"Your door girls are recycling free drinks coupons and have copied the entry stamp for their friends. Check your ticket sales versus your door clicker. Unless, of course, your doormen are in cahoots with the door girls. I suspect this is the case, given everything else going on here."

"Jesus H. Christ."

"Oh, and one last thing."

"There's more?" the manager asked. He was shaking his head, looking lost.

"The *broken* handheld terminal for credit cards—the one that never seems to work? In reality, it's a credit card cloning machine your staff uses to clone customer credit cards right in front of them."

Corvina almost gasped. So he was smart as well.

The manager stopped writing. "Can you send me some kind of report?"

"I've already sent it . . . to your boss."

"What? Why would you do that?"

"Because he's the one who hired me to read your team. There he is now."

Corvina followed Bryan's gaze to the entrance, where the hapless manager's boss had just walked in.

"But how is this all possible?" the manager asked, panic in his voice. "We don't have any liquor shortages or cash shortages or any guest complaints. There were no signs."

"Of course there were. I discovered all this after only a few evenings spent reading your staff," Bryan said.

"Then how come I couldn't see it?" the manager asked. Corvina was thinking the same thing.

"That's simple." Bryan leaned forward one last time. He rested his elbows on the table, and in a voice just above a whisper Corvina and the manager had to strain to hear, he said, "Your staff are all in on it together."

"So why the international phone call and urgency to meet?" Bryan asked her once they were alone. The manager and his boss had disappeared into the back of the bar, presumably to the office where the manager would be reamed out and fired.

"I need assistance in an investigation, and you came highly recommended," Corvina answered.

"For what?"

"It's hard to explain."

"Try me."

"I'm a flying winemaker. I work for Universal Wines."

"Ah, you're not a Master of Wine, are you?" Bryan took her card out of his pocket to study it once more.

"No, but I understand you pursued an MW?" Corvina asked.

"Why did you call me?" Bryan asked. Corvina sensed a sudden change in his demeanor.

"I'm hunting bugs," Corvina stated.

"Excuse me?" Bryan set his drink down.

"You've heard of phylloxera?"

"Ah, by bugs you mean aphids!" Bryan responded with enthusiasm. Gone was the chill present only moments before, when she'd asked him about the MW. "And by *heard of phylloxera,* you mean recently, I suppose."

"Yes and yes."

"I've been thinking a lot about that."

"Really?" Now it was Corvina's turn to be surprised.

"Yes. I'd heard reports of an infested vineyard in California. I mean, I suppose it was bound to happen in previously uninfested areas, in particular those where the vines aren't grafted to be resilient against attack—like in Chile for instance, where the terroir is sandy. But for supposedly grafted and resistant rootstock, it sure is unusual."

"Exactly. And for the infestations to be found in vineyards thousands of miles apart is highly suspect. Italy—"

"And Napa," Bryan finished her sentence.

"Wait. How do you even know about this?" she asked.

"I have RSS feeds to keep me up to date on trends and events in the wine industry. There have been other infestations."

"Why are *you* looking into this?" Corvina asked, wondering if, in fact, Bryan was the best person to ask to assist her in her bizarre quest. She hoped he wasn't some kind of conspiracy nut.

"Individual winemakers, distribution companies, regions, and countries will have no interest in solving the problem holistically. They'll be too narrow in their focus and won't see the bigger picture. The wine industry is global, and this is a global issue."

What he said made sense to her, but she felt like he was hiding something. Was it just professional interest that drove him, or did he have a personal reason to want to help?

"I think someone is behind this," he said.

"Like who?" Corvina asked.

"I haven't the foggiest, but if someone is behind the infestations, they have resources and truly understand every winemaker's worst fear," Bryan said. "Tell me what you know so far."

Corvina told him of her recent trip to Italy, the discovery of the aphids, and her investigative trip to California. She liked how he listened intently, interjecting only once in a while with a clarifying question.

"Sounds like you're going to need all the help you can get. Lucky for you, I'm available," Bryan said.

"Perhaps. I've just begun looking into the matter." She was still not sure what to make of Bryan. "So where would *you* go from here?" she asked, looking around the wine bar.

"Chile," Bryan said, thumbing his phone screen.

"What's happening in Chile?" Corvina asked. She leaned forward, trying to get a better view of Bryan's phone.

"My RSS feed just got a hit on an arrest of a Chilean national in California."

"Arrested for what?"

"Spreading aphids in a Napa Valley vineyard. They're already calling him an environmental terrorist."

"This could be the lead I'm looking for." Was partnering with Bryan the right decision? She felt like she was on the back foot with him. He was obviously intelligent, had the right experience and background, and perhaps most important, he was available. Despite her nonexistent alternatives and the mounting pressure she felt to continue her investigation, she still wasn't convinced.

"Thank you for your time, Mr. Lawless. I'll be in touch if I think you can be of assistance in my investigation." She pushed back her chair and winced as it scraped loudly on the floor. She stood and shook Bryan's hand, replaced her tribal-patterned scarf, and shouldered her bag. As she walked down the wooden switchback steps, she resisted looking back at him.

CHAPTER 7

HEATHROW INTERNATIONAL AIRPORT
TERMINAL 5
LONDON, ENGLAND

Bryan searched the sea of faces in Terminal 5 from his position next to the British Airways check-in counter. An online search the night before had shown him that BA had the only flight from London to Santiago, Chile, that day. When he checked in, he was able to confirm the flying winemaker was on the same flight. Now he was waiting for her to arrive.

It was easy enough for him to determine what flight she would be on, but finding the hotel she planned to stay at took more time. He called over a dozen hotels before he was able to confirm she had made a reservation at the Marriott. He had pretended to be her fiancée wanting to surprise her with a bottle of champagne in the room. It was the only way he could get the hotels to confirm her booking status.

He was excited about joining forces with her to investigate the spread of phylloxera. Maybe Candy was right—he should use his skills to contribute to the industry and stop sniping at it from the outside. If pairing up with the flying winemaker gave him a chance to resit the Master of Wine exam, he was going to embrace the opportunity. With his MW, he could get his career, and his life, back on track.

He saw Corvina approach a hundred meters away. She was dressed smartly in a dark-gray pantsuit, the only pop of color coming from a green-and-fuchsia silk scarf worn in a loose knot around her neck. She walked slowly, dragging a small black suitcase on wheels behind her, the bounce in her step from the night before gone. The life of a flying winemaker sounded glamorous, but the reality of hours in the air and on the road away from home didn't appeal to him.

He saw her ask an employee a question. She was directed to the row of self-serve check-in kiosks where he was standing. He watched her approach. Less than nine meters away, her eyes met his; he watched as her expression changed from confusion to anger.

"What are you doing here?" she asked.

"I'm catching a flight to Santiago."

"Santiago, Chile? That's where I'm going. Are you following me?"

"I got here before you. How could I be following you?"

She slapped her confirmation papers down on top of the self-serve kiosk and proceeded to check in.

"Shame we couldn't stay in Argentina. I've never been and would love to taste Argentinean malbec in situ," Bryan said. He leaned against the kiosk and waited for Corvina to retrieve her boarding pass. No direct flights were available, necessitating a brief stopover in Buenos Aires, Argentina, to catch a connecting flight across the Andes.

"Maybe I'll leave you there. Wait, how did you know I was flying via Argentina?"

"Lucky guess. Have you been to Chile before?"

"Of course. Universal Wines has some vineyards there. I speak Spanish, so I've been flown over a few times even though it's not my region," she said. She slipped her passport and boarding pass into her shoulder bag.

He got the impression Corvina was well traveled and had possibly seen more vineyards and wine regions than he had, despite his training and studying for the Master of Wine examination.

"How did *you* come to the conclusion to go to Chile?" he asked her.

"I'm going to Chile to speak with the man's family. I called the police station in California, where they're holding him. They won't let anyone near him except for his lawyers. His family in Chile are worried sick about him," she said. He was relieved to see and hear her body language and tone of voice softening.

"That's what I'm doing too. You're welcome to join me," Bryan said.

"Join you? This is my investigation! I met you just last night, remember? Are you always so difficult?" she asked.

And just like that her fiery temper was back. He led her through security, and they waited in silence for their plane.

Onboard, their assigned seats were next to each other—a request he had made when he checked in earlier than her. Once the wheels were up, he resumed the conversation about the reason for their impending visit.

"Why do *you* think a Chilean national would want to intentionally spread phylloxera?" Bryan asked. He had his own theories but wanted to get her opinion, hoping it would give him a better sense of why she was pursuing the matter.

"Remember, he was caught in an American vineyard. We have no idea if he was responsible for infesting the vineyard in Italy. But he's obviously willing to travel."

"You think there are multiple suspects at play?"

"Who knows? Maybe there's one mastermind behind this and he's paying people off to spread the aphid on his behalf."

"That's possible. Wouldn't it have been easier to hire someone in California to do the job?"

"Okay, if he wasn't hired to do the job, why did he leave Chile to spread aphids in a Napa Valley vineyard?" Corvina asked.

Bryan sat back, deep in thought. He was silent for a few minutes before he spoke again.

"Have you heard of the Chilean grape scare of 1989?" he asked her.

"I recall there being an incident of sorts."

"In March 1989, the US Embassy in Chile received an anonymous call. The caller said Chilean grapes bound for the US had been injected with cyanide. Inspectors from the Food and Drug Administration, the

FDA, found some punctured grapes with white marks on them. So they impounded the lot of fruit before they could be distributed further."

Bryan continued recounting how the incident had unfolded. "The grapes were sent to two separate labs, one in Philadelphia and one in Cincinnati. The lab in Philadelphia found traces of cyanide in the grapes, but the lab in Cincinnati didn't. Unfortunately, the Philadelphia sample was destroyed during the testing.

"The FDA's scientists didn't find traces of cyanide in any of the other grapes. What they should have highlighted at the time is that cyanide dissipates over time and would have done so in the period it was shipped. Also, the markings should have been yellow-purple patches instead of white circles. The white circle marks they pointed to as proof they were injected with cyanide were most likely left by talc residue, which Chilean grape growers sometimes use in pesticides as a stabilizing agent."

"So how did the lab in Philadelphia find cyanide?" Corvina asked.

"They messed up the testing," Bryan continued.

"So then what happened?"

"The FDA urged small groceries and the public to dispose of any Chilean grapes. They also had over two million crates of fruit impounded nationwide to be destroyed or left to rot."

"That must have had a major impact on the Chilean market."

"Between twenty thousand and fifty thousand Chileans lost their jobs."

"Wow. So then the FDA must have had to admit their lab mistake."

"Of course not. The FDA announced they had averted a major tragedy. Since then it's been used as just another example of the FDA overreacting."

"That's a pretty big mistake."

"The FDA claimed they were just being cautious."

"Because of the anonymous phone call. Did anyone ever take responsibility?" Corvina asked.

"No. As it turns out, the anonymous caller called back and told the Embassy it had all been a big lie and they had had their laugh."

"How horrible."

"It gets worse. Twenty-four hundred Chilean fruit growers and shippers sued the FDA for a million dollars each for destroying an entire year's worth of grapes. The way the system was set up, the Chileans had to file twenty-four hundred individual claims if they wanted to sue the government. The FDA denied all of them, leaving the Chileans no choice but to file a suit in federal court.

"The FDA's defense was that there was no case because of the 'discretionary function exemption.' It states the government can't be sued for stupid policy decisions."

"But they messed up the tests!"

"Yes, and that's the argument the Chilean grape growers and shippers used—that the FDA's tests had found cyanide when there was none. But they weren't successful. After six more years of litigation, the Supreme Court declined to hear their appeal. The best they can hope for now is that the incident is used as a bartering chip in trade negotiations between the two countries."

"So you think this is a revenge scheme?" Corvina asked.

"Could be. It's a powerful motivator, particularly if you were a grape grower or your family was in the business. But then it doesn't explain the phylloxera in Italy or how the two incidents could be connected."

"So you think I'm wasting my time? I thought going to Chile was your idea?"

"I didn't say it was a good one, just a timely option," Bryan said. He leaned back and closed his eyes to get some rest. With over fifteen hours of flying ahead of them, it was going to be a long trip.

Eighteen hours after leaving Heathrow, they checked themselves into the Santiago Marriott Hotel. They rode the elevator up to the twenty-third floor.

"Care for a nightcap?" Bryan asked when the elevator reached their floor. "There should be a chilled bottle of champagne in your room."

She found her room was not far from the lift—and right next to his.

"Not tonight. I need to sleep after that flight," she said after a pause. A pause to consider taking him up on the offer? She didn't know. Maybe she was just overtired. Or maybe she was considering having just one drink. Her suspicions of Luis's indiscretions shot to her mind.

"We should celebrate the start of our case together," Bryan said. He leaned casually against the wall. He *was* good-looking and she *was* miles away from home, the thought came unbidden to her mind.

"This isn't a case—it's a serious investigation. This is my job," she said firmly. Her senses returned.

"How do you know how serious it is if we don't know what's going on yet?"

"We will soon find out. We just need to start investigating."

"Good idea. I always find champagne helps me think."

"I am going to bed. I suggest you do the same."

"That's what I'm trying to do," he said.

"I am going to my bed, and you are going to yours. *Buona notte!*" she said with finality, shocked at his brazenness.

"Okay. See you at breakfast?" Bryan asked. He was still smiling.

"*Sí*," Corvina said with a wan smile.

"Enjoy the champagne!" he said as he disappeared into his room.

She entered her room and closed the door behind her. It was dark inside. She could hear Bryan moving about in the room next to hers. She checked her phone to see if she had missed calls or messages from Luis. Nothing. She tried calling him, but the call went to voicemail. Was he screening his calls and ignoring her?

She leaned back against the door, pulled off her scarf, and closed her eyes, trying not to think about the tall, dark, and handsome man she had just traveled with to the other side of the world.

CHAPTER 8

NAPA VALLEY, CA, UNITED STATES

"Can you see them?"

"Not really." Malcolm Goldberg was on his hands and knees in the dirt, staring at the dug-up roots of a vine, looking for bugs. As a staff writer for the *San Francisco Chronicle*, it wasn't how he pictured pursuing a Pulitzer.

The winemaker, Ted Crandall, hovered above him, blocking out the midday sun, making it even more difficult to find what he was looking for. He poked his pen around some of the vine's thick, gray gnarled roots and looked for the small bugs known as phylloxera.

"They're there all right. Just gotta look for 'em," Ted said.

"Okay, yeah, I think I see them. Ugly little things, aren't they?" Malcolm said when he thought he spotted something on the vine's roots. He pulled himself up and wiped the dirt from his palms and brushed off the knees of his slacks, stained brown from kneeling on the ground.

"I noticed them only a couple days ago, when the leaf canopy changed color. Folks up at the university confirmed it just this morning."

"I know. I called them on the way here," Malcolm said.

"It's too late to save my vineyard . . . but maybe not too late to save others."

"Is that what prompted you to call me?" Malcolm asked.

"No, my wife did. She thinks the world should know. She thinks everyone has a right to know everything," the winemaker said. Malcolm followed the man's gaze to the large brick house set among the vines.

"Is phylloxera spelled with one 'l' or two?" Malcolm asked the winemaker as they walked out of the vineyard toward Malcolm's car.

"I don't care how it's spelled, just how it can be killed. I hope your article gets the damn government to act faster than they did back in the nineteen eighties, when it almost wiped out California's vineyards."

"Never mind. Spell check will get it," Malcolm said. He thanked Ted for his time, shook the winemaker's hand, and walked away.

After he climbed into his car, he opened his laptop and returned to the article he was writing on the mysterious resurgence of phylloxera in Napa Valley.

His phone rang just as he was finishing the article. He'd almost had it, the perfect sentence to finish his article. With the ring of the phone, it vanished from the tip of his prefrontal cortex.

He glanced at his phone's screen. It was his editor. He couldn't ignore her.

"Are you finished with the piece on the vineyards?" she asked in her staccato voice. Her staffers called her "Chief" to her face and didn't have the courage to come up with an appropriate nickname to call her behind her back, though many came to mind. Malcolm's favorite monikers included the word "dragon," in reference to her Asian heritage.

"All done," Malcolm replied. He ran a final spell check. "Just sending it now." He amended the spellings when prompted while at the same time he watched the winemaker pace around the vineyard. He reached for his plastic cup of coffee, remembered it had gone cold hours ago, and returned his attention to his laptop's screen and spell check.

Spell check completed, he attached his article to an email.

"Want to read it before I send it to press?" Malcolm asked. His index finger hovered over the mouse pad.

"Do I need to?" He could hear her rifling through papers.

"No," he said.

"Get on with it, then."

Malcolm clicked "Send," and his email with attachment disappeared into the ether, from where it would be extracted and added to the next morning's edition of the *San Francisco Chronicle.*

"Done," Malcolm announced.

"Great," his editor said. "I need you to get down to the hospital and see what else you can dig up on the school fire you covered yesterday. Speak to the parents, do the human-angle thing, but try to speak to the kids as well. If it was arson, as the police seem to think, maybe it was one of the kids."

"If it bleeds, it leads, right?" Malcolm said with distaste at the thought of asking juvenile burn victims to relive their experiences. Twenty-seven of their classmates had perished in the flames.

"Right. And if it burns, it turns," she answered, and ended the conversation.

Malcolm closed his laptop, set it on the passenger seat, and started the car, already thinking about his next story.

CHAPTER 9

SANTIAGO, CHILE

"So you've come to ask questions about my brother?" The most beautiful woman Bryan had ever seen hurled the question at him like an accusation.

Following breakfast, he and Corvina rented a car and drove out to see the Chilean's family, a forty-minute drive out of Santiago. Now he was sitting beside Corvina on a two-seater sofa opposite Carlos's sister, Christina, who sat on a matching chair and glared at him with her big, dark eyes.

A small boy, about five years old, scampered through the living room.

"That's Eduardo, Carlos's son," Christina said, her tone softened. She brushed aside a strand of thick raven-black hair and tucked it behind her left ear.

"Why do you think Carlos went to California?" Bryan asked, matching her soft tone but cutting to the chase. He had to resist staring at her. Aside from long, thick black hair, she had a generous mouth framed by full lips and had curves that even her loose-fitting clothing couldn't completely hide.

"*No tengo idea,*" Christina responded in Spanish. She brought her hand to her mouth and quickly brought it back down, but not before Bryan noticed she chewed her nails.

"There must have been some reason. What motivation could he have had?" Bryan pressed her with the open-ended question.

Christina didn't speak. She was looking at the floor.

Bryan saw Corvina was about to say something, so he raised a hand to signal to her to wait. He could sense that Christina wanted to talk but that it was a painful subject and she needed time.

"Revenge," Christina finally said. She continued looking at the floor.

"Revenge for what?" Bryan asked.

"Our father killed himself after we lost the business because of what the Americans did in 1989. He tried for a few years to recover the business, but he had lost his will," she said bitterly. A tear ran down the left side of her face, and she wiped it away with the back of her hand.

"The year of the grape scare," Bryan whispered.

"Good, you're familiar with what happened." She looked at him again, only now he observed the bitterness in her eyes was gone; in its place was anger. "Yes, we lost an entire season's worth of our crop. It destroyed the business. Like most farmers, we subsisted season to season. To have an entire year's worth of grapes become worthless was too much. My father had to declare bankruptcy after years of building up his business. It never recovered, and he took his life a few years later."

"What about your mother?" Corvina asked.

Bryan sensed the empathy in her question. Corvina had told him on the flight to Chile that her own father had invested his whole life into the family winery and vineyards, and he suspected she was imagining what *her* father would do if everything he worked his whole life for was suddenly taken from him. He followed her gaze to a picture of a handsome couple on the coffee table next to her.

"She died three years ago—natural causes—but her spirit died years before," Christina said.

"When was the last time your brother traveled outside of Chile?" Bryan asked, changing the topic back to Carlos. He wanted to keep Christina focused so his trip to Chile was not a waste of time. He was happy to help Corvina in her investigation, but he would do it on his own terms.

"Never. This was the first time. As far as I know, he's never even traveled farther than fifty kilometers from home. I didn't even know he had a passport. He spends all his time here with us, his family, and at the winery where he works."

"He works at a winery?" Bryan asked. He was surprised that a man whose family was destroyed by the Chilean grape scare would choose to work in a winery.

"*Sí,* he's an assistant winemaker."

"Where?"

"It's a big winery called Errázuriz, not far from here. I can show you how to get there if you want."

"Absolutely," Bryan replied.

"Why do you want to see the vineyard where he worked?" Corvina asked when they were outside walking toward the rental car with the directions Christina had provided.

"It's been awhile since I've wandered through a vineyard and enjoyed fresh air and sunshine on my face."

"Are you serious?"

"Never. Look, this guy Carlos had to start spreading phylloxera somewhere," he replied. "Where he worked is probably ground zero."

A massive cloud of billowing black smoke signposted Errázuriz's vineyards long before they arrived. The smoke rose up into the sky, merging with low, dark clouds threatening a downpour.

Bryan stared at the smoke in awe as Corvina drove into the vineyard grounds and up a winding gravel path to the edge of the vineyard itself. An industrious scene of men pulling and burning vines greeted them.

A giant pile of timber consisting of round wooden stakes used to train the vines lay in a tangle of wires and leaves, tossed haphazardly by the men who were digging them out of the ground. Behind them, other men were tending to the vines with flamethrowers.

"Well, that's not something you see every day," Bryan said.

"*Hola.* No tours today," a swarthy man shouted at them. He walked over to their car. Complementing his bulk, he had a rounded nose and cherubic face but looked like no angel.

"He must be the winemaker. He doesn't look happy," Corvina said. She stopped the car and killed the engine.

"We're not here for a tour," Bryan said, once out of the car. He surveyed the vinous inferno all around him. Vines burned as far as his eyes could see through the smoke and up to the surrounding mountains. Thick tendrils of smoke cut into the darkening sky. The roar and crackle of burning vines was almost deafening.

"As you can see, we're busy. I'll have to ask you to leave," the man protested. He shielded his eyes from stray drafts of smoke and ash that blew down the sloping, burning vineyards.

"You're the winemaker here?" Bryan asked. He shielded his eyes from the smoke as well. He saw Corvina cover her face with her scarf to help filter out the smoke. Today's scarf bore a colorful, multipatterned print.

"*Sí,*" the man responded.

"Why are you burning your vines?" Bryan asked him.

"They're cursed by the devil himself!" The winemaker spat on the ground.

"Cursed?" Corvina asked from behind her scarf.

"By a bug. A bug *Americano*!"

"You mean phylloxera?" Bryan asked.

"Yes, the American pestilence!"

"That's why we're here." Corvina held up a hand in a gesture of supplication.

"You know how to stop the bugs?" the winemaker asked.

Bryan saw him look back at his burning vineyards, nestled in the Aconcagua Valley. A look of panic swept across the winemaker's face.

"Of course," Bryan said.

"We do?" Corvina looked at him.

"But first"—Bryan gave Corvina a pointed look—"we have to find out where the aphid came from and why it is spreading. There are different ways to stop different varieties of phylloxera."

"How did you know our vineyards were infested?" the winemaker asked.

"We didn't. We came to Chile to meet the family of Carlos, your assistant winemaker. He was arrested in California for allegedly spreading the aphid in a vineyard," Corvina said.

The winemaker made a grunt that could be deciphered a dozen different ways.

"When his sister told us he worked here, we drove out to see what else we could learn."

"I don't think you'll learn much here," the winemaker said.

"I'm Corvina, and this is Bryan," Corvina said. Bryan detected hesitation in her voice when she'd introduced him. What was he to her? Friend? Colleague? Partner?

"I am Roberto, chief winemaker here at Errázuriz. Let's go inside, away from the smoke and flames. I cannot bear to watch my precious cabernet sauvignon vines go up in flames." He swept his arm indicating the vineyard on fire. "These ones here are over thirty-five years old."

"This is all cab sauv?" Bryan asked.

"No. Those up there"—Roberto pointed into the distance to the right to vines on steep, sloped terrain—"are my syrah. Only about fifteen years old, but still producing great fruit. Everyone thinks Chile produces only carmenére, but our noble varieties are just as good and getting better by the year."

Roberto led them into the principal building, deceptively large and made of white brick in a colonial style. A wraparound veranda covered in vines added to its charm.

Inside, the walls were of the same white brick and stucco. The floors were reclaimed brick and solid wooden planks. The mezzanine level was constructed entirely of wood, with thick-beamed rafters. Chandeliers, recessed spotlights, and shafts of light from outside illuminated the cavernous yet intimate space. Wooden carvings in bas-relief adorned the walls along with framed prints of maps and certificates of recognition for the vineyard and its award-winning wines. To their left, a set of stairs led down to a barrel room.

Roberto showed them to a tasting area. He busied himself behind the bar and set down five tasting glasses for each of them, along with two Errázuriz-branded tankards for spitting.

"While you're here, you may as well taste some of our wines," he said in a booming voice that made Bryan think he was normally a spirited bon vivant—when his vines were not being razed.

"No, that's okay," Corvina said.

"We would love to taste your wines." Bryan shot her a look and nudged her with his elbow. "I've tasted some before. They have a great reputation, and it would be an honor to taste them with the winemaker himself," Bryan said. He read Roberto as a man who needed a distraction.

"So Carlos was arrested? In California? *Idioto!*" Roberto said from behind the bar. "No wonder he hasn't come to work."

Bryan was amazed at the winemaker's resilience. Outside, his vines were burning, yet he had the stoicism to continue on as though the world would soon right itself. He watched the winemaker bring out a bottle of white wine from a countertop wine chiller and pour them each a generous tasting portion, including one for himself.

"My 2011 Fumé Blanc, made from grapes handpicked from vineyards near the Pacific coast in the Aconcagua region and fermented in stainless steel tanks and aged in oak. The season was cold and dry so there were only moderate yields, yet it was a harvest of high quality and intensity. This sauvignon blanc, you'll discover, is citrusy, herbaceous, and refreshing." Roberto held up his glass to observe its appearance. He inhaled deeply of the wine and took a sip and swished it around his mouth. He reached for the tankard spittoon, glimpsed his burning vineyards outside, and set the tankard back down and swallowed.

"Are you surprised Carlos went to the US and was arrested?" Bryan asked, nosing the wine. "This smells fantastic, by the way."

"Yes and no. He's worked for the past two years straight and never traveled. I guess he was saving up for the flight. He always had a fire in his heart for what the Americans did to his father and their family business. But to curse their land with phylloxera isn't something I would have expected."

"Yeah, it's more of a last resort kind of action," Bryan said. He took his first sip of the Fumé Blanc, grabbed the bottle's cork, and studied it.

"Carlos is a simple boy," Roberto said, and slapped the bar counter to punctuate his statement. "Don't get me wrong—he's clever and is an excellent assistant winemaker. But how he came to know about phylloxera . . . well, there could be only one way."

"Wikipedia?" Bryan asked.

Instead of answering, Roberto went back to the small counter wine fridge where his whites were stored. He pulled out another bottle and poured them each a glass.

"This is my unoaked chardonnay. The grapes are from the Casablanca Valley." Roberto lifted the glass toward the nearest window. "You can see it has a pale-yellow color." He sniffed from the glass deeply. "It has an intense nose, giving tropical flavors of passion fruit and citrus." He swirled the wine, inspected, sniffed again, and took a full sip. "The same aromas of fruit carry through on the palate, and its refreshing acidity makes it a vibrant wine with an enjoyable texture and persistent finish."

"*Delicioso,*" Bryan said. He made no move to spit out his wine.

"Delicate and exquisite," Corvina added. Bryan noticed she, too, ignored the tankard spittoon when tasting the second wine.

"So how do you think Carlos learned about phylloxera?" Bryan asked to guide the conversation back to the purpose of their visit.

"I took in a student of viticulture for a season two years ago. He spent his time studying the rootstock of every varietal imaginable. He also helped around the vineyards, working for nothing but room and board and the opportunity to study in return."

"What was his name?"

"David Slater," Roberto said. A fierce look swept across his face.

"Was he studying anything specifically?" Bryan asked. The name David Slater didn't sound familiar to him.

"Aside from my daughter? He did many studies here, but nothing specific that I can recall. He kept to himself and didn't talk about his work. He always had questions, though. So, onto the reds, *sí*?"

With a flourish, Roberto spun on his heel and retrieved a bottle of red wine from a meter away under the bar. Using fresh glasses, he poured each of them a half a glass of the deep-red wine. Bryan reached for the cork and held it up to examine it more closely.

"The varietal Chile is famous for—carmenére. Straight from the alluvial soils of the *Valle de Aconcagua.* The grapes are handpicked and aged for eight months in French and American oak barrels before being cold stabilized and lightly filtered. It's a fine representation of our indigenous varietal." Roberto held up his glass in a toast. "To carmenére."

"To carmenére," Bryan and Corvina responded in unison. With only a light breakfast lining his stomach, the wine was going straight to Bryan's head.

"On the nose you'll smell roasted peppers, sweet spices, and delicate floral notes."

Bryan inhaled deeply of the wine in the glass. "Yep, I'm getting lots of peppers."

"The palate is intense with similar flavors and is well balanced with smooth tannins and a lingering finish," Roberto said.

"A fantastic grape sadly absent from many wine-growing regions," Corvina mused.

"A varietal not without its charm," Bryan espoused. He was eager to get more answers out of the winemaker and was glad to see his hunch had paid off; the more wines Roberto opened, the more the winemaker seemed to open up.

"You were asking about David, the student." Roberto pointed his glass at Bryan as he continued to enjoy the carmenére. The Errázuriz tankards sat untouched on the counter.

"Yes, do you know if he was studying phylloxera?" Bryan asked.

"I don't know, I'm afraid. He took many soil samples and studied the rootstocks for hours on end. He also visited a lot of neighboring vineyards asking for root samples and tours of facilities. He took a lot of notes on his laptop and told me his studies were going well, but he never shared his work or findings and I never asked. I was more concerned about keeping him and my daughter apart. She's at college now."

"It sounds like he would be worth speaking with, especially in light of what happened with Carlos. It seems unlikely Carlos would have access to a strain of deadly phylloxera."

"It's unlikely," Roberto muttered. "But he did have access to something wonderful." The winemaker perked up as though suddenly recalling an important piece of information. "My 2005 vintage of Don Maximiano Founder's Reserve." Roberto set down his empty glass and dashed toward a small room off the main tasting room. He returned moments later cradling a heavy-looking bottle with a black label.

"Now this is a wine to be reckoned with," he announced as he cut off the foil and removed the cork with an Errázuriz-branded waiter's friend. "A souvenir for my beautiful guest." He offered the wine opener to Corvina.

"*Gracias,*" Corvina said.

"And something for you," he said, and passed the bottle's cork to Bryan.

Roberto poured the entire bottle into a large glass decanter and swirled the wine around to aerate it.

"This is our bordeaux-style blend from grapes picked in the Aconcagua Valley," Roberto announced with pride.

"What is the ratio?" Corvina asked.

"Eighty-five percent cabernet sauvignon, seven percent cabernet franc, five percent petit verdot, and just a dash of shiraz at three percent," Roberto recited as he reverently poured half a glass for each of them from the decanter. "Like much of Europe, 2005 was a *mucho fuerte* year for our wines, especially for the cabernets.

"To make Don Maximiano, the grapes are handpicked and sorted carefully on a sorting table to remove extra plant materials and less-than-perfect grapes. Once pressed, they're fermented in stainless steel tanks and pumped over three times a day to encourage a consistent maceration."

In the glass, the wine was deep red in color and by sight alone could be identified as a big, bold, and special wine.

"The bouquet is complex, with a mix of notes from cherry, black currant, truffle, and cloves. To add some spice, you can also detect the smell of black pepper and cigar box," the winemaker expounded as he thrust his nose as deep into the glass as it would go.

"It smells amazing," Corvina said.

Bryan took his first sip and was impressed by the muscular, tannin-filled wine reflective of the cabernet sauvignon–led blend. The flavor of dark fruits cascaded over his palate and through his mouth, rounded off by the small amount of shiraz giving the wine an ever-so-slight sweetness. He noticed Corvina seemed to be enjoying the wine as much as he was.

"The aging in the French oak barrels imparts additional flavors of chocolate, caramel, and cloves. The finish is long, as is its aging capability. It's just beginning to drink well now, but it will become more complex for years to come."

The winemaker held up his glass in a toast.

"To your success in stopping phylloxera," he said.

"*Salud!*" Corvina and Bryan raised their glasses.

"Did the visiting student have an avid interest in wine?" Bryan asked, noting with concern a slight slur in his speech.

"Not that I recall. He was more focused on his studies and research, but he was familiar with wine and wine-making techniques," Roberto replied.

"Where can we find him?" Bryan asked.

"I have no idea. But he wrote on a regular basis to a professor of viticulture at Brock University," Roberto replied.

"Where is that?" Corvina asked.

"Ontario, Canada."

"Do you remember the professor's name?" Corvina asked.

"*Sí, sí,* of course," he said, opening his eyes as though waking from a pleasant dream. "I'm sure I have some old letters from him. David never left a forwarding address." Roberto left and returned after a few minutes with a small stack of envelopes addressed to David Slater. In the top left-hand corner was the professor's name with a return address at Brock University in Canada. He handed them to Corvina.

"I never opened them, thinking one day he might come back. Now, if he's the reason I have phylloxera in my vineyards, I hope he never does," Roberto said. Bryan sensed a change in the man's demeanor. It seemed like the anger present earlier was creeping back.

"Thank you for your hospitality, the information, and the impromptu, yet excellent, wine tasting," Bryan said as he climbed off his bar stool. He helped Corvina off hers and turned to leave.

Roberto escorted them out of the building. They all walked with a light step. The smell of smoke assaulted their senses once they were outside and once more reminded Bryan of their purpose. He approached a pile of vines and found a few phylloxera he could take away as samples. He would have them analyzed when he could.

"I wish you could take them all away," Roberto said after them as they neared the car.

"I think we should check out more vineyards here in Chile to see if any others have been infested," Corvina suggested after they said their goodbyes and they were both in the car.

"If one is infested, others will be too. We already know it's here," Bryan said.

"In that case, I should go back to California and report what I've found to my company."

"Just send them an email. No need to go back. That's a waste of time."

"I can't believe I'm chasing a bug around the world!" Corvina said.

"Then don't."

"What do you mean?"

"Don't chase the bug—chase the man."

"Who? Slater? We have no idea where he is. He could be anywhere in the world."

"True, but we know where he was," Bryan said.

"You mean Canada?"

"Yes. If anyone can help us find Slater, it will be the professor he was corresponding with at the university."

Corvina didn't answer him, but he noticed she also didn't disagree with him.

As they drove away, leaving the hellish scene behind them, Bryan couldn't help but consider in silent horror the burning of a vineyard. If phylloxera led a man like Roberto to set fire to his own livelihood, what else might it lead winemakers around the world to do? It was a sign that didn't portend well of the aphid's return to the globe's terroir under vine. To Bryan, it gave credence to Corvina's theory that someone was orchestrating the spread of phylloxera, and he fully intended to help her find out why. If he could solve that mystery and help bring an end to phylloxera's swathe of destruction, he might find his own redemption and finally atone for the indiscretions of his past.

CHAPTER 10

COMODORO ARTURO MERINO BENÍTEZ INTERNATIONAL AIRPORT
SANTIAGO, CHILE

"Earth to Corvina." Bryan waved a hand in front of Corvina's face. "What has you so engrossed?" It was the day after they'd visited Errázuriz, and he was seated next to her in the terminal awaiting their flight to Toronto. He was energized by the outcome of their talks with Carlos's sister, Christina, and the winemaker, Roberto, at Errázuriz. They had another lead to pursue, and he felt Corvina had come around to the idea of being partners in the investigation. She no longer appeared to be angry with him for coming to Chile.

"*Lo siento.* I was reading an article in the *San Francisco Chronicle,*" she said. She looked up from her phone.

"What's the article about?" Bryan asked, peering at her screen.

"Everything we're looking into. It's titled 'Philomena Strikes Napa Winery!'"

"Philomena? Don't you mean phylloxera?"

"I didn't write the article—I'm just reading it, and it says Philomena. 'In just one week, an aphid known as Philomena has infested several vineyards around the world. It struck first in Italy, followed by a prominent winery in Napa Valley, California, and most recently at Errázuriz in Chile, outside Santiago.' He goes on about the vineyards and how much damage was caused. Then he writes about how the aphid attacks the root of the vine, blah, blah, blah. Oh wait, he says the cause of the infestations isn't known." She scrolled down farther.

"He writes about the nineteenth-century outbreaks across Europe. 'Over a period of several decades, Philomena destroyed most European vineyards, those in France especially, virtually collapsing the European wine-making industry. The American aphid was accidentally imported to Europe by English botanists who brought samples of aphid-infested vines back with them in the mid-nineteenth century. The aphid first ravaged vineyards in England before it crossed the Channel.'"

"Anything else?"

"He writes about how Philomena was thwarted. Thwarted? Is that a word?" She looked at Bryan.

"Yes, a perfectly good one."

"It is awkward to read. Like a piece of cork in a nice glass of wine."

"I didn't make up the language. I just speak it," Bryan said.

"Anyway"—Corvina rolled her eyes in a way he found cute—"he writes about how the discovery that the aphid was repelled by grafting European vines onto American rootstock, still used to this day, led to the replanting of Europe's vineyards."

"Does he suggest what could be causing the current attacks or tell us something we don't already know?"

"No, he just speculates on what farther spread could do to the industry."

"How can he have put it together so quickly? Especially to include Errázuriz in Chile?" Bryan asked.

"I don't know. I only discovered phylloxera in Italy last week. There's a link to some other articles he's written too," Corvina said. "I'm going to call him."

"Right. I'll get us some coffee."

"Any luck?" Bryan asked when he returned. He handed a Tim Hortons cup to Corvina and sat next to her.

"I found the journalist online. His LinkedIn profile listed his cell number under his contact information. I called and asked how he knew about the spread of phylloxera. He said he only knew what he'd written in the articles. He heard about the attack in California and then kept his eyes open for other attacks in case there was a pattern."

"How did he know about the winery in Italy where you first discovered phylloxera?"

"The ex-winemaker of the winery has been posting all over social media that the vineyard is infested."

"What a prince."

"You have no idea."

"And Errázuriz?"

"He figured out where Carlos worked and called the winery directly."

"How does that help us?" Bryan asked, taking a sip of his tall double-shot skinny latte.

"It doesn't. I told him about our investigation."

"How did he react?"

"He was excited. He asked if he could help in any way."

"Let me guess—in return for keeping the lead on this story?"

"Quid pro quo."

"Okay, so how can he help?"

"If he can help with research while we investigate, that will speed things up."

"Yes, because we haven't been moving fast enough already. Do you really think we need another person helping with our investigation?" Bryan asked. He was worried that his own involvement might be diluted with more people investigating. He had already begun to think of the investigation as his and Corvina's.

"He already knows more than us, and he obviously has good resources. I think we should take advantage of any help we can get. Don't you?"

"Yes, yes of course," Bryan said. "So he'll call us when he learns more?"

"Even better. He's going to meet us at the airport in Toronto."

"Malcolm's flight arrived before ours, so he should already be here," Corvina said as they cleared customs in Toronto.

"Do you think that's him?" Bryan pointed to a man sitting on his own, typing on a laptop. He was dressed in loafers, brown corduroy trousers, and a beige collared shirt. Curly brown hair and glasses completed the scholarly look. An overnight travel bag rested on the floor at his side.

"Could be."

"He looks like a reporter," Bryan said.

"*Looks* like a reporter? What does a reporter *look* like?"

"Like him, you know—always concentrating, bookish, slouched over a computer or notepad. It's easy to read people."

"Can you read me? What do you think I look like?"

"A waitress, or a flight attendant with that scarf," he said without looking at her, knowing his comment would get a rise out of her.

"A what? A waitress or a flight attendant? What's wrong with this scarf?" She held up her embroidered Missoni cashmere scarf.

"Nothing. It's fine."

"*Basta.* You're intolerable."

They approached the man, who continued staring at his screen until they were standing right in front of him.

"Malcolm?" Bryan asked.

"Yes?" He stopped typing and looked up. "Oh, hi!" he said. He stood and extended a hand. "You must be Corvina and Bryan. How wonderful to meet you. You've just flown in from Chile? You must be exhausted."

"We're fine, just anxious to get moving again," Corvina said.

"It's okay—we have coffee," Bryan said, hoisting his Tim Hortons cup and stifling a yawn.

"Let's go, then," Malcolm said. He tucked his laptop into a shoulder bag and grabbed his travel bag.

"What made you name the aphid Philomena?" Bryan asked as they walked through the arrivals hall, Malcolm between them. They passed a group of flight attendants, all wearing silk scarves. "Nice scarves, ladies," Bryan called out and smiled at Corvina, who blushed like a young pinot noir and immediately removed her scarf.

"An accident. What I didn't realize—or catch when I ran the spell check on my article—was that phylloxera isn't listed in my word processing program's dictionary. It autocorrected every appearance of the word and changed it to the closest word it could find. In this case, Philomena," Malcolm said. "Unfortunately, no one else caught it either."

"Well, it certainly caught on. All of the press are now calling the bug Philomena," Corvina said.

"It's gone viral, so to speak," Bryan added.

"I suppose they name hurricanes and tropical storms after women, so why not other forms of destruction?" Malcolm said.

"That's right—hell hath no fury like a woman," Bryan said.

"That's not the entire quote. Oh, never mind." Corvina rolled her eyes. Bryan continued talking with Malcolm while Corvina rented a car at one of the myriad of rental agencies positioned in small kiosks lining the arrivals hall. Bryan had to admit, the man was clearly intelligent and had connected the dots of the various attacks as fast as Corvina had. What the journalist did not have was Bryan's extensive wine knowledge and contacts throughout the industry.

"What made you write the first article?" Bryan asked.

"Honestly? My editor. It's not like I was looking for a vineyard infestation story to write about," Malcolm laughed. "I prefer human interest stories."

"But you've written more than one article on the topic."

"After the first story on the vineyard in Napa, I set up some Google Alerts to let me know if there were any more incidents. It's always nice to put a story into a larger context. That's how I found out about the infestation in Italy. When Corvina called me, I knew we were onto something. My research tells me that if the phylloxera isn't stopped quickly, it will just keep on spreading until it's too late. This could be a big story."

When Corvina returned with the car, Bryan took the passenger seat, forcing Malcolm to take the back seat. Corvina navigated the car out of the airport and merged onto the highway leading south. The GPS took them down Highway 427 where they would get on Gardiner Expressway and merge onto the QEW, or Queen Elizabeth Way.

"Where is Brock University?" Malcolm asked after they had been driving for the better part of thirty minutes while sharing their respective findings. They drove over a monstrous bridge named the Burlington Bay Skyway, leading past factories and smokestacks belching out noxious clouds that dominated the shoreline to their right.

"In a city called St. Catharines, an hour south of Toronto," Corvina said.

It wasn't long before the early evening drive became picturesque, taking them past small towns, including Grimsby, Beamsville, Vineland, and Jordan, homes to vineyards such as Vineland Estates, Cave Spring Cellars, and Henry of Pelham.

"Some of these vineyards have interesting names." Malcolm pointed out directional signs for wineries such as Megalomaniac, Organized Crime, and Foreign Affair. "I didn't realize Canada had such an extensive wine-growing region."

"They're prolific—especially in Southern Ontario," Corvina said.

"Most of the time when you hear about Canadian wines, it's in reference to ice wine," Bryan agreed.

"But isn't it too cold in Ontario for the grapes to grow?" Malcolm asked.

"For much of the year, yes," Corvina answered. "Most of the vineyards are in a microclimate between Lake Ontario and a natural elevation of land called the Niagara Escarpment. This explains why most of the area under vine is dedicated to white grape varietals. Grapes such as riesling and gewörztraminer, but also pinot grigio and chardonnay, are well suited to cooler climates. The reds in Ontario tend to be on the heavier side with merlot, cabernet sauvignon, and shiraz growing better than more delicate varietals, such as pinot noir."

Following the voice of the GPS, they exited the QEW onto Highway 406, taking them through Ridley Square and past the city's coed private school, Ridley College. A short drive across the Burgoyne Bridge led them past the local rock music radio station, 97.7 HTZ FM.

The last leg of their drive led them down Glenridge Avenue, a narrow, tree-lined street. The giant trees' branches arched over the street, providing sun-speckled shade. Each lawn appeared more immaculate and vibrant green than the last.

"What a beautiful city," Corvina said.

"They call it 'The Garden City,'" Malcolm said, looking at his laptop.

"I can see why." Bryan leaned forward to admire the view.

A winding hill at the end of the road led them toward the university where Bryan hoped they would find the answers to who was responsible for Philomena.

CHAPTER 11

NIAGARA-ON-THE-LAKE
ONTARIO, CANADA

"We're going to pick grapes in this weather?" Malcolm cried from the back of the rental car. Corvina glanced at the rearview mirror and smiled at the journalist's complaint.

Outside, the sky was black and full of stars. Stretching for miles on her right, the vast mass of the Niagara Escarpment was invisible in the inky darkness. The temperature outside the car was minus sixteen degrees Celsius—freezing cold. Inside, she had the car's heater blasting to little effect. Malcolm sat in the back seat rubbing his hands together, while in the seat next to her she could see Bryan bouncing his legs up and down to keep his circulation going to stay warm. The clock on the dashboard read 00:35, just over nine hours since they had arrived in Canada. It seemed to her to be one of the few things in the car that wasn't frozen. A song about corduroy roads played on the radio.

"It's the only time you can pick grapes to make ice wine," Corvina replied brightly from behind the steering wheel. "For grapes to make ice wine, they must be picked once they have been frozen on the vine at a minimum of minus eight degrees for at least seventy-two hours. That's the Canadian standard regulation."

"Don't the Canadians have regulations against forcing foreigners to do manual labor in the dead of night in the freezing cold?" Bryan asked.

"It was the only way Professor Taverne would agree to speak to us. He said some of his volunteers had called in sick so he needed more bodies to help bring in the harvest at a vineyard the university works with."

"I thought grapes were picked by machine?" Malcolm asked.

"In many cases they are, but to make ice wine, the grapes have to be handpicked," she said.

When the GPS announced she was nearing their destination, Corvina slowed and turned off the rural highway. She drove up a long paved road to the winery and parked among several dozen cars and trucks. Some were running with the occupants still inside. With the ground covered in snow, it was impossible to tell where the lot ended and the grounds skirting the frozen, ghostly vineyard began.

"We're here. Let's go," Corvina said. She opened the door and let in a blast of icy air that sucked the warmth out of the car. She pulled her Burberry scarf, wrapped in a classic Parisian knot, more snugly around her neck. The soft, tartan-patterned cashmere warded off the chill. The sound of gas-powered generators met her ears, and bright lights powered by the generators shone onto the snow-blanketed vineyard.

Corvina spied a cluster of thirty to forty people all dressed for the weather and standing in a semicircle. There was animated conversation among some, others bounced on their toes to stay warm, and the remainder stood looking forlorn with resigned postures. Two men stood in front of the group.

"There's Professor Taverne," Corvina said, and pointed to the man on the right wearing a bright-blue jacket. She gave the professor a little wave, and he nodded in acknowledgment. The professor of enology and viticulture was in his midforties, had a pale complexion, and could have been described as handsome had he looked after himself better. He didn't look like someone who spent much time in vineyards.

"Let's go, people—we haven't got all night!" the man standing next to Professor Taverne shouted. He was a full head taller than the professor and looked like he was accustomed to the outdoors and giving orders.

"Who's the drill sergeant?" Bryan asked.

"I'm not sure. He must be with the winery," Corvina said.

"My name is Mr. Morley. I am the head winemaker here at Pirri's Vineyards," the man next to Professor Taverne bellowed. His deep voice carried clearly into the night.

"First and foremost, thank you for coming tonight. Nobody present is required to be here . . ."

"Speak for yourself," Bryan whispered.

Malcolm chuckled.

Corvina glared at them.

"So thank you for coming on such a god-awful morning at a god-awful time to help me and my team bring in the harvest of cabernet franc, riesling, and vidal for next year's ice wine. Let me tell you how we're going to work tonight.

"No matter how cold your fingers get, do not, I repeat, *do not* cover them with any kind of material to get warm. Not your hat, your scarf, or gloves. The warmth generated will thaw the grapes you pick, and this will increase the yield of juice from each grape. Each grape is meant to yield only a small amount of juice to make the best possible ice wine. One bottle per bunch of grapes. Any more than that and the wine's sweetness, and therefore its quality, will be compromised. There's a box of fingerless gloves and a box of vine cutters next to the generator.

"You will be working in teams of four—two people on each side of the vine, sharing plastic crates to hold the grape bunches. You and your group will pick row by row. Your row will be lit by the spotlights mounted on those pickup trucks." He waved toward a row of idling vehicles.

"The grapes will be pressed on-site as fast as possible, as soon as you get them to the end of the row, so they don't thaw. Just like the truck lights, the pressing machines are mobile and will follow your progress. Don't fall behind, or you'll be picking in the dark and running crates farther than you have to.

"Make sure to collect your gloves before you go into the vineyard. For those of you who didn't bring your own, you can also pick up a pair of kneepads. You're going to need them, as the ground is frozen. With a little luck, we'll be finished in about three hours. Happy picking!"

When everyone began dividing into groups, Corvina introduced herself to the professor.

"Miss Guerra, I'm glad you came. I was a bit worried you and your friends might not show. Frozen grape picking isn't for everyone," the professor said. "You're lucky we're picking in Niagara-on-the-Lake. It's three to four degrees warmer here due to the microclimate created by the Escarpment."

"Real lucky," Bryan said.

"We're happy to help—aren't we, guys?" she asked Bryan and Malcolm. She held up a pair of kneepads with as much enthusiasm as she could muster, her breath visible in the chilly night air.

"Thank you for seeing me," Corvina began the conversation with the professor once they began picking.

"It worked out well. I needed more volunteers," the professor said, and nodded toward where Bryan and Malcolm were already low to the ground picking frozen grapes with the other volunteers.

"They are happy to help—only minimal arm twisting was required," Corvina said to the professor, who was on the opposite side of the vine they were picking.

"I'm sure." The professor smiled back.

"Professor Taverne, we came to talk to you about the recent spread of phylloxera," Corvina began. She also wanted to know if the kindly professor could be working with Slater.

"I doubt it will spread farther. Grafting technology has proven too strong for it to persist."

"You don't think phylloxera is a threat?" she asked, surprised.

"Perhaps as much as global warming is. Though your colleague's articles are entertaining, and I can see why the idea is catching on."

"I would say the infestation and subsequent loss of vineyards in Italy, California, and Chile seems pretty threatening, wouldn't you?" She felt her face grow hot despite the subzero temperature.

"A vineyard here, a vineyard there, spread out around the world. Hardly anything to get worked up over." The professor chuckled.

"We have reason to believe there is someone behind this. I could use your expertise to help me figure out who and why," she said, trying to appeal to his intellectual side. She forced herself to take a deep breath between clenched teeth. She didn't understand why people couldn't see the threat phylloxera posed. She could only imagine what it must have been like for those people in nineteenth-century France trying to convince their peers phylloxera was a threat.

"You should find one of my ex-students to speak with about the aphid—David Slater. He can tell you everything about phylloxera." The professor shuffled down the row of vines, and Corvina mirrored him so they picked face-to-face.

"Can you tell me what he was working on?" Corvina asked. She chose not to reveal she was already aware of the professor's relationship with Slater.

"He was researching phylloxera, among other types of aphids. He was also working on a neurotoxin to combat phylloxera—a genuine preventative method, in case it ever came back in a mutated form resistant to American rootstock. His research and experimentation into phylloxera was groundbreaking. But who needs a solution to a problem that's already been solved?"

"Was he close to discovering this neurotoxin?" Corvina asked.

"I believe he was—no small feat. Recall that it took years to discover the aphid was the source of the vineyard's destruction across Europe in the nineteenth century and many more years to figure out how to stop it. Its life cycle is incredibly complex. The problem is, he became paranoid toward the end of his time here at the university."

"In what way?" Corvina asked. She felt she was getting close to the crux of the conversation.

"He registered patents on every discovery he made. He stopped sharing his research with me, even though I was mentoring him. He even left the program before finishing. I encouraged him to do some fieldwork—he chose Chile—but he was meant to come back and complete his studies."

"What was he like? I mean as a student." Corvina didn't know how close the professor might be to his ex-student or whether he may even still be in contact with him, so she was careful to keep her questions neutral.

"Brilliant, introverted, with an unquenchable curiosity and tenacity that drove his research. We got on well at first, but once it was obvious he was surpassing even my knowledge and experience, he became sullen and secretive." The professor brushed a layer of snow off a bunch of grapes before dropping them in the crate.

"That must have been difficult," Corvina said. She reflected on her relationship with her father and how he seemed to close himself off to her once her wine-making skills had grown to match, and eventually surpass, his own.

"What's your interest in finding him?" Professor Taverne asked. He stood up and arched his back. Corvina hoped he wasn't signaling an end to the conversation.

"We want to ask him about the recent outbreaks of phylloxera," Corvina replied. She stood to stretch as well. Her back and shoulders already felt cramped. "We think he may know something, like maybe how to stop it." She didn't share her thoughts with the professor that she and Bryan suspected Slater was responsible for the spread of phylloxera.

"You're looking for the right man. If anyone can stop what's happening to those vineyards . . ." Professor Taverne's voice trailed off like the plume of his breath in the freezing air.

"That's what we're hoping. But we're also afraid that Slater may already be involved," Corvina said after building a small degree of rapport with the professor.

Professor Taverne looked up sharply. "Do you think he's responsible for this phylloxera reemergence?"

"We were hoping to ask him ourselves. If he's not somehow involved himself, he may know who is. Do you know where we can find him?" she asked.

"I haven't a clue," the professor said. Corvina searched his face for signs of deception but found none. She believed him and was grateful for the information he had shared with her, but she was unsure of her next move.

"I see why they gave us kneepads," Bryan said from deep within the vineyard. He was crouched on both knees leaning into the vines in front of him to shear off the next snow-covered cluster of frozen grapes. The uneven ground was all jagged edges, stones, and ice.

To his right, the blinding light of the spotlights illuminated their work. To his left was pitch black. The sound of the generators rumbled on in the background, forcing the pickers to shout as they got closer to the end of the rows, where the generators were loudest. Howling, freezing winds off Lake Ontario hurtled through the vineyard's rows.

"Microclimate my ass," Bryan grumbled.

"Just f-f-focus on the grapes," Malcolm said.

"These aren't grapes—they're marbles. I'm surprised they can get even *one* drop of juice out of them," Bryan said.

"How long have we been out here?"

"Thirty minutes."

"Feels like double that."

"*Tempus fugit* when you're having fun."

"Ha! Is this your first time grape picking?" Malcolm asked.

"Yes," Bryan answered.

"Really? I assumed this is something you would have done before, given your knowledge of wine."

"I like to learn about wine in less harsh conditions," Bryan said. He stood up and shuffled to the next vine. He took a knee and slid the plastic crate full of grapes farther down the row.

"Me too. I hope Corvina's conversation with the professor is proving fruitful so we can find Slater and get out of here."

"Are you talking about David Slater?" a woman in her twenties with blonde hair poking out the sides of a Toronto Maple Leafs toque asked from across the row of vines.

"Yes. Do you know him?" Bryan asked. He stopped picking. He peered through the vines, waiting for the woman's response.

"Of course. Professor Taverne doesn't stop talking about him. He was one of his star students. He's here tonight."

"Here? Where?"

"He went over there." The Maple Leafs fan pointed in the direction Bryan knew Corvina was picking grapes with the professor. "He said he was looking for Professor Taverne. He's wearing a red toque."

"Let's go," Bryan said to Malcolm, and stood up. He dropped his vine cutters into the crate of frozen grapes. "Thank you," he called over his shoulder to the young woman.

"We better hurry," Malcolm said from across the row of vines. "If Slater's here and knows we're looking for him, we could be in danger."

"My thoughts exactly. And Corvina's on her own right now!" Bryan ran down the row of vines as fast as the uneven terrain and his cramped legs would allow.

"There's the professor. I recognize the blue jacket," he said when he saw the professor twenty meters away. "But I don't see Corvina. She should be across from him. Do you see her?" he asked Malcolm, who was running in the row next to him.

"No. Wait, I think I see Slater. There—he's in the row behind the professor. Wearing a red toque. Do you see him?" Malcolm shouted over the vines.

"No, where?" Bryan looked around wildly, fearful for Corvina's safety. All of a sudden, he saw a man appear behind the professor ten meters away.

"Slater!" Bryan called out across the vineyard.

The man in the red toque looked up.

Slater had a pair of vine cutters in his hands, raised above his head.

Bryan saw a bunch of grapes fly across the row of vines, striking Slater in the face. Slater shouted in surprise and turned to run when he saw Bryan bearing down on him.

"Nice shot," Bryan said to Corvina as she crawled through the row of vines to join the professor. He appeared to be in shock. When Bryan saw the professor was unharmed, he bolted after Slater. He could see him running ahead, the bright generator-powered lights illuminating his back.

Slater reached the end of the row and turned right. When Bryan reached the end, he turned right but then stopped. The lights barely illuminated the vineyard this far out, and Slater could have run down any number of rows in the adjacent vineyard.

Bryan spotted fresh footprints in the snow and ran in the same direction. He followed the footsteps for a full five minutes, running down rows and crawling under vines.

He stopped when it became so dark he could no longer see in front of him. He was running farther and farther from the winery, chasing a desperate man familiar with the area who was prepared for the weather and armed with vine cutters. He inhaled deeply to catch his breath and scanned the silent, snowy vineyard, but his quarry was gone.

"There's Bryan." Corvina pointed at a dark figure emerging from the vineyard behind the winery. She was standing with Malcolm and the professor by the rear entrance, underneath a vent pumping out warm air, looking for signs of Bryan or Slater.

"I almost had him, but he got away," Bryan said as he approached.

"You shouldn't have gone after him. He could have hurt you," Corvina said. For the first time, she worried her investigation might put others at risk.

"It was impulsive, I know. I just wish I could have stopped him," Bryan said. He brushed the snow and dirt off his trousers.

"Well, thankfully you're safe," she said. "At least we've confirmed Slater is involved with the phylloxera outbreak. Why else would he run away like that?"

"I think his being here tonight removed any doubt," Malcolm said.

"I'm sorry about how this has all turned out. I can't believe we're talking about the same person," Professor Taverne said.

"Can you alert the authorities for us? And be careful," Corvina said.

"Of course. I'm sorry for all the trouble."

"It's not your fault, Professor. We must be going now. I think that's enough excitement for one night. Please extend our thanks to Mr. Morley and our apologies for leaving before the grapes are all picked," Corvina said. She gave the professor a hug and led Bryan and Malcolm back to the parking lot.

"At least we got what we came for," she said once she was inside the car with Bryan and Malcolm.

"If we came for frostbite, then Malcolm and I were equally successful," Bryan said.

"My knees are killing me, and I can't get the stickiness off my fingers," Malcolm said.

"I can't even feel my fingers," Bryan said. "Or my toes, or knees, or nose."

"Thank you, guys, for stepping up—or kneeling down," Corvina said. "It was worth it to get the opportunity to speak with the professor about Slater. Now we just need to find him again." She peeled off her gloves and breathed warmth into her hands.

Corvina called her CEO, but not surprisingly it went straight to voicemail given the late hour. She called Vicente and updated him on their progress as the car's engine warmed up and the heater struggled to warm them.

"That was my boss," she told Bryan and Malcolm, who had been listening to her side of the conversation.

"Everything okay?" Bryan asked.

"After I told him what Professor Taverne told me and that Slater was here, he said the CEO wants me to go to Washington DC, to investigate an anti-alcohol, pro-Prohibition group called the Drys. He believes they may be behind the attacks on the vineyards. Maybe Slater's working with them?"

"But Slater is here in Canada!" Bryan shouted.

"At least we'll be going south," Malcolm said through chattering teeth.

"It's a complete waste of time," Bryan said.

"Actually, it's perfect," Malcolm said. "We can go to Virginia while we're there."

"What's in Virginia?" Corvina asked. She put the car in reverse and backed out of the winery parking lot.

"The United States Patent and Trademark Office, the USPTO. We can look for the patents Slater registered," Malcolm said. "That might help us track him down or at least give us a better idea of what he was working on and maybe even a way to stop the infestations."

"I don't think this is the right move," Bryan said.

"I don't disagree, but my company is funding the investigation, and the CEO must have his reasons," Corvina said. As she guided the car's rising and falling tires over packed crests of snow, she reflected on the equally bumpy investigation she had embarked on—and thought Bryan may be right.

CHAPTER 12

ST. CATHARINES
ONTARIO, CANADA

Corvina was woken by her ringing cell phone. Her room was pitch black.

"*Hola?*" she answered.

"Corvina, is that you?" a man's voice asked in Italian.

"*Sí*," she answered, a little more awake. She looked at the clock beside her bed and groaned. It was seven in the morning. She must have slept through her six-thirty wake-up call.

"It's Enzo. From Barbara d'Aversa Wines," the voice said after Corvina failed to inquire. Her mind was still booting up.

"Of course, Enzo," Corvina replied. "Sorry, I'm in Canada and still half asleep." The thought arose that he was calling to tell her his vineyards were infested with phylloxera. She sat bolt upright in bed and fumbled for a light switch.

With a winery and vineyards in the Piemonte region of Italy, Enzo was one of Corvina's first clients. They had been through five seasons together and had developed a friendship based on trust and good wines made using sensible growing and wine-making practices. When they first met, Enzo insisted he wanted to be a traditional winemaker and get the best out of his grapes without taking any shortcuts. The winery had been in his family for generations. After his father passed away, he suddenly found himself at the helm of a business he had never fully understood.

"Sorry to wake you, but it's important. It's about your replacement."

"Enzo, Sergio isn't my replacement," Corvina said, relieved it wasn't phylloxera that was troubling him. "He's just covering for me temporarily. I'll be back in your vineyards in no time," Corvina assured him. She had, in fact, no idea how long her investigation into "Philomena" would keep her engaged. It had already taken her to three countries in less than two weeks.

"Corvina, I'm not looking for market share or Parker points. I sell what I can and cellar the rest, and we've made some beautiful wines, you and I. My reputation in the market is solid, and in the region I'm well respected, thanks to you. I trust your judgment, and I need your opinion. He's trying to convince me to use reverse osmosis."

Corvina shuddered. The practice of reverse osmosis became widely used in the 1990s when many winemakers delayed their harvests to make bigger and fruitier wines. The process allowed winemakers to make wines that didn't require lengthy cellaring before being consumed. The unwanted side effect of later harvest times was higher alcohol content, which Corvina preferred to avoid.

Reverse osmosis worked by eliminating excess alcohol in wine using the same technique as used to desalinate water. In addition, it removed undesirable chemicals like ethyl acetate and acetic acid, which could otherwise cause wines to taste like vinegar. But Corvina felt it stripped wine of crucial aromas in the process.

"Let me talk to Sergio. I'll make sure he understands what your wines are all about."

"I know some of my fellow winemakers use the process, even though they would never admit it."

"I would never recommend you practice reverse osmosis. I think it's as bad as adding wood chips to wine to add flavor and bypass barrel aging," Corvina said.

"*Grazie*, I agree. It takes the wine away from its natural roots and destroys its connection with the terroir and nature itself."

She got out of bed and called Sergio as soon as she and Enzo finished talking.

"Sergio, why are you telling Enzo to use reverse osmosis?" she asked when he answered.

"Well, hello to you too, Corvina. Because he insists on reusing his barrels and not getting the flavor he could out of them."

"Have you ever thought maybe he doesn't want fruit bomb wines?"

"It would be an improvement."

"Your limited opinion is well noted. Just deal with whatever he called you for and leave his wines alone," Corvina said.

"He didn't call me for anything," he replied. Corvina could hear the smugness in his voice.

"So why were you even at the winery?" Corvina asked.

"I'm visiting all of your clients to help them improve their wines."

"Don't! You have no idea what they want and no idea what you're doing!" Corvina shouted into the phone. Someone in the room next door banged on the wall. "I have to go. Stop interfering with my customers." She ended the call.

Her cell phone rang again before she had a chance to set it down. It was her mother calling. She briefly entertained not answering; she wasn't used to so much drama in her life before her first cup of coffee.

"Hi, Mamma. Everything okay?"

"*Sí, sí,* of course. I just wanted to make sure *you* were okay. You've been away from home over a week now."

"I'm fine, just tired from all the traveling. I'm in Canada now and leaving for America shortly. How's Papà?"

"Your father is considering a change of barrel and wants to know what kind of oak barrels you think he should use for the reds."

"He wants my advice?" Corvina asked, shocked.

"Oh, *querida,* he does everything you tell him these days—or everything you tell me to tell him, that is."

"You're kidding."

"No, I'm not. Do you know that he visited a few of your customers recently?"

"He did what?" Her overtired mind briefly pictured him traveling with Sergio.

"He went to see some of your customers in the region. He wanted to see for himself what kind of advice you were giving them."

"And?"

"I've never seen him so quiet. I can tell he's very proud of what you're doing."

"But he never listens to me. He's always so . . . so . . ."

"Obstinado?"

"Sí."

"A trait he comes by honestly. And now you know where you get it from."

"I'm persistent, Mamma."

"Sure you are, honey. Oh, you can talk to him yourself—he's coming back inside. He was out tinkering with the tanks. He thinks he can get a few more pressings out of them."

"Papà, when are you going to replace those ancient tanks and get with the times?" Corvina asked her father when he came on the line, a question she had asked a million times.

There was a knock on her door.

"Papà, hold on. I need to get the door," she said. She donned a bathrobe from the washroom and opened the door.

"Almost ready to go?" Bryan asked. He was fully dressed and had his suitcase at his side.

"Give me a few minutes," Corvina said, and held up her phone to illustrate why she was not ready.

"Need help getting dressed?" he asked.

"I certainly do not."

"Okay, meet you in the lobby," Bryan said. Corvina nodded and closed the door but not before noticing Bryan looked her up and down in her bathrobe.

"Papà, are you still dressed?" she asked. "I mean there? Are you still there?"

"I'm still here, *mia cara.* Listen, I've had those tanks for years. They've served me well. They are a part of our winery's tradition."

"I respect tradition, Papà, but buying new equipment has nothing to do with tradition. And there's so much more we can do with the wines," Corvina said.

"You should come back. Marco could really use your help rebuilding his winery since you made his winemaker leave. The phylloxera is getting worse," her father said, changing the subject.

"Papà, the phylloxera is spreading in vineyards around the world. It's not just Italy."

"Don't worry about our vines—they're grafted."

"So were Marco's. This version of phylloxera attacks American rootstock. It doesn't care whether the vines are grafted or not. Our vines are at risk."

"We're pretty isolated out here, so I think we should be fine," he said.

"I'm sure they thought the same thing in Santiago, Chile. Papà, this thing is spreading everywhere. All vines appear to be susceptible."

"Let's wait and see," her father said with finality.

Why did no one seem to understand the true threat Philomena posed? She knew she was not going to convince him of it over the phone.

"Okay, Papà. Please look after Mamma. I have to go. Talk to you soon. *Te quiero.*"

She took a quick shower and packed. She tried to process everything she, Bryan, and Malcolm had learned about Carlos, Philomena, and Slater and the threat they posed to the wine industry.

She raced downstairs to the car where Bryan and Malcolm were waiting for her and put her suitcase into the trunk. They had an hour-long drive to the Toronto airport to fly to Washington, DC, where they would investigate the Drys and the phylloxera patent. She joined them in the car and looped her cashmere scarf around her neck. She shivered from the cold and at the thought of what Slater could be up to at that moment.

CHAPTER 13

K STREET
GEORGETOWN
WASHINGTON, DC, UNITED STATES

Corvina found the Drys anti-alcohol lobbyist group headquarters in a six-story concrete office building near Farragut Square on K Street. Infamous for its think tanks and advocacy groups, K Street was synonymous with Washington's lobbying industry.

The lengthy walk from her hotel in Arlington across Key Bridge into Georgetown refreshed her body and mind. It was warmer than Canada but still brisk. The main strip, M Street, was made up of narrow sidewalks, small high-end shops, and a host of restaurants and bars that catered to nearby Georgetown University. She wished she could spend the day shopping instead of looking into conspiracy theories. She had seen some pretty scarves in a shop window.

Aside from asking her to look into the Drys group for a possible connection to the phylloxera attacks, Vicente had not given her any further information to suggest why James Harvey had made the request. She agreed with Bryan that they should have stayed in Canada to pursue Slater; but as the company was paying for and supporting her in her investigation, she didn't have much choice but to pursue the lead.

She had sent the CEO an email asking him what he thought the link might be between the Drys and Philomena, but he hadn't answered. Could it have anything to do with *his* recent visit to the capital?

Corvina was one step out of the elevator onto the third floor when a woman charged at the elevator, almost colliding with her.

"Are you Corvina?" the woman asked. She stabbed at the button for the lobby and the one to close the doors. "If so, come with me," she said. She gave no time for Corvina to answer.

Corvina stepped back into the elevator before its doors squeezed shut on her.

As soon as the elevator returned to the lobby, the woman flew out, marched across the lobby, and was walking down the street before Corvina could catch up.

"You must be Stacey. Where are we going?" Corvina asked. She followed in Stacey's wake.

"We're spearheading a protest on Capitol Hill, and I need to be there. I hope it's okay if we walk and talk. It's not far," Stacey said. She set a fierce pace.

As Stacey power walked, Corvina sized her up. Only slightly shorter than Corvina's five-foot-nine frame, the lobbyist had dark-red hair, piercing green eyes, and a no-nonsense attitude. The woman wore Steve Madden combat boots, gray jeans, a midlength black jacket, and a plain, frayed gray scarf.

Corvina suspected the woman had a military background.

Stacey couldn't have been more in contrast to what Corvina had expected the head of the anti-alcohol group to look and behave like. She'd been expecting a crotchety old lady angry at the world. She struggled to keep up as Stacey barreled down the street. Pedestrians gave way as she approached.

"What would you like to know?" Stacey began without preamble.

"What are the Drys lobbying for exactly?"

"Total prohibition of alcohol throughout America."

"That's ambitious." Corvina raised an eyebrow.

"Happened once already."

"Not successfully," Corvina dared to say.

"The same and worse could be said for the war on drugs, another form of prohibition, but it doesn't mean we should stop trying. Alcohol is a drug like no other—and perhaps worse than others, because it's so accepted despite the consequences."

"But alcohol is prevalent in so many aspects of society."

"So are physical abuse and bullying," Stacey shot back.

"Don't you think Prohibition illustrated how essential alcohol is to society?" Corvina asked. In many ways she agreed with the lobbyist. She understood the adverse effects alcohol had on individuals and society. But it was an integral part of a system she had grown up with and spent her studies and career working within. When she thought of wine making, she could see only the positive side.

"Essential? Dysfunctional, you mean. Just because alcohol has been around longer than most other drugs doesn't legitimize it—it just makes it that much harder to combat."

"But there are already laws around the sale and consumption of alcohol."

"A lot of good they do. A patchwork of legislation exists here in America. The original Prohibition set this country back decades in terms of any meaningful legislation against alcohol. Let's just say television shows like *Boardwalk Empire* aren't a good representation of Prohibition."

"What kind of activities do the Drys engage in to achieve their goals?" Corvina asked. The sound of a large crowd could be heard ahead, though they were still a full city block away from Capitol Hill.

"Fundraising, sponsoring studies into the adverse effects of alcohol, forging and leveraging partnerships with other groups, lobbying politicians on the municipal, state, and federal levels, and, of course, protesting to raise awareness."

They rounded the corner, and Corvina saw where the noise was coming from. A crowd several hundred strong was shouting en masse, extolling the virtues of sobriety and the ills of alcohol toward Capitol Hill.

The protesters were vocal and highly visible with their signs and placards. The messages included such witticisms as "No wine? That's fine!," "Go Philomena!" with a picture of a cartoon aphid eating the placard where a bite-shaped cut had been made, "You Booze, You Looze!," "Repeal the Repeal!," and her favorite, "Lips that touch liquor shall never touch mine."

"As you can see, the protests in and of themselves aren't necessarily great for our public image, as they tend to attract the fringe element of our supporters. These are our 'Tea Party' supporters," Stacey admitted, referring to the once-popular fringe element of the Republican Party. "What's your interest in the Drys?"

"I work for Universal Wines out of California, though I'm based in Barcelona."

"Yeah, I could tell from your accent and clothes that you're not American."

"I'm looking into the spread of phylloxera," Corvina said, not sure how to take Stacey's observation on her speech and fashion sense. She tugged at her scarf, the same cashmere Burberry she had worn in Canada, and wrapped it tighter against the chilly weather.

"You're investigating the terrorist attack on the vineyard in California?"

"I wouldn't call it a terrorist attack," Corvina countered.

"Have you seen the papers? They've made that poor boy from Chile look like he was single-handedly trying to take down the California wine industry. They take their grapes seriously out there. A foreigner spreading a bug to destroy a piece of the heartland is easily construed, or misconstrued, as a deliberate attempt to subvert the American way of life. In other words—terrorism. Despite the cute name, rest assured the wine industry has taken notice and is worried about Philomena."

"It sounds like you've given this a lot of thought," Corvina said. She sidestepped a small terrier being walked by an elderly man. He was holding up a sign that read "Bring Back Volstead!"

"Of course. As the head of the Drys, I need to be aware of and understand the impact of anything that happens in the drinks industry. I figure it won't be long before they start knocking on my door asking if I have any connection to the boy from Chile or whether I breed phylloxera in my basement." Stacey laughed. It was a harsh laugh.

Corvina strode alongside Stacey and searched her eyes.

"Holy shit!" Stacey stopped suddenly. "That's why you wanted to see me, isn't it?"

"I'm looking into all possibilities."

"Well, you're barking up the wrong tree with the Drys. We lobby for the prohibition of *all* alcoholic beverages—beer, spirits, *and* wines. And we have our hands full with alcohol in America. I don't have the time or inclination to wage war on alcohol on other continents."

"What about the attack on the vineyard in California?"

"What about it? We don't condone terrorist attacks on producers. Revisit your paradigm," Stacey said.

"How do you mean?" Corvina asked.

"You shouldn't be looking for someone who has an agenda against the entire drinks industry," Stacey said. "That's too obvious. You should be looking for who would benefit the most from the destruction of the wine industry—brewers, spirit makers, global beverage companies like Diageo, Maxxium, and InBev. Perhaps they're building up their beer and spirit categories while shedding their wine portfolios. Who knows?"

"You have a point," Corvina conceded.

"You're damn right I do. Look at the targeted vineyards and find out what they have in common. Or follow the money!" Stacey shouted over her shoulder as she waded into the crowd of protesters, leaving Corvina alone surrounded by strangers.

CHAPTER 14

UNITED STATES PATENT AND TRADEMARK OFFICE
ALEXANDRIA, VA, UNITED STATES

"Did you know that before Roswell, New Mexico, and Area 51 became synonymous with UFOs, the original X-Files were credited to the USPTO?" Malcolm asked Bryan. "The first ten thousand American patents, issued between 1790 and 1836, were later designated with a letter 'X' before their patent numbers. The patents were destroyed in a fire in 1836. Less than three thousand of the patents were recovered and are now known as the X-Patents."

"Fascinating," Bryan said. He kept his eyes on the sun-dappled road while Malcolm read up on US patent history on his laptop. He drove along a one-way two-lane highway that cut through picturesque, forested countryside following the Potomac River on the left. A parallel running path was well traveled by cyclists and joggers.

"In February 2013, the Federal Court of Australia ruled in favor of a patent for the naturally occurring BRCA1 gene, in effect allowing for a patent on natural evolution. And in the US, the Supreme Court ruled in June 2013 that human genes isolated by scientists and naturally occurring DNA sequences can be patented if the genes were sufficiently isolated, like in the cases of adrenalin and insulin. Genetically engineered DNA sequences and genes created in the lab could also be patented."

"That's scary," Bryan said.

He hoped Malcolm's hunch that Slater had patented his research into phylloxera with the USPTO panned out. With luck, Slater had also patented the method to destroy his strain of phylloxera and prevent its spread.

Bryan drove south for twenty minutes on the George Washington Parkway. The route took them into the heart of Alexandria, where he found the campus of red brick buildings making up the USPTO. Once inside, Bryan spotted the patent clerk and could tell by her demeanor that she was an open and honest soul. He told her the purpose of their visit. She immediately set to work.

"Gentlemen," the patent clerk announced, her ebony skin glowing with a sheen of perspiration upon her return from her search to address Bryan's query. She wore dark trousers and a red silk blouse.

"I have some good news for you. There is a patent filed with the USPTO with phylloxera in the title—*Apparatus for the Destruction of Phylloxera*, patent number 317.802." She placed a folder on the counter and slid it across to Bryan. Her fingers were as big as his thumbs, and her forearms as big as his calves.

"Great! You found that quickly," Bryan said. He picked up the file.

"What a fantastic stroke of luck!" Malcolm exclaimed, standing next to him.

"Everything is digitized these days, even records going back over a hundred years."

"Well, we won't need anything going back that far," Bryan said, and laughed.

"I don't understand." The patent clerk tilted her head and looked at them askance.

"How do you mean?" Bryan asked.

"This patent is from the nineteenth century. The apparatus was patented in the United States on May 12, 1885; in France on July 31, 1883; in Italy on December 22, 1883; and in Spain on April 21, 1884."

"Who was it patented by?" Bryan asked with a growing sense of dread. He doubted a neurotoxin to kill Philomena was developed in the 1880s.

"A Frenchman named Ludovig Laborde."

"I don't think that will be of much use," Malcolm said.

"I agree," Bryan concurred after quickly skimming through the file. "We're looking for something more recent, say in the last five years?"

"Why didn't you say so?" the clerk asked with a raised eyebrow. She disappeared into the back office.

"Would this be it?" she asked when she returned ten minutes later with a sheaf of papers in hand.

"Let me see." Bryan reached for the freshly printed document. He leafed through the pages, but he needn't have passed the first page. It held the name they were looking for: David Slater.

"This is it, perfect. Thank you."

"I know why I didn't find it the first time," the clerk said.

"Why?" Malcolm asked.

"If it's living or organic, it is under a biological patent," she said.

"How long is the patent valid for?" Malcolm asked.

"That one is for ten years," the patent clerk replied.

"Are there any contact details for the patent attorney or the inventor?"

"I can't give you contact details, I'm afraid, but it looks like this patent was filed from Canada."

"Yes, that's what we believe," Bryan said.

"In that case, they could have had a Canadian patent attorney handle the filing. A reciprocity agreement exists between Canada and the US for filing patents," the clerk said.

"He probably chose to do it himself to keep it as discreet as possible," Malcolm said. "Who registered the patent?"

"The creator of that strain of phylloxera. He sent in the application in a PDF."

"You can do that?" Bryan asked. This was all new to him.

"Yes, of course. Inventors or their patent attorneys can file their application electronically as PDF documents. They pay a filing fee online or create an account with us."

"Can you check to see if there are any other patents registered under David Slater?" Bryan asked.

"That's all of them." The clerk pointed to the papers in Bryan's hands. "I brought them all out."

"It's essentially the same patent for several different types of phylloxera," Bryan observed. He skimmed the pages in the file.

"Why would he file a patent for something he would use to commit a crime?"

"Maybe he didn't create it with the idea of intentionally spreading it; that idea may have come later."

"Any mention of how to stop it?" Malcolm asked.

"Each patent references a neurotoxin, but there's no description," Bryan answered. He leafed through more pages.

"We have to find that neurotoxin. That will be the way to stop it," Malcolm said.

"Hey, does this have something to do with that bug Philomena?" the clerk asked.

"Maybe. We're investigators and have been asked to look into any patents on the subject," Bryan said.

"Wow, really? What, like with the FDA?"

Bryan just smiled enigmatically and was grateful Malcolm kept mum.

"Oh my God. This is so cool," the clerk said.

"We'd appreciate your discretion in this matter," Malcolm said. He adopted an official tone to his voice.

"Oh, of course. Anything I can do to help," the clerk said.

"Well, we would really like to talk to the owner of the patents," Bryan said.

"I'm not sure how helpful that would be?" the clerk said, but she made it sound like a question.

"Why's that?"

"They no longer own the patents."

"What do you mean?"

"They were purchased by a holding company."

"Can you tell us the name of the holding company?" Malcolm asked.

"That I *can* tell you, and it should be easy enough to find online. As you asked the first time, I thought I would check in advance on this one. It looks like this company buys a lot of patents. It might be a patent troll."

"Someone who buys patents and sits on them, hoping they can sell them in the future for a profit," Malcolm explained.

"Exactly. Or in some cases, hold them to ransom," the clerk said. "Here it is. Let me jot down the name of the company."

"Thank you. You've been incredibly helpful." Bryan took the piece of paper, and they left the desk.

"So the whole time he was telling his professor and the world he was working on a cure for naturally occurring phylloxera, he was in fact genetically engineering a new super strain that would be resistant to American rootstock, the traditional and only method of prevention," Malcolm said as they left the USPTO.

"It looks like it, yes," Bryan agreed.

"What now?" Malcolm asked when they stepped into the sunshine.

"Let's go back to the hotel. We need to look deeper into the holding company." Thirty minutes later they were sitting in the lobby at the Key Bridge Marriott hotel, taking advantage of the hotel's free Wi-Fi to power their search on Malcolm's laptop.

Malcolm Googled the name of the holding company.

"The company has offices around the world, but it looks like its headquarters are based in Hong Kong. Oh, and look here." Malcolm pointed to the screen. "Though publicly traded, the company is effectively run and owned by one man, Zhang Tao Lung."

"Never heard of him."

"He's only one of the richest men in the world. He and his twin brother have a fierce reputation."

"So now all we need to do is schedule a meeting with a Chinese billionaire and ask him why he bought the patent for a bug that's destroying the world's vineyards." What on earth had Corvina gotten him mixed up in?

CHAPTER 15

EMERGENCY DEPARTMENT
GEORGETOWN UNIVERSITY HOSPITAL
WASHINGTON, DC, UNITED STATES

"When you said you were going to meet the head of the protest movement the Drys, I didn't realize you intended to join their protest," Bryan said when he found Corvina in the emergency department of Georgetown University Hospital.

"It wasn't my intent. It was the only way I was going to be able to speak with her. Where's Malcolm?" Corvina looked around for the reporter, but in the chaos of the ward he was nowhere to be seen. She clutched her scarf tightly in her hands.

"He said he had some research to do. I'm sure he would have come had he known you were here and not at the coffee shop where we were meant to meet. You look a bit beat up. Is she okay?" Bryan asked the male nurse practitioner who was tending to a bruise on Corvina's neck.

"Just a few cuts and bruises," the nurse said.

"I'm fine," Corvina said. "I think someone's elbow connected with my face," she said while feeling the contours of her face, searching for any additional injuries.

"Did you learn anything aside from not to join a protest in a foreign city?"

"Yes, as a matter of fact. Despite what you think, the protest was peaceful until a few troublemakers got into a scuffle with the Capitol Police. I just happened to get in between them. The Drys are definitely committed to their cause, but not to the extent that they would destroy vineyards around the world," Corvina said. Following her conversation with Stacey, she had observed the crowd of protesters for a while longer to see if she felt any of them capable of launching a global attack on the wine industry. As Stacey had said, they appeared to represent the fringe element of the anti-alcohol movement, but none of them raised any alarms. The next thing she knew, she was being heaved to and fro between the protesters and the police and carted off to the hospital to get fixed up.

"Their beef seems to be more with the spirits and beer industries, the beverage categories that tend to be linked to the negative effects of alcohol. They also don't seem to care what happens outside of the United States. It's unlikely we're dealing with anyone from this organization."

"I don't disagree," Bryan said. "But then why did your CEO send you here? It seems like a long shot when we have better leads to follow and Slater is on the run." Bryan pulled himself onto the gurney Corvina occupied and sat down beside her. He placed a hand on top of hers, wrapped inside her scarf, and squeezed her fingers through a layer of cashmere.

"I've been wondering that myself," Corvina said.

"I'll be right back. I'm going to write you a prescription for some painkillers," the nurse said.

"Thank you," Corvina said.

"The trip wasn't a total bust," Bryan said after the nurse left. "It worked out well that we were able to check out the USPTO." Bryan recapped his and Malcolm's discovery of the filed patents and their new owner, the Chinese billionaire industrialist Zhang Tao Lung.

"So what *about* the spirits and beer industries?" Bryan asked. "They would benefit from the destruction of the wine industry, as people would buy their products if wine was no longer available or if prices skyrocketed."

"That's what Stacey suggested," Corvina said. "It would be worth checking out the recent activity of the major beverage companies and players in the beer and spirits categories."

"I'll ask Malcolm to look into it," Bryan said.

The nurse returned with a prescription for painkillers and gave her directions to the on-site pharmacy.

"Malcolm should also look at any major asset purchases or sales as well as mergers and takeover bids," Corvina suggested as they slid off the gurney and made their way to the pharmacy. She let go of Bryan's hand—grateful he was there, but not yet ready to trust herself in another relationship—and draped her scarf over her shoulders.

"The market share wine has gained in the last thirty years, especially here in America, must have come as a surprise to many competitors," Bryan said. "Since 2004, the world's wine supply hasn't been able to keep up with market demand. Global wine production peaked in 2004 and has been falling since."

"I've heard of peak oil but never peak wine," Corvina said.

"Many believe we'll soon be facing a global wine shortage. Production has been severely limited in recent years by poor weather conditions and vine pull."

"This is the worst possible time for vineyards to be attacked by an unstoppable, genetically engineered aphid," Corvina said. "Especially in Europe. Vineyards everywhere will be equally affected." Her thoughts turned to worry as she thought about her European clients and her parents' vineyards in Italy.

When she and Bryan met Malcolm an hour later at a wine bar in Georgetown, she was looking forward to finding out what his research had uncovered.

The bar was packed with local university students, but Corvina managed to find them a high table with three chairs. She ordered a bottle of white wine for their table. Their server went about pouring them each a glass and then left the bottle in an ice bucket and its cork on the table. Corvina noticed Bryan study the bottle's cork for a minute before he slipped it into his pocket.

"Should you be drinking wine while on painkillers?" Bryan asked her.

"I'm not pregnant, and I promise not to operate any heavy machinery," she quipped. "I think I'll be okay with a glass of wine."

"Nice wine. It has an interesting smell—what is it?" Malcolm asked, holding the glass up to his nose.

"New Zealand sauvignon blanc, and it smells like cat's pee," Bryan announced.

"Oh, has it gone off?" Malcolm asked, and set his glass down.

"No, it's a telltale aroma of the varietal, especially for New Zealand sauvignon blanc," Corvina said.

"I should have ordered the riesling," Malcolm said. He looked warily at his glass.

"Then you would be smelling petrol, if it was very good," Bryan said.

"Petrol?" Malcolm asked. He shook his head.

"Wine has many peculiar smells," Corvina interrupted.

"Dare I ask what bad wines smell like?"

"Wet cardboard if it's corked, or toe jam if it's an older white wine past its best-by date," Bryan said, and laughed.

"Are you serious?"

"Some of my favorite aroma terms are ashtray, horse sweat, wet dog, tar, charcoal, forest floor, pencil shavings, fresh-cut garden hose, and grandma's purse."

"What wines smell like tar?" Malcolm asked.

"Malbec and nebbiolo," Bryan said.

"And pencil shavings?"

"Merlot," Corvina said.

"And fresh-cut garden hose?"

"For me, a decades-old Châteauneuf-du-Pape," Bryan said.

"I disagree. It would have to be dry American or Australian riesling," Corvina said. "Just close your eyes and imagine you are in a winery. Now smell the wine," she encouraged him.

Malcolm smelled the wine once more. "Yep, smells like cat's pee," he said, raising his glass. "Cheers."

"It seems we've exhausted what we can discover in Chile, the Niagara Region, and DC. So what next?" Bryan asked.

"I might have the answer," Malcolm said. He turned his attention to his phone.

"What?" Bryan asked.

"I did some research after we discovered who had purchased Slater's patents, but Zhang Tao Lung remains elusive. There's not much in print about him, and he doesn't interview. I asked my editor if she still had contacts in Hong Kong, where her family is based. Seems like she does, and I now owe her big time."

"What could she tell you?" Corvina asked.

"Our reclusive billionaire and his brother have a penchant for wines."

"How does that help us?" Corvina asked.

"He's hosting something called a 'vertical wine tasting' one week from today. What's a vertical tasting?" Malcolm asked.

"It's a wine tasting where everyone remains standing," Bryan said, "as opposed to the much more enjoyable horizontal wine tasting where everyone is—"

"It's a tasting of different vintages of the same wine," Corvina interrupted. "It allows you to taste how the wines age over time. Does it mention the producers' names?"

"Just one. It's French."

"What is it?" Corvina asked.

"Château Lafite."

Corvina gasped.

"Is that a good one?" Malcolm asked.

"It's among the oldest and most recognized wine producers in the world," Bryan said.

"Where is the tasting?" Corvina asked.

"Hong Kong." Malcolm looked at his screen and confirmed. "How do we get a ticket?"

"You can't buy a ticket for that kind of event," Bryan said seriously.

"So how do we get in?" Corvina asked.

"You wouldn't believe me if I told you," Bryan said.

CHAPTER 16

CROSBIE'S BONDED WAREHOUSE
HOUNSLOW, LONDON

Max Perfetto located the bottle of vintage Château Lafite and removed it from its cradle. He sighed in appreciation at the first growth's vintage, 1899. Some lucky sod would be drinking this heavenly claret, and this was the closest he would get to the wine. He imagined it sold to a wealthy Arab in Knightsbridge or an aristocrat with a block of flats in Mayfair. He triple-checked the requisition number for the single bottle of wine, which was to be collected by a representative of Universal Wines.

He then applied the same level of scrutiny to the accompanying letter of provenance from the château and winemaker confirming the label, the bottle, and its contents were genuine. The letter further confirmed the bottle had originally been purchased as part of a case directly from the château, demonstrating the chain of custody.

Since the incident with the *contraffatto* wine at the Crosbie's auction, Max Perfetto had suffered countless indignities: humiliating sympathy from his family, as if he'd come down with a terminal illness; scorn and ridicule from his industry counterparts who didn't return his calls; shocked disbelief from his fellow Masters of Wine; and severe reprobation from his employers.

He was lucky he hadn't lost his job altogether. It would be a long time before he was responsible for purchasing and authenticating vintage wines for the auction house again. For the two weeks since the incident, he had been relegated to the less glamorous side of the wine auctioning business. He found his days filled with inventorying, purchase requisitions, and other menial tasks far below the status his Master of Wine degree should have afforded him.

Once he confirmed he had the right bottle and it was supported by the correct documentation, he inspected the bottle further to ensure there was no chance it could have been replaced by a fake.

He inspected the capsule for signs of tampering, and he held the bottle up to the light to determine how far the wine came up the shoulder of the bottle. It reached midshoulder height, supporting its authenticity. Such an old wine would have experienced trace evaporation over time—known as ullage—and be centimeters away from the cork, which proved to be the case in this instance. An extremely old vintage with wine right up to the cork was either a fake or had been re-corked at the château, a practice widely abandoned since counterfeit wines began to flood the markets in the 1980s.

Though his perfunctory inspection didn't include such detailed verification measures as carbon and nuclear dating, he was confident the bottle and its contents were genuine. Not one to wallow in self-pity, he'd studied counterfeit wines following the incident to ensure he would never be caught out again. His research was shocking to say the least. He hadn't realized just how widespread the counterfeiting of wines had become. It was believed over 50 percent of Château Lafite in China was fake.

Assured that this bottle wouldn't come back to haunt him, Max gently placed the bottle, label facing upward, into a briefcase with a black foam interior designed to fit its contours perfectly. He secured the bottle further with two Velcro straps so it wouldn't fall out when the case was opened. The case would protect it from sunlight, vibrations, and direct impact, and if it were to go missing or get pinched, a GPS tracking unit inside allowed the auction house to trace its whereabouts. He slid the letter of provenance behind the top portion of foam, where it would be secure between the foam and interior of the case.

He drove to central London with the briefcase tucked securely behind the passenger seat and returned to Crosbie's on Bond Street with time to spare before the Universal Wines representative would arrive to collect the wine.

At a minute before the appointed time, Max received a call from reception confirming his ten o'clock appointment had arrived. He checked the bottle one last time, smoothed down his hair, and made his way to reception. He couldn't wait to find out who had purchased the wine and maybe even learn what occasion was to be commemorated with the opening of the bottle.

There, standing in reception, was his nemesis—Bryan Lawless.

"What are *you* doing here?" Max seethed. He cast his eyes about for his appointment.

"Hi, Max. How are things?" Bryan asked.

"What do you want? I don't have time for you. I have an important transaction to make." Max craned his neck and looked anxiously over Bryan's shoulder.

"Yes, I know—a bottle of 1899 Lafite," Bryan said.

Max snapped his attention back to Bryan. He was leaning on the counter and tapping the briefcase.

"How could you possibly know that?" he asked.

"Max, you disappoint me. It's just like how I knew the Pétrus you were auctioning was a fake. I do my homework."

At that moment, a stunning woman came into reception.

"Is that it?" she asked, pointing at the briefcase in Max's hands.

"Yep. You just need to sign for it, and we'll be on our way to that dinner party in Hong Kong," Bryan said. Was the woman with Bryan? Max dared not ask aloud.

The woman laid down her driver's license and Universal Wines identification card for Max to see. He checked her identification and slid the requisition sheet over the desk toward her as though in a trance.

A signature later, and the bottle was in their custody.

Max clenched his fists in silent rage as Bryan Lawless sauntered out the door, whistling and swinging the briefcase like a child's lunch box.

"We have time for a quick lunch before we go to the airport?" Bryan asked her once they returned to his car.

"Sure. It would be nice to get a decent meal before such a long flight," she answered.

"How about a brasserie near Green Park Station?" Bryan suggested.

"Sounds good."

Corvina opened the case to check on the bottle once they were seated in the restaurant. Satisfied it was still intact, she closed the case and set it down between her feet.

The waiter came over to take their drinks order.

"Madam, I couldn't help but notice you're carrying a bottle of wine with you. Would you like me to open it so you may enjoy it with your lunch?" the waiter asked.

Corvina placed the case on her lap and opened it again so the waiter could see the bottle. He looked down smiling and then gasped when the label's details sunk in.

"Not today, thank you," Corvina said.

"No, of course not." The waiter shook his head and walked away.

After the waiter had returned and taken their order, Corvina called home.

"Hi, Mamma. I'm back in Europe. I'm in London now," she said when her mother answered the phone.

"Oh, *querida*, it's so good to hear your voice." She heard her mother choke back a sob. "You need to speak with your father."

"Corvina," her papà said, coming on the line. The sound of his voice alarmed her.

"Papà, what's wrong with Mamma?"

"Your mom is fine. She's just upset."

"What's going on?" Corvina pressed her phone to her ear when he didn't respond. "Papà? Are you still there?"

"The phylloxera is here," he whispered.

"Oh no! What are you going to do?"

"What can I do? I spoke with Antonio in the next commune. His vines have phylloxera too. He doesn't think he'll be able to keep the winery going if he can't harvest next year."

"What will he do?"

"He says he'll sell as soon as possible to avoid going bankrupt and losing everything. He won't get a good price. With his vines covered in phylloxera, whoever takes over will have to pull the vines and hope for a miracle. It will take at least four years before any new plantings are ready to harvest."

"And what about you, Papà?" Corvina repeated her question.

"We'll make wine as long as we can," he said. She could hear the despondency in his voice—something she had never heard before. He always sounded so confident.

"Papà, you have to pull the vines. You can't just let phylloxera destroy the vineyards."

"And then what? Phylloxera is killing the vines. American rootstock no longer works."

"We'll find a solution, Papà. Just wait," Corvina said, but realized he was right. There was no way to stop Philomena.

"I admire your optimism, dear. It won't be our best vintage, but at least we'll go out with a fight. *Tutto comincia nel vigneto,*" he said in a voice barely above a whisper.

"Papà, I'll send someone from my company to look at the vineyards. Maybe it's not too late," she said with little conviction.

"It's too late for Marco and for our vineyard but not for the rest of the country. If you're going to stop Philomena, *cara*, you have to do it now!" her father said.

"Did I hear right? Your family vineyard is infested?" Bryan asked as soon as she ended the call.

"Yes, the neighbor's vineyard too," Corvina said. She felt like she had stepped out of her own body for a moment and nothing was real.

"What are you going to do?" Bryan asked. He placed a hand on her shoulder and gave it a gentle squeeze. She was touched at his level of concern.

"*We* are going to find out who's responsible for spreading Philomena and figure out how to stop it spreading further. I won't let everything my family worked so hard to build be destroyed by an aphid. It's time to put an end to this once and for all," Corvina said with fierce determination.

CHAPTER 17

CHRONICLE BUILDING
SAN FRANCISCO, CA, UNITED STATES

While Corvina and Bryan returned to London to prepare for their trip to Hong Kong to pursue the patent lead, Malcolm used every available resource and investigative trick he knew to dig into Slater's past. He soon discovered that aside from Slater's time at Brock University and working in Chile at the Errázuriz winery, there wasn't much to go on. An interview in the Brock University paper printed in his first year linked him to an anti-GMO student group, but no quotes were attributed to him.

Saving the easy part for last, Malcolm looked up the Brock University online yearbook for the year Slater graduated and identified several students who were in the same year who also studied viticulture. He recalled the days when he would have searched the Yellow Pages and printed college directories. With a few more keystrokes, he was able to find some phone numbers. He was always amazed at how much personal information people shared online.

The first few numbers were a bust. Either there was no answer or the people he spoke with didn't remember Slater.

He got lucky on his seventh call.

"Yeah, I knew Slater pretty well. We were lab partners. Who did you say you were again?"

"My name is Malcolm. I'm a reporter with the *San Francisco Chronicle*. I'm writing an article about phylloxera."

"Oh, you mean Philomena?"

"Yes, that was a typo—" Malcolm started to explain.

"Oh, wow, you wrote *that* article?"

"Yes, I did," Malcolm said, unaccustomed to stardom.

"Cool."

"Do you know how I can reach Slater?" Malcolm asked.

"Why do you want to talk with Slater?" the student asked in a guarded tone.

So much for building rapport.

"I was told he was an expert on phylloxera, and I need an expert opinion to include in my next piece."

"Neat. I don't know where he is, to be honest. We fell out of touch. I thought he went to work down in the States."

"Do you know where?" Malcolm pressed.

"Some multinational, I think. An agricultural company—seeds, chemicals, that kind of thing."

"Do you remember the company name?"

"It was something like DuPont or Monsanto . . . No, I think it was Dusanti. Yes, that was it, Dusanti."

"Why do you think that?"

"He met some guy from Dusanti who was at the university during a job fair. They seemed to hit it off."

"Do you remember who he met?"

"No, but I could find out. I may still have the guy's business card somewhere. Let me have a look around. I'll send you a text if I find it."

"Okay, thanks. I appreciate your help."

"No worries."

While he waited for the Canadian student to text back, Malcolm Googled the company and brought up its home page.

He read that Dusanti International was based in Missouri and had offices and production facilities around the world. They worked in many fields, but their focus was in agriculture, specifically seed manufacturing, pesticides, and other methods of pest prevention. He scrolled through product listings, facility locations, mission and vision statements, the previous year's annual report, and the corporate social responsibility pages of the site.

His research was interrupted by a text message from the Canadian student. It was the name and contact details of the man Slater had met from Dusanti—his next lead to tracking Slater down.

Malcolm texted a thanks back to the student and called the number for the Dusanti employee.

"Hello?" a man replied.

"Hi, is this Donald?"

"Yes," the man answered.

"My name is Malcolm Goldberg. I'm calling from the *San Francisco Chronicle,* and I'd like to ask you a few—"

The man hung up on him.

Getting the man from Dusanti to talk would be harder than he thought, but it was the only lead he had.

CHAPTER 18

INTERPOL COMMAND AND COORDINATION CENTRE
LYON, FRANCE

"What the hell is this?" Alison Pittard shouted. She stormed into Claude Duval's office waving a report in her hand as though it were on fire. She wore a light-gray pencil skirt and a white blouse. Medium-length brown hair framed a pinched face permanently set in a scowl.

Claude Duval, author of the report in question, looked up at his boss through his gray-blue eyes and then returned his attention to the man sitting in front of him. At forty-seven years old and originally from Marseille, Claude had a slight paunch he regularly threatened to get rid of but never did, perpetual bags under his eyes, thinning black hair, and no time for office politics.

"Henri, we'll continue your appraisal later," Claude apologized to his direct report. "Something seems to have upset our section head."

The appraisee, Henri, was just shy of thirty years old. He wore a collared blue shirt with the top button undone and no tie. A fop of brown hair hung loosely over one side of his forehead and touched the rectangular black frames of his glasses. The glasses and his wide-set eyes gave him a perpetual quizzical expression. Henri stood to leave but was roughly pushed back down into his seat by Alison. "Stay where you are. This will only take a minute."

Impossible on most days, Claude found that Alison Pittard, branch section head, had become unbearable since she had demoted him from the Terrorist Division of the Lyon Command and Coordination

Centre, or CCC, to the Wildlife Crime Division. The demotion was meant to force him to quit; Claude didn't oblige her in her plans.

"It's my proposal to launch Operation Philomena," Claude responded calmly. "If you had read the executive summary, you would understand." Claude laced his hands behind his head and leaned back in his chair.

"Sit properly. You will show me respect!" she shouted.

Claude remained seated as he was. Henri squirmed in his chair and looked at his phone.

"You want to launch an investigation into a bug?" Alison asked.

"It's not just a bug," Claude explained calmly. "It's a threat to the world's vineyards. And it falls directly into Interpol's Wildlife Crime Division's jurisdiction. It's an environmental threat that's already crossed numerous borders. As the leaders in wine production, I thought it appropriate that the French CCC of Interpol spearhead the efforts to tackle the problem."

"It's a bug. I will not go to my superiors to propose a worldwide hunt for a bug."

"I would have thought you would want to stop Philomena. If it gets to France, just think of the damage it could do to our vineyards."

"We're not launching an operation against a bug," Alison repeated. "You will stay in this office and work on what I tell you to work on. Garbage is what you will work on." With that, Alison tossed his Operation Philomena report onto his desk and marched out of his office. A large rejection stamp from her office marred the front cover.

"*Incroyable*," Henri said when he was sure Alison was well out of earshot. "What a bitch."

"Now, now, Henri. That's no way to speak of your superiors," Claude admonished.

"How is that *superior* behavior? She can't treat you like that," Henri persisted.

"Henri, enough. Let's finish up your appraisal."

An hour later, with Henri's appraisal complete, Claude stood and closed the door to his office, something he rarely did. He closed the window blinds and turned off the overhead light. His desk lamp provided enough light to illuminate the office. It was past seven o'clock in the evening. Most of the office would be empty, and Alison would most definitely be gone. Though she demanded her team burn the midnight oil, Alison managed to leave the office by six most evenings.

He turned to the back wall of his office. He paid no attention to the white projection screen outlining in dry erase ink the various phases of Operation EuroHaz, his current assignment. Operation EuroHaz targeted the illegal transportation of hazardous waste across the borders of European countries—the garbage project Alison had assigned to him.

Claude was in charge of coordinating inspections, ensuring violations were properly identified, and launching sub-investigations into offenders. The operation was running smoothly. His team had everything under control, with many offenders caught to their credit. His role now was mainly administrative as he checked in regularly with all team members and completed detailed progress reports for his superiors. His precision and punctuality in submitting them drove Alison to distraction.

Confident that Alison would not return, Claude let the screen roll back up into the ceiling to reveal a large map of the world covering almost the entire wall. Small black flags were pinned into each location where the phylloxera aphid, Philomena, had been reported. Small yellow flags were pinned into each location his primary suspect had been to in the last year. Several of the pins overlapped almost perfectly.

Aside from a few outlier locations, most recently Washington, the travel history of the Spanish-Italian flying winemaker—his suspect—and Philomena were almost identical. Her travels seemed to follow Philomena around as if she was checking on its progress.

Malcolm Goldberg's articles on the origins and spread of Philomena flanked the map. The *San Francisco Chronicle* journalist had become the de facto authority on Philomena.

Claude's investigation into the spread of Philomena led him to discover the link to Corvina Guerra. The pattern of the spread of the aphid indicated that it couldn't be accidental or natural, and it showed no signs of letting up. If it caused even half of the damage that phylloxera in the nineteenth had caused to the world's vineyards, Claude knew it would be a catastrophe. Unfortunately, Claude believed this new strain of phylloxera was going to spread farther and more rapidly than its predecessor and cause much more damage. It was already shaping up to be the botanical equivalent of the Spanish flu pandemic of 1918, which killed between twenty and fifty million people. The difference was that Philomena had the potential to kill 90 to 100 percent of the world's vine population. He believed it posed a far greater threat to Europe than the illegal cross-border transportation of hazardous waste he was currently tracking.

Operation Philomena was going to be his big break. Launching and running the operation would give him the exposure he needed to get out of the Wildlife Crime Division and back on the Fusion Task Force, responsible for fighting terrorism, or on Project Millennium, targeting Eurasian criminal organizations.

He was careful to follow all protocol in conducting his research, preparing his proposal, submitting it to his superiors, and documenting his work. He also discussed his plans with key individuals he'd made allies with to ensure the credit for the operation couldn't be taken from him.

It was time now to go off protocol and take the next step to making Operation Philomena a reality. He knew he was taking a career risk, but if he wasn't successful in launching the operation, he didn't want to continue working under the incompetent and tyrannical leadership of Alison Pittard anyway.

Returning to his desk, he logged onto I-24/7, Interpol's secure network linking member countries to each other and allowing them to search international criminal databases. As a director at one of the three Command and Coordination Centres, he had the authority to send out Interpol-wide notices, a message that would alert policing authorities worldwide. Notices were color-coded depending on the threat level.

With a few clicks and typed entries, he sent an Orange Notice indicating a threat pertaining to Philomena. Orange Notices were normally reserved for terrorist activity or impending natural disasters. He also sent a Red Notice to indicate a wanted person, referring to Corvina Guerra.

Within minutes, the two notices would reach all National Central Bureaus located in 190 Interpol member countries. The Orange Notice also requested that all members share any reports on Philomena with the Command and Coordination Centres in Lyon, Buenos Aires, and Singapore, naming Claude Duval as operation leader. All three CCC offices were open and manned twenty-four hours a day, three hundred sixty-five days a year.

"Your time is running out," Claude said as he studied the black and yellow flags on the map. He leaned back in his chair, hands laced behind his head. Now all he could do was wait for the fireworks to begin as senior leadership throughout Interpol discovered his transgression.

CHAPTER 19

WAN CHAI DISTRICT
HONG KONG

"We're here," Corvina said as their taxi lurched to a halt in the middle of traffic. The driver pointed out the passenger window and shouted something in Cantonese.

En route to their destination, she had watched the city pass by in a blur of narrow ramps, one-way streets, and bright lights. Hundreds of people on the streets weaved between cars, trucks, scooters, and bicycles. And there was honking—lots of honking.

"And I thought London was densely populated and chaotic." Bryan put voice to her thoughts.

She opened her purse on top of the briefcase holding the bottle of 1899 Château Lafite and leafed through British pounds, Canadian dollars, US dollars, and recently exchanged Hong Kong dollars. When they had arrived at their hotel the night before, she was relieved to find that the shipping company DHL had safely delivered the bottle.

"It's times like this that I love the euro," she said. She paid the driver with a hundred-dollar note.

Bryan got out first and opened the taxi door for her. She stepped out in high heels and immediately felt conspicuous. She wore an elegant off-the-shoulder black evening dress, whereas Bryan had kept it simple and rented a tuxedo that afternoon. Corvina had to admit that tall, dark, and handsome wore it well. The taxi driver took off without looking back.

"Are you sure this is the right place?" Bryan asked. She saw him looking around, taking in every detail as he had when they first met in the bar in London. It was dark outside, but the street was lit well enough to show them that gentrification hadn't reached this part of the city. The ground was still wet after a day of sporadic rain showers.

"The confirmation I received was explicit in both the dress code and location," Corvina said. "This is the address they emailed me. Then again, this is the first billionaire's vertical tasting I've ever attended," Corvina said. "We're exactly on time." Corvina checked her watch to confirm it was in fact nine o'clock while she stifled a massive yawn. She was used to jetting all over the world and across time zones, but the last two weeks had been draining—Italy, Barcelona, California, Santiago, St. Catharines, DC, London, and now Hong Kong.

They stood at the mouth of a narrow street, no more than an alley, that bisected the block of buildings surrounding them and connected to a parallel street on the other side a hundred meters away. Corvina took some comfort in the fact that they weren't entering an alley with a dead end.

"Do you really think he's going to be here?" Bryan asked.

"Zhang Tao Lung? The confirmation said he was the host. And from what little I've read of him online, he loves bordeaux," Corvina said. "It will be a huge waste of our time and money if we don't get the chance to talk to him. But I couldn't get an appointment no matter how hard I tried. I even asked my boss, Vicente, and he asked his boss, our CEO, to try to make an appointment—but no luck. This is our best chance." She held up the case.

"How do you want to approach him once we confirm he's inside?" Bryan asked.

"I think we need to be subtle. We can't just accuse him of wiping out vineyards around the world," Corvina cautioned.

"I don't know that we have the luxury of subtlety. We're going to have only one shot at this. I think we have to catch him off guard."

"Don't you think that will upset him?" Corvina asked.

"He's a billionaire. I don't think he's going to be intimidated by us."

"What do you suggest?"

"We get right in his face and ask him about the patent he purchased on phylloxera and if he has a patent on the means to stop it. Then we ask him about the spread of Philomena. We should be able to tell a lot just by how he reacts."

"I'm not sure. Let's get inside and talk further once we know he's there," Corvina said. She wasn't committed to Bryan's aggressive approach.

Halfway down the alley, beyond a row of dumpsters, she saw a small cluster of people standing at a doorway. A blue light above them cast a pale glow.

"That must be it," Corvina said with as much courage as she could muster. She was only too well aware that she was in an alleyway in an unfamiliar neighborhood of Hong Kong carrying a small fortune in a bottle of wine, accompanied by a man she still barely knew. She lifted her scarf—a bright-purple paisley print she had picked up at the airport in Santiago, Chile—and covered her mouth and nose, as she had seen so many Hong Kong residents do with surgical masks. The alley carried a pungent aroma.

"Don't worry. I won't let anything happen to us," Bryan said. She admired his confidence. How much of it was bravado? As they neared, the door was opened and two people entered, leaving only two others behind in the alley.

Corvina and Bryan approached a young man in a dark suit and black shirt with no tie. He had the build of a professional athlete and blocked the doorway. He was having a heated conversation with the remaining person outside.

"But this bottle is over a hundred years old," the man shouted at the doorman. He spoke with an American accent.

"That may well be, sir. But I'm afraid Lafite didn't make an 1885 vintage."

"Tell me what's wrong with this bottle. This capsule? This label?" the American persisted.

"They could all be genuine, sir, but it doesn't change the fact that there's no such thing as an 1885 Lafite."

The American fumed, but the doorman's body language brooked no argument.

"Sir, if you'll stand aside, I have guests to attend to." He glanced at Corvina and with one look told her she had better not waste his time.

The American stood aside and began typing into his iPhone.

"Looks like we're up," Bryan said.

"It's not a Rodenstock, is it?" the doorman asked Corvina when she stepped up to the door with the bottle of wine still in its protective briefcase.

Corvina dropped her scarf over her left shoulder and laughed at the reference. She disarmed the man with a smile. "Of course not. We brought an 1899." She produced the letter of provenance from Château Lafite to prove the bottle was genuine and had an unimpeachable chain of custody.

"Show me the bottle," the doorman demanded after careful inspection of the letter. He looked up and down both sides of the alley.

Corvina felt like she was taking part in an illegal activity—and maybe she was. She opened the case so the bottle was resting on the bottom and the label was facing upward for the doorman to examine. He produced a small penlight and looked at the seal, the capsule, the ullage, the label, and the condition of the bottle itself.

"You seem to know your wines," Bryan commented.

"I hope so. I'm head sommelier at the Ritz-Carlton," he said without looking up from his inspection. "Go on in." He opened the door for them. "One of my colleagues will escort you to the tasting room where your wine will be further inspected and then decanted. Enjoy the evening."

Inside, another well-built man led them down a dark hallway. Corvina spied a pin in the shape of a bunch of grapes on his left lapel indicating that he, too, was a sommelier. Maybe at Mandarin Oriental?

He led them down a spiral staircase twisting two stories down into a cavernous space.

When she reached the bottom, she stepped onto a solid concrete floor that abutted cinder block walls running up to the ceiling high above, punctured by steel beams crossing the massive space. Indirect lighting lit the walls and hanging industrial lamps pin-spotted a long bar and numerous cocktail tables around the room.

"It looks like a Prada casting call," Bryan said, side sweeping the room with his eyes.

Corvina looked around and realized he was referring to the men and women servicing the event. In addition to the bouncer-slash-sommeliers, an array of beautiful service staff poured wines from decanters and cleared empty Riedel glasses. Others passed around canapés covered with smoked salmon, caviar, and shaved truffles from silver trays filled with dry ice that created trails of white mist around the room. At the edges of the room, several local men with earpieces kept an eye on the guests.

A Korean female DJ sporting purple hair was playing tracks in a corner, filling the room with house music loud enough to create a sophisticated lounge atmosphere while still allowing guests to converse easily.

The sommelier led them to a large bar at the far end, opposite a stairwell. A tall, beautiful European woman with long blonde hair beckoned them. The second sommelier left them with her without a word and retreated across the room and back up the spiral staircase.

Corvina laid the briefcase on the table between herself and the blonde woman and opened it. She unfastened the Velcro straps and removed the bottle of 1899 Lafite. She set it in a cradle provided on the bar and placed the letter of provenance on the counter.

"Thank you," the woman said once she was finished with her inspection.

"Are you a sommelier as well?" Bryan asked, leaning forward and smiling at the woman.

"No," she replied with scorn in her voice. "I'm a buyer for Berry Bros. & Rudd here in Hong Kong."

"Oh, sorry," Bryan replied. Corvina tried not to smile. It was the first time she had seen him read somebody incorrectly. She guessed his hyper-observational skills had a weakness when it came to beautiful women.

"Now that we've established your wine is genuine, welcome to our Lafite vertical hosted by Mr. Zhang Tao Lung. He'll be joining us soon. Only fifteen guests are attending. Most come alone and don't bring their partners."

"We're newlyweds," Bryan said, taking Corvina's arm.

"Congratulations," the woman said before Corvina could respond. "Each attendee will get to taste fifty milliliters from each bottle. Vintages range from 1850 to 1982, and professional tasting notes will be provided for each bottle after the event, though you're welcome to make your own observations." As she spoke, a sommelier retrieved their bottle and opened it with great care farther down the bar. Their 1899 was decanted into a Riedel decanter and set beside a collection of other decanters already filled with incredible vintages. The sommelier placed the empty bottle and cork on the same silver tray the decanter occupied, thus ensuring the vintages weren't mixed.

"Once all the wines are decanted, we'll announce the tasting has begun. In the meantime, we're pouring Lafite 2005 and this year's *en primeur* for you to prepare your palates. Spittoons are positioned around the outside of the room should you require them."

"How did you get an *en primeur* sample?" Corvina asked in disbelief.

"We had a barrel shipped over this morning from the château." The blonde looked across the room.

"Of course you did," Corvina said, following the woman's gaze. She was shocked to see a large oak barrel. It was at an angle, and she could just make out the château's name and logo on the side. One of the sommeliers was pouring a glass of wine from a long glass pipette used to pull wine from the top of the barrel.

Corvina pulled Bryan away from the bar where he was examining the 1899 bottle's long, wine-stained cork.

"Let's find Zhang Tao before the tasting begins, *honey*," she whispered.

"Agreed. But first, let's grab a glass of the *en primeur* so we don't look suspicious, *darling*," Bryan suggested. He pocketed the cork.

She followed Bryan across the room to where the sommelier drew and poured them each a fresh glass from the barrel.

Glass of Lafite *en primeur* in hand, she looked around the room for Zhang Tao Lung. Not counting the four security men on the perimeter, there were two male Asian guests in the room. One was speaking with a gorgeous woman with long black hair who was wearing a black cocktail dress, black Jimmy Choos, and diamond jewelry. Two jade hair sticks held her hair in place. The other man was standing alone at a cocktail table tasting one of the wines on offer and writing notes in a small notepad.

"I'll talk to Mr. and Ms. Black, and you can check out the oenophile," Corvina said, and walked over to the first couple.

Bryan was approaching the lone Asian gentleman across the room when he heard his name.

"Oh no," he said aloud. He turned to see Candy Turner standing before him. He should have guessed she would be at this event. She looked great in her little black dress and her signature bright-red lipstick. Her brown hair was tied up.

"Hi, Candy. I didn't know you were in Hong Kong," he said. He looked for Corvina over Candy's shoulder. He spotted her across the room engaged in conversation with the Asian couple.

"What vintage did you bring?" Bryan looked at the bar where the vintages were breathing.

"I didn't bring anything. I was invited for my credentials. And yourself?"

"I came with the 1899 vintage." He held up the cork for her to see. "I booked late, so it was one of the few vintages left still available to get me in."

"Expensive choice. I see you still have that fetish for stealing wine corks."

"It's not a fetish. Is that the *en primeur* you're tasting?" Bryan asked. He hoped she would leave soon.

"Dear God, no. I find *en primeur* much too rough. I'm on the 2005. It's come a long way and seems to be fulfilling the expectation of becoming one of bordeaux's great vintages."

He didn't disagree with her; *en primeur* wine was an acquired taste. He continued to scan the room for Zhang Tao Lung. The gentleman on his own with the notepad seemed too reserved to be a billionaire host.

"Are you thinking of working in Hong Kong?" she asked him. "It's a fascinating place to do business—especially since the sales tax on wine was eliminated in 2008. Recently, even more so because of the added complexity and scrutiny the counterfeit wine market brings. China is a country where even breakfast cereal cornflakes are counterfeited, so it should come as no surprise that luxury items as lucrative as vintage bordeaux are counterfeited in abundance. Apparently, there are more bottles of 1982 Lafite in China than were ever produced."

"Really? That many?" Bryan feigned surprise. He suddenly recalled how she used to bore him to tears with her recounting of stats and figures.

"A massive amount of fake wine is bought and sold in China and sadly here in Hong Kong as well. That's why they're so stringent with provenance at events like these. Where did you get your bottle of ninety-nine?"

"From the château via Crosbie's," Bryan answered.

"Max must have been thrilled to see you," she said, her voice laced with sarcasm.

"Speaking of thrilled, have you talked to anyone at the institute about my exam?" he asked.

"I've made inquiries. I know who supports you and have confirmed who stands opposed. I think those opposed will be willing to reconsider. It's been five years, after all . . . and even I've forgiven you by now," she said.

Bryan was taken aback by her flirtatious manner. Did his reexamination come with that price tag?

"But tell me, what are you working on now? If I could give the institute something to make them see you in a different light—a recent award you've won, a charitable cause you're supporting, an article that doesn't incite riots among wine aficionados—it would be helpful."

"I'm working on something big right now," he said. He scanned the room again for Lung.

"Who are you looking for?" Candy asked him.

"Our host, Mr. Lung, has yet to make an appearance," he said.

"Shall we go and have a look at the lineup?" Candy pointed her glass toward the bar.

"Sure." Bryan left his glass on the cocktail table in anticipation of the vertical tasting set to begin and followed Candy to the bar. He spotted Corvina easily enough with her bright-purple scarf. She was still engaged with the Asian couple across the room.

Each silver tray was brought over to a long, dark wooden table and set between rows of sparkling glasses. A sommelier for every vintage appeared on one side of the table. The other guests began to amble over to the tasting table.

Bryan reached the bar and placed himself in front of the 1982 vintage, the first of the vertical collection that would be served.

"Friend of yours?" Candy asked. Bryan turned to see she was nodding toward the spiral staircase.

A fierce-looking man wearing a leather biker jacket met Bryan's eyes and strode toward him. He bore no resemblance to the rest of the service staff, and he didn't look like any wine aficionado Bryan had ever met. Two of the security men from the perimeter of the room joined the newcomer and headed straight for Bryan.

"Come with us," one of the men said, his voice a hiss. Across the room, Bryan saw Corvina being grabbed by the arm by a similarly fierce-looking man.

"Hey, let go of my wife!" Bryan shouted. He grabbed the man who held him by the shoulder and suddenly found himself spun around with his arm wound painfully high behind his back. He was guided toward a small door at the back of the room.

Bryan saw the other guests in the room watching the altercation in mild alarm, but no one said a word or moved to act. Candy Turner, on the other hand, was looking at him in shock. When his eyes met hers, he saw her lips move as she mouthed "Your wife?"

"Ladies and gentlemen, the tasting will begin," the blonde announced as Bryan was manhandled out of the room. He regretted that he was not going to meet Zhang Tao Lung—but even worse, he wasn't going to taste any of the wines.

CHAPTER 20

INTERPOL COMMAND AND COORDINATION CENTRE
LYON, FRANCE

Entering his office early the next day, Claude made no effort to hide the map with the black and yellow flags on it identifying all the coordinates Philomena and the flying winemaker had visited. When he finished updating the map at a quarter to eight, there were many more black flags.

The aphid had spread to dozens of additional vineyards in Tasmania, New Zealand, Chile, Napa, and Italy. His Orange Notice on I-24/7 had resulted in hundreds of responses from all over the world. Over one hundred vineyards were now identified as being infested by Philomena. Many infestations had been reported to local authorities earlier, but Interpol was the first to collate all the data.

"*Mon dieu*," Claude said when he looked at the map full of pins. "So many wineries and lives on the verge of destruction." The threat level was even higher than he'd anticipated.

This was what Claude liked best about Interpol. The organization allowed law enforcement agencies around the world to communicate and work with one another to tackle problems that transcended borders and politics. Without his threat notice, no one would have been alerted to look for the aphid infestations or realized they were related and most likely perpetrated by ecoterrorists.

He called Henri. He needed help responding to all the messages received overnight in answer to his notice. There was a good chance it would be his last day with Interpol, so he wanted to make the most of the time he had. He also wanted a witness to be present when his boss, Alison Pittard, confronted him, as she surely would the moment she entered the building. Claude had learned long ago that she cared little for the people she worked with and was single-mindedly focused on her own development and promotion.

"Morning, boss," Henri announced when he came into the office. He carried a steaming cup of coffee and a muffin from Starbucks. He set them down on the desk alongside Claude's own takeaway coffee, croissant, and a single canelé. The Bordelaise pastry—with its darkened caramelized crust and soft, rum-soaked custard center—was Claude's only vice.

"Good morning, Henri. We have a busy day ahead of us. Operation Philomena has been launched, and the response from the NCBs has been overwhelming. We must put an end to this menace and save those vineyards that are still unaffected," Claude said.

"And before it reaches France," Henri added to the conversation before adding sugar to his coffee. "I saw the notices you sent, and I've been tracing the responses. Miss Pittard changed her mind after I left last night?"

"No, she didn't. I launched Operation Philomena and sent the notices in direct contradiction to her instructions."

Henri's Adam's apple bobbed up and down, though he hadn't begun drinking his coffee or eating his muffin.

"Don't worry. I'll make sure everyone knows I acted alone," Claude said.

"But, boss, this won't end well for you. You saw how she reacted last night. And that was just to your proposal."

"I understand, but Operation Philomena is too important not to launch. If the aphid crosses our borders, our vineyards will be annihilated. I've been reading up on what happened in the late 1800s when phylloxera first spread across Europe." Claude pointed to a book with the title *The Botanist and the Vintner* lying on his desk. "It was like the

Black Plague for grapes. A repeat occurrence wouldn't only destroy the wine industry, it would have a major impact on the French economy."

At that moment, they heard the door to the outer office open, followed by the telltale sign of Alison's walk. All noise in the hallway and offices outside ceased.

Henri cringed and held his breath.

Alison came around the corner and marched into Claude's office.

"You think you're clever, don't you?" she asked without preamble.

"I don't know what you're talking about," Claude responded from his desk chair.

"You know exactly what I'm talking about—Operation Philomena, your crazy idea that a bug is taking over the world."

"What of it?"

"You sent out notices against my command."

"I don't deny it," Claude answered.

"How dare you think you can disobey me. I'm your boss, and you will do as I tell you!" she shouted.

Claude didn't rise to her baiting.

"I finally have you where I want you," she continued. She regained some composure. "I gave you a direct instruction not to launch Operation Philomena, and you went ahead and did it anyway. I look forward to processing the paperwork for your termination for gross insubordination," Alison shouted, her temper peaking again.

"*C'est quoi cette bordel?*" A new voice entered the fray.

Claude was surprised to see Secretary General Arsenault standing in the doorway. Exuding authority, the man had jet-black hair without a hint of a receding hairline, stern green eyes, a furrowed brow, and a sturdy jawline. Though shorter than most men in the building, his perfect posture and bearing made him seem taller.

"Secretary General Arsenault?" Alison said in surprise. "What are you doing here?"

"I work upstairs, Pittard, not on the other side of the planet." He stepped into Claude's office and eased the door shut behind him.

It was rare for the secretary general to visit the lower levels of CCC. Claude couldn't recall a time the man had ever entered his office.

Henri bounded out of his seat, offering it, but the secretary general waved him back. Three long strides took him to the back of the office, where he glared at the map, the little black and yellow pins, and the articles by Malcolm Goldberg.

"I came to find out who's responsible for the hot mess of this so-called Operation Philomena," the secretary general said. "My phones have been ringing off the hook, and my email is flooded."

Alison smiled, but her eyes were as cold as ice.

Claude steeled himself for the imminent moment she would throw him under the bus and assert herself as the disrespected authority who had tried to stop Claude and his misguided operation.

"Sir, Operation Philomena was a mistake. I declined the proposal just last night and instructed Duval to drop the matter and focus on Operation EuroHaz," Alison said.

"And?" the secretary general prompted.

"And," Alison went on, "I'll retract the two notices and issue an Interpol-wide apology on behalf of the Lyon CCC."

"Well, Duval? Do you have anything to say for yourself?" the secretary general asked. He turned away from the map to face Claude.

"Sir, I take full responsibility for my actions. I proposed Operation Philomena based on my concern about the new strain of the phylloxera aphid infesting vineyards around the world. I also sent both notices last night to alert our NCBs that Philomena constituted a continued threat against agricultural interests worldwide and was most likely perpetrated by ecoterrorists."

"How serious of a problem are we talking about here?" the secretary general asked.

"It won't take me long to retract the notices. Aside from a bit of unnecessary scaremongering, I don't think Duval's notices have caused any irreversible damage—just embarrassment to our CCC," Alison said.

"I meant how serious of a problem is Philomena likely to be?"

"Sir?" Alison asked.

"Very serious, Secretary General," Claude answered. "My notices led to dozens of responses confirming the presence of Philomena in many vineyards—over one hundred at last count—and it appears to be spreading on its own."

"And what happens when a vineyard is infested?"

"Well, as there's no method of prevention at this time, all of the vines have to be pulled and burned. The soil also has to be burned and left to rest. After a year or two, new vines can be planted. That is, *if* a method to stop the aphid can be found. I understand that infested vineyards won't produce new grapes suitable for wine making for about ten years."

"And the aphid hasn't reached France yet?" Arsenault asked, still studying the map.

"Not as far as we can tell. But if it keeps spreading and can't be stopped, it's a matter of when, not if."

Alison stood stark still. Henri shrank farther into his chair. Claude remained philosophical. He'd done everything he could; now it was up to his superiors to act.

"Why wasn't I sent a proposal?" the secretary general asked.

"Sir, I can get one for you. Give me until noon," Alison said, and glanced at Claude.

"No need," Claude said. He opened his desk drawer and pulled out a file. "I have a copy right here." He handed the file to the secretary general but kept his eyes on Alison.

She looked like she wanted to leap across the room and tear the file from the secretary general's hands. Claude saw her face cloud over when her eyes caught the rejection stamp with her signature on it a moment before the secretary general saw it for himself.

He looked up sharply at Alison.

"Alright, I've seen and heard enough. Duval, I want a detailed report in my office by two o'clock outlining what resources you need and your action plan to hunt down and stop this aphid and the ecoterrorists behind it. If it gets to France, we'll have a national emergency on our hands. I'll start preparing for that contingency." He turned toward the door to leave.

"Yes, sir," Claude answered.

"And don't even think of sending out any more notices until you and I have talked," the secretary general added.

Alison smirked.

"Pittard, in my office—now," he said, and marched out of the office.

"This isn't over," Alison whispered to Claude as she followed the secretary general out.

"Now what, boss?" Henri asked when they were alone again.

"We pull everyone off Operation EuroHaz and reassign them to Operation Philomena. Get everyone in the office to the conference room, and set up a video call with everyone in the field. We have a bug to stop."

CHAPTER 21

WAN CHAI DISTRICT
HONG KONG

Bryan strained to see Corvina behind him, but his escort didn't permit him to turn around. He could hear Corvina's shouts of protest, reassuring him that she was near.

Over the course of his lifetime, Bryan had found himself in many uncomfortable situations, some more harrowing than others. Being led into a darkened room in a Hong Kong basement with his arm hiked up behind his back counted as the most uncomfortable and the closest he'd ever felt to a life-threatening situation. And he'd only known Corvina for a couple weeks!

The door they were led through closed behind them, and they were taken down a short corridor that emptied out into a small and sparsely appointed room. Bryan could no longer hear the DJ's music, only a distant thumping of the bass. A large flat-screen TV silently broadcasting Chinese news hung on one wall. The floor was lightly carpeted in flat gray squares, and the cinderblock walls were painted a pale yellow. The room was dimly lit by several fluorescent light fixtures hanging from the ceiling. It reminded Bryan of any number of rooms in movies where the hero gets tortured.

The men herded him and Corvina toward two metal folding chairs in the middle of the room. Taking the cue, Bryan sat down. Corvina sat down beside him.

Another metal chair sat facing them, but none of the men made a motion to occupy it. Instead, they stood at the perimeter of the room with their arms folded in front of them.

Silence filled the room as they waited.

"I'm sorry I got you into this mess," Corvina said.

"It's not your fault. I'm the one who found the connection to Zhang Tao Lung with Malcolm in Virginia. Besides, I'm here of my own free will."

"Why is this investigation so important to you?" Corvina asked. "I get why Malcolm is helping us—he gets to write the articles. What do you get out of it?"

"Redemption. I made a serious error in judgment which changed the direction of my life, and ever since then I seem to be compounding it at every opportunity."

"The Master of Wine?"

"Yes, how did you know? I was expelled and . . . it doesn't matter."

"Do you need the Master of Wine designation that badly?"

"It's not just the title. Getting expelled from the Master of Wine program became the defining point of my life. Everyone knew it was my lifelong dream, and I put my heart and soul into achieving it."

"So when you were expelled, you felt you had become a failure?"

"Not just me—my peers, employers, friends, and family. I was ostracized. No one in the industry wanted to be associated with me. Imagine going to medical school for years and then leaving without becoming a doctor."

"Is that why you take such a critical view of the industry? I've read some of your articles."

"Probably. Infamy is the next best thing to fame, is it not?"

"And if you get the MW, then what?"

"I can get steady work, for one thing. My consultant work is good, but it's unpredictable. Having the MW will help me get reliable and better paying work."

"Is that it?"

"Honestly, no. I worked my ass off to become a Master of Wine. I owe it to myself to finish what I started."

"Did you cheat?" Corvina asked after a lengthy pause.

"No, I didn't. I was dating Candy, who was an invigilator for the exam, but I never cheated. Why spend a decade studying for something and then cheat at the last minute? It doesn't make sense. The institute didn't see it that way."

"I believe you."

"Hey, guys, we're missing the tasting," Bryan said loudly. "Any chance you can fetch us a glass of the eighteen ninety-nine?"

A tall Chinese man walked through the door. The three men in the room took an involuntary step back when he entered the room. The room seemed to grow even more silent.

It was Mr. Black—the man at the tasting who had been accompanied by the woman with jade hair sticks, whom Corvina had been talking to earlier. Much closer now, Bryan could see the man's high, angular cheekbones and small, narrow mouth. He was almost skeletal in appearance.

Bryan glanced at Corvina, but she just stared straight ahead at Mr. Black.

Mr. Black removed his jacket with care and draped it over the back of the folding chair. A black shirt revealed a slim, well-built frame. He stepped in front of the chair in a precise manner and sat down, crossing his left leg over his right. Bryan felt uncomfortable under the inscrutable and calculating glare of the man's deep-set dark eyes. The man's expression and intent were impenetrable. Bryan couldn't read him.

Mr. Black asked a question in Cantonese.

"Why are you here?" one of the men behind Corvina and Bryan shouted.

Bryan almost jumped out of his seat.

He had been so focused on the new man in the room, he had forgotten they were not alone with him. The man behind them was there as a translator.

"We're looking for Mr. Zhang Tao Lung," Corvina answered.

Mr. Black looked first at Corvina and then at Bryan and spoke softly in Cantonese.

"Why are you looking for Mr. Lung?" the man behind them translated once more.

"We want to speak with him about one of his purchases—a patent for a genetically mutated aphid."

"What business do you have with Mr. Lung?"

"That depends on why he purchased the patent and what he intends to do with it. The creation specified by the patent is causing damage to vineyards on a global scale. I'm a winemaker, and my colleague is a wine expert. We need to know how it can be stopped," Corvina said.

Mr. Black appeared to consider Corvina's words. He steepled his fingers in a gesture of contemplation, and with a barely perceptible nod, dismissed the men from the room.

They left quickly, closing the door behind them.

Mr. Black's gaze seemed to bore right through them. Bryan looked over at Corvina, who held the man's stare.

"You're a persistent couple." Mr. Black spoke in English with just a hint of a Chinese accent. "And not husband and wife as you claim."

Bryan registered his words in mute surprise.

"You tried many avenues to contact Zhang Tao Lung, and when those didn't work, you somehow secured a bottle of 1899 Château Lafite and traveled around the world posing as a couple to gain access to an event he would host and attend. Few would go so far. What are you truly seeking?"

"We want to see Mr. Lung," Corvina said.

"And what would you ask him?"

"What is his involvement? Why did he purchase the patent? And what are his intentions? He may have the power to stop the phylloxera," Corvina said.

"Why is this important to you?" Mr. Black asked.

"My customers' and family's vineyards are at risk. Wine making is everything to me," Corvina said softly.

Bryan flinched. It dawned on him how personal this investigation was to her. She had much more to lose than he did.

"I think you need to speak with my brother, Feng. He's the one who's interested in biotechnology. And next time, you should announce the purpose of your visit in advance to avoid any unpleasantness."

Bryan was stunned as his mind made the connection.

"Wait," Bryan said. "You're Zhang Tao Lung?" he asked. The man they were looking for was sitting right in front of them.

"Yes. I must always exercise such precautions when meeting new people. I have many enemies. I was curious to meet you. As I said, your persistence intrigued me," Zhang Tao said. He uncrossed his legs and stood. The door opened, and two of the men returned to the room.

"We wish to meet your brother," Bryan said, though he really wanted to leave as soon as possible. He had a bad feeling about their encounter with Zhang Tao Lung and wanted to get as far away from the man as he could.

"And we're in a hurry. We have a flight booked for tomorrow to return to London," Corvina added.

"You're leaving so soon?" Zhang Tao asked.

"Yes, we came here only to meet the purchaser of the patent," Bryan said.

"Can you tell us where we can find him?" Corvina asked.

"Where all billionaires go for enjoyment—Dubai." Lung smiled for the first time. To Bryan, it was scarier than the man's bodyguards and his basement interrogation room.

CHAPTER 22

WALMART SUPERCENTER
KANSAS CITY
PLATTE COUNTY, MO, UNITED STATES

Malcolm walked by aisle after aisle of outdoor furniture, toys, video games, movies, music, books, and auto and home improvement items. He searched for the Seattle's Best coffee shop where he would meet his contact. After a few more attempts over the phone, he had finally convinced the biologist at Dusanti who had assisted David Slater to meet him. He hoped Donald could tell him more about Dusanti's involvement in the development and propagation of Philomena. He sent Corvina a message through WhatsApp to let her know he'd arrived. He wondered if she and Bryan had made any further progress.

Though he'd been to Walmarts before, he was always overwhelmed by the store's size. He peered down aisles that stretched as far as his eye could see. They all had high ceilings, and every available surface seemed to be dedicated to retailing millions of SKUs. The fluorescent lighting was perfectly distributed, and Muzak played over the sound system.

It all made for a sterile environment and made him question why he was here at all—miles from San Francisco, to meet a man who may or may not know anything about the story he was pursuing. Was there even a story? Or were he, Corvina, and Bryan just tilting at windmills and chasing shadows?

He observed dozens of customers wandering the aisles, loading up on inexpensive goods, assisted by overfriendly staff in blue uniforms. Ubiquitous, bright-yellow smiley faces promised everyday low prices.

Walking past the home and garden center, a sale item caught Malcolm's eye. He entered the aisle and approached the object that had piqued his interest: a carefully rolled length of garden hose. He looked up and down the aisle to confirm he was alone. Recalling his conversation with Corvina and Bryan in Washington, DC, about peculiar wine smells, he lifted the hose off its hook and brought it to his face.

He smelled the hose. It smelled like he expected it would—like a run-of-the-mill garden hose.

Is this what a good wine was supposed to smell like? He struggled to see how such a scent would be a desirable trait in a wine. He brought the hose closer and sniffed it more thoroughly. Still smelled like a garden hose.

Maybe he needed to smell the inside of the hose, not the outside. He grasped the nozzle and placed it underneath his nose. He closed his eyes, imagining that he was in a winery and holding a glass of fine wine in his hand. He inhaled deeply; though it smelled fresher and more rubbery, it still smelled like a garden hose.

"Can I help you, sir?" a voice asked.

Malcolm opened his eyes and spun around.

An older Walmart employee stood staring at him.

"Um, no, I was just . . . um . . . checking the quality of the garden hose," Malcolm said. He could feel the blood rushing to his face.

"By smelling it?" the man asked.

"I wanted to see how new it was," Malcolm said.

"Okaaaaay," the Walmart employee said. "Would you like to buy it?"

"No, thanks. I'm just here to meet someone." Malcolm put the hose back where he found it and left the aisle as quickly as possible. His face was still burning.

He spotted the Seattle's Best coffee shop and made his way over.

He looked around the coffee kiosk. He assumed the man he'd spoken to was neither retired nor shopping with his family, leaving the gentleman in khaki trousers, a plain blue shirt, and brown loafers who was sitting alone at the table farthest away from the counter as his likely contact. The biologist was drinking from a paper cup and bouncing one leg on the other.

"Donald?" Malcolm asked when he approached.

"Yes. You must be the reporter?" Donald asked, and looked around the store. Malcolm looked around himself—bright lights, Muzak, average Americans shopping. He couldn't think of a less threatening environment. The smiley faces were a bit creepy though.

"Malcolm, yes. Sorry I'm late. Let me get a coffee and join you. Can I get you anything?"

"No, I'm fine," Donald said, and continued to look around the store.

"Thanks for agreeing to speak with me. May I ask how you and Slater first connected?" Malcolm asked after he returned with his coffee and eased into the seat opposite Donald. He sensed that small talk and rapport building would be wasted on this occasion, so he cut straight to the chase.

"Dusanti keeps a close eye on biological and agricultural patents registered in every country. When Slater registered his patent for a genetically modified phylloxera aphid, it was immediately flagged by my team. We reached out to him and expressed interest in helping him."

"Helping? How?" Malcolm leaned forward, both hands wrapped around his paper coffee cup.

"Funding, mainly."

"What was Dusanti going to do with modified phylloxera?" Malcolm leaned closer.

"To begin with, just study it and hope to find a real-world application. Genetically modifying biology to target specific plants is no easy feat, and we thought the same modification process could be applied to target other plants."

"How did Slater do it?" Malcolm asked.

"We suspect he succeeded through a clever combination of genetic mutation and Mendelian mutation."

"Mendel? You mean like the monk who grew peas?" Malcolm asked. He vaguely recalled the story from his high school biology class.

"Exactly. Stick enough phylloxera aphids in a tank with *Vitis vinifera* and after dozens, or hundreds, of generations and mutations, they will eventually eat any rootstock put before them. They adapted through evolution and Slater's genetic tinkering to attack resistant rootstock."

"If it's so easy, why hasn't anyone done it before?" Malcolm asked.

"What on earth for?" Donald asked.

"Fair point. What would be an example of a real-world application for such a modification?" Malcolm asked.

"It could be applied to the pollination of crops or elimination of specific pests, for instance."

"How much funding did Dusanti provide?" Malcolm asked.

"I don't know. It's not like he kept a record of receipts and filed his expenses. We just wanted him to continue pushing the development of the aphid."

"Well, mission accomplished. Wine-growing regions around the world are now under attack," Malcolm said. He tried to keep the disgust out of his voice but failed.

"That was never the intent," Donald replied. His leg stopped bouncing, and he leaned forward. "Who knew Slater planned to release it and spread it around the world?"

"What did you think he was going to do with it?" Malcolm said, incredulous. He took a deep breath, realizing he was not going to get anything out of the biologist if he berated him for his complicity.

"I made the connection that he was spreading the aphid only after I read about it in the press," Donald continued. "Your article, in fact. If I had known how destructive the aphid would be, I never would have let it go so far." Donald's voice trailed off as he stared into his coffee.

"You should have thought of that before you sponsored him. So now what for Dusanti? You develop a cure, mass-produce it, and sell it at an exorbitant cost to the wine industry?"

"The plan was to develop a resistant rootstock that we would effectively own. But we can't." Donald looked up, eyes wide.

"What do you mean, you can't?" Malcolm asked.

"Slater was supposed to provide us with the means to stop Philomena but never did, and he's been incommunicado for weeks. It looks like he double-crossed Dusanti once he no longer needed the company to fund his research and development work."

"Do you know for a fact that he actually had the means to stop Philomena?" Malcolm asked.

"No, he never showed us anything. We took him at his word."

"Why are you telling me this?"

"I now lead the team that's been tasked with developing a solution."

"A solution? Like a new resistant rootstock to graft? Or a neurotoxin?" Malcolm asked, recalling the patent file he and Bryan had discovered in Virginia.

"Yes."

"To profit from, of course," Malcolm interjected.

"Yes," Donald confessed. "But we've hit nothing but dead ends."

"So when do you think you will have a cure?"

"It's not a matter of *when* but *if*. I'm starting to feel that nothing can stop Philomena," Donald said. "And if we don't find a solution fast, it will be too late."

"What do you mean, too late?"

"Once Philomena achieves a critical mass of infestation in each wine region, there will be no way to stop its spread and the destruction of the vineyards it infests."

Malcolm saw the biologist's leg bouncing faster than ever.

CHAPTER 23

INTERPOL COMMAND AND COORDINATION CENTRE
LYON, FRANCE

"Our mandate is threefold," Claude said as he addressed his team seated in the conference room and those watching online via a secure video link on I-24/7. "Arrest the ecoterrorists spreading the phylloxera aphid known as Philomena, stop it from spreading farther, and monitor its impact on infested vineyards."

Claude Duval felt like he'd been reborn. Operation Philomena was his to run at full tilt.

He had the opportunity to manage an operation under the auspices of his current assignment on the Wildlife Crime desk using his experience and skills developed over years on the Fusion Task Force hunting terrorists—the best of both worlds.

"Refer to the Lyon CCC message board, where we'll be posting as much relevant information as possible for you to get up to speed on the suspected ecoterrorists and the aphid."

Henri gave him a thumbs-up sign from his seat at the conference table to indicate the video link had been disconnected. Only those individuals in the conference room could now see and hear him.

"Any questions?" Claude asked his team.

"Why aren't we apprehending the suspect in Dubai if we know she's there?" a senior member of his team asked.

"Even though France has an extradition treaty with the UAE, we want to see who she meets in Dubai and learn more about her and the man she's traveling with before we show our hand. I'll head up the team that meets her when she lands at Heathrow tomorrow."

His teams in the field who would normally be liaising with border and highway patrol units were now dispatched to liaise with wine industry organizations. In France they included *L'Office National Interprofessionnel des vins (ONIVINS)*; *Confédération Européenne des Vignerons Indépendants (CEVI)*; *Vignerons Indépendants de France (VIF)*; *Comité Interprofessionnel du Vin de Champagne (CIVC)*; *Conseil Interprofessionnel du Vin de Bordeaux (CIVB)*; and the *Comité d'Action des Vignerons de Bordeaux (CAVB)* and their equivalents in every wine-producing country on the planet.

With the conference call delivered and Operation Philomena officially recognized by all three Central Command Centres and launched to every National Central Bureau, Claude returned to his office.

This morning there was one more yellow flag to add to his map. His Red Notice had prompted a worldwide search for the flying winemaker. Within hours, an Emirates airline flight manifest revealed she was traveling from Hong Kong to Dubai.

He instructed the Abu Dhabi National Central Bureau to keep tabs on her while she was in Dubai but not to approach or apprehend her. As her return flight was to London, he planned to intercept her at Heathrow.

Report in hand and email sent in advance, Claude made his way upstairs to where Secretary General Arsenault had his corner office with sweeping views down the Rhône River and the sprawling Parc de la Tête d'Or, a vast expanse of city parks with a lake in the middle. Claude walked into the office and saw that the secretary general was on the phone. He motioned for Claude to take one of the two seats in front of his desk.

"*Oui*, sir, I can assure you we're pulling out all the stops and putting our best people on the job." He smiled at Claude when he said this. "Operation Philomena is our top priority. No, I'm not fond of the name either, but that's what they call it in the American newspapers, and it seems to have caught on. I agree, the name *and* the aphid should have stayed Stateside. *Oui,* just as it should have in the 1800s. No, sir, I was not aware it was imported from America by British botanists. What were they thinking? I'll update you once I have more information. Thank you, sir." The secretary general ended the call.

"That was the minister of agriculture," he said.

"They're taking the threat seriously, then?" Claude asked, secretly delighted.

"You better believe it. But the next time you want to go global with an idea, give me a heads-up."

"Yes, sir. Sorry, sir. Here's my report. I've emailed you a copy as well."

"Merci. I scanned through it—looks thorough. Aside from the impact on the wine industry and knock-on effects to the economy, what other effects are we likely to encounter?" Secretary General Arsenault demanded.

"Interpol in London has requested a confidential report to be drawn up by a small group at the London School of Economics to tell us exactly that. They'll be here later this week to share their views. But it's not difficult to imagine. Border security will tighten up everywhere. Land under vine will lose its value and be purchased at bargain prices by competing wineries, foreign buyers, and property developers. Consumer hoarding behavior will deplete stores and merchants of all wine in a matter of weeks. Prices will skyrocket, along with counterfeit wine. There will presumably be a lower demand for cheese and other products traditionally paired and bundled with wine. And millions will be out of work and lose their livelihood."

"*Putain!* You're going to need all the help you can get. I'll approve your manning and resource requests." He stabbed Claude's report with a thick finger.

"Thank you, Secretary General. Everything I need is outlined in my initial proposal and further detailed in the report you requested." Claude breathed a sigh of relief, as he had already committed the resources he would need that morning.

"Speaking of support, I want to discuss with you the role I see for Alison Pittard on Operation Philomena."

"Excuse me? What possible role could she have?" Claude asked. "She rejected the entire proposal." He tried to remain calm but felt his blood boiling.

"She may not have vision, but she has strong ties to the other CCCs. She can contribute in leveraging the network."

"So do you. I can use your leverage," Claude said. He felt he was on losing ground. "The only reason she has such strong connections with CCC leadership is because she spends all her time managing upward."

"Enough. You're overreacting. I've already spoken with her. She's not happy about the arrangement either, but the way I see it, it's a win-win situation—you get to run Operation Philomena, and she gets her wings clipped."

"I don't think it's a good idea and respectfully disagree with your decision, sir."

"Your concern is noted. Now go stop this bug."

Claude stood and left the office. He restrained himself from slamming the door.

CHAPTER 24

DUSANTI INTERNATIONAL
GLOBAL HEADQUARTERS
PLATTE COUNTY, MO, UNITED STATES

"No comment," the CEO of Dusanti International said for the ninth time, making Malcolm want to punch the man in his weak-looking cleft chin.

The man sat across from him and looked at him with dull brown eyes set underneath low eyebrows. He had a wide forehead, pasty white skin, and pattern baldness. He looked like an accountant or middle manager, which made Malcolm think he was the type of man who was often underestimated. The fact that he was CEO of a major multinational company and a leader in its field reminded Malcolm not to make that mistake.

When Horatio Jackson smiled after each "no comment," he revealed all his teeth like a wolf when it snarled.

After he'd met Donald and confirmed the connection between Slater and Dusanti, Malcolm called the chief executive officer's office for a quote. He was surprised to not only be connected to the CEO directly but to be asked to come in "while you're in our neck of the woods anyway" to meet the man and ask his questions face-to-face. He had expected to be passed on to some lackey in the PR department; instead, he was now sitting opposite the CEO, who sat leaning back in a black leather swivel chair behind an expansive desk made of glass and steel.

It was turning into a trip of strange encounters—first the rendezvous in Walmart, and now an impromptu meet-and-greet with a powerful industrialist he intended to accuse of destroying the global wine industry. The story on Philomena was not the standard puff piece his editor usually assigned to him. Now he just had to milk it for all the print he could. But in order to do that, he needed more than "no comment."

"Mr. Jackson, I appreciate your time, but what can you tell me about Dusanti's connection to the phylloxera aphid that's infesting vineyards around the world?" Malcolm asked.

"You mean Philomena, the cute nickname you coined?" Jackson asked with derision.

"Um, yes, that was actually a typo." Malcolm found himself on the back foot.

"I hope your spell check is more effective if and when you print anything about me or Dusanti."

"Indeed. So phylloxera?"

"I have no comment on that," the CEO said. He leaned farther back in his chair.

"Are you familiar with the name David Slater?" Malcolm asked.

"No comment."

"One of my sources told me that David Slater was approached by Dusanti. Slater developed the genetically modified aphid that's now destroying grape crops around the world. My source also tells me that his work was funded by Dusanti."

"No comment."

"I'm sorry, Mr. Jackson. When we spoke on the phone I was under the impression that you were prepared to speak with me on the topic of the phylloxera aphid."

"I agreed to see you. What I choose to say is my prerogative."

"And what would you choose to say if I said I believe Dusanti is behind the creation of Philomena and intends to profit from its spread by selling the only means to stop it?" Malcolm challenged the CEO. The fact that they were speaking alone, behind closed doors, with no PR representative or legal counsel led Malcolm to believe the man had something to hide.

"I would choose your words carefully, Mr. Goldberg. Writing unfounded statements such as what you are proposing is the quickest route to libel. How is it that you've come to write about Philomena in the first place, if I may ask?"

"I was writing a story on an infested vineyard in Napa. I had no idea that it was phylloxera or that the aphid was already infesting other vineyards around the world."

"And how did you come to make the gossamer-thin connection of Philomena to Dusanti?" Jackson asked, his wolfish smile returned.

"Another one of my sources."

"You seem to have many sources, Mr. Goldberg, but very few facts. And I noticed in the *Chronicle* that you're not sharing a byline with anyone. Writing this story alone, are you?"

"I prefer to work alone," Malcolm said, careful not to reveal his collaboration with Corvina and Bryan, who he knew were at that moment in Dubai looking into the involvement of another powerful figure.

"Thank you for your time." The CEO ended the interview as if on a cue. "Now I really must bring this interview to a close and return to my affairs." Jackson stood abruptly and gestured toward the door.

Malcolm stood less quickly. Had he said something to set the CEO off, or had he revealed something unintentionally? He felt like something had shifted in the dynamic of the interview and not in his favor.

"Thank you for your time, Mr. Jackson. It's been illuminating." Malcolm didn't extend his hand. He turned to leave the office and crossed the distance to the door in three strides. He opened the door to let himself out.

"Oh, just one more question," Malcolm said halfway out the office door. He turned to face Dusanti's CEO. "Would you prefer to be labeled an ecoterrorist or, as the French say, a *terroirist*? I'll be sure to spell your name correctly when I go to press."

Malcolm left the office before Jackson could respond.

CHAPTER 25

BURJ AL ARAB HOTEL
JUMEIRAH DISTRICT
DUBAI, UAE

"What do you mean? We are meeting Feng here tonight? I thought his brother arranged for us to meet him tomorrow at Zheng He's, the Chinese restaurant in the resort next door," Corvina asked Bryan. She looked up at the bulging white façade of the Burj Al Arab, Tower of the Arabs, as they entered the world's only seven-star hotel. Powerful spotlights lit up the front of the hotel. It stood out like a beacon in the night set against the inky-black backdrop of the warm Arabian Sea. The short walk from the taxi to the front door was like walking through a sauna.

"We're scheduled to, but when I found out he was dining here tonight I thought we could meet him beforehand," Bryan answered her. He wiped a sheen of sweat from his forehead.

"How did you find out?" Corvina asked. She nodded to the liveried doorman who held the door open for them.

"My colleague Christine, the head sommelier at the Ritz in London, used to work with the head concierge here."

"Is Feng expecting us?"

"Of course not," Bryan said. "This way we catch him off guard."

"Catching a billionaire off guard didn't work out so well for us the last time," Corvina said. She nervously recalled the mess they had gotten into trying to meet Zhang Tao Lung in Hong Kong.

"Don't worry. I'll think of something," Bryan said.

Corvina admired Bryan's ability to switch off. Her mind was racing. The aphid's mutation, presence, and spread continued to confound her, and she needed to make sense of everything they had discovered. It was all a jumble in her mind, and she was frustrated that she wasn't seeing the bigger picture. Was there one? They still didn't know for sure who was responsible for the spread of Philomena, how the aphid was being spread, why it was being spread, and most important, how it could be stopped.

She had initially struggled with the decision to accept Lung's offer to fly them to Dubai but came to terms with it given the Château Lafite she had donated to his vertical tasting. Thankfully there had been some left for her and Bryan to taste when they rejoined the tasting the night before. Also, if he wasn't the owner of the patent on the genetically modified strain of Philomena, it was hard to argue a conflict of interest existed.

Corvina followed Bryan into the hotel through tall glass doors and tried not to gawk at everything in sight: the reception and concierge desks nestled inside giant seashells; the twenty-four karat gold leaf paint that seemed to cover every surface; the stepped choreographed fountain splashing in perfect synchronicity; the two giant aquariums; the intricately colored floor mosaics; and the gold-plated elevators that whisked guests to the top of the hotel, which housed a restaurant, bar, and helipad.

Once she was well inside the blessedly cool air-conditioned lobby, she removed the hijab covering her head. She had purchased the black-and-gold Arabic geometric print silk scarf upon arrival to Dubai. An Emirati woman in the store showed her how to wear it. Now she tied the two ends together and draped the scarf twice around her neck in a more familiar faux infinity style. She dabbed away the sheen of perspiration covering her face with a tissue.

Corvina looked up into the atrium of the hotel.

"Taller than the Eiffel Tower," Bryan said over her shoulder.

She followed Bryan to an escalator that took them past one of the giant aquariums and up to the mezzanine level.

"I feel like we're wasting our time out here," Corvina said after a moment of silence.

"The patent is the only lead we have," Bryan said. "Besides, your boss thought it was a good idea."

When she'd called Vicente, who in turn called James Harvey in California, she was surprised that they both thought going to Dubai was a great idea.

"I know, but this is the third city—after Washington and Hong Kong—that we've been to that doesn't even have vineyards. I feel like we should be closer to where Philomena is spreading." *It all begins in the vineyard.*

"Let's play this lead out. Feng didn't just buy the patent on a whim."

A tall, blonde Lithuanian hostess greeted them at the restaurant's reception desk and escorted them into a gold-plated elevator. She took them back down a level.

"You ready to meet Zhang Tao's brother?" Bryan asked.

"Yes. I want to know why he purchased the patents. It makes him look culpable in the matter, but I don't see the connection," Corvina said. A tightness in her gut accompanied their short descent.

They exited the elevator and passed a smoking lounge where tall glass cases displayed boxes of Cuban cigars, French cognac, and Scottish single malt whisky. Corvina counted dozens of magnums of red wine on display in similar glass cases lining the walls between the lounge and restaurant.

The entrance to the restaurant was a ribbed golden tunnel arching over a dark marble floor that stretched out for three meters before they reached the opening. The tunnel ended with a view of the floor-to-ceiling oval aquarium that dominated the center of the room. Corvina was impressed to see the entire restaurant flowed around the giant aquarium, which housed dozens of species of fish and numerous sharks.

Tables for two were set around the aquarium while round tables for four hugged the outer wall, each encircled by blue high-backed chairs with curved tops.

Precariously tall champagne flutes and blue charger plates adorned ironed white tablecloths. Even the menus were embedded with an oyster shell, a nod to the restaurant's name, *Al Mahara*: The Oyster Shell.

Corvina entered the restaurant with Bryan at her side. The thick, blue broadloom carpet and unobtrusive music playing softly in the background created a subdued and tranquil environment where diners were engaged in hushed conversations. Each table was occupied by guests, save one on the other side of the aquarium reserved for her and Bryan.

She thought the venue was a bit over the top, but in a city where man-made islands, gravity-defying skyscrapers, and extravagant luxury hotels were the norm, perhaps not.

Just as they took their seats, the peace was shattered by a raised voice coming from one of two private dining rooms. "I don't want a pinotage, and I don't care if it's from Stellenbosch! I want a bordeaux!" the voice shouted in a Chinese accent. Corvina met Bryan's eyes in understanding. It must be Feng.

"What is it with South African wines in this hotel? Get me a bordeaux!" the voice shouted. A sommelier in black trousers and a white coat bolted out of the private dining room, narrowly missing being hit by the wine list hurled at him.

Her illusion of a calm conversation with Zhang Tao's brother shattered, Corvina thought next about how she and Bryan were going to confront the man with their suspicions.

Never one to miss an opportunity, Bryan reached into his jacket pocket and removed the black pin of grapes he'd pinched from the vertical tasting in Hong Kong. He pinned it to his lapel while the drama in the adjacent private dining room unfolded.

Without wasting a moment or taking the time to explain his plan to Corvina, he scooped up the wine list from the floor and passed under the archway leading into the private dining room where Feng Lung was entertaining. Fish swam overhead and to his sides, as the arch was made of glass and formed part of a larger aquarium.

Bryan opened the bulky leather-bound wine list and quickly found the bordeaux section.

"Good evening, sir." Bryan started momentarily when he saw that Feng looked exactly like his brother; Zhang Tao hadn't mentioned they were identical twins. Thankfully, Feng didn't even look up as he eyed the wine list spread before him. "We have an excellent selection of bordeaux available in magnum format. I'd be happy to make a selection for you that will please you, or alternatively we can discuss what kind of wine you like."

"Select. Isn't that what sommeliers are paid for?" Feng asked.

"In that case, sir, I would recommend either the Château Margaux or the Château Haut-Brion. The 1975 Haut-Brion is my favorite. Shall I start the table off with a magnum?" Bryan asked, pointing to the astronomical price of the bottle before closing the wine list. He sized up the rest of the guests at the table while Feng was distracted by the list. The man nodded and waved him away.

The manager of the restaurant strode in just as Bryan was leaving the table. "I'm sorry, Mr. Lung," the manager said. Turning to Bryan, he asked, "Who are you?"

"I'm—" Bryan began.

"He's my sommelier, that's who he is!" Feng shouted while pivoting in his chair to look at the restaurant manager.

"But he's not—" the manager stammered.

"Yes! He is!" Feng commanded, standing now. "I want a bordeaux. He's offered me a bordeaux. Now get me a bordeaux!" Feng screamed.

Bryan left the private dining room with the restaurant manager following hot on his heels.

"What do you think you're doing?" The manager grabbed Bryan by the arm in the middle of the restaurant. Diners stopped in mid-conversation and turned in their seats. Bryan saw that Corvina was studying the menu.

Bryan smiled and led the manager through the golden tunnel and out of the restaurant.

"Well?" the manager asked. He had an Italian accent and wore a black suit with a burgundy-striped tie. Bryan could tell he was a man used to being in control—but now was not one of those times, as his raised voice revealed.

"I'm taking care of *your* customer. Now you can either tell me where to find the magnum of bordeaux I just sold to him, or you can go back in there and take the order yourself," Bryan said.

At that, the manager looked uneasily toward the private dining room where Feng Lung and his party were being served their starters.

"It'll have to be decanted, so you better hurry and decide," Bryan said, reminding him of the time-sensitive nature of Feng's request.

The manager let go of Bryan's arm and patted his sleeve as though to smooth the crease he had made.

"I'll get the decanters," the manager said. "Suresh," he called to the sommelier who had left the room unceremoniously and was now being consoled by a hostess in the lounge, "help this gentleman locate the wine for Mr. Lung's party."

While Bryan was sourcing the magnum of bordeaux for the table, Corvina watched Feng leave the private dining room. He held a cigarette in one hand and was making his way toward the lounge. Corvina smiled as he walked by. He stopped in front of her table.

"Dining alone?" he asked.

"I'm afraid it looks like my date has stood me up," she replied.

"That won't do. Come join me in the lounge, then you can join our table for dinner."

"*Grazie.* I think I will," she said. She removed the napkin from her lap and stood to join him. While Bryan ingratiated himself to Feng in his adopted sommelier role, she now had the opportunity to approach Feng on his other flank and court the man with a subtler approach.

CHAPTER 26

AL MAHARA RESTAURANT
BURJ AL ARAB HOTEL
DUBAI, UAE

The only guests in Al Mahara's smoking lounge were Corvina and Feng. Bryan raised an eyebrow when they entered, but he walked out with the magnum of bordeaux without giving Corvina a second glance.

He entered the private dining room where Feng's guests were finishing the white wine that had accompanied their intermediate course and set to work to decant the magnum. Out of the corner of his eye, Bryan saw Feng and Corvina return. A waiter set an additional chair to Feng's left and laid down another place setting on the corner of the table for Corvina, who sat between Feng and the sheikh of a neighboring emirate.

Working over a side table behind Feng, Bryan slipped the magnum into a cradle specially designed to hold the bottle at an angle. The restaurant manager passed him a corkscrew. Bryan used it to remove the foil and withdraw the cork. He wiped off the top of the bottle with a cloth napkin and examined the cork without smelling it. He presented it to Feng, who made an impatient gesture. Bryan slipped the cork into his pocket and lifted the bottle of wine.

Fumbling with his lighter, the restaurant manager lit a candle for Bryan to pour the wine over. He poured himself a small amount into a glass, swirled it around, inhaled its aroma, and had a quick taste. The wine was without fault. None of the guests paid him any attention, not even the four men forming two separate security details for Feng and the sheikh he was meeting—the former two wearing dark suits, the latter two wearing white ankle-length kandoras and red checkered turbans. They stood against the walls watching the guests in silence.

Satisfied that the wine tasted as it should, Bryan held the shoulder and neck of the bottle just above the candle. He poured the magnum into the first decanter and ignored the restaurant manager.

Switching decanters, Bryan ensured that as much wine as possible was aerated on its way into the clear glass vessels. Once he saw the sediment begin to accumulate in the shoulder of the bottle, illuminated by the candle, he slowed down until he stopped altogether, leaving the sediment and just a small amount of wine. He heard the restaurant manager release his breath.

Bryan set the second decanter next to the first on a side table where the wine would have time to breathe further before the main course arrived. He left the room with the restaurant manager in tow.

"Who are you?" the restaurant manager asked. Gone was his arrogant posturing.

"It's not important who I am. But don't worry, I'm a trained sommelier. Now go get another magnum of the Haut-Brion if you want to smash your revenue targets this evening."

Bryan returned to the private dining room and began pouring wine from the first decanter to the head of the table. He noticed Feng's gaze lingered on his lapel pin. Feng looked up at his face and just as quickly looked away.

Bryan continued pouring the bordeaux into Feng's glass.

"A lot can change over time," Feng said, deftly returning to the conversation at the table. "Wine, for instance, had its origins here in the Middle East." He held up his glass.

"From humble beginnings come many great accomplishments," the sheikh sitting to Corvina's left responded, extending his arms with palms facing upward. Bryan couldn't tell if he was referring to the origin of grapes, the hotel they dined in, or the phenomenal rise of Dubai since it gained independence from Britain in 1971.

Bryan approached Corvina next with the wine, acting as though he had never met her, and poured her a glass of the Haut-Brion.

"And what does a desert dweller know about wine?" Feng laughed. He leaned back as his main course was served—a three-hundred-gram Kobe beef fillet prepared medium rare. Three other waiters served the rest of the table.

"As you mentioned, the Middle East has a rich history of wine making. The Phoenicians were responsible for widely spreading the knowledge of how to grow and cultivate grapes and turn them into wines. The origins of the syrah grape can be traced to Iran, where the grape was first grown in the town of Shiraz, giving the grape its name. And Lebanon today boasts such famous wineries as Château Musar and Château Ksara," the sheikh responded with pride.

Bryan had to bite his tongue to stop himself from correcting the sheikh about syrah's origins. DNA analysis proved the grape was in fact indigenous to the Rhone Valley in France.

"You're absolutely right," Feng said, getting into the theme. "Not too long ago, didn't archaeologists find the world's oldest wine cellar here in the Middle East? A room full of jugs used to store wine? In Israel, if I recall?" Feng asked with a wicked smile.

The sheikh glared at him and just as quickly broke out into a grin himself. "There's hope yet for the infidels," he said graciously and laughed. The table laughed with him. Bryan poured each guest a fresh glass of bordeaux. He wished he could have a drink himself to calm his nerves as he tried not to let the decanter shake in his hands.

While a toast was made and the main courses served, Corvina felt two hands on her legs at once. Feng and the sheikh both rested a hand on her knees under the table and began squeezing.

Corvina stood abruptly. "Gentlemen, I need some air."

Bryan followed her out to the smoking lounge.

"Is everything okay?" he asked.

"Getting groped by two decrepit *pervertidos* is not how I envisioned my evening. We need to get Feng someplace where we can confront him about the patent."

"I agree," Bryan said. "And I have an idea."

"Don't even think about suggesting I seduce him and go up to his room with him," Corvina said.

"The thought hadn't crossed my mind. I was going to suggest that you just talk to him at the table. Everyone has had a few drinks, and they all seem to be having separate conversations."

"I'll try," Corvina said, wondering how she was going to turn the conversation to Philomena and patents filed in North America.

They returned to the private dining room separately.

Corvina sat down and drank some of the Haut-Brion. It was divine. Feng had his glass cupped in the palms of his hands, his elbows on the table.

"I thought you looked familiar." Corvina looked Feng in the eyes when she sat back down. "I did a quick search on my phone. You're the industrialist from Hong Kong."

"Your phone is correct," Feng said, glancing down at the phone she held tantalizingly in front of her chest.

"No wonder you have such expensive taste." Corvina raised her glass in reference to the pricey bordeaux Bryan had served them.

"Wine is one of my passions."

"Shame that there's that bug going around destroying vineyards right now."

Feng set his glass down on the table and looked at Corvina with an open expression.

"I mean," Corvina continued, worried that she had overplayed her hand, "it's a shame that such beautiful wines are at risk."

"I'm not worried about that," Feng said.

"Why is that? Do you own a pesticide company?" Corvina smiled, flirting with the industrialist. She adjusted her scarf to reveal her neckline and more cleavage.

The men at the table laughed, their attention turned to the conversation between her and Feng. Feng laughed too. Corvina was glad to see the wine seemed to be having an effect on him.

"No, but close. I own the patent to the bug itself." Feng smiled and drank from his glass.

"You own the patent for Philomena?" Corvina asked her host.

"I purchase hundreds of patents. It's a hobby of mine." Feng looked at her with renewed interest.

"Like a patent troll?" She leaned forward, elbows resting on the table.

"I take a long view of the future."

Corvina resisted the urge to straighten up and hide her cleavage from Feng's gaze.

"Sound investment advice, but why would you buy a patent for a bug?"

"I hedge my bets. Someone designed a bug that would be devastating if it were released. Why? I don't know. But with misfortune and disaster come opportunity."

"But it needs to be stopped." Corvina sat up straight and repositioned her scarf to cover her neckline.

"Do you have a means to stop it?" he asked.

"No."

"Neither do I." He sipped from his wine glass. "If I did, I could make a tidy profit selling it to every winery in the world. I suggest we let nature take its course. Speaking of nature taking its course, why don't you come see me later," Feng said. He took out his keycard from his inner coat pocket and slipped it into her clutch. She could see his room number written on the paper pouch the card was tucked inside. Feng then slid his hand onto her leg again.

Before Corvina could express her revulsion or ask Feng any more questions, the room was suddenly filled by a platoon of men, some wearing long white kandoras and others in the uniform of the Dubai police. Four members of hotel security flowed in swiftly as well, filling the small private dining room.

Feng was surrounded by his security detail as the new arrivals swarmed toward the table. The sheikh was quickly surrounded by his security detail as well and just as quickly surrounded by the local security forces.

To Corvina, it seemed like the entire room stood at once and began shouting simultaneously in a cacophonic mix of Arabic and Cantonese. Confusion reigned, and everyone seemed to be yelling at one another all at once.

Corvina found it difficult to discern what was happening since she spoke neither language filling the small room. She seemed to escape the brunt of the initial confrontation but then was grabbed by a policeman and dragged out of the room by one arm. Bryan dashed out of the room behind them.

"No prostitutes in the hotel! Take her away!" the Dubai policeman said, and shoved Corvina toward Bryan and a security guard from the Burj Al Arab who had materialized at his side.

"How dare you! *Puto!*" Corvina shoved the policeman back. He staggered backward and tripped over someone's legs. His shouts were drowned out by the rest of the men in the room.

The hotel security guard took one of Corvina's arms and led her out through the ribbed entrance to the elevator. Bryan took her other arm and motioned to the security man to take it easy. She struggled against both men's grips and screamed obscenities in Spanish and Italian at the policeman, who was struggling to get back on his feet. It took the security guard and Bryan working together to get Corvina up the lift to the mezzanine level. She didn't make it easy for them.

"I'll take her from here. We don't want to cause a scene at His Highness's hotel, now do we?" Bryan said, referring to His Highness Sheikh Mohammed bin Rashid Al Maktoum, ruler of Dubai and ultimate owner of the Burj Al Arab.

The security man let go with obvious relief yet continued to watch their progress as Bryan urged her down the escalator, past the aquarium, across the lobby, and out the front doors.

"Let go of me!" Corvina tore her arm away from Bryan's hand once they were outside.

"Sorry. At least we got out of there unquestioned. I wouldn't want us to get caught up in an international incident in the Middle East." Bryan summoned an awaiting taxi.

"I'd like to see them try!" Corvina said, shouting back at the hotel.

"*Inshallah,*" Bryan said. He put his arm around her and guided her to the taxi.

"What are we even doing here, Bryan? I can't believe we came all the way to Dubai for nothing," Corvina fumed as the taxi whisked them across the bridge, the broad white belly of the Burj Al Arab receding in the rearview mirror. She didn't bother to replace her head scarf.

CHAPTER 27

TERMINAL 5, HEATHROW AIRPORT
LONDON, ENGLAND

As soon as the "fasten seat belt" sign extinguished, Corvina switched her phone on. A flood of emails, messages, and missed calls filled her screen and inbox—none from Luis, she noted. She shouldn't have been surprised, and she chastised herself for hoping. She sent him a quick text just to let him know she was back in Europe, but she didn't expect a reply.

Next she texted her boss in Spain to say she was back in London and would be connecting shortly to Barcelona. She knew he would want to meet right away and get a full report.

Scrolling through her messages, she was annoyed to see several emails from her clients, all complaining about Sergio's intrusive approach to their wine making. Before she could read any of them in any depth, her boss called her back.

"You have to talk to Sergio. He's becoming unbearable," Corvina protested before Vicente even had a chance to welcome her back.

"*Hola* to you too. That won't be possible," he replied.

"*¿Por qué?*" Corvina demanded, not reading the tone in his voice. "It's completely unacceptable that he's upsetting my clients."

"Corvina, Sergio has disappeared."

"*¿Que?*" Corvina asked in shock.

"He was on his way to see one of your clients along the Mosel. The police in Germany don't seem to have any leads."

"Meaning they don't know what happened?"

"His rental car was found in a ditch with blood inside. He hadn't checked out of his hotel, and he didn't make it to the winery where he had an appointment to meet your client."

"When did this happen?"

"Two days ago. Corvina, there's something else to consider," he said. "Sergio was meeting with *your* clients."

"And?"

"When I mentioned it to the police, they suggested that Sergio might have been kidnapped or killed because someone thought he was the flying winemaker investigating Philomena."

"*¿Que?* Why would anyone want to kidnap me?" Corvina asked. She held a hand up to Bryan, who looked at her with growing concern.

"The spread of Philomena doesn't seem to be accidental," Vicente said.

"So you no longer think that Philomena is spreading by chance?"

"It seems unlikely, given what your investigation has turned up so far and the fact that dozens more vineyards on opposite sides of the planet have been infested. Whoever is infesting vineyards around the world might have found out that someone who works for Universal Wines is investigating."

"And wants to stop me," Corvina said.

"It's just a theory, but—"

"Let's talk when I get home. I need to digest this."

She hung up and filled Bryan in regarding Sergio's disappearance. Then she scrolled through her phone some more and saw several missed calls from Malcolm. She clicked on his number to call him back.

"Malcolm, it's me, Corvina. We just landed in London. I saw you tried calling."

Corvina listened as Malcolm recounted his interviews with the biologist and the CEO of Dusanti, then she gave him a brief update on what she and Bryan had learned in Hong Kong and Dubai. The passengers began to disembark, so she cut the call short and dropped her phone into her shoulder bag.

"Do you have a jealous husband?" Bryan asked from behind her.

"I don't think that's an issue you need to worry about," Corvina said. She wasn't sure whether to smile or cry. "Why?"

"I think we're being followed," Bryan said.

Corvina glanced back but didn't see anybody who looked familiar or who seemed preoccupied with them.

"Who?" she asked.

"One of the Arabic men back there. I noticed him check us out on the plane, and he was just looking at us and speaking into his phone."

"I think you're being paranoid." Once she was out of the plane's chilly interior, she replaced her woolen pashmina with the black-and-ochre silk Jim Thompson scarf covered in a repeating elephant pattern she had purchased in Hong Kong. She tucked her pashmina into her shoulder bag.

As she stepped out of the jet bridge into the concourse, a man in a light-gray suit approached her and Bryan.

"Corvina Guerra?" he asked, in a French accent.

"Yes?" Corvina asked surprised.

The man reached into his jacket pocket. Corvina's eyes widened and her hands reached instinctively for the scarf around her neck.

"I'm just getting my ID," the man said as he withdrew a small, navy-blue leather folder. He flipped it open and extended it for them to see.

"My name is Claude Duval with Interpol. We need to talk."

"Interpol?" Corvina asked. "Why would someone from Interpol want to talk to me?"

"You're a person of interest in an ongoing investigation," Claude said.

"What investigation?" Corvina asked.

"You're the only person who has been to many of the areas afflicted by this so-called Philomena bug."

"It's an aphid," Corvina corrected him.

"So you don't deny it?" Claude asked, surprised.

"Deny what? Traveling? I'm a flying winemaker."

"Wait a minute," Bryan intervened. "So as far as you can tell, not one other person has been to the afflicted areas?"

"No one with her background and qualifications. Why do you think Interpol is so interested in speaking with your colleague?"

"Of course I've been to some of the areas involved—I'm investigating the spread of the aphid on behalf of my company, Universal Wines," Corvina protested.

"You can tell me all about it once we reach the Interpol offices in London."

"Am I under arrest?" she asked, trying to keep the anger and panic she was feeling out of her voice. Her mind was reeling.

"No. As I said, you're a person of interest in an ongoing investigation. If you don't cooperate, you'll be placed on a No Fly list. The person responsible for spreading Philomena has been labeled an eco-terrorist, putting things into a totally different context. It's easier if you come voluntarily," Claude said.

CHAPTER 28

INTERPOL NATIONAL CENTRAL BUREAU
LONDON, ENGLAND

Dark gray clouds filled the sky over central London, giving the streets a muted quality. Claude observed that the threat of precipitation hung ominously in the low cloud cover. The drive from Heathrow to the Interpol National Central Bureau took just over an hour with traffic and Henri's careful driving. Claude knew he was unaccustomed to navigating London's streets and driving on the opposite side of the road.

When they arrived at the London NCB, Claude led Corvina and her colleague out of the car and through the basement parking lot. He entered a lift that took them up into the building. Given her colleague's proximity to Corvina on her recent travels, Claude decided it would be best to question him as well, but together, not separately. He sensed they would speak more freely together than if separated. They were here for an interview after all, not an interrogation.

"Can I send a message to my boss in Barcelona?" Corvina asked. "I was supposed to meet him at our offices in Barcelona this afternoon."

"Of course," Claude responded, looking up at the changing numbers until the car reached the fifth floor. The doors opened.

"Can I tell him Interpol is detaining me?" Corvina asked.

"I remind you that you're not under arrest. That said, I wouldn't broadcast it too loudly that you are a person of interest in an ongoing Interpol investigation," he said. His lips drew a straight line across his face. He felt a natural urge to reassure her, but it wasn't his role to do so.

Henri stepped out of the elevator first, leading them down a lengthy corridor to a meeting room featuring expansive floor-to-ceiling windows with a dramatic view of the River Thames. To the left Claude could see Blackfriars Bridge spanning the blue-gray waters, and, in the distance to the right, the London Eye dominated the skyline.

"Have a seat." Claude gestured to a large boardroom table with six leather chairs on either side and one at each end. Corvina and Bryan sat beside each other while Claude and Henri took the seats opposite.

"Sorry to disrupt your travel plans. Your cooperation in our investigation is appreciated," Claude began.

Corvina and Bryan just stared at him. He knew what they were both thinking—that he hadn't left them with much of a choice. So be it. He was chasing terrorists.

"You're familiar with the spread of the phylloxera aphid nicknamed Philomena by the media?"

"Yes, and I know the reporter who gave the aphid its nickname."

"I see." Claude mentally filed that piece of information for further thought later. "And are you aware of the threat that the aphid poses to wineries and vineyards around the world?"

"Of course I'm aware. I already told you I'm a winemaker," Corvina said. Claude could sense she was straining to be civil. "I first came across this new strain of phylloxera in Italy three weeks ago. I requested that my company, Universal Wines, allow me to investigate further," she said.

"Is that why you went to Santiago?"

"We went to talk to the family of the man accused of spreading Philomena in California. We also visited the winery where he worked as an assistant winemaker."

"And what did you discover?" Claude asked. He was pleased that she was being so forthcoming. He hadn't known what to expect from her.

"No one who knows him believes he is capable of doing what he's accused of doing. The vineyard where he worked was infested, and they were pulling up and burning the vines when we arrived," Corvina explained.

"And why did you go to Canada? Toronto, was it?" Claude probed.

"We flew into Toronto, but from there we drove south to a city called St. Catharines. We were trying to track down a student who had worked in Santiago and who we believe is responsible for the development of the aphid. We spoke to one of the student's professors at Brock University and just missed the student himself."

"The development?" Claude asked, perplexed.

"The phylloxera aphid currently infesting vineyards has been genetically modified. Funded by a company called Dusanti, we believe."

Claude leaned forward in his seat at this new revelation.

"It can attack American rootstock, the roots of the vines grafted onto the majority of vines today to protect them from phylloxera. American rootstock isn't immune to this new strain of phylloxera."

"Okay, then you next went to Washington, DC, correct?"

"Yes. My boss's boss, the head of Universal Wines in California, had requested that I look into a group of anti-alcohol pro-prohibitionists called the Drys. They're a lobbying group based in Washington. And after our visit to Brock University, we suspected that the student had registered a patent on his genetically modified phylloxera. While we were in Washington, we visited the US Patent and Trademark Office in Virginia to learn more."

"What did you discover?" Claude asked. He was impressed by the steps they had taken to investigate the aphid's spread—a threat that Interpol acknowledged existed only several days ago.

"The Drys don't seem to be involved, and I don't think they would have an interest in a global pandemic. Their interests are much more insular. At the patent office, we found the patent that the student had registered for the genetically modified version of phylloxera. The patent had been purchased by a man from Hong Kong named Feng Lung."

"You've covered a lot of ground," Claude said.

"I find it hard to believe that I'm the only person who raised a red flag in your system," Corvina said. "Surely there have been other travelers to these countries, though maybe not to the same cities. I mean, there are dozens of ways to get to the infested vineyards once you're inside the country. Surely there are other potential suspects out there."

"We're looking into all possibilities," Claude said. "Bear in mind that we're talking about a global threat. We have a lot of ground to cover."

"I'd also cross-check any travelers who have been to more than one of the specific destinations or who have flown into secondary cities nearby," Bryan said. Claude didn't react but was taken aback at the man's investigative instincts. Just the night before, Claude had instructed his team to do just what Bryan had suggested.

"And up to a year before the infestation was reported or discovered," Corvina added. "The aphids wouldn't be immediately apparent. They have a complicated reproductive cycle."

"I can check that," Claude said. He hadn't thought of that. It dawned on him that despite his readings, he knew little about the aphid.

"Here's my business card." Claude slid his card across the table to her. "Please send me your travel schedule for the last twelve months with corroborating documents as soon as you get home. Some of this may explain why you were in all of these areas and help clear your name."

"That would be a relief," Corvina said. "Let me give you my card."

Claude reached out for her card while she retrieved one from her clutch.

"Oops, what's that?" she asked. She pulled a hotel keycard out of her clutch. "Here, you can have this too." She slid the card across the table to Claude. He stopped it and held it up. It was a keycard holder and key from the Burj Al Arab hotel. Claude raised an eyebrow in question.

"Feng Lung gave it to me in the restaurant of the hotel in Dubai," she said.

Claude raised both eyebrows.

"I never used it, in case you're wondering," Corvina said. Her tone suggested she was not happy with his wordless insinuation.

"Leading to my next question," Claude said. "If you're really investigating the spread of Philomena—visiting infested vineyards and speaking with industry experts—do you have any suspects yourself?"

Before Corvina could answer, the door swung open violently and Alison Pittard entered the room.

"So you enjoy destroying vineyards, do you?" Alison Pittard demanded. She marched to the head of the table.

"What? No! I—" Corvina said. She looked at Claude.

"Look at me when I'm talking to you." Alison slapped her hands together. "You've been to numerous infested vineyards, yet you deny your involvement?"

"What are you talking about?" Corvina loosened her scarf; it reminded Claude of a man removing his tie before a fight.

"Just tell us why you're doing it and how to stop the stupid bug!" Alison slammed her hands on the table, making Bryan and Henri jump in their seats. Claude was used to her tactics and barely blinked an eye.

"Alison—" Claude began saying, but Corvina interrupted him.

"Listen, lady, I don't know who you are, but if you'd let me get a word in edgewise I could answer your questions," Corvina said in a raised voice.

"Why were you at these vineyards?" Alison asked.

"I've already answered that." Corvina looked at Claude.

"You'll answer me," Alison said.

"I'm investigating the spread of the *aphid* known as Philomena on behalf of my company, Universal Wines, as some of our wineries and those of our clients were infested," she said. To Claude, Corvina's tone sounded like one a person would use to address a simpleton.

"Do you have any proof of that?" Alison asked. "It looks to me like you're behind these terrorist attacks. You just happened to be at many of the vineyards that were attacked."

"She didn't just *happen* to be anywhere, you silly cow." Bryan stood up. "She told you why she was at the wineries that were infested. It could also stand to reason that there is more than one person responsible for the spread of the aphid," Bryan shouted, visibly upset at Alison's demeanor.

"*Et voilá!* If you'd like to volunteer yourself as a suspect, that's fine with me," Alison challenged Bryan.

"That's not what I'm implying. If Corvina is the only passenger who shows up on all of the manifests and she's not responsible, then one alternative is that two or more individuals are traveling around the world spreading the aphid or perhaps even shipping it across borders and overseas."

"Sure, sure," Alison replied dismissively. "That's not an alternative I'm currently looking into."

Claude suppressed the urge to correct her. Operation Philomena was still *his* investigation.

"*Alors*, why don't we all take a breath and calm down," Claude suggested. The boardroom was thick with tension.

"Look, the flight manifests and my travel arrangements will show you that my visits to the afflicted areas took place *after* the aphid had infested the vineyards," Corvina said as if he hadn't spoken.

"We'll see about that," Alison said with determination.

"If you're not going to charge me with anything, we'll be leaving now." Corvina stood, trembling with anger. "Otherwise I want a lawyer." She crossed her arms and fixed her stare on Alison.

"You're free to go," Claude said. This earned him a fierce look from Alison.

"Just don't plan on any lengthy trips," Alison said.

"My job entails flying to wineries around the world, so unless you're going to ground me, I'll go wherever I damn well please. Let's go, Bryan." Bryan left the room first, followed by Corvina, who slammed the door as violently as Alison had opened it.

"That could have gone better," Claude said with an accusing glare at Alison.

"Perhaps if you'd let me conduct the interview from the start we would have caught her in a web of her own lies," Alison said. She stood and paced around the table. "She knows something. Next time, you wait for me." She jabbed her index finger in Claude's direction.

"Alison, I told you when we were going to pick her up and where we were going to interview her. You're the one who insisted on coming to London with us. It's your choice whether you want to show up or not."

"Oh, so now it's my fault that she's gone free?"

"Gone free? What are you talking about? We didn't have anything to hold her on."

"I'm not the one who didn't apprehend her as soon as her location was discovered. I'm not the one who brought her and her sidekick in for questioning together instead of interrogating them separately. And I'm not the one who learned nothing from the only suspect we have. I didn't even ask to be a part of this ridiculous investigation. You created this mess by going behind my back—you fix it." With her final barb, Alison left the room as angry as she had entered only moments previously.

Claude looked at Henri, who just rolled his eyes.

"Let's get back to Lyon and back to work. We need to dig deeper into our suspect's story and the company she works for," Claude said while closing the thin folder on Corvina in front of him.

"So you still think it's her? That she's the ecoterrorist we're looking for?" Henri asked, following him out of the boardroom.

"I haven't made up my mind yet. I do agree with Alison on one thing—Corvina knows a lot more about what's going on than we do and perhaps more than she's letting on. Whether she's responsible or not, I want to speak with her again. In the meantime, let's flag the Canadian student she was looking into as soon as possible and start looking into *his* background and travels. An ecoterrorist is still on the loose."

Corvina left the Interpol office as fast as she could. She shared a black cab with Bryan to the nearest Tube station. After a short ride down the Strand, they parted company at Charing Cross Station, where Bryan caught the Tube home and Corvina continued in the black cab to the airport to catch another flight to Barcelona. She'd found a flight online and booked it over her phone en route.

She was desperate to return home to recuperate after all the traveling, but first she would have to swing by the office to debrief Vicente. He hadn't replied to her text message informing him of her interception between flights.

The moment after she collected her luggage from the carousel in Barcelona hours later, she summoned an Uber to take her to the office. She preferred the black cabs in London, with their ample space for luggage and outstretched legs.

"Vicente, it's me. I just got to the office. Are you available?" Corvina was on her phone even as she was stepping out of the Uber driver's car thirty minutes later.

"Yes, of course. Meet me in my office. See you in a minute," he replied.

Corvina rushed through reception and into the lift that would take her to Vicente's office. When she arrived, somewhat breathless, Vicente was waiting for her at his desk. He stood to greet her.

"Corvina, come in. Take a seat." He gestured to one of the two chairs in front of his desk. "Did you run all the way here?" he asked. Concern marked his words as she left her luggage by the door and sat down to catch her breath.

"*Lo siento.*" She took another breath. "I was just anxious to see you. I've had a rough couple of days," she said. She thought back to the terrifying experience in Hong Kong, the fruitless trip to Dubai where she was branded as a billionaire's whore, and most recently the good cop/bad cop interrogation by Interpol only hours ago.

"Tell me about what happened this morning in London first," Vicente said. He came around to the front of the desk and sat in the seat next to her, something she had never seen him do.

Corvina took a deep breath and told Vicente everything Claude Duval and Alison Pittard had asked her and what she in turn had revealed to them. Vicente made appreciative noises of understanding and concern, asking an occasional question for clarification, but otherwise he let her recount her morning without interruption. When she was finished telling him everything, she felt as though a great weight had been lifted from her shoulders.

Without a word, Vicente stood and paced the room. "What? What is it?" Corvina asked. When his steps took him near the office door, he closed it gently.

"Vicente, *que pasa*?" Corvina asked.

Vicente walked back to the desk. Instead of returning to his seat or the seat next to Corvina, he sat on the front of the desk itself, one foot off the ground, the other still firmly planted. He crossed his hands over his raised knee.

"Corvina," he said before taking a breath, "I have to let you go."

"You're firing me?" Corvina gaped at him.

"*Sí*," he said, looking into her eyes.

Corvina bolted up out of her chair and strode halfway across the office. She spun around.

"On what grounds?" she demanded. She felt her temples throbbing.

"I informed headquarters that Interpol had detained you for questioning as a person of interest, and they insisted I let you go. The CEO is worried about the negative press and has expressed concern about your actions recently."

"My actions?" Corvina was incensed.

"Your flying around the world on this quest to stop Philomena—"

"With the company's blessing!" she shouted, bewildered.

"Your talking to the media about crazy theories of genetically modified aphids—"

"Malcolm is a reputable reporter, and the theory of genetic modification isn't just a theory—we found the patent proving it! The aphid has been weaponized!" Corvina shouted.

"Nevertheless," Vicente continued, "the requisition of a priceless bottle of wine with nothing to show for it." He shrugged in futility.

"Approved by headquarters!"

"And now Sergio is missing and you're being hauled in for questioning by Interpol—Interpol, for Christ's sake, Corvina!" Vicente's normally calm demeanor cracked as he raised his voice. His size and anger made him an intimidating force. "This isn't the local police. They think you're a terrorist! An *eco*terrorist!"

Corvina slumped in her chair and threw her hands to her face. Was this really happening?

"I don't know what happened to Sergio," Corvina protested. She looked up at Vicente. Her eyes were moist as she fought back a flood of tears. She tugged fiercely at her scarf, hand over hand.

Vicente raised his hands, a gesture to calm her down. It seemed to have an equal effect on him as well. His posture relaxed as he returned to his seat on the desk, and he spoke in a measured tone.

"Corvina, no one's saying you had anything to do with Sergio's disappearance. But as I told you this morning, the police in Germany suspect whoever *was* responsible may have mixed up their flying winemakers. If that's the case, you should be more worried about your own personal safety than your job or some damned bug. Me, I'm more worried about my protégé."

"It's not just a bug," Corvina whispered.

"Corvina. If there's anything I can do, please, let me know," Vicente said firmly. He was signaling the end of the conversation.

"*Gracias*, Vicente," Corvina relented. The decision was out of Vicente's hands. Shooting the messenger would achieve nothing. Arguing would get her nowhere.

"Anything at all—a reference, an introduction, just . . . well, whatever . . ." Vicente's voice trailed off. She could feel his gaze on the top of her head. Corvina had never heard him at a loss for words. He eased himself off his desk and shifted his bulky frame toward the door.

He turned to look at her one more time before leaving the office.

"I'm sorry, Corvina," Vicente said with genuine sympathy. He left Corvina alone with her darkening thoughts.

How did things get so bad so quickly? Then she remembered—*it all began in the vineyard.*

She left the building with her head wrapped in a scarf held low so no one could see her tears. The Uber she'd ordered arrived within minutes. Corvina climbed in the back seat and gave the driver her address.

She fumed and stared out the window. First Sergio took her role, then she traveled the world on a wild aphid chase with no thanks from anyone, then some Interpol bitch accused her of being an ecoterrorist, and then she was fired!

"*Hola, se puede ir más rápido?*" Corvina slapped the back of the driver's seat, urging him to go faster. She wished she was driving so she could speed up and get as far away from work as fast as possible.

She thanked the driver before he had come to a full stop outside her home and was out the door and opening the trunk for her luggage before he could get out and assist her.

She hauled her suitcase up the stairs to her empty apartment. She unpacked her trainers and iPod, changed into her running gear, and hit the street, pounding her ears with music and the pavement with her feet within minutes. She needed to clear her head and put literal and figurative distance between the events of the last twenty-four hours—hell, the last twenty-four days.

Forty-five minutes of endorphin-inducing hills and wind sprints later, she felt a million times better. Her anger at Sergio for approaching her clients was replaced with worry. What had happened to him? Despite their differences, she hoped he was okay and that he would return soon.

On the final sprint up the road leading to her apartment, she spotted a woman with a suitcase outside the door to her apartment. She immediately suspected the woman was looking for Luis.

The woman turned around, and Corvina stopped in her tracks. She could have cried with happiness.

Rachel Miller was standing on her doorstep.

"Rachel!" Corvina forgot all about her disheveled and sweaty state. She closed the distance between them with two long strides and wrapped her friend in a tight hug.

"I'm glad to see you, too" Rachel said, and laughed.

"How? I mean, why are you here?" Corvina asked.

"After you came to San Francisco, Ed saw how happy it made me to see you again. Ed and I haven't had a vacation for a while, so he suggested we should visit. But when he emailed Luis to tell him we were coming, Luis told him you two had separated. Why didn't you tell me?"

"I'm sorry, I wanted to but . . ."

"Never mind, I'm here now. Tonight's drinks are on me."

"This is such a wonderful surprise," Corvina gushed. "But I look a sight," she said. She looked down at the state of her clothes and appearance. "Let me jump into the shower to freshen up."

She let herself and Rachel into the apartment and entered the bathroom, where she stripped off her running gear. The bathroom was still in the same state of disrepair as when she had last left it. Luis hadn't touched it since they had split up.

When she closed her eyes to wash her hair, she remembered she had just been fired at work. Vicente would probably be on the front nine by now, golfing with his buddies. She flushed with shame at the unbidden thought. Vicente was a good man and had always treated her like a daughter. His protégé, he had called her. He wasn't responsible for her termination. He may have pulled the trigger, but he hadn't loaded the gun and pointed it at her.

Cleaned and refreshed, they took an Uber to the city's famous Passeig de Gràcia Boulevard. Once there, Corvina led Rachel into a wine bar she was familiar with, La Vinoteca Torres. The bar served most Torres wines by the glass and was a Spanish oenophile's dream.

In the time it took the women to have two drinks and share a few mouthwatering tapas, Corvina unloaded on Rachel, who listened with rapt attention, about her separation from Luis and all that had happened since she had last seen her friend in California.

"So what now? I mean, job-wise?" Rachel asked.

Corvina signaled their waiter to replenish their wine. Her scarf, a Bombay paisley silk chiffon, was draped loosely around her shoulders. She hadn't felt this relaxed since before she'd discovered the aphids in Tuscany three weeks earlier.

"I have no idea. I haven't even thought of it. I mean, I was only fired"—she looked at her watch—"four hours ago. I've been a flying winemaker for years and love what I do. It never even occurred to me to have a backup plan."

"I wouldn't worry about work. The wine industry will always offer plenty of work for someone as knowledgeable and experienced as you."

"Thanks, Rachel," Corvina said.

"But not if there isn't a wine industry to work in." Rachel raised her voice.

"Wait. *¿Que?*"

Their waiter came over with two glasses of wine and a bowl of fresh olives. He cleared their empty glasses.

"You said it yourself," Rachel continued. "The wineries of the world are under attack, and vineyards are being destroyed. Something is destroying your livelihood."

"Or someone," Corvina said, staring into her glass of wine. She looked up suddenly. "Disaster capitalism," she almost shouted.

"What's that?" Rachel asked.

"Naomi Klein's coined phrase, *disaster capitalism*—the exploitation of a natural disaster to benefit economically, a concept from her book *The Shock Doctrine.*"

"What does that have to do with anything?" Rachel asked.

"If someone is spreading Philomena, how would they stand to benefit?" Corvina asked rhetorically. "They could use the infestations to their advantage. Wineries with infested vineyards will sell for a bargain as wineries around the world collapse."

"So who's going to stop Philomena from destroying all of them and letting someone benefit from this disaster? Your replacement, Sergio?" Rachel asked.

"He can't. He's missing," Corvina said, melancholy creeping into her voice.

"Your company?"

"Unlikely," she said, getting angry just thinking about her last conversation with Vicente.

"The bitch at Interpol?"

"Definitely not. She's clueless," she said in disgust.

"Bryan?"

"Not by himself," she said. She reluctantly acknowledged that she missed his company.

"Well then?" Rachel raised an eyebrow.

"You think I can stop Philomena?" Corvina asked.

"That's my girl."

"You're drunk," Corvina said, and laughed.

"*In vino veritas,*" Rachel said as she held up her glass.

"*In vino veritas,*" Corvina replied, and raised hers in salute. "You gave me some great advice in San Francisco two weeks ago." Had it really been only two weeks? It seemed like months since she had shared a cocktail with her friend.

"Want to know my advice this time?" Rachel asked. She leaned forward, elbows on the table.

"Yes." Corvina leaned in as well, like they were conspiring.

"Same as last time—find an expert," Rachel said.

"I'm normally the person people call when *they* need an expert. I guess I'm just not used to asking for help."

"Who does a consultant consult, right?" Rachel asked.

"Are you saying I should replace Bryan?"

"No. You seem to get on well with him. Find someone else who can help you and Bryan figure out what's going on. Why are the two of you trying to figure this out on your own? This is the second time you've asked *me* for help. Don't be so proud that you won't ask anyone else."

"I think I might know someone," Corvina said. She recalled a name she had read in the letters Professor Taverne had sent to Slater in Chile, which Roberto, the winemaker at Errázuriz, had given her. As soon as she thought of it, another thought occurred to her. She mentally berated herself for not thinking of it earlier.

She looked up Bryan's name in her phone. Her hands trembled with excitement as she typed. She had to go back and fix typos before finally sending Bryan the message: "I hope you haven't made any plans for the weekend."

CHAPTER 29

FRANSCHHOEK
WESTERN CAPE, SOUTH AFRICA

"Look, I'm sorry you wasted your time, but I can't help you. I've never met this Slater person you keep asking about," Jacob Boerefijn said.

Following her conversation with Rachel two nights ago, she had called the famous viticulturist and ampelographer and got him to agree to see her and Bryan. She then convinced Bryan to fly with her to South Africa to meet with him, despite no longer having the backing of Universal Wines.

Corvina was familiar with Jacob's work even before she found him referenced in one of Professor Taverne's letters to David Slater. After reading the letters on the way from Santiago to Toronto a week ago, she had completely forgotten their contents as she had been so intent on tracking down Slater herself.

Every grape grower or winemaker in the world knew of Jacob Boerefijn. His research was widely published, and he had written much of what made up modern-day viticulture theory and practice in hundreds of peer-reviewed articles and textbooks used in many university viticulture programs. Corvina had read many of his articles over the course of her career. With his advanced work in the field of natural resistance and grafting in viticulture, Corvina suspected Slater must have made contact with him at some stage of his own research and development of Philomena. She also hoped Jacob had some insight on how to stop the new strain of phylloxera.

"Aren't you worried about phylloxera spreading to your own vineyards? Philomena is a global problem. You can't just stick your head in the sand," she said to the man who had withered from demigod in the wine industry to the next obstacle in her quest and pain in her backside in under an hour.

"We haven't had any reported cases in South Africa so far—luckily for me," Jacob said, pointing to the vineyards next to the greenhouses on his land. He was a bear of a man, standing over one hundred eighty-five centimeters tall with broad shoulders and a solid physique. Dark-blue eyes looked out from a well-tanned and bearded face. He had a steady gaze that looked accustomed to seeing far into the distance. Corvina knew he was in his early fifties after reading his bio on Wikipedia, but he looked ten years younger.

"Are your vines grafted?" Corvina asked.

"Like I already told you, only the sémillon and shiraz are grafted. Franschhoek has largely been unaffected by phylloxera in the past due to its protected position in the valley, so I've always grown the native grapes without grafted rootstock. That's not to say I'm not concerned. It seems that Philomena is a hungry bitch and will eat through any rootstock, grafted or not. I'm not so naïve to think this part of the world is out of reach."

"Mr. Boerefijn, we came all this way to see you and could really use your help," Corvina said.

"I don't know what you think I can help you with, but come on in while you're here anyway." The man finally relented, and he led her and Bryan into the main building of his estate, a large white Dutch Cape–style building with wooden-framed doors and windows.

The inner foyer was packed with small boxes, parcels, and envelopes. Judging by their postmarks and stamps, Corvina noted that they came from around the world. She looked around the room and saw packages were piled and scattered everywhere.

"Those are root samples that winemakers and grape growers have sent me from their vineyards to test and deliver a verdict on since Philomena hit the papers a few weeks ago," Jacob said.

"A verdict on what?"

"Whether they're resistant to Philomena," Jacob said. He picked up and examined a few of the newly arrived packages.

"How many have you tested?" Corvina asked.

"Dozens, but none are resistant. My team and I haven't found a single varietal or clone of any varietal that can withstand the aphid. I had even started with the American rootstocks—the one rootstock that's always resisted attack from phylloxera." Jacob led them through the house and out into the back, where he took them into a greenhouse the size of a football field. "Welcome to my office."

"Impressive," Bryan said.

"There must be some way to stop it," Corvina said. She looked out on row upon row of vines. All were labeled, highlighting their origin, varietal type, and clone identity.

"Not that I've found. Don't forget, to this day there still isn't a cure to stop the original *Phylloxera vastatrix.* The only reason it was stopped in the past was because native wild vine species in the US—like *Vitis berlandieri, Vitis riparia,* and *Vitis champini*—all developed a natural resistance to phylloxera and could be grafted onto the European vine, *Vitis vinifera.*"

"And they're still used to this day?" Bryan asked.

"Yes, but they've undergone a lot of change. Over the years, breeders generated many new crosses between the American species of vines. Some didn't protect against phylloxera as well as the originals, but others were successful and were propagated further. Crosses like *110 Richter, 1103 Paulsen,* and *5A Teleki* are among the most successful. This is partly because of their resistance to phylloxera, but it's also because they have other properties that allow vines to produce higher grape yields and grow better in different soil types like limestone and clay or in soil that has high salinity or acidity.

"Before it was discovered that grafting American rootstock onto vines could stop the aphid, the cures trialed in vineyards ranged from the ridiculous to the sublime. Grape growers and winemakers tried everything, including cow urine, powdered tobacco, walnut leaves, crushed bones dissolved in sulfuric acid, a mixture of whale oil and petrol, hot wax applied to pruning lesions in the leaves, volcanic ash, tea leaves—even marching bands were paraded up and down rows of vineyards in futile attempts to kill the aphid by sound. None of it worked.

"By 1874, the French Ministry of Agriculture became so desperate to stop the aphid and the devastation it was wreaking in the French countryside, it offered a reward of three hundred thousand French francs for the cure. As no actual cure was ever discovered, the reward remains uncollected to this day in the vaults of the Banque de France.

"The last time phylloxera ravaged Europe's vineyards, many winemakers abandoned their land and moved abroad to places like Algeria, Chile, and Argentina to find fresh territory to start anew. France took decades to fully recover," Jacob said. "If the current strain of phylloxera spreading around the world can't be stopped, or at least slowed, there will be no fresh territory to run to, including the Western Cape of South Africa where we stand. We're looking at the end of global wine production for the next ten to twenty years. And at the rate Philomena is spreading, I predict each affected wine region will reach the point of no return in just a few more weeks."

"That's not a comforting thought," Corvina said. "I have no doubt the aphid will reach wineries in every wine-growing region if it's not stopped. While we still don't know why he's doing it, we believe David Slater is spreading Philomena—but not without support. He must have had serious backing to have developed Philomena and financing to travel the world and remain undetected. I suspect he has accomplices who have helped him along the way," she said, and looked at Jacob.

"Are you accusing me of collaborating with the ecoterrorist the papers are reporting is responsible for Philomena?" Jacob asked her, and took a step closer to her and Bryan. It was an intimidating gesture, but Corvina wouldn't be cowed.

"Are you? You're the foremost expert on viticulture, and by virtue of that title, also an expert on all types of vineyard pests, including phylloxera," she retorted.

"Honestly? You come to my place of work, my country, and accuse me of such a heinous act. You must really be desperate."

"Mr. Boerefijn," Bryan said, and stepped between Corvina and Jacob. "I think what Corvina's trying to say is that as an expert in your field, surely you must have some insight into how Philomena can be stopped. Perhaps somewhere among all these boxes or your correspondence, Slater may have reached out to you for your expertise and you may have even inadvertently assisted him by responding to him," he said. Corvina admired his determination to defuse the situation, but she required the fuse to be lit.

"No, I'm accusing him of collaborating with Slater. And if it comes out later that I'm right"—she pointed at Jacob—"you'll be labeled as a collaborator who helped bring about the death of our industry," Corvina said with conviction in her voice.

"How dare you," Jacob said. He took a deep breath and drew himself to his full height. "I think it's time you both left." He marched back to the door they'd used to enter the greenhouse and held it open. "I'd say it was a pleasure meeting you both, but it wasn't. Don't contact me again."

"You should write a book," Bryan told her once they had left Jacob's estate. "It could be called *How to Make Wine and Offend People.* Was that really necessary?"

"He wasn't helping. And Philomena isn't spreading any slower," Corvina replied.

"I understand, but perhaps accusing him of being part of the problem wasn't the best tact," Bryan said.

"Funny, I picked that up from you in London. Or don't you recall when we first met in the bar on Fleet Street?" she asked him.

"Touché," Bryan said. "I suppose you're right. We don't have time to mollycoddle these people. And I agree with you—he's lying about something," he replied.

Within five minutes they found themselves on Huguenot, Franschhoek's main street. Corvina took deep breaths to calm herself down. Her heart was pounding and her mind racing.

The smell of roses and fresh-mown grass permeated the air throughout the picturesque town. It helped calm her frazzled nerves. The sidewalks along the street were cast in cooling shadow by pine, oak, lemon, cypress, and towering eucalyptus trees.

Huguenot Street was lined with dozens of high-end restaurants, art galleries, sculptures, beautiful gardens, B&Bs, and cafés where locals and tourists alike enjoyed the warm evening weather. Similar to the buildings at Jacob's vineyards, many of the structures were designed in Dutch Cape style. Traditionally thatched dark-brown roofs added to the natural look and feel of the town.

"We came at a good time. I read that in late November and early December the town hosts the Franschhoek Cap Classique & Champagne Festival and you can barely move for all the tourists and visitors," Bryan said.

As if to punctuate his statement, a wine tram full of German and Swedish tourists singing drunkenly off-key drove past them.

Corvina forced herself to take in her surroundings and distance herself from the argument with Jacob. She was distracted by the vibration of her phone. She swiped in her password and checked the screen.

"It's a message from Jacob. It says 'Let's Talk.'"

"Really? Are you surprised?" Bryan asked her.

"No . . . vindicated," she said, and smiled.

Twenty minutes later, they were back at Jacob's.

"Let's find a place to talk. It's not every day you learn that you may have helped an ecoterrorist destroy the one thing you've dedicated your whole life to. I could use a drink," he said when he opened the door to let them back in. "I know a nice restaurant in Stellenbosch at the Jordan winery. They do a great set menu using local, seasonal ingredients paired with regional wines. The springbok medallions are to die for, and the view of the sunset is spectacular."

Corvina thought the restaurant sounded ideal. It would give them time to find out what Jacob knew and to discuss his work and his thoughts on how to combat this threat. A botanist had helped stop phylloxera at the end of the nineteenth century; she was pinning her hopes on history repeating itself and Jacob being the one to find a means to stop Philomena.

"You're right," Jacob said once they had ordered dinner and their first glasses of wine had arrived. "David Slater did contact me."

"When?" Corvina asked. She didn't touch her glass of chenin blanc for the time being; she wanted to have a clear head for the discussion.

"The first time was about two years ago."

"Two years ago!" Bryan raised his voice. "Why didn't you tell us this to begin with? Do you know how culpable this makes you look?"

"Bryan, calm down. He's telling us now," Corvina said. She rested her hand on his. How ironic that she was now the calm mediator in the discussion.

"Like you, he called me to ask about phylloxera," Jacob said.

"And what did you discuss?" Corvina questioned him.

"He wanted to know how vines defended themselves against attack from phylloxera—why some vines succumbed and others didn't. We had detailed conversations. I thought I was just helping a graduate student with his thesis paper. I had no idea I was helping him develop a super-aphid."

"There was no way you could have known," Corvina reassured him.

"We talked on the phone several times, then he said he would come see me here in South Africa."

"When was that?" Corvina asked.

"Last year. Ten months ago."

"He came here, to South Africa?" Corvina asked, surprised.

"Yes. I showed him around my facilities, and we had some lively discussions right there in my greenhouses."

"What was the purpose of his visit?" Corvina asked.

"He asked me to show him the vines in person, how each grape varietal differed and how they defended themselves. We spent a lot of time in the vineyards."

"The vineyards next to your greenhouses?" Corvina asked. She worried her suspicions were right. *It all begins in the vineyard.*

"No, we visited several wineries. I took him to some of the best in the region and those where I know the winemakers."

"Only in Franschhoek?" she asked. Her suspicions grew stronger, and her stomach clenched with dread as if she had drunk too much wine on an empty stomach.

"No, there and all over Stellenbosch and Paarl."

"Oh no," Corvina said.

"What?" Jacob asked. "What are you thinking?"

"I think you helped Slater spread Philomena when he came to South Africa," she said, and glared at the viticulturist.

CHAPTER 30

N2 HIGHWAY, STELLENBOSCH
WESTERN CAPE, SOUTH AFRICA

The next morning, Bryan tried hard to erase the events of the night before from his memory, but the tension in Jacob's car was almost unbearable. Jacob drove while Bryan sat beside him in the passenger seat on the left-hand side of the car. Bryan could feel Corvina fuming in the back seat. He glanced back and saw she was staring out the window. Her sunglasses covered any expression in her eyes, and a dark-green scarf covered her head and the sides of her face. But he knew she was pissed. And why not? The man she had hoped would help them destroy Philomena had in fact helped Slater develop it and possibly even spread it. Unsuspectingly, of course, but it didn't change the fact that Slater couldn't have done as much damage without the viticulturist.

Now they were driving to Stellenbosch to retrace Jacob's steps and see the wineries he and Slater had visited. If Corvina was right, some, if not all of them, would be showing signs of Philomena infestation. Bryan had to admit that Slater was clever. What better cover to spread a genetically modified aphid among susceptible vineyards than in the company of the world's greatest viticulturist and ampelographer.

With the morning sun rising in the east, the vistas of rolling hills, distant mountains, and vineyard after vineyard were painted in vivid Technicolor. Jacob pointed out well-known wineries such as La Motte, Boschendal, Delaire Graff, Tokara, and Neil Ellis as they drove past long, winding entrances and spotted rolling vineyards in the distance.

"I love vineyards," Bryan said as they drove past plot after plot. "It's nature, but organized." His attempt at humor fell on deaf ears, and he refrained from further attempts to lighten the mood.

As they neared the town of Stellenbosch, Bryan spied locals hitchhiking on the side of the road, most waving a few notes of the local currency to incentivize commuters. Jacob slowed down to point out yellow boxes on the side of the road that served as speed traps and to point out the shantytowns on the outskirts of the town. Bryan took in every detail.

"How is the pinotage grape doing these days?" he asked.

"Getting better every day," Jacob responded.

"It doesn't have a great reputation abroad," Bryan said. He hoped his comment hadn't offended their host. He was thinking back to some of the pinotage wines he had tasted in London and more recently of Feng's shouted comments at the Burj Al Arab in Dubai.

"Pinotage has a bad rep abroad largely due to poor examples being exported. In reality, it's a beautiful and versatile varietal. One hundred percent pinotage wines are excellent—smooth like a merlot, spicy like a syrah, and fruity like a cab sauv, all at the same time."

"Kind of like zinfandel in the States," Bryan suggested. He was heartened to see his tactic to get Jacob talking had worked. Lively conversation would help ease the tension, and he hoped it would draw Corvina out.

"A few wine estates grow zin here, Blaauwklippen Winery for instance. But there's a big difference between pinotage and zinfandel. The zinfandel grape is originally from Croatia, so although it's seen as America's varietal since that's where it grows and shows best, it's not originally from the States. Pinotage, on the other hand, was created here in South Africa. It's a cross between pinot noir and cinsault, or hermitage as we call it in South Africa."

"Who created it?" Corvina asked. Bryan was relieved to hear her joining the conversation. He knew her expertise was in making wine; she didn't have the same in-depth knowledge of viticulture history as he did.

"The South African government commissioned viticulturists back in 1924 to develop a grape varietal the country could call its own. It's been South Africa's varietal ever since, though other countries are now experimenting with it."

"If what I think is true happened, and Slater did spread Philomena when he visited almost a year ago, I'm surprised that we've not heard of any attacks in the area," Bryan said.

"I doubt that anyone would volunteer that kind of information," Jacob said.

"Why not? Wouldn't they want to warn others and enlist help to fight the aphid?"

"It comes down to pride. If a wine grower's vines are attacked, the last thing they're going to think of is their neighbor. They'd switch to survival mode. Or they'd deny what's happening right in front of their eyes."

"Well, we know what that looks like," Corvina said.

Bryan saw her give Jacob an accusing glare in the rearview mirror.

"Let's focus on what we can do here today," Bryan said.

"There should be a map in the glove box." Jacob pointed across the dashboard.

Bryan opened the glove box. Inside was a pair of garden clippers, a pair of gardening gloves, and a battered copy of *Platter's South African Wine Guide.* He found and opened a well-used map that illustrated the various wine regions and wine estates dotted around Stellenbosch.

He stared at the map in disbelief. It was covered in different colored icons resembling small bunches of grapes that indicated every Stellenbosch wine estate's location.

"There must be over a hundred wineries in Stellenbosch alone!" Bryan exclaimed.

"Over one hundred thirty, if I recall," Jacob said.

"It'll be like looking for a needle in a haystack," Bryan said.

"A needle in a haystack would be easy to find compared to finding an aphid in a vineyard," Jacob countered. "And we have about twenty vineyards to check."

"How should we approach this?" Bryan asked Jacob.

"We can divide the wine estates by region. I took Slater to a few wineries in each area. You'll see from the colors of the grape icons that there are five primary wine regions in Stellenbosch—Greater Simonsberg, Stellenbosch Berg, Helderberg, Stellenbosch Valley, and Bottelary Hills. They're divided by geography more than anything else and often connected by the same road, making it easy to stay within each region. I'll cover Helderberg because I'm most familiar with the wineries there and know the people in the area. Corvina, you can cover Bottelary Hills and Stellenbosch Valley while Bryan checks out the wineries Slater and I visited in Greater Simonsberg and Stellenbosch Berg. I've arranged a driver for each of you, and they'll have the same map as that one." He pointed to the map in front of Bryan. "We're meeting them at the plaza after the next robot."

"Robot?" Bryan looked out the windshield.

"Sorry, streetlights. We call them robots here," Jacob said.

Jacob pulled into the plaza, and they got out of the car. Jacob introduced Corvina and Bryan to the young men who would drive them to each wine estate and wait for them while they carried out their separate investigations.

"Let's keep in touch by phone throughout the day and update each other on our progress," Bryan said.

"Agreed. We can aim to regroup at six unless we find Philomena earlier," Jacob suggested.

"Let's hope it's not here to find," Bryan said. He scanned the map of wineries and the dozens of potential targets Philomena could be making its way through now.

After they had split up and left for their assigned regions, Bryan's driver chauffeured him to the grounds of the Kanonkop Wine Estate, just off Route 44 in Greater Simonsberg, the area assigned to him to search for Philomena. Bryan admired the large cannons that flanked the entrance to the estate. Named after its strategically defensive position, it was a well-established winery renowned for its pinotage and situated in the middle of the vineyards. He tried to put himself in Slater's mind; he imagined if he was trying to inflict as much damage as possible on the vineyards, starting at the epicenter of a major wine region seemed to make the most sense.

Walking up to the main visitors' building, where tastings were carried out and tours began, Bryan let himself in and approached the desk. A young woman in jeans and a yellow blouse was straightening out brochures and tasting notes.

"*Howzit?*" he asked in a local colloquialism he had picked up after hearing the informal greeting and question by several people in Franschhoek. "Is it too early for a tasting?" he asked.

"Good morning." The young woman looked up. "Could you give me twenty minutes? We're not open yet."

"That would be fine. I'm not in a hurry. Mind if I walk around and explore outside?" he asked.

"Please, go ahead," the woman said without looking up at him.

"Thank you," he said. He walked back outside into the sunshine and headed straight for the vineyards. He pulled out his cell phone and found his location on Google Maps. While the map didn't specify what area was under vine, it did give him an idea of the vineyard's boundaries between the surrounding roads. That gave him enough information to plot out a search grid. He wanted to cover as much area in his assigned vineyards in as short a time as possible by their self-imposed six o'clock deadline.

He started with the pinotage plots of vines. Putting himself in the mind of the ecoterrorist once more, he thought it was fitting that anyone attacking South Africa's vineyards and wine industry would target the national grape. He sincerely hoped they wouldn't find signs of Philomena in any of the Cape's vineyards—where wine making dated back as far as 1655—but he wasn't optimistic.

The vines towered up to his shoulders. He examined the leaves, looking for telltale signs of infestation. When he found nothing but healthy vines he extended his examination to the stalks of the vines, looking for signs of the aphid itself. He kneeled down and checked the roots, digging down into the dirt with his bare hands to see if he would unearth some of the aphids or at least uncover some evidence that they were gnawing the rootstocks.

He moved from vine to vine, traversing row after row.

He looked at his watch and was amazed to see twenty-five minutes had already passed. He stood to move to the final group of vines he'd planned to inspect. He placed his hands on his hips and leaned back, stretching his stiffening back. From his upright position he peered over the vines' canopy and let out a long sigh. A sea of green foliage stretched into the distance. The leaves rippled in the warm morning breeze, giving it the appearance of a vast ocean photosynthesizing in the sunlight.

Around him, he could barely see the vineyard for the vines.

Finding a needle in a haystack would be a hell of a lot easier.

CHAPTER 31

MEERLUST WINE ESTATE
STELLENBOSCH VALLEY
WESTERN CAPE, SOUTH AFRICA

Corvina circled Welmoed Winery on her map and crossed off the Spier Wine Estate, where she had just visited. She had already visited Die Bergkelder, DeMorgenzon, Bonfoi, Neethlingshof, Stellenbosch Hills, and Jordan, where they had dined the night before. She felt she could cover most of the wineries in Stellenbosch Valley in one day. The Bottelary Hills region would have to wait for a second day.

Meerlust in Stellenbosch Valley off Route 310 was her eighth winery, and it had taken her until noon to reach it. Thankfully Stellenbosch Valley was the smallest of the five wine regions and represented only around a dozen vineyards on Route 304 and the M23.

She planned to check every winery Jacob had taken Slater to on her numerous routes within Stellenbosch Winery and Bottelary Hills. Unlike Jacob, who told her he would focus his search in the vineyards themselves, Corvina's approach differed in that she intended to speak to the winemakers before checking on the vineyards. She felt comfortable with winemakers and could easily relate to them. If anyone knew the state of their vines, it was the winemakers.

Shortly after she introduced herself to the staff at the entrance to the Meerlust visitor center, the head winemaker himself came out to greet her. He ushered her to the back of the visitor hall and positioned himself behind a makeshift bar. After setting down several glasses, he withdrew a bottle of wine from underneath the counter. In the corner of the tasting room, two dogs lay on the floor panting in the shade. The cool interior offered respite from the hot midday sun.

"While you're here, you must try our Rubicon. It's what we're famous for." He opened a bottle of the red wine and poured two glasses.

"Sounds good. I feel like I've just crossed the Rubicon, so I might as well taste it too. Thank you." Corvina removed the scarf she was wearing to keep the sun off her head and accepted the proffered wine without objection. She admired, swirled, inhaled, sipped, and nodded appreciatively, making a few appropriate comments to compliment the winemaker.

"Nice," she said after taking a few sips. She set her glass down, wondering how to broach the subject of Philomena without causing offense or raising suspicion. She decided to be as direct as possible.

"What would you do if your vines were infested with phylloxera?" Corvina asked without preamble.

"What do you mean?" the winemaker asked. His glass stopped halfway in its journey to his lips.

Like the winemakers before him, he just stared at her. Aside from grafting American rootstock onto the vines—or *les pieds Americains*, as the French referred to the rootstock—there was no defense, no backup plan. It was why Philomena had had such a disastrous effect on the wine industry in the 1800s before grafting saved the vines.

Between the time phylloxera was discovered and the time a new planting was completed and the vines produced grapes worth harvesting, she knew a good seven to ten years would pass, as Jacob had warned her the night before; and the grapes grown would allow winemakers to make only entry-level table wines. It would be a long time before the vines were mature enough to make quality grapes worthy of producing blockbuster vintages.

Corvina determined the aphid hadn't yet been detected at Meerlust. She was glad for the negative detection yet despondent to realize that yet another winemaker hadn't begun thinking about the ramifications if Philomena reached his vineyards. It was only a matter of time, and it would all begin in the vineyard.

She thanked the winemaker again for the Rubicon tasting and his time and then returned to the car.

"Please take me to the Jacobsdal Wine Estate off the M12," she said to her driver. She took a drink of water from her plastic bottle of Evian to clear her mouth of the wine and called Bryan for an update.

"Hi, Bryan. Any sign of Philomena?" she asked when his voice came on the line.

"Not yet, but I'm making progress," he said.

"How many wineries have you checked?" she asked.

"Seven so far," he replied.

"Okay. Keep moving. I've been to eight already. We have to check as many wineries as possible before sunset." She hung up the phone and leaned back into her seat. She closed her eyes and pinched the bridge of her nose, shaking her head from side to side.

It was going to be a long day.

CHAPTER 32

KLEINE ZALZE WINE ESTATE
STELLENBOSCH BERG
WESTERN CAPE, SOUTH AFRICA

Bryan asked his driver to turn off a busy road and onto a narrow drive leading to the Kleine Zalze wine estate. In addition to the vineyards, wine-making facilities, and visitors' center, he read signage that the estate was also home to a highly rated restaurant and clusters of premium condominiums.

When they reached a small white guardhouse with a lowered barrier on either side, Bryan leaned over to speak to the guard through the driver's side window.

"*Howzit,* I'm here for a wine tasting," he said.

"I'm sorry, sir, but we're closed to visitors today," the guard responded. He held a clipboard but didn't look at the paper it held.

"How come?" Bryan asked.

"Private function," the guard said.

"That's a shame."

The guard shrugged. "You can turn around just ahead, then come back the way you entered."

"Okay, thank you," Bryan replied. He smiled and waved to the guard.

The guard pressed a button inside the guardhouse to raise the barrier.

The driver drove forward. When he reached a crossroad where he could pull in for a three-point turn, Bryan told him to keep driving straight onto the property.

"You sure? He told us to turn around," the driver said.

"I know what he told us, but I want to go farther and see what private function is happening today. I didn't see any signage indicating there was a function. He also didn't ask if I was attending the function. How did he know I'm not a guest or one of the organizers?"

They carried on until they reached the parking lot for the tasting rooms and visitor center as well as a restaurant called Terroir.

Bryan exited the car and approached the first person he saw. A young man was driving a small forklift carrying a pallet of wine boxes. Each box had the Kleine Zalze name and logo stamped on the sides. The forklift driver was guiding the pallet into a small storeroom next to the restaurant.

"Hi there," Bryan said, and waved. "I'm here for the private function."

"Sorry, sir, but we're closed today," the forklift operator said. He brought the forklift to a stop with its load hanging in midair. He looked like a springbok caught in headlights.

"Oh, I could have sworn the event was being held here," Bryan said. He feigned confusion and scrolled through his emails on his phone, pretending to look for a confirmation.

"Can't be here, sir. We're closed for renovations."

"My mistake. I must have gotten my wires crossed. I'll go back out in that case."

The forklift driver looked relieved to see him leave.

"See, no event. Let's get out of here," Bryan said to his driver as soon as he got back in the car.

They drove out in a hurry, not stopping to hear the abuse hurled at them by the guard at the gate, who had seen them drive on against his instructions.

"Stop here," Bryan said once they were off the estate. The driver came to a stop alongside the vineyards.

"Wait for me here," Bryan said. He left the car and jogged over to a meter-high stone wall. It was painted white and intended more as a property marker than a serious deterrent to trespassers. Bryan clambered over it and dropped into the vineyards beyond. He jogged between neatly planted rows of vines until the sound of men's voices ahead made him slow down. He proceeded with caution until he could see activity a few rows away.

At the end of a row of vines on a dirt road between plots, Bryan saw a group of men spraying vines with over-the-shoulder pesticide sprayers and installing net screens over entire rows of vines. A small flatbed truck was being loaded with vines that had been pulled out of the earth, roots and all.

Bryan knew he wasn't watching harvest activities. The men were spraying and segregating vines against infestation. The vines on the truck must already be infested.

He took a picture of the activity and sent it to Corvina and Jacob with a short message:

"I found Philomena."

CHAPTER 33

KLEINE ZALZE WINE ESTATE
STELLENBOSCH BERG
WESTERN CAPE, SOUTH AFRICA

Within twenty minutes of Bryan's text message, Corvina and Jacob arrived at Kleine Zalze. Jacob used his contacts in the region to get them access, and soon they were deep in the vineyards speaking with the grape growers and winemaker.

It was just after five o'clock in the evening. The setting sun cast long, dark shadows from trees surrounding the winery.

Corvina walked over to where Bryan and Jacob were working between two rows of vines.

"How are you two getting on?" she asked.

"Under the circumstances? Great," Jacob said. "I'm getting lots of samples."

"Let's hope it's enough to find a way to stop them," Corvina said.

"They're just bugs; there has to be a way," Jacob said.

Corvina excused herself and took the opportunity to call Claude at Interpol.

"What are you doing in South Africa?" he asked as soon as the call went through.

"Fighting Philomena. We're the only ones who seem to be taking this seriously. Wait, how did you know we are in South Africa?"

"We? Don't tell me you convinced Bryan to go with you?"

"He didn't need convincing. And you haven't answered my question. How do you know where I am?"

"Interpol still has an alert set on you, so I always know where you are. And you haven't answered *my* question—what are you doing in South Africa?"

How much she should tell Claude? He obviously still didn't trust her. The fact that he continued to monitor her travels was evidence enough.

"We came to meet an expert viticulturist, and we discovered Slater had come to see him too. This was long before anyone knew about Philomena."

"And?"

"We're too late," she told him. "We found an infested vineyard in the Stellenbosch Valley. There's a good chance we can stop its spread in the one vineyard where we found it, but if others are already infested then the entire region is at risk."

"Well, at least that's something," Claude said. "I'll send a pair of investigators out there to look into things and speak to the winery reps. The investigators can help secure resources to quarantine the area."

"Okay. We've alerted the local authorities, and the viticulturist is on-site taking samples for study," she said. She could see Bryan and Jacob in the vineyard with a few men from the estate collecting samples and examining the vines.

"Any sign that Slater was there?" Claude asked.

"He was here some time ago, but he's long gone now."

"No matter. We may get another chance to catch him," Claude said.

"What do you mean?" Corvina asked.

"Slater just got off a flight in Oporto, Portugal."

"When?" Corvina felt a twinge of panic realizing how close Portugal was to Spain, the location of many of her clients' vineyards.

"This morning. I couldn't get anyone mobilized to intercept him upon arrival, but the National Central Bureau in Portugal is on the case. I thought you might like to know."

"Do you have any idea where he went?" Corvina asked, and waved Bryan over.

"No," Claude said. His terse response made Corvina wonder what he wasn't telling her.

"Okay, Bryan and I will be on the next plane to the Douro."

"No, you won't, Corvina," Claude said. "This is an Interpol investigation. Slater is wanted by authorities in several countries, and you're still a person of interest as far as Interpol is concerned. Leave chasing Slater to me. Let me know what else you find out about Philomena in South Africa."

Claude ended the call before she could respond. She pocketed her phone and took a deep breath, a plan already formulating in her mind.

CHAPTER 34

OPORTO, PORTUGAL

Corvina held tight to the hand bar above the door to her right as the SUV raced across washboard secondary roads.

In her short but well-traveled lifetime, Corvina had flown countless miles and encountered fierce turbulence on more flights than she could remember. She had fought traffic in Beirut, Cairo, and Damascus, where the lines on the road and traffic signals served as guidelines, not rules. She had driven in Rome, a city that all roads led to, but once there, seemed to lose all sense of order and control. She had also bungee jumped, rode a motorcycle, galloped on horseback, and jumped out of a plane skydiving.

All her experiences hadn't prepared her for a cross-country ride with a teenage boy at the wheel of a Toyota Land Cruiser who'd been instructed to hurry.

"Where did you find this driver?" Bryan shouted over the blaring music and rattling truck.

"He's the son of one of my clients," Corvina answered. She kept her eyes on the road ahead.

"Is he even old enough to drive?"

"I didn't ask," she said.

"I still think we should have stayed longer in South Africa with Jacob. I think we could have learned more there about what and who we're up against."

"We know who we're up against, and he's in Portugal. Our best chance of stopping Philomena is by stopping Slater."

"Claude is going to go berserk."

"You don't think I know that? But he and Interpol can't stop me, or us, and I'm willing to take the chance. For the record, I'm glad you are too."

"You didn't give me much of a choice."

They were headed to Graham's Quinta dos Malvedos on the opposite side of the Douro River, one of the Iberian Peninsula's major rivers according to the map bouncing wildly in her lap. They were racing down the back roads of Oporto to avoid the much longer route of the A1 motorway. The Quinta was located less than twenty-five kilometers away from the Oporto airport, where they had landed only thirty minutes ago. With no luggage to retrieve from the carousel and the airport catering mainly to small domestic flights and budget airlines from across Europe, they were able to speed through customs and get out quickly. Antonio, her client's son, was waiting for them. He was tall, thin, and looked to be in his late teens, with unruly, curly black hair and dark eyes. He wore khaki shorts, sandals, and a dark-green sweater. His smooth, olive complexion led Corvina to think he was still too young to shave. Thinking back to Bryan's question, Corvina did *hope* he was old enough to drive.

Antonio turned to Corvina. "Is my driving okay? You said to hurry."

"It's a little bumpy, but keep going, *obrigado*," Corvina said. She had to balance the need for speed with their safety if they were to have a chance to catch up to Slater and the spread of Philomena. "How long will it take us to get there?"

"Another ten minutes. Don't worry, I'll drive safe." Antonio turned and smiled.

Corvina almost expected him to say he had learned to drive from watching *The Fast and the Furious* movies.

"Are you sure we're going to the right place?" Bryan asked. She could tell he was still not convinced this was the best course of action.

"Graham's Quinta dos Malvedos is one the most established of the major port houses. It's also one of the highest, situated up on the

Douro Valley. If I was Slater and wanted to spread Philomena, I would start there. The aphids would have an easier time spreading downward than upward."

"You know they can fly, right?" Bryan asked.

"Oh, shut up. At least the weather is more reasonable here than in South Africa," Corvina said, recalling the grueling day of looking for Philomena in the Stellenbosch vineyards under the hot African sun.

Ten bone-rattling minutes later, Antonio drove up a long, winding gravel drive flanked by vineyards leading to Graham's Quinta dos Malvedos.

He pulled to a stop so they could get out.

To their right, the Douro River sparkled far below and flowed swiftly between the banks of the Douro Valley, rushing toward its outlet in Oporto. Terraced vineyards extended all the way down to the valley floor, where they met a road and railroad tracks.

To their left, the valley continued its steep slope upward. Evenly spaced vineyard terraces carved into the valley wall rose as high as the eye could see. At the top of the staggeringly high valley, the elevation reached over two thousand meters in some areas, even steeper than the vineyards found along the banks of the Rhine and Mosel Rivers in Germany. The aspect and pitch of the wine-growing area of the Douro Valley—Douro Vinhateiro—created an ideal microclimate and exposed the grapes to the sun for as long as possible throughout the day. In recognition of its importance to trade and culture, the Douro Vinhateiro was classified by UNESCO as a World Heritage site.

Corvina looked up and down into the vineyards, knowing if she examined the vines more closely she would find tinta amarela, tinta cão, tinta barroca, touriga franca, tinta roriz, and touriga nacional grapes growing to one day be turned into deep-red port wine. Portugal boasted upward of forty indigenous grape varieties.

"So what now?" Bryan asked.

"We find the winemaker and owners and ask them to show us their vines." She waved Antonio out of the Land Cruiser. "We are going to find the owner to speak with him. Can you come with us? My Portuguese is a little rusty," Corvina said to the boy.

Antonio bounded out of the SUV and joined them to walk up the unpaved road to the estate.

She heard a vehicle approach behind them. She and the others moved to the side of the road to let the merlot-colored Jeep Cherokee squeeze past.

Corvina looked into the passenger side window as it passed, expecting to see a Portuguese driver and possibly the owner or winemaker of the estate. A white man in his thirties wearing a baseball cap was at the wheel. He turned to look at her.

"That's Slater!" Bryan shouted.

Corvina saw Slater's eyes widen as he realized he was recognized. The Jeep bolted forward, sending up a cloud of dust and small rocks, which dug into her legs.

"Back to the truck!" Corvina shouted, sprinting for the Land Cruiser. Antonio was in the driver's seat before she was even in the vehicle, and Bryan clambered in a moment later, still coughing from the lungful of dust inhaled when Slater made his getaway. The Land Cruiser shot forward with music blaring.

Despite Slater's head start, Antonio closed the gap and within a minute was trailing only a hundred meters behind Slater's Jeep. The narrow road leading into the vineyards was thick with dust as the two SUVs sped upward on paths meant for the slower climbs of wine-loving tourists and cautious winemakers.

Corvina turned the music down and was relieved to see that Antonio's speed and driving skills weren't somehow inextricably linked to the volume of the vehicle's sound system. He forged ahead, navigating the narrow dirt path with aplomb.

In front of them, Slater raced onward and upward through the vineyards, climbing higher and higher up the stepped valley wall.

Antonio chased him up treacherous switchbacks and virtually perpendicular climbs cutting straight through the neatly planted rows of vines.

"Is there a way out?" Corvina asked. She leaned into the dashboard, worried that they may lose him. Once again, her desire to catch and stop Slater outweighed her concern for their personal safety.

"Yes, but only on paths like these. If he's not used to the driving conditions, he could wipe out," Antonio replied.

Corvina looked out her window and was shocked to see how high they had driven in such a short time. She couldn't see the road underneath them since they were so close to the terrace ledge. The valley seemed to drop down at an impossibly steep angle. The Douro far below seemed smaller at this height, and she could barely make out vehicles and buildings near the river.

Only meters ahead of them, Slater's vehicle struggled to make another steep climb as it overshot a crucial hairpin turn in the path. One moment the Jeep was making slow but inexorable headway, and the next Corvina saw the wheels spin out and the car begin to slide sideways, tilting dangerously. The Jeep's tires spun desperately, seeking purchase in the loose soil and friable gray schist. Dark slate-like sheets broke up under the weight of the vehicle. Its rear tires ripped through vines and their trellises.

Antonio slowed down as they caught up to Slater's Jeep.

The first roll happened in slow motion; the Jeep rolled onto its side, then onto its roof. It looked as though the vehicle would stop, but then everything accelerated. The Jeep flipped over and gained momentum, tumbling rapidly downhill.

Corvina screamed and watched in stunned horror as Slater's vehicle rolled over and over again through the stepped vineyards. It crashed through the vines and the man-made walls of the sweeping terraces, down the side of the Douro Valley. It seemed to go on forever. She couldn't see where it stopped.

Bryan broke the stunned silence that had descended in the car. "Antonio, take us down," he whispered.

When they arrived at the crash scene, they found the mangled Jeep resting against a broken cork tree where the final impact had occurred.

A clear trail of destruction could be seen leading almost to the top of the valley wall, close to two thousand meters away. All of the Jeep's windows were shattered, and every surface of the vehicle was scratched and dented. One of its tires was still slowly turning.

Antonio drove as close as he could to the Jeep and came to a gravel-crunching halt in a cloud full of dust. From inside the Land Rover, Corvina could see that there was no sign of smoke or fire.

"Stay here," Bryan said, rushing out of the Land Cruiser and over to Slater's vehicle.

She watched Bryan struggle to open the crumpled door. He gave up after a few tries and instead pulled Slater out of the vehicle through the shattered windshield. He dragged him away from the vehicle, and she saw him press two fingers to his jugular, feeling for a pulse.

Corvina got out of the Land Cruiser and ventured closer to the crash site. Bryan turned at her approach.

"He's dead," Bryan said as he removed his hand from Slater's neck.

"Oh my God," Corvina gasped, her hand flying to her mouth. "Are you sure?" she asked in disbelief. Hadn't it been only two weeks since they'd chased him through the vineyard in Ontario? It felt like yesterday, yet it also felt like ages had passed.

"Pretty sure. He wasn't wearing his seatbelt."

"Be careful," Corvina said as Bryan surveyed the upside-down roof of the wrecked Jeep Cherokee where all the loose items in the vehicle had collected. Corvina could see Slater's wallet and his cell phone.

"What do you think these are?" Bryan showed Corvina a small case filled with clear plastic vials.

"They look like aphids," Corvina said. She had still not recovered from the shock of witnessing Slater's fatal accident. She couldn't get the image of the tumbling Jeep out of her mind's eye.

"I also found a ticket to an upcoming awards dinner in London and his phone," Bryan said. "I'll check his messages and emails before the police or Interpol arrive."

"Any smoking guns?" she asked Bryan. He was already looking through Slater's phone. She couldn't understand how he could appear so calm after what they had just seen.

"Even better—pictures," Bryan said.

"Pictures of what?" Corvina asked. She leaned over his shoulder, purposely turning her back to Slater's lifeless body.

"Wineries and vineyards. Lots of vineyards. It looks like he was cataloging where he went." He scrolled through hundreds of images captured on the smart device.

"Why would he do that?" she asked.

"Maybe he was recording where he'd been for someone else, or maybe he was making a record of the location in case he wanted to come back and check on his work."

"We should be able to use the pictures to see where else he went then, right?"

"Not only that, but with today's technology, let me check . . ." Bryan pressed a few buttons on the phone. "Yes, just as I thought. Each picture is geotagged."

"Meaning what?"

"Meaning the GPS coordinates where each picture was taken are recorded within each picture file. We can pinpoint where he took each photo and identify each vineyard he visited, even if he took pictures of just the vines and vineyards. Look, here's pictures of Kleine Zalze in Stellenbosch." Bryan held up the screen for her to see. She recognized the buildings.

"With these pictures and their GPS coordinates, we can warn all of the vineyards he infested," Corvina said.

"You should call Duval at Interpol," Bryan suggested.

Corvina was already bringing up the Interpol agent's details. When he answered, she relayed the details of Slater's death and what they had discovered.

"Leave everything as you found it. Don't touch anything . . . or anything more," Claude admonished her. He confirmed that he would have the Interpol agents, who would arrive on scene shortly, review the photos and identify all the locations Slater had visited.

"We're heading back to London soon. We'll let you know when we get there so we can coordinate a time and place to meet. Thanks, Claude." Corvina ended the call.

"You two seem to have built up more rapport," Bryan said.

"When I'm not being apprehended between international flights and interrogated, I can be quite pleasant."

"More honey, less vinegar, right?"

"Interpol has resources we don't. I don't care how Philomena is stopped just as long as she—I mean, *it*—is."

"Careful. You don't want to begin anthropomorphizing the aphid. You may develop Stockholm syndrome and want to protect her," Bryan said.

"Unlikely," Corvina said. "Keep looking through his things." She looked back at their vehicle.

"Antonio! Anything?" Corvina called out to the teen, who was waiting for them next to the Toyota Land Cruiser. He shook his head and gave her and Bryan a thumbs-up signal; the coast was clear. The local police and Interpol were still on the way, giving Bryan more time to carry out their roadside investigation on Slater's vehicle and personal effects, against Claude's instructions to leave the site untouched. Corvina left the sleuthing up to Bryan; she didn't want to touch a dead man's possessions.

"You should call Malcolm too," Bryan suggested.

"Good idea," she said, thankful for the distraction. She called the reporter's phone without checking the time difference. She was sure he wouldn't mind being disturbed at any time of day or night for news like this.

"Tell me what you've learned," Malcolm said when he answered. "I can write and file my story from here and email it to my editor in time for the next print run."

She told Malcolm about her run-in with Interpol in London, their discovery in South Africa, and the events in Portugal, but she asked him to keep Slater's death unreported until Interpol had investigated. Just as she finished answering a few dozen questions for him to write his article, Corvina heard a shout from Antonio. She looked in his direction and spotted several vehicles making their way toward the crash site.

"The cavalry has arrived," she said.

"More like the cleanup crew," Bryan said. "Slater is dead, and we now have the location of the vineyards he's infested. It looks like our work here is done."

"I hope so," she said, but inside she didn't feel any hope at all. A man was dead, and she couldn't shake the feeling that it was her fault.

"Check out these WhatsApp messages," Bryan said. "It looks like he was communicating with two different people about Philomena. One seems to be giving him instructions, and another seems to be an accomplice of some sort."

"That proves he wasn't working alone," Corvina said.

"Take down these numbers," Bryan said, and read them both aloud.

"Based on the dialing codes, one is an American number and the other is an Italian number," Corvina said once she had entered both into her phone under the contact names Philomena 1 and Philomena 2.

Bryan continued scrolling through the photographs on Slater's phone. Corvina looked on.

"Wait, stop! Go back!" Corvina cried out when Bryan flipped past an image of a building set among vineyards.

He scrolled back and held the phone out for her to see the image more clearly. She held a hand over the screen to shield it from the sun and squinted to see the photo.

It took her a moment to grasp the meaning and importance of what she was seeing. The picture was of the front of the Universal Wines headquarters building in California, a building she herself had recently visited. It wasn't a smoking gun, but it connected Slater to Universal Wines—her own company. Why had he gone there? Did he meet anyone? A thousand questions raced through her mind.

She pulled out her phone and hit redial.

"C'mon, pick up, pick up," she said. "Malcolm! I think you were right—Slater was working with someone! I think he knows someone at Universal Wines!"

CHAPTER 35

INTERPOL COMMAND AND COORDINATION CENTRE
LYON, FRANCE

The press conference had already begun when Claude arrived. He walked up the center aisle and found a seat. He was all too aware the entire room had noticed his late entrance.

What a day to be late, he thought.

In the front of the room, the prime minister of France was speaking.

Claude was surprised to see he had come all the way to Lyon just to speak with the press at Interpol headquarters, even if it was related to the impending threat of Philomena. The man was in his early fifties, had black hair graying at the temples, bushy eyebrows, and bags under his blue eyes. His dark-blue pinstriped suit contrasted starkly against his pale white skin.

"Not since the infamous 1976 Judgment of Paris—where American wines were judged to be better than our French treasures—has our wine industry been under such a threat." The prime minister gestured to a man in a gray suit with a long, narrow face seated behind him on his left. "The minister of agriculture and I are making sure that all available resources are at law enforcement's disposal to help prevent this new wave of phylloxera from reaching our vineyards."

Though anxious to get back to work and follow up on all the leads Slater's phone was providing his investigators, Claude was grateful for the support from the highest levels. He also felt vindicated at launching Operation Philomena. Unfortunately, he was also starving. Due to the heightened building security, his takeaway coffee and canelé had been confiscated.

"Years ago, when phylloxera last terrorized our vineyards, the French government offered a reward of three hundred thousand gold francs for a cure. To this day, the reward is still uncollected. The president has given instructions for the reward to be raised to three million euros to be given to whoever finds the cure or method to stop Philomena. It's essential that our wines, integral to the cultural and gastronomical heritage of our country, be preserved," the prime minister finished. He left the stage without taking questions.

When Claude returned to his office, his phone rang. It was Secretary General Arsenault's secretary asking if Claude could come up. He quickly scanned the field reports that had come in overnight from the National Central Bureaus around the world. The news wasn't good. Despite Slater's death the day before in Portugal, Philomena was spreading at an alarming rate. The panic in its wake seemed to be spreading even faster.

He met Alison Pittard in the elevator on his way upstairs. She glared at him without greeting.

Alison's animosity toward him went back to when Interpol had decided to set up a Command and Coordination Centre in South America, and Alison was promoted out of Lyon to help open the CCC in Argentina. Claude joined Interpol as her replacement on the Fusion Task Force. His promotion into her vacated position immediately produced better results and feedback from the team. Alison learned of this while she was in Buenos Aires. Once the CCC in Argentina was up and running, she was promoted again back to Lyon, but as division head, effectively becoming Claude's boss. After six months of stonewalling him in his role on the Fusion Task Force, making it impossible to be effective and undermining him at every opportunity, she demoted him by transferring him laterally to the Wildlife Crime Division.

He hadn't joined Interpol to play politics; he joined to stop crime. Despite his best efforts, he knew he would never be able to bridge the divide between them.

"Now what have you done?" Alison glared at Claude as they approached the closed door to Secretary General Arsenault's office. Claude knocked while Alison just opened the door and let herself in.

Claude stopped before he crossed the threshold.

Standing in the office speaking with the secretary general were the prime minister of France and the minister of agriculture.

"Tell me what you're doing to stop Philomena," the prime minister asked Claude without preamble.

"What we know so far is that the aphid appears to have been genetically modified, its spread is not by accident, and there's currently no way to stop it," Claude began. "Cases have been reported from around the world. France has so far remained unaffected, or at least we've not had any reports of infestation yet."

"I understand you brought some suspects in for questioning," the prime minister said, urging him on.

"We identified a person of interest and questioned her in London. She's a flying winemaker and says she's investigating the aphid's spread on behalf of her company, Universal Wines. Some of the company's vineyards have been infested. We identified her as a person of interest as she had visited many of the infested countries and, of course, because of her line of work."

"And you think she may be responsible?" the prime minister asked.

"Yes, sir—" Alison interjected. She stopped speaking when the minister of agriculture swiveled his head toward her and gave her a withering glare. He was a tall, weedy man with close-cropped, curly black hair, full lips, piercing dark eyes, and patrician features.

"Please continue," the prime minister said to Claude.

"She knows more about the aphid than we do and helped us narrow the search for the real ecoterrorist—David Slater, a Canadian viticulturist."

"Are you close to apprehending him?"

"We had tracked him to Portugal, but he was killed in a car crash there just yesterday."

"An accident?"

"Yes, while being pursued."

"By your agents?"

"No, the flying winemaker and an Englishman were chasing him." Even to him, it sounded like Corvina could have been working with Slater. Had the two been in cahoots and fallen out? What really happened in the Douro Valley? Maybe Slater had been killed to silence him. These thoughts and doubts swirled around in his head.

"So as far as you're aware, the aphid has not yet penetrated our borders?" the prime minister asked.

"No, sir. But we don't yet have a full understanding of how many other countries the viticulturist visited—and we don't know if he was working alone. Philomena doesn't manifest itself right away. It could be weeks or months after an initial infestation that the aphids appear."

"And if that were to happen here in France, what does the worst-case scenario look like?"

"Tens of thousands of grape growers and wine producers will be put out of work. Millions of acres under vine will be destroyed and left fallow. It would be an agrarian disaster on an unparalleled scale." Claude looked at the minister of agriculture as he said the last sentence.

"You're just scaremongering," Alison interrupted.

"When we want your opinion, we'll ask you for it," the minister of agriculture said to Alison, speaking for the first time since they had entered the room.

"Is this true?" the prime minister asked Claude.

"Mr. Prime Minister," the minister of agriculture spoke before Claude could answer, "what Agent Duval is telling you is based on fact, and not only that, but on precedent. What he's failed to tell you," he said as he looked at Claude, "is that the situation could be much, much worse. The last time phylloxera—*the dry-leaf devastator*, as they called it—infested our vineyards, a method to stop it was discovered. And even then it took over forty years for wine production to recover."

"How fast can it spread?"

"A single female aphid can produce millions of descendants in two-thirds of a year without even mating. Aphids reproduce asexually," the minister of agriculture stated.

"Then it's more crucial than ever that Philomena doesn't reach France." The prime minister glared at everyone in the room. "Secretary General Arsenault, you and your team have my full support, and every resource I can call on is at your disposal. Act as if the bug is already here. We're at war and must act accordingly."

CHAPTER 36

LUNG INDUSTRIES INC. HEADQUARTERS
WAN CHAI DISTRICT
HONG KONG

Zhang Tao Lung stood as still as a Terracotta Warrior and stared out his office window.

Though his body didn't move, his mind was racing.

The two Germans sitting in front of his desk were waiting for him to respond.

He checked his phone one last time for the message he'd been waiting for. In less than thirty minutes, his instructions would be carried out in Beijing.

"Gentlemen," Zhang Tao said, turning around to face them. "I'm afraid our business is now concluded."

"Excuse me?" one of the men said.

"Did you not hear what we said?" the other asked.

"Gentlemen, I heard every word," Zhang Tao said, taking his seat behind the desk. "You've been buying up shares of one of my companies in China and are now threatening me with a hostile takeover if I don't sell out to you and capitulate. Have I understood correctly?" Zhang Tao asked. He studied his shirt cuffs and tugged on the left one so that it protruded the same distance from his jacket as the right.

"Yes, that is exactly what is going to happen," the first German said.

"Gentlemen, please excuse me." Zhang Tao turned to leave. "I must go. You see, I don't respond well to threats." Zhang Tao fastened the button of his charcoal single-breasted jacket.

"We are in the middle of a discussion regarding the future of one of your companies—you can't just leave. We will have your company, whether you like it or not."

"This is highly unusual," the second German protested.

"Thank you for the clarification." Zhang Tao leaned over his desk and pressed a button on his phone with a long, manicured finger. He spoke to one of his personal executive assistants in English. "Has Feng arrived yet?" he asked in a friendly tone.

At the mention of his brother's name, Zhang Tao saw the two Germans stiffen. They looked at one another and whispered in their native tongue.

"Yes, sir," Zhang Tao's assistant responded over the phone's speaker.

"Thank you. I shall be right out." Zhang Tao walked around his desk.

"Where are you going?" the first German asked.

"I'm leaving. As I said, I don't respond well to threats. You can speak with my brother directly." Zhang Tao left the two German men sitting in their chairs and exited the office through the main doors, closing them behind him. He knew what thoughts would be racing through *their* minds.

Ten minutes later, an office side door opened.

Had the Germans not known about the Lung brothers, they would have guessed Zhang Tao Lung had returned in a different suit.

Their worst fears were realized when Feng Lung stood behind his brother's desk and stared down at them.

"You are Karl Etzel and Stefan Kolman?" Feng asked the two men.

"Yes," the first German replied.

"Of Rheinwolf Pharmaceuticals?"

"Yes," the second German answered.

"Good. I wouldn't wish to waste my influence in China on the wrong *gweilos*."

"We have come to discuss the purchase of one of your companies, specifically—"

"DO NOT INSULT MY INTELLIGENCE!" Feng screamed at the two men.

The Germans recoiled in their seats.

"You come to my brother's office with threats! You come to my brother's office to intimidate Zhang Tao! You come to my brother's office to piss in my face!" Feng's face turned crimson as he screamed each accusation, jabbing a finger at them to punctuate each verbal explosion.

"*Nein, nein.*" Karl waved his hands in front of him.

"You've bought some shares, and you think this gives you the right to take what my family has built?" Feng asked the two men, his eyes darting from one to the other.

"We wanted to discuss—"

"There will be no discussion!" Feng shouted, slamming his fists onto the desk. Everything on the desk's expansive surface—papers, pens, laptop, and desk lamp—jumped into the air, startling the Germans into silence.

Feng snapped his left arm up to look at his watch.

"As of ten minutes ago, your visas to return to China were canceled. As of nine minutes ago, your work permits to conduct business in China *and* Hong Kong were revoked. As of eight minutes ago, your wives' credit cards were blocked. And as of seven minutes ago, your children were taken out of their classrooms at their international schools."

"You can't—"

"IT'S DONE!" Feng screamed, his face now purple.

"You've not heard the end of this," Stefan sputtered.

"You dare threaten me?" Feng stood to his full height.

"Of course I'm not threatening you, but this is hardly any way to conduct business," Stefan said.

"If you're not out of my sight in the next thirty seconds, I'll have you taken out of the office and beaten to within an inch of your life."

"You can't threaten us like that!" Karl said.

"It's not a threat," Feng said, and smiled. "Get the hell out of my office!" Feng shouted for the final time.

"You've lost your mind," Karl said, stuffing a sheaf of papers into his briefcase as fast as he could.

The Germans left the office, both making calls on their phones as they fled.

When the interruptions to his day were concluded, "Feng" returned to the window and Zhang Tao dropped his twin brother's persona.

The threat eliminated, Zhang Tao could be himself again.

He unclenched his fists and focused on his breathing to slow the furious beating of his heart.

He let all of the tension run out of his body by concentrating on one area at a time, mentally pushing thoughts of business away.

The view from his floor-to-ceiling windows stunned the few visitors he invited to his eighteenth-floor office. From where he stood, Zhang Tao could see much of Wan Chai, where his offices were based; the harborfront of Hong Kong Island, including the convention center and Star Ferry; and across the water to Kowloon and the International Commerce Centre, home of the Ritz-Carlton hotel.

Zhang Tao preferred the nefarious Wan Chai district, as it was "old" Hong Kong and clutched onto the city's history more fiercely than any other neighborhood. And because of the area's less desirable attributes, it incurred fewer taxes, saving Zhang Tao a fortune in overhead.

It also allowed him to remain closer to his off-the-books activities.

Only after he'd reviewed the entire day in his head and reflected on what he would do the next day to block the threatened hostile takeover did he relax and return to his desk.

He had one last thing to do, a task he'd been putting off for weeks.

Normally he enjoyed visiting his brother, but lately he seemed to think of any excuse to put it off.

He sat in his desk chair, all dark-green leather and Manchurian walnut wood crafted decades ago in Shanxi.

The chair was affixed to the floor.

An immovable chair provided the benefit of maintaining his posture while he worked and while he had visitors; however, this chair was affixed for a more practical reason.

He pushed a button on his desk phone indicating to his staff he wasn't to be disturbed.

With a sigh, he pressed a number of buttons under the left arm of his chair in a precise order.

His chair descended, along with an entire section of floor. Silent hydraulics brought Zhang Tao into the private, hidden space below his office.

The lights in the room automatically came on, revealing a mini-museum of antiquities and the most contemporary and luxuriously appointed panic room ever designed.

Feng was across the room.

Zhang Tao stood up before the chair had finished its descent and strode across the room to confront his flesh and blood.

"Good evening, Feng," Zhang Tao said. He smiled sadly, looking into his brother's face.

His brother's countenance was frozen in a serene expression. He gazed downward in eternal supplication.

Zhang Tao examined his brother's neck through the thick glass.

The bruises left by Zhang Tao's hand had long ago been covered up and any signs of lividity erased by the expert technician Zhang Tao had paid to preserve his brother's body.

When Zhang Tao's twin brother died, the death was never officially recorded. Zhang Tao also killed the technician and removed his body from the panic room, whereas Feng's body remained. Zhang Tao had him put on display for his personal gratification and to serve as a reminder—trust no one.

Murdering his twin brother had proved advantageous in three ways. First, it meant Zhang Tao no longer had to compromise on anything. Second, it meant that all the company profits were his and his alone. Third, it permitted Zhang Tao to impersonate and adopt his brother's fierce persona to get anything he wanted, whether in the board room or in the smoky back rooms where he conducted his Triad business.

Zhang Tao thought deeply about the man and woman he'd met at his Lafite vertical tasting the previous week and again in Dubai when he was acting as Feng.

Were they a threat? He didn't think so, but perhaps it was time to remove his co-conspirators in California now that the aphid was successfully spreading around the world.

He reviewed for the thousandth time in his head how he could possibly be connected to what was happening in the world's vineyards. When he was satisfied his connections to the threat in the vineyards were as thin as gossamer threads, his thoughts returned to more pressing matters.

CHAPTER 37

INTERPOL COMMAND AND COORDINATION CENTRE
LYON, FRANCE

"Morning, boss. You have twenty new phone messages," Henri announced to Claude the second he walked in the front door of Interpol. "I've printed off the critical emails you need to read." He handed Claude a thick sheaf of papers. "Secretary General Arsenault wants to see you, and the people from the London School of Economics are here."

Claude felt like he'd been cast into a bureaucratic nightmare.

Since France had declared war on Philomena, battlefield reports—as he had come to think of them—flooded in from Interpol's National Central Bureaus all over the world.

A hotline and email address had been created to handle the influx of calls and emails sent by concerned citizens, terrified vignerons and winemakers, and even individuals claiming to be responsible for the spread of Philomena. It took Henri and two full-time administrators to prioritize the messages and print the critical ones each day.

"They're here already? We just spoke with them Friday evening," Claude said, trying to scan and absorb the subject lines of the many emails.

"I guess, like us, they didn't take the weekend off."

Claude looked back at his assistant. He looks as tired as I feel, Claude thought.

"Where are they now?" he asked.

"In the conference room on level two."

"In that case, we may as well ask the secretary general to join us," Claude said. He bypassed his office and headed straight to the conference room with Henri in tow.

Claude hadn't spoken to his wife in three days, as he climbed into bed past two in the morning and was back out the door by seven. He was running on coffee, adrenaline, and canelé. When the brasserie he frequented for his morning coffee and canelé recognized him from headlines in *Le Figaro,* they broke tradition and arranged a delivery to his office each morning free of charge. Gift-wrapped bottles and wooden cases of exceptional wine from Bordeaux, Burgundy, Rhone, and Champagne had also started appearing at his home and office, sent by desperate winemakers seeking favor in the country's preemptive war on Philomena.

Claude entered the small conference room where Henri had left the economists from the London School of Economics. There were three of them, two men and a woman. They were conferring over their notes next to the coffee machine. Claude was relieved to see Henri had brought him his coffee and canelé.

"Good morning. I'm Claude," he announced.

"Hi, I'm Douglas," the tallest of the three economists replied, an Englishman of about fifty. He wore a dark suit, round spectacles, and was bald. "These are my colleagues, Davis and Hilary." Douglas gestured to a black man in a blue suit and a fair, pert, blonde woman in a red blouse and black skirt, both in their midthirties.

Claude shook each of their hands in turn. Douglas was the one he had spoken with over the phone the previous Friday, asking for assistance to help clarify the aphid's impact on a wider scale. Claude knew Philomena was devastating to grape growers and winemakers, but he wanted to better understand, and ensure his bosses understood, its wider implications.

"Claude," Secretary General Arsenault said when he entered. "Give me an update on the spread of phylloxera."

"Sir, if you'll permit me, I think the economists from London I've engaged can give you a comprehensive update."

Secretary Arsenault looked at the three economists for the first time. Claude quickly introduced them to the secretary general, who sat down at the head of the conference table facing a screen on the opposite wall.

"Well, carry on," he said when no one spoke.

Douglas stood up and motioned to his colleague Hilary to turn on the projector. A map of the world appeared on the screen.

"Here in France, workers in the wine industry have gone on strike as grape growers, bottlers, and wineries have laid off workers in anticipation of Philomena's arrival and the expected impact on their business," Douglas said.

"We know this already," Secretary General Arsenault interrupted. He looked at Claude.

"Yes, perhaps, but in Burgundy and Bordeaux, we're getting reports that winemakers and estate owners are hiding their wines in walled-up cellars designed to keep looters at bay, much as was done during the Second World War when German soldiers were pillaging wine from the best French châteaus' cellars for the führer."

"That's a good thing, isn't it?" Secretary Arsenault asked.

"No, the behavior indicates that looting will begin soon, if it hasn't already," Hilary interjected. "Cellar thefts occurred regularly long before phylloxera began spreading again. Any drop in production and supply, perceived or real, will result in increased theft."

"Speaking of the Germans," Douglas continued, "traffic on the Rhine and Mosel Rivers has all but stopped. Only crafts vital to trade and national security are being allowed to pass through military checkpoints."

"That must be crippling their economy," Arsenault said.

"It certainly won't help," Douglas answered.

"What about the Americans?" Claude asked.

"You've heard of the Drys?" Douglas asked.

"Yes, but I didn't think they were involved," Claude said, recalling what Corvina had told him about her visit to their headquarters in Washington, DC.

"They're not, but their movement seems to have increased in popularity and taken on an almost religious fervor as members and their supporters lobby the government for the reenactment of Prohibition. They're seeking to return the country to its puritanical roots, asserting that Philomena was God's first step in a master plan to rid the world of alcohol."

"At least we don't have those nuts to contend with," Arsenault said, and snorted.

"Americans are coming to blows in stores over dwindling wine stocks and panic buying what's left on the shelves," Davis exclaimed, speaking for the first time.

"Bulldozers are lining up on the edges of vineyards in Napa and Sonoma, where Philomena is spreading," Douglas said. "They're positioned to wipe the aphid-infested vines off the face of the earth, much as they had in the late 1980s and early 1990s when phylloxera attacked ARx1 rootstocks, previously thought to be immune to the aphid. It's feared that developers will move in quickly afterward to take advantage of the crisis."

"What about across the channel? What are the Brits doing?" Arsenault asked.

"It's mad cow time all over again," Davis said excitedly. Douglas gestured to his colleague to tone it down and then picked up the conversation.

"The measures used to contain and destroy bovine spongiform encephalopathy, or mad cow disease, have been reintroduced but this time targeting the phylloxera aphid," Douglas said.

"Are the measures working?" Arsenault asked.

"It's too early to tell, but if the United Kingdom's shores could be protected from the spreading aphid, it could soon find itself in the enviable position of being one of the few wine-producing countries in the world."

"*Mon Dieu*, the world has gone mad." Arsenault shook his head. "Anything else?"

"Of course, the impact of the aphid's spread is global. I'll let Hilary continue from this point, since her team's research covered the Southern Hemisphere," Douglas said, and took his seat. Hilary stood up and pointed to Australia on the map.

"In Australia, New Zealand, and Tasmania, nationalistic tensions have escalated. Mainlanders are calling for restrictions on travel to Australia from both islands, citing fears that ungrafted vines in both countries were originally responsible for the spread of phylloxera and would lead to the ruination of hardier, ungrafted Australian vines. Airlines have slashed their routes."

"And what did you find out about South America?" Claude asked, recalling that Corvina and Bryan had traveled there.

"In Chile," Hilary said, "vineyards continue to be burned as grape growers and winemakers try to salvage what uninfested vines they can by destroying those that have already succumbed. The aphid was discovered in Argentina and Brazil soon after it was first reported in Chile, and similar accounts of vineyard destruction have been reported."

"How is global travel being affected?" Secretary Arsenault asked.

"As expected," Douglas said. Hilary retook her seat at the table.

"Major airports in gateway cities around the world have heightened their security. The move has prompted journalists to recall safety measures implemented following the attacks on the World Trade Center in New York and the Pentagon in Virginia. Many smaller airfields in rural areas—particularly those anywhere near vineyards—have closed down altogether, halting all air traffic into, out of, and over the areas.

"Last, wine exports the world over have plummeted as protectionist tariffs have shot up in wine-producing nations, and wine producers, wholesalers, and distributors are hoarding supplies in anticipation of skyrocketing prices once demand outstrips supply."

Claude took a deep breath. He almost longed for the quieter days when he was hunting and fighting actual terrorists.

"And everything you've just told us is based on facts on the ground?" Secretary General Arsenault asked.

"This isn't all just theory—it's happening now!" Davis said, standing up. "Because of Philomena, the worldwide wine industry just got bitch-slapped by Adam Smith's invisible hand!"

"What my colleague is trying to say is . . ." Douglas began saying, his face turned red.

"I get it," Arsenault said, frowning. Claude saw Henri was struggling not to smile.

"Is there any positive news?" Arsenault asked.

"Very little. Without a method to stop and kill the genetically modified aphid altogether, we predict it will reach every vineyard on the planet," Hilary spoke up, pointing to a spreadsheet sprawled out before her.

"By when?" Secretary Arsenault asked.

"A matter of weeks, maybe days. At the rate we've seen it spreading, there's a good chance it's already present in most wine-growing regions," Hilary said, looking at Douglas. The man nodded in affirmation.

"*Mon Dieu*," Secretary Arsenault said.

"And within a few short years, it will create the unthinkable," Douglas said.

"What's that?" Secretary General Arsenault asked, leaning forward.

But Claude already knew.

"A world without wine," Douglas said.

CHAPTER 38

CHAMPAGNE ACADEMY ANNUAL GENERAL MEETING & TASTING
INSTITUTE OF DIRECTORS, 116 PALL MALL
LONDON, ENGLAND

The Nash Room of the Institute of Directors was packed, and Claude had never felt so out of place in his life.

Upward of three hundred guests, few looking under the age of thirty, crowded into the expansive hall. If the Champagne Academy membership roster on the back of the annual report Claude was leafing through was anything to go by, these men and women represented the who's who of the UK drinks industry. Members were identified as buyers, shippers, distributors, sommeliers, Masters of Wine, brand ambassadors, restaurateurs, and hoteliers.

Claude stood on his own, scanning the crowd and keeping an eye on the doorway for Corvina and Bryan, who were late. The guests all seemed to know one another, and the resultant din of conversation was overwhelming despite the high ceilings. Thick broadloom carpet and heavy drapery did little to absorb the myriad voices and clinking of champagne flutes. He himself abstained from both the idle small talk and the free-flowing champagne.

He scanned another page of the annual report he'd been handed upon arrival. The Academy's crest was splashed across the cover. The first page introduced the Champagne Academy:

The Champagne Academy was established in 1956 to foster the appreciation of Grand Marque Champagnes through the education of promising young members of the wine trades in the UK and Ireland. Every year only sixteen successful candidates are invited to attend the comprehensive study program of Champagne.

Claude surveyed the room and the Grande Marque Champagne Houses represented. Alongside three walls of the room were evenly spaced trestle tables holding giant stainless steel champagne buckets full to overflowing with ice chilling dozens of champagne bottles. Guests were offered champagne at each table just by holding out their glasses.

The annual report listed each of the sixteen Grand Marque Champagne Houses. It was an impressive collection:

Bollinger
Charles Heidsieck
G.H. Mumm
Heidsieck & Co Monopole
Krug
Lanson
Laurent-Perrier
Louis Roederer
Moët & Chandon
Perrier-Jouët
Piper-Heidsieck
Pol Roger
Pommery
Ruinart
Taittinger
Veuve Clicquot

Until that evening, Claude wasn't aware that such an organization existed. He didn't realize champagne required promoting.

He checked his watch again and looked around the room for Corvina and Bryan, who had asked him to meet them at the strange event. He straightened his name tag though it required no interference and checked his phone for missed calls or messages though it hadn't rung or vibrated. Henri was still screening all his calls and doing a good job of it.

That morning Claude had met the Interpol chief of London to make plans to apprehend David Slater's accomplice. The single ticket Corvina and Bryan had found on Slater in Portugal led them to believe Slater was going to meet his accomplice at the International Wine Challenge Awards Dinner in London. The evidence Claude's team had found on David Slater's phone in Portugal connecting his accomplice to the spread of Philomena was sufficient to make an arrest. The problem was they didn't know who Slater's accomplice was, so Claude, Corvina, and Bryan had come up with a plan.

"What madness is this?" Claude asked Corvina and Bryan when they finally arrived. Bryan was wearing a tuxedo, and Corvina wore an elegant black dress accessorized with a colorful scarf covered in bunches of purple grapes and green vines.

"It's a champagne tasting," Bryan said. "We had our annual general meeting this afternoon. Now all members and guests are invited to taste each house's champagne, both a non-vintage and a vintage offering, served by magnum."

"And you're a member?" Claude asked.

"Yes, for years. I completed the course ages ago."

"How does one sign up?" Claude asked.

"You have to be nominated by one of the sixteen Grande Marque Champagne Houses. Each house nominates four individuals in the UK drinks industry each year. Only one from each house gets selected."

"Who nominated you?" Corvina asked.

"I don't know. The nominations are confidential."

"I really think we should be going. The wine awards dinner will be starting soon," Claude interrupted.

"Relax, Claude, we have plenty of time," Bryan said. They were standing beside a table displaying Charles Heidsieck Champagne. Bryan signaled three glasses to the young lady behind the table. Claude noticed Bryan discreetly pick up the champagne bottle's cork and put it in his pocket.

"*Merci,*" Claude said when he was offered, and reluctantly accepted, a glass.

"*Je vous en prie,*" the young woman answered in perfect French, and smiled at Claude. Claude couldn't help but smile back.

"Looks like you're starting to enjoy the investigation," Corvina said.

"I can see how working with champagne has its attractions," Claude said.

"I need to go find my colleague," Bryan suddenly said. "He has the extra ticket we need for us to attend the International Wine Challenge Awards Dinner tonight."

"Okay, hurry."

Between sips of the delicious non-vintage Charles Heidsieck, Claude updated Corvina on Interpol's investigation into the photos and messages found on Slater's phone. He didn't share everything with her but enough to get her to cooperate without suspicion. He was still on the fence about her involvement.

"I find it hard to believe someone from Universal Wines could be involved," Corvina said.

"As do I, which is why I've authorized tonight's operation," Claude said. "It might be our best bet of bringing this adventure to an end."

Bryan returned at that moment waving an envelope in his hand.

"I got the ticket," he said.

"Good, let's go," Claude said. Even the minimal amount of brut champagne he had drunk was making him light-headed, and he wanted to remain sharp.

"Give me a minute to freshen up. I'll be right back," Corvina said, and disappeared into the crowd.

"Are these events held throughout the year?" Claude asked Bryan, trying to make small talk while they waited for Corvina to return.

"Yes, though not for much longer if Philomena isn't stopped," Bryan said. "At the rate it's spreading, even Champagne may soon succumb. And if that happens, there may no longer be any champagne to promote, Grande Marque or otherwise."

"You have a lot of nerve showing up here," Claude heard a woman's voice behind him say. He turned to see a pretty woman with bright-red lipstick confronting Bryan.

"What do you mean?" Bryan asked.

"First of all, when did you get married?" the woman asked Bryan.

Claude raised an eyebrow. Bryan was married?

"She's actually—" Bryan tried answering.

"And second of all, are you and she in on it together?"

"In on what together?"

"Don't be coy with me. I know you're still a wine industry news junkie. You mean to tell me you haven't read the article about your precious *wife*, the woman spreading phylloxera?"

"What are you talking about?" Bryan asked.

"I think she means this." Claude showed Bryan an article he'd pulled up on his phone, written by Malcolm Goldberg. It had been posted within the past hour and revealed Corvina as a person of interest in an ongoing Interpol investigation into the spread of Philomena. It was not flattering. Claude's immediate concern was that there was a leak at Interpol. How else could the reporter have learned of Interpol's interest in Corvina? Had she told him?

"And to think I was willing to get you back into the institute to resit your exam. I'll be sure to do everything in my power to keep you out forever," Candy said centimeters from Bryan's face. She stormed out of the reception hall.

Claude looked around the room. It seemed as though everyone was looking at their phones, and the intensity of conversation ratcheted up a few notches.

Corvina returned moments later.

"*Que pasa?* Everyone seems to be a in a foul mood all of a sudden."

"I think we better go," Bryan said. Claude couldn't agree more.

"We have to get you out of here," Claude said, and nodded to Bryan to help him escort her out of the building before the crowd turned. He motioned to Corvina to cover her head with her scarf.

Claude drained his glass, steeling himself to get Corvina out fast and incognito. He savored the taste and hoped it would not be his last.

CHAPTER 39

INTERNATIONAL WINE CHALLENGE AWARDS DINNER
GROSVENOR HOUSE HOTEL, PARK LANE
LONDON, ENGLAND

"*Cazzo!*" Corvina exclaimed as she looked over the railing. She was in a mood for swearing after reading Malcolm's article about her.

She was with Bryan on the balcony level of the Great Room at Grosvenor House Hotel on their way to attend the International Wine Challenge Awards Dinner. They arrived early to the event that Slater was meant to attend but wouldn't be making due to his spectacular demise in Portugal. She still cringed every time she thought of Slater's Jeep tumbling down the Douro Valley.

She looked down on the Great Room floor at over a hundred tables prepared for the evening's dinner. Each table was set for ten and bedecked with branded showplates, polished WMF silverware, tasteful floral centerpieces, tealight candles, programs and menus, and dozens of polished Riedel glasses.

By counting the rows of tables, Corvina could see that over a thousand guests were expected to attend the evening's gala event. She knew those in attendance represented the biggest names in the wine industry worldwide and all would be vying for dominance in their field.

A large stage dominated the front of the floor where the awards would be presented.

Corvina had read that the Great Room, originally designed and used as an ice skating rink, was converted into Europe's largest ballroom to host prestigious events for England's rich, powerful, and influential. The hotel was currently managed by Marriott International, serving as its flagship JW Marriott Hotel in Europe.

"This place is massive," Corvina said once she recovered from the shock of seeing the Great Room for the first time. Hundreds of guests had already arrived and were gathering in small groups around hosted bars, where they drank sponsored champagne. Others were doing the same as Corvina, leaning over the railing and marveling at the space below where the dinner and awards would soon be held. She nervously played with Slater's invitation in her clutch.

Bryan extended his arm. She looped her arm around his and followed him back to the entrance foyer, where she collected a printed guest directory. She saw dozens more guests arriving by the minute. They formed a long, orderly queue of tuxedos and evening dresses on the switchback stairs leading from Park Lane to the Great Room three stories below. Corvina flipped through the forty-page booklet, looking for Slater's name.

"You've got to be kidding me," Corvina said aloud when she found it.

Slater was listed under one of three tables booked in the name of Universal Wines, her own company—*former* company, she corrected herself.

They found an electronic poster board displaying a two-meter-tall illuminated table plan.

She snapped a quick picture of the guest list and the table plan, zooming in on table seventy-three, and sent the images to Claude through WhatsApp. One of the nine other guests at the table was there to meet Slater. Her job was to find out who without compromising herself.

"While I join the Universal Wines table in place of Slater, what are you going to do?" she asked Bryan. His ticket allowed him to join a different table, where his contact from the Champagne Academy would be seated.

"Go to the bar, of course," Bryan said, and smiled at her. "I'll keep an eye on you from up here."

"I can take care of myself."

"I didn't say you couldn't."

"You were implying it," she said grumpily.

"Is it too late to unimply it?"

Her answer to his question was interrupted by a booming voice.

"Ladies and gentlemen! The International Wine Challenge Awards Dinner is about to begin!" a toastmaster bellowed from across the room. He was dressed in a red jacket and a white bow tie and gloves. His deep baritone voice carried over the heads of guests and through the reception areas. Men and women stopped in mid-conversation to hear his announcement.

"Please make your way down the stairs on either side of the bal cony to your tables," he cried. With assured confidence, the toastmaster herded the thousand or more guests toward the twin curving staircases and down into the Great Room. In less than fifteen minutes, the majority of the guests had found their tables and resumed their conversations. Loud music played from speakers hung from the ceiling eighteen meters above to get guests in a celebratory mood. The din was overwhelming.

With a glass of Laurent-Perrier Grand Siècle in hand, Corvina weaved through dozens of large round tables. In her other hand, she held tight to her clutch holding the ticket Bryan had liberated from Slater's vehicle. She tossed her Ferragamo silk scarf over her shoulder, trying to appear casual. Corvina recognized numerous people in the room who waved, smiled, or stopped her to say hello. She found table number seventy-three in the middle of the room, two rows of tables away from the stage.

Nine guests had already arrived, leaving only one seat free—Slater's.

Someone at the table was Slater's contact at Universal and the person she believed was ultimately responsible for the spread of Philomena around the world. She hoped none of them had read Malcolm's article, outing her as a person of interest with Interpol.

She was furious with Malcolm. His treachery put her reputation in serious jeopardy. How would she ever get another job?

Corvina approached the table and sat down as casually as possible in the empty seat. She nodded and smiled at the other guests as she did.

Seated on her left was James Harvey, the CEO of Universal Wines—the man responsible for her termination.

Was Slater the CEO's right-hand man?

"Sorry I'm late." Corvina addressed the table. She avoided eye contact with Harvey.

Judging by the lack of reaction from the rest of the table, the other guests were apparently not aware that she had been fired or that she hadn't even been invited to the event. Many recognized her, since she had been with the company for a significant period of time.

Harvey leaned toward her as a waiter unfolded her napkin and placed it on her lap.

"What are you doing here?" he asked through clenched teeth.

"I'm joining you for dinner. A colleague of mine couldn't make it, so he gave me his ticket." She flashed the black-and-gold envelope that held Slater's ticket. Was he mad about her attendance because she no longer worked for the company or because of something else?

Before Harvey could speak further, the showplates were removed from their table and a choice of still or sparkling water was offered to each guest. Corvina turned her attention to the stage and drank the rest of her Grand Siècle. The glass was whisked away within seconds of her setting it down on the white pressed linen tablecloth.

Despite the time she'd had to process the connection, her head was still spinning that someone at Universal Wines was involved with Philomena. Incidents like her being fired started to click into place. Maybe she was getting too close to finding out who was responsible. Was Sergio's disappearance in Germany somehow connected? Maybe he, too, had been investigating the aphid's attacks on vineyards.

She looked at the guest directory once more and studied the list of names of the people seated at the three Universal Wines tables. She didn't recognize all of them. It was possible Slater was there to meet someone at another Universal Wines table.

Her thoughts were interrupted by the man sitting to her right. She recognized him from a company conference she had attended the previous year.

"Albariño?" He held out a bottle he'd plucked from an ice bucket in the middle of the table.

"*Sí, gracias,*" Corvina answered. He filled one of the seven glasses that formed a line above her knives.

She could feel the tension radiating from her ex-CEO. She purposefully ignored him, daring him to make a scene.

The first course—lightly seared Hokkaido scallops—was served, and the table tucked into the dish set before them. Corvina tasted the wine, made some mental tasting notes, and delighted in the pairing. The match with the Spanish wine was close to perfect.

"Corvina, I heard you are chasing Philomena. How is that going?" one of the men across the table asked over the long and low floral centerpiece. He spoke with an English accent. She recognized him from her frequent trips to London.

Corvina put down her cutlery and wiped at the corner of her mouth with her napkin. The rest of the guests paused in their conversations to hear her reply.

"Well"—she looked to her left—"in the past four weeks, the investigation has taken me to London, Chile, the Niagara Region in Canada, DC, Hong Kong, Dubai, and South Africa."

"Wow! Any luck finding out where it came from?" another man asked.

"Yes, as a matter of fact." She picked up her glass of albariño and took an appreciative sip. She looked around the table to see if anyone looked unduly concerned. Everyone at the table was looking at her, waiting for her to expand on her answer. The CEO's eyes were riveted to her face.

"I'm working closely with Interpol out of Lyon, so I can't reveal any more I'm afraid," she said, and laughed. She twirled her silk scarf around her fingers playfully. "I did recently enjoy a trip to Portugal, however." She smiled at the table.

Corvina picked up her cutlery, stabbed another piece of scallop, and tasted it with the wine. It really was an exceptional pairing.

The CEO coughed and stood suddenly, excusing himself from the table.

Corvina stood up and excused herself from the table as well. She followed Harvey across the room, weaving between tables.

She caught up to him at the base of the stairs leading to the balcony level. Corvina saw Bryan looking down at her and signaled to him to stay where he was. She then saw Claude further along the balcony looking at her as well. Corvina gave him a signal to hold tight.

"Where are you going?" she asked the CEO of Universal Wines. She forced herself to maintain a friendly tone of voice.

"I have a call to make," he said. He had his phone in his hand.

"To David?" she asked.

"Who?" Harvey stopped climbing the stairs.

"David Slater, the man who gave me this ticket." Corvina withdrew Slater's ticket and showed it to Harvey. She concealed it just as quickly with her scarf and returned it to her clutch.

"I don't know what you're talking about," Harvey said.

"We don't have time for this," Corvina said. She had seen his eyes flicker in recognition when she had said David's name. She looked around as if suspicious they were being watched. She would have found this humorous if not for the situation and the fact that they *were* being watched by Interpol.

"How do I know I can trust you?" Harvey asked. "You just said you were working with Interpol." His thumb hovered above his cell phone.

"They approached me as a suspect. I convinced them to let me help. You recruited me, remember? You asked me to investigate Philomena and keep you updated in order to keep Universal Wines above reproach. If we were investigating it, we could hardly be accused of engineering the spread of Philomena. That's why you sent me to Washington—to plant suspicion on the Drys organization, right?" she guessed.

"I sent you to Washington to get you as far away as possible from Slater. You surprised me when you flew to Chile and connected Slater to Philomena so quickly. The Drys were a red herring."

"Slater found me before I could locate him again, after we missed each other in Canada. After he looped me in, he asked me to come to this dinner to warn you."

"Warn me about what?" Harvey asked, looking worried. That was when she knew he was Slater's contact. She had drawn him into the conversation, and before he knew it he was asking questions implying he not only knew Slater but was there to meet the ecoterrorist.

"He was worried that Interpol would track him down. He even thought his phone calls were being monitored."

Harvey looked at his phone and returned it to his jacket pocket.

"Shit, if they find Slater, he'll lead them back to me. We need to talk about this after the dinner. For now, let's go back to the table so we don't draw attention to ourselves," he suggested.

Corvina led the way back to the table and returned to her seat. The next course had been served.

"Is Interpol no longer following you?" Harvey asked her in a hushed voice. Now he was looking around the room.

"No, they no longer need to."

"What do you mean?" Harvey asked, looking visibly relieved.

Corvina stood up and waved her napkin.

"Because I told them I would be here," she said, and smiled at Harvey, who looked at her in shock. "Try the albariño—it's divine," she said. As she walked away, she saw a dozen men rushing toward table seventy-three. Harvey bolted.

Behind her, she heard a massive crash as Harvey was tackled into a table by a member of Claude's Incident Response Team. She cringed at the sound of silverware, crockery, and dozens of glasses and wine bottles crashing to the floor.

CHAPTER 40

UNIVERSAL WINES WINERY
NAPA VALLEY, CA, UNITED STATES

Malcolm stood inside the vat room at the winery where James Harvey's assistant's body had been discovered earlier that morning. It was a cool afternoon, and the stale air inside the vat building was a few degrees cooler than the still California air outside.

He looked around in puzzlement.

As soon as he heard about the incident over the police wire—less than twelve hours after Harvey's arrest by Interpol in London—Malcolm went to investigate. He hoped there was a connection to the spread of Philomena. At the same time, he hoped to hear from Corvina soon. He had not heard from either her or Bryan since his article about her being an Interpol person of interest was published, and he worried his piece may have gone too far in insinuating her involvement. He made a mental note to call her later in the day.

"Why on earth would he have come here in the first place?" Malcolm asked the silent vats. He pushed thoughts of Corvina out of his mind.

Maybe he didn't come here on his own, Malcolm thought. The police called the death an accident, but that didn't sit right with him.

Maybe he was brought here to be killed, or maybe he was killed somewhere else and his killer disposed of the body here.

Murder was likely. But when he thought about it more, he found it increasingly difficult to entertain as an option. First of all, according to the police, there was no indication that someone else had been present, nor were there any signs of violence or evidence pointing to manslaughter.

Malcolm tried to conjure up a scenario that would explain how Harvey's assistant got on top of the twelve-foot-high vats. If someone had killed him, it would have been much easier to kill him on the catwalk than to kill him somewhere else and bring his body up the spiral staircase and drop him into the vat.

As Malcolm climbed the spiral staircase, his steps echoing, he ruled out Harvey's assistant being killed elsewhere. The staircase was steep and narrow and would have made carrying a grown man up the steps almost impossible.

That left suicide, an even less likely scenario given the bizarre fashion that the man had met his end.

He stared at the top of the vat, willing it to reveal what had happened. The only sound in the winery was the buzz of the halogen lights above and the hum of hidden machinery.

Maybe it *was* an accident. That brought Malcolm back full circle to his original question; if Harvey's assistant hadn't come here to kill himself, why on earth was he here? Had he come of his own accord, or had his boss sent him?

If he did die by accident, what was he doing opening the vat in the first place? The police had ascertained through an interview with the winemaker that the vats full of wine were sealed during the daytime.

Maybe Harvey had instructed him to put something into the wine? Or maybe he was going to take a sample because something had already been added? Malcolm followed this line of reasoning, but it didn't seem to connect with what was happening with Philomena and Corvina and Bryan's parallel investigation into the spread of the aphid. What was happening in vineyards around the world was happening in the fields, not in fermentation tanks.

If Harvey's assistant had opened the vat of fermenting wine, he could have been overcome by the carbon dioxide and fell in on his own. A tank full of wine would be full of carbon dioxide, the by-product of fermenting grape juice. Odorless, tasteless, and invisible, carbon dioxide is a silent killer. Harvey's assistant literally wouldn't know what hit him. Exposed to the freshly released carbon dioxide, it would have rendered him unconscious with just a few breaths.

Having done some research on carbon dioxide poisoning in wineries beforehand, Malcolm was surprised to learn that even with the industry's advanced technological safety measures—and winemakers who should have known better—every year a handful of winemakers around the world succumbed to the deadly gas and died in or next to the passion of their pursuit.

Up on the stainless steel tanks, Malcolm ducked underneath the yellow crime scene tape bisecting the catwalk. He peered down through the open hatch and into the vast, empty seven-thousand-gallon tank below. It had been emptied once the body had been removed. The hatch at the side of the tank near the bottom was ajar, letting in enough light for Malcolm to see the interior stainless steel surface.

Malcolm got down on hands and knees and peered into the dark container. He couldn't see much, but the smell of fermented wine was overwhelming. No amount of cleaning would remove the odor. He experienced a moment of panic thinking that he might stick his head into a pocket of carbon dioxide and share the same fate as the Universal Wines employee.

He looked around but saw only stainless steel surfaces. He stood and felt light-headed. Cautioning himself not to panic, he realized he had just stood too quickly. After he descended to the ground level of the winery via the spiral staircase, he stuck his head into the hatch at the bottom of the tank and looked around from another angle. Something on the ceiling of the tank caught his attention—a small dark patch.

He returned to the top of the tank and lay on his stomach. Reaching into the vat as far as his arm would go, he swept his hand back and forth until he felt a solid object protruding from the stainless steel ceiling. He explored the object with his hand. It felt metallic and small.

At first it seemed to be part of the tank. Was it a temperature or carbon dioxide sensor perhaps? Malcolm pulled on it and was surprised when it slid toward him along the stainless steel. It was magnetized!

He pulled the object closer until he could see it at the edge of the hatch. It was a small metallic box. He maneuvered his other arm into the hatch and with a determined tug freed the metallic box from the stainless steel tank.

Standing, he placed the box into his jacket pocket—hoping it wasn't an explosive device—and descended the spiral staircase. He ducked under another yellow ribbon of crime scene tape, left the winery, and returned to his car.

Without preamble, he flipped open the case and saw a USB memory stick and a row of plastic vials. He assumed they contained samples of Philomena.

He fired up his laptop, inserted the USB, and opened the files within.

The memory stick contained dozens of folders. Malcolm found one labeled "Targets." Opening the folder, he discovered dozens of files, each named after wineries. He checked a few of the files. Each file contained a huge amount of information on the winery it was named after, from location and history to grape varietals grown and types of rootstocks used. Much of the information could never have been found online; it was either proprietary or too technical in nature to be shared on any company websites. There were also two itineraries filed separately.

Ten minutes later, he pried himself away from his laptop and called Corvina.

"Corvina, it's Malcolm."

"What do you want?" Her voice was cooler than the vat room.

"Corvina, I know you're probably upset—"

"Upset, Malcolm? Your article made it look like I'm the one responsible for killing the world's vineyards!"

"Corvina, I'm sorry. That wasn't my intent. My editor insisted I include the information about you being questioned by Interpol."

"Well, that's small consolation to Bryan and me, who will never work in the wine industry again."

"Corvina, if I hadn't written the article, someone else would have."

"Malcolm, stop. With Slater dead, the conspiracy is over. We can leave it to Claude and Interpol to find out why they did it."

"But that's the thing—it's not over. Slater had an accomplice. There was someone else working with him."

"Probably James Harvey, but he's been arrested," Corvina said.

"No, I mean someone else. An accomplice that was helping Slater *spread* Philomena."

"What? Are you sure?" Corvina asked.

He was relieved to hear her voice had lost its bitter edge. "I'm sitting in my car at a Universal Wines winery next to their corporate headquarters where James Harvey's assistant's body was found just a few hours ago. The police just left, and I managed to sneak in. I found a memory stick that I think Harvey's assistant was looking for before he died. It looks like Harvey hid the documents there for safekeeping, along with samples of the aphid. Going through the documents, I found two separate travel plans that seem to correspond with the spread of Philomena."

"Two travel plans? You mean there *was* someone else spreading the aphid aside from Slater? Do the documents reveal who the other person is?"

"No, but there's something else. I might know where he or she is going next. Have you heard of Vinexpo?" Malcolm asked.

"Of course," Corvina answered.

"When does it start?" Malcolm asked. He started his car to get back to his office, where he would write his next article.

"Tomorrow, in Bordeaux," Corvina said.

"Then you need to get to Bordeaux right away. And there's something else you need to consider."

"What?"

"Once they've finished spreading Philomena, you'll only have a bug to chase, and the real culprits will disappear. You have to catch them while they're still at large." His car fishtailed down the drive bisecting the vineyard and the valley before him. He hoped they weren't already too late.

CHAPTER 41

CHÂTEAU PETIT-VILLAGE
POMEROL, BORDEAUX
FRANCE

Corvina was woken up by the sound of birds outside the window. A church bell rang in the distance, counting off the hours. It was eight o'clock in the morning.

She flung the fluffy white duvet off her body and jumped out of bed. She cursed herself for oversleeping, but it was the best sleep she'd had in weeks. Despite staying up late reading the files Malcolm had emailed her, she was bursting with energy. She wiped the sleep from her eyes and brushed back her hair with one hand.

She donned a bathrobe that hung from the wall in the bathroom, checked her appearance in the mirror, and stepped outside the bedroom into a small kitchenette shared by the separate rooms of the guesthouse.

She and Bryan had arrived in Pomerol just after midnight. Following her phone call with Malcolm, they had booked the first plane out of London to Bordeaux. She had called Claude with the information Malcolm had discovered, and they arranged to meet in the city of Bordeaux the next day.

Fresh croissants made by a local baker were left on the dining table in a brown paper bag by their host. Corvina removed a croissant for herself and found a plate and knife to spread rhubarb compote across the delicate French specialty. It was one of the best things she'd eaten in ages.

Bryan joined her in the kitchenette, wearing a T-shirt and a pair of black boxer briefs.

"Morning," he said, rubbing the sleep out of his eyes.

"Good morning. Put some clothes on, for goodness' sake. There may be people in the other rooms. Espresso?" she asked.

"Yes, please. I thought you might like to see more of me," Bryan yawned.

"Keep dreaming," Corvina said. Though nothing had happened the night before, the thought had crossed her mind. She and Luis had been separated over six months, and she was positive he wasn't honoring his wedding vows. Not including her father, Bryan was turning into the most reliable man in her life.

She made fresh espresso using the small machine provided in the kitchenette. The machine whirred and poured, making quick use of the capsules she dropped inside. She handed the first cup to Bryan when he returned fully dressed.

"Enjoy," she said. She drank her own with a few practiced sips, a method learned in a thousand different Italian coffee bars with her father.

"How often have you been here?" Bryan asked.

"At least a dozen times. I've been consulting with the winery's technical director, a woman named Marielle, for the last three years. I called her after Malcolm told us Slater or his accomplice had been to her vineyard. I asked her to check the vines for herself."

"And what did she find?" Bryan asked. He sipped his espresso.

"At first she thought it was just the usual nematodes that sometime infect the vines with their virus, turning them yellow. But then she realized it was much more serious."

Corvina left Bryan to sip his espresso and look out upon the vineyards while she took a quick shower and changed. She came out to join him minutes later wearing snug dark jeans, a figure-hugging black sweater, and a colorful scarf with a butterfly motif and carrying a pair of trainers by the laces that bound them together.

"Where are you off to?" Bryan asked.

"To check on the neighboring properties for signs of infestation. If Malcolm is right, the vineyards throughout the region are probably already infested. I want to see for myself. That's why I wanted to come here before meeting Claude in Bordeaux. I won't be long, and then we'll be on our way." She tied on her sneakers and sprung up, ready to go. Corvina opened the heavy steel gate leading outside and let herself out of the guesthouse. She closed the gate behind her, careful not to let it clang shut.

Once outside and heading into the vineyard, she called her parents. Her father picked up on the second ring.

"*Ciao, Cara.* Your mamma and I read an article about you in the newspaper. Is it true?" her father asked.

Corvina's gut sank. She hadn't spoken with her parents since her trip to Hong Kong.

"Papà, do you honestly think that I'm spreading phylloxera?"

"Of course not, dear! I meant is it true that you've been fired from Universal Wines?"

"Oh, that. Yes, that part is true," she said. "Vicente let me go after I was questioned by Interpol." She had no desire to lie to her father.

"I'm sorry to hear that. It's why I was surprised that the man from your company came by yesterday."

Man from her company? She had completely forgotten she had asked Vicente to send someone to check on her parents' vineyard following her father's discovery of phylloxera.

"Vicente called on you?" Corvina asked.

"No, one of your work colleagues. He came by and inspected the vineyards with me. I showed him everything, but it felt like he was already familiar with the vineyard. Your mother had him in for tea and wouldn't stop pestering him. He was a nice man and asked how you were doing and where you were."

"Who did they send?" Corvina asked. She felt her whole body tense.

"Sergio."

Sergio was alive! How could that be? And why was he at her parents' winery?

"Oh," was all she could manage to say as more questions ran through her mind.

Why would Sergio go to her parents' winery before contacting the company? Did Vicente know? Was his appearance in any way connected to Harvey's arrest? The only reason she could think that Sergio would resurface without making contact was if he was somehow involved in the spread of Philomena.

Could Sergio be Slater's accomplice? And Harvey's? Maybe Harvey had introduced them. As Bryan had suggested to Claude and Alison at Interpol in London when Corvina was first brought in as a person of interest, there had to have been more than one person spreading the aphid to get around the world undetected. Malcolm and the files he discovered seemed to confirm this. Now she thought she knew who it was. All of these thoughts spun wildly in her mind while she held her phone pressed to her ear.

"Corvina? Are you still there?" she heard her father asking.

"Yes, sorry. I'm still here. Did Sergio say anything else? Did he mention where he was going next?"

"No, but he left you a message."

"A message for me? What did he say?"

"Hold on, I wrote it down. Let me find the paper."

Corvina listened to the sounds of her father putting the phone down and shuffling around the kitchen, where the house phone was located. She could picture it clearly.

"Here we go," he said when he came back on the line. "He asked me to tell you he was working on a project to level the field, it would be getting a lot of exposure soon, and he would make sure you got the credit for helping."

"Level the field? What did he mean by that?"

"I don't know; he just asked your mother and I to pass on the message."

"*Grazie,* Papà."

When she finished the call, Corvina closed her eyes and took a deep breath. Sergio had visited her home. He had been in the vineyards with her father and inside the house with her mother. She had never liked the man, but she had never feared him as she did now. Had he visited before? Was he responsible for infesting her parents' vineyard?

She put her thoughts of home and Sergio's visit aside to focus on the task at hand. She had to see for herself that Philomena was in Bordeaux as Malcolm had suggested following his discovery of James Harvey's files.

She took in her surroundings. A cloudless sky floated above a sea of green vine canopy as far as she could see in any direction. The sight was breathtaking and beautiful. Yet Corvina knew that terror could lie just beneath the surface, like a calm blue sea full of sharks.

Situated on a rise in the heart of Pomerol, the vineyards of Château Petit-Village benefited from their elevated position as they were subject to a slight breeze that kept the leaves dry. The higher placement also allowed for better drainage—and faster spread of phylloxera.

To her left, but out of sight, was Château Cheval Blanc. Straight ahead she could see the new, contemporary concrete buildings of Château Le Pin. To her right, not far from the church, was Pétrus.

Named after the pine trees growing around the château, Le Pin was one of the preeminent producers in Pomerol. Corvina marched up and down the vineyards, keeping a low profile to avoid being caught. Some of the paths between the vines had tire tracks in them where they had recently been weeded. The soil composition was made up of gravel and stones, many the size of bottle corks, and blue clay that helped the soil retain water and release it when needed. While hardly an ampelographer, Corvina recognized the distinctive patterns of merlot leaves shielding the grape bunches around her.

It didn't take long to find what she was looking for. After a few passes between the vines, she discovered the same evidence of aphid infestation she had first seen in Italy on the leaves but particularly on the roots below the soil. She took a few samples of the pustules and aphids as well as a few pictures with her phone.

It looked like Malcolm was right; Philomena had penetrated the heart of Bordeaux.

Having seen enough in Le Pin's vineyards, she snuck away and headed down the road to Château Cheval Blanc, where she found more signs of aphid infestation.

Last among the immediate neighbors that she recognized, Corvina went to Pétrus. Unlike the other producers in the area, Pétrus didn't have "château" before its name; as no one lived on the property, the title of château didn't apply nor was it necessary.

A quick inspection of the vines' roots around her confirmed the presence of Philomena.

Deep in the vineyard, she let out a small yelp when a man peered at her between the vines.

"*Que fais-tu là?*" he asked. *What are you doing there?*

"Oh, hello—I mean, *bonjour, comment allez-vous?*" she replied. Her French was not as strong as her native Spanish and Italian or her accented English.

"*Et bon, que fais-tu?*" he asked again.

"*Um, je cherche les aphids, um . . . les petits chose,*" Corvina said. She held her thumb and forefinger together to illustrate that she was looking for something small. After several more hapless attempts, Corvina took out the samples she had taken from the other vineyards to show him and continue explaining what she was doing.

"*Je cherche Philomena.*"

The winemaker looked at her. He looked at the test tube in her hand. He looked at his vines. Then he looked at her again, this time in panic as it dawned on him what she was trying to say. He turned and ran.

Corvina herself ran in the opposite direction toward Château Petit-Village as fast as she could. She no longer worried about being seen or caught.

When she reached the grounds of Château Petit-Village, she found Bryan and Marielle sitting outside in two chairs near the vines, chatting over a glass of wine. A third chair between them was empty. Bryan was twirling a cork between his fingers.

"I see you two have met. A little early, isn't it?" Corvina asked. She tried to catch her breath.

"I wanted Bryan to get a taste of our latest vintage," Marielle said. Corvina leaned down and kissed Marielle on both cheeks in greeting. The petite woman was in her midfifties and had short blonde hair that always seemed perfectly set. She was wearing hiking boots, black trousers, and a gray jacket over a white shirt.

Bryan raised his half-filled glass of red wine. "This is straight from the barrel, not even bottled yet," he said.

"Nice," Corvina said.

"Would you like some?" Marielle asked.

"No. Wait, on second thought—yes, I could use a drink."

"What did you find?" Marielle asked as she offered a glass to Corvina.

"Your neighbors show signs of infestation as well."

"But why haven't they said anything?"

"Same reason as you, I suppose. Perhaps they're not sure what it is or they think it's something harmless. Or perhaps they haven't detected it yet. It's still in the early stages."

"Not so early. If it continues, we won't have a harvest this year," Marielle said.

"Now what?" Bryan asked the two women.

"Now the real panic will begin," Corvina said.

"We have to meet Claude at Vinexpo Bordeaux in an hour," Bryan said.

"Then we had better get driving," Corvina said. She looked at her watch.

Corvina was almost finished packing the trunk and Bryan was in the car when Marielle returned from the winery to say goodbye to them. She was carrying a small package.

"This came for you, Corvina," she said, handing the package to Corvina.

"What is it?"

"I don't know. It's from America."

Corvina inspected the sender's details. It was from Malcolm. She opened the package and saw that he had sent her the small case of vials he had found in the California winery, the scene of Harvey's assistant's death.

"Thank you. It's from a journalist in San Francisco who's been helping us," she told Marielle.

Corvina reached into the back seat for the stainless steel briefcase they had used to transport the bottle of 1899 Lafite to Hong Kong. She hadn't had the chance yet to return it in London, so she used it to keep her papers inside. Underneath the foam padding, it also contained the vials of aphids they had discovered in Slater's vehicle in Portugal. She planned to mail them to Jacob for study in South Africa.

She lifted another portion of the padding and tucked Malcolm's vials underneath and out of sight.

"Wait just a moment," Marielle said. She came back moments later with a bottle and handed it to Corvina.

"You should have something in that case. A bottle of our 1990 should fill it nicely. Oh, and a wine opener."

"Thank you, Marielle," Corvina said, taking the bottle. She strapped it into the case and tucked the wine opener in next. She passed the case to Bryan, who placed it in the back seat.

After Corvina finished loading up and returned to the car, she heard a news alert come across the radio. Bryan translated the broadcast for her. An announcer was describing the discovery of Philomena in Pomerol's vineyards.

"That was fast!" Corvina said. "The winemaker at Pétrus must have reported it."

"Or someone else detected and reported it," Bryan said.

She gave Bryan directions and settled in for the drive as he navigated the gravel driveway of Château Petit-Village and turned right.

Within minutes they passed the walled commune of Saint-Emilion and were driving down Highway D121 toward the city of Bordeaux.

Corvina was amazed at the speed of the French army.

Truck after truck sped past them down the narrow secondary highway heading deep into the Bordeaux region, all on a mission to protect the nation's vineyards.

Roadblocks were set up at the entrance of each vineyard they passed and the walls surrounding renowned wine districts and appellations.

She and Bryan hadn't anticipated such organized chaos on the roads or such a swift response from the French military. She became impatient as Bryan drove at a crawl behind a long line of cars making their way through a checkpoint ahead. She assumed many of the commuters were also headed to Bordeaux to attend Vinexpo.

When it was their turn to roll up to the checkpoint, a man dressed in military garb peered in at them and asked for their identification.

"What is the purpose of your visit to the Bordeaux region?" he asked in heavily accented English as he inspected Corvina's and then Bryan's passports.

"I'm a consultant to the wine industry." Corvina produced one of her business cards. "I was visiting a client." She chose not to reveal the château she'd visited or even that they had been in Pomerol. The Philomena aphids she had collected from Pomerol's vineyards were in the case on the back seat. She hoped it wasn't searched and that the pounding of her telltale heart didn't betray her.

While the man scrutinized their passports, another man with a mirror on a stick inspected the underside of the vehicle.

"And you, sir?" The man looked inside the car at Bryan.

"I'm a wine writer, writing about this year's vintage."

"*Bon.* Can you please step out of the car and open the trunk?" the soldier asked.

They both complied and watched as their luggage was inspected.

"What are you looking for?" Bryan asked.

"Bugs and anything suspicious. Have you two seen anything suspicious?" the soldier asked.

Corvina shook her head. She had to force herself not to look in the direction of the case. She hoped the man had not read Malcolm's article, otherwise he might recognize her as Interpol's person of interest.

"Open the back door of the car please," the soldier with the mirror commanded. Corvina tried to act calm as Bryan opened the door.

The soldier set down his mirror and pointed at the case on the back seat.

The case containing the bottle of wine and wine opener given to them by Marielle.

The case containing the vials of aphids she had collected from Pomerol's vineyards.

The case containing the vials Malcolm had sent to her from California.

"Can you open the case for me, sir?" the soldier commanded Bryan from his side of the car.

Corvina's phone rang. She almost jumped out of her skin. It was Malcolm.

"Now is really not a good time to talk," she whispered, and turned away from the guards.

"I wanted to check that you received the package I sent okay," Malcolm said.

"Yes." Corvina couldn't take her eyes off the case. She could see it clearly through the rear passenger window.

"Great. I don't know if you opened it yet, but it contains everything I found at the winery where Harvey's assistant died."

"I received everything." She watched as Bryan slid the case toward him and angled it so that he could open the latches simultaneously.

"Did you also know that the vials I sent don't contain the aphid, like those you found on Slater in Portugal? I've been reading the files—it turns out that the vials contain the neurotoxin Slater designed to destroy his own creation!"

"What!?" Corvina whispered, turning away from the car.

"Madam?" the guard asked. He looked up at her. "Is everything okay?"

"Yes, yes, fine. Sorry."

"Corvina, are you still there?" Malcolm asked.

"Yes."

The guard opened the case toward Corvina, so all she could see was its top.

"Did you hear me? We have it! We have the means to stop Philomena!" Malcolm was saying excitedly in her ear. He sounded a thousand miles away.

Corvina watched helplessly as the soldier reached into the case.

"What is this?" the soldier asked.

Instead of lifting the vials of aphids or Malcolm's package out of the case, the soldier lifted out the bottle of wine.

Corvina couldn't find the words to answer. Malcolm was saying something in her ear.

"It was a gift from the winery we visited," she heard Bryan answer calmly.

"Nineteen ninety—that is a good year for Pomerol," the soldier said with admiration as he inspected the bottle's label.

"They must want a favorable review from me," Bryan said, and laughed. The soldier laughed with him. Corvina tried to laugh but only managed to smile wanly. She thought her heart was going to burst.

The soldier returned the bottle to the case and motioned for Bryan to close it. The inspection was over. Corvina wanted to dive back in the car but forced herself to open the door slowly and ease herself into her seat so as not to raise suspicion.

"*Allez-y*, be on your way." The soldier handed them their passports and waved them through the checkpoint.

"How did they not see the vials or Malcolm's package in the case?" Corvina asked once the car was in motion again and the checkpoint far behind them. She checked her phone, but Malcolm had ended the call.

"Because I have the vials in my pocket and Malcolm's package is right here," Bryan said, reaching under his seat. "I heard about the roadblocks on the radio while you were loading the car, so I took the precaution."

"Good thing you did, but next time please let me know. I almost had a heart attack," Corvina said.

"What did Malcolm want?" Bryan asked. He passed the package to Corvina.

"To tell me that the vials he sent didn't contain more aphids—they contain the neurotoxin that can stop Philomena!"

"That's terrific news! Even more reason to meet Claude at Vinexpo," Bryan said.

"Do you mean give it to Claude? Why would we do that?" Corvina asked.

"Um, because he's from Interpol?"

"I think we should send the neurotoxin to Jacob. At least he'll know what to do with the solution," she said. She wanted the neurotoxin in Jacob's hands as soon as possible so he could begin testing it and sharing its power to kill Philomena with the world. She worried that if she handed it over to Claude, it would end up mired in Interpol red tape and would be of no use to anyone.

"After everything that happened, you still trust the man?" Bryan asked her. It sounded like an accusation.

"I trust his passion."

"Well, I don't. I think we should hand everything over to Claude."

"And you trust him?"

"I trust him to want to fight Philomena," Bryan said.

"Let's talk about it when we get to Bordeaux," she said.

They were stopped twice more at checkpoints by military personnel as they approached Bordeaux. Their passports were checked again, and they were waved through without further incident.

"How do they expect to stop Philomena with checkpoints?" Corvina asked.

"They can't. We're proof of that. But what else can they do? It doesn't matter. They're too late. Philomena is already here," Bryan said.

Corvina called Claude at Interpol while Bryan drove on. What should have been an hour-long drive would take them almost two hours because of the checkpoints and military traffic.

"*Oui?*" Claude answered when her call was put through to him.

"Claude, this is Corvina. We're on the way to Bordeaux. What's going on out here? Military checkpoints and truck convoys are everywhere."

"The discovery of Philomena in Pomerol has started a nationwide panic. Château Petit-Village and Pétrus on the Right Bank are not the only ones infested."

"Oh no. I feel responsible," Corvina said.

"For what? If not for you, we wouldn't even know where to begin. At least now we have somewhere to start investigating. The military has been preparing for weeks, and checkpoints at major junctions have been in place for days. When will you get to Bordeaux?" Claude asked. She could hear the strain in his voice.

"If we don't hit any more checkpoints, we'll be there within an hour," Corvina said.

"Okay, hurry. Vinexpo has just opened."

She called Malcolm back and put him on speakerphone.

"Hello?"

"Sorry, I couldn't talk much earlier. We were at a checkpoint." She told Malcolm about her confirmation of Philomena's presence in Pomerol's vineyards and her conversation with her parents.

"So you think Sergio is Slater's accomplice and he was helping him and your CEO to spread Philomena?" Malcolm asked.

"It makes sense. Why else would he not tell anyone he is still alive? And why would he go to my parent's vineyard? It's like he's warning me."

"Maybe he is. I've been thinking about the pattern in which Philomena has been spreading."

"What pattern?"

"When phylloxera spread in the nineteenth century, its spread and trajectory were subject to the distance the aphid could travel on its own and via trade routes where it could hitch a ride. Its path was subject to chance and opportunity. Philomena today is being disseminated by design. It's being spread according to a preconceived plan. It's not random," Malcolm said.

"I think they chose well-known vineyards to make as big a statement as possible," Bryan said, joining in the conversation.

"You might be right. They appear to have chosen centrally located vineyards to facilitate the aphid's spread throughout the rest of each region," Malcolm added.

"But we already know Philomena's in Bordeaux. We just saw it in Pomerol at Pétrus and Château Petit-Village. Maybe Burgundy and Champagne are the next targets," Corvina said.

"How does Vinexpo fit into all of this?" Malcolm asked.

"Consider the context," Bryan said. "The last time phylloxera struck, it was shortly after the Classification of 1855. That, of course, was a coincidence. This year a new classification will be announced. Perhaps this time phylloxera's presence isn't a coincidence. Half of the wine world is gathered in one place, and the rest of the world is waiting for the new classification results."

"Oh my God—you're right!" Corvina exclaimed. "We've been so busy chasing Philomena that I forgot all about the reclassification to be announced this year."

"Sorry, non–wine geek here. What's the Classification of 1855?" Malcolm asked.

"In 1855, Paris was to host the world exhibition," Bryan answered. "Napoleon ordered a ranking of France's best Bordeaux wines so that he could show them off to visitors. Brokers ranked the wines based on trading price and the château's reputation—both linked to quality—and the Classification of 1855 was the result. With the exception of a few minor changes in rankings, it still holds today and has had a significant impact on the wealth and importance of many châteaus for the last century and a half."

"And there's going to be a reclassification *this* year?" Malcolm asked.

"Yes, winemakers have been pushing for a reclassification for years. It'll be announced at the end of Vinexpo," Bryan said.

"That's unfortunate timing with Philomena just being discovered in Bordeaux," Malcolm said.

"I don't think the timing is a coincidence," Bryan said. "If Philomena is going to make an even bigger statement than it already has, it will be in the next day or two as Vinexpo kicks off—and on the eve of the reclassification. I think Philomena's invasion of France has just begun."

CHAPTER 42

VINEXPO
PARC DES EXPOSITIONS EXHIBITION CENTER
BORDEAUX, FRANCE

"Claude, are you already here?" Corvina asked when Claude picked up her call.

She and Bryan had just arrived at Vinexpo Bordeaux.

Bryan drove with one hand, looking for a parking space in the vast underground parking lot.

"We've been here for over an hour. What took you so long?" Claude asked.

"I told you, we got held up by checkpoints. We're coming in now," she said. She disconnected her call with Claude and took a moment to touch up her lipstick. Once done, she squeezed the tube into the front pocket of her jeans.

As soon as Bryan found a space to park, she and Bryan got out of the car and ran for the nearest entrance where they could collect their passes, arranged for en route and online.

"*Bienvenue* á *Vinexpo*. Welcome to Vinexpo," a young lady greeted them at the main entrance. She scanned the bar code on the badges she gave them and showed them into the exhibition hall. Corvina draped the bright-red lanyard with her entry badge around her neck.

It was just before noon, and the exhibition center was already full. It felt to Corvina like entering the world's largest cocktail party—if cocktail parties were held in aircraft hangars and fine wines were offered to every guest by the winemakers themselves.

"Do you think we're really going to find Sergio here?" Bryan asked.

"We have to. If we don't, Philomena will keep spreading." Corvina shook her head at the magnitude of the event swirling around them.

She continued through the exhibition, passing hundreds of booths and exhibits featuring wines from all over the world. Every booth was littered with pamphlets, bottles, wine glasses, and spittoons. Attendees crowded around the booths, all holding out small wine glasses for the privilege of a taste.

She passed a host of exhibitors hawking improbable remedies and solutions designed to thwart, circumvent, or outright halt the scourge of Philomena. All were aimed at the naïve, the gullible, and the desperate. Countermeasures on offer included sprays, sonic devices, bottled cat urine, and ground-up crystals.

"Can we find the Universal Wines area? This case is heavy." Corvina held up the steel case she had transported from London to Hong Kong to Dubai to Portugal back to London and now to France. "Oh look, there's the stand right over there," she said, and pointed to the middle of the exhibition.

Due to its size and influence in the global wine industry, Universal Wines commanded a significant amount of floor space. Dozens of wines under its portfolio were represented and showcased in smaller exhibits within the dedicated Universal Wines area.

"*Hola*, Corvina!" a familiar voice boomed. Corvina spotted her former boss, Vicente. He was wearing a black suit with a white shirt open at the collar. She hadn't forgiven him for firing her yet.

"Hi, Vicente. This is Bryan Lawless," Corvina said when they entered the booth.

"Ah yes, Mr. Lawless, the gentleman you've told me so much about who has helped you in your investigation." Vicente took one of Bryan's hands into his own huge hand and shook it.

"Hi," Bryan replied.

"We believe the person responsible for spreading Philomena is here at Vinexpo," Corvina said.

"I thought the man responsible died in Portugal," Vicente said. He looked confused.

"He did, but he wasn't acting alone," Bryan said.

"Oh no, then the nightmare's not over," Vicente said.

"Not until we stop whoever is behind this," Corvina said.

"The good news is we're going to find whoever was helping Slater and put an end to this," Bryan interjected. "But we better get going. We have a lot of ground to cover." Bryan took the case from her hand and set it next to several unopened boxes of Argentinean malbec.

"Vicente, would it be okay if I left my case here? It's a bottle of wine from a friend."

"Sure, I don't see why not."

Corvina followed Bryan out of the stand and away from Universal Wines and Vicente. She felt guilty for not telling Vicente about her conversation with Sergio earlier that morning.

"Why didn't you let me tell him about Sergio?" Corvina asked, struggling to keep up with Bryan as he led her away.

"Corvina, I know he was your boss, but don't forget he did fire you without hesitating when he was told to by the CEO. We don't know who else is involved in all of this, and I don't know if you should trust Vicente. At least not with something so important," Bryan said.

"You may be right, but I hate to keep him out of the loop. He has always been so good to me," Corvina said, looking over her shoulder.

"Yes, until he fired you. Let's go to the upper level to get a better vantage point," Bryan said.

She followed him as he cleared a path through the inebriated crowds. They skirted the outer perimeter of the exhibition until they found a staircase. She kept a close eye out for Sergio. Once they were higher up, they could make more sense of the exhibition's layout and organization. She looked out onto the exhibition in awe. The space was huge, and the sound of thousands of people talking, clinking glasses, and laughing was almost deafening.

"How are we ever going to find one person in this hive?" Bryan asked.

"I have an idea. Give me your phone." Corvina took out her phone and retrieved the numbers she had taken down from Slater's phone in Portugal, which she hoped was the accomplice's phone number. She leaned over the railing overlooking the ground floor of the exhibition and dialed the second number—Philomena 2—with Bryan's phone.

"Holy chardonnay!" Corvina said as the phone rang in her ear.

"What? Who do you see?" Bryan asked.

"Sergio! He's right there, heading toward us." Corvina pointed between a row of exhibitors. "He's wearing dark jeans, a black shirt, and a navy jacket." She pointed at a man in his midthirties walking through the crowd.

At the same time, Sergio took his phone out of his pocket and answered.

"Hello?" Corvina heard Sergio say. It was him! That confirmed it; Sergio was Slater's accomplice!

"Sergio? Are you sure?" Bryan asked.

"Yes!" She cupped her hand over Bryan's phone so Sergio couldn't hear her. "Do you see him? He's right there." Corvina pointed again at a man of average height and build with close-cropped blond hair, pinched features, and thin lips. His dark eyes cast furtively about as though he were hunting someone or trying to evade detection—or both.

"I see him. Wait, that's Sergio?" Bryan asked in surprise.

"Yes, why? Do you recognize him?" Corvina asked.

"Of course; he and I were on the Champagne Academy course in the same year. But we all called him Serge."

Sergio looked up and saw her and Bryan staring at him. He looked at his phone and then stopped and did a double take when he recognized Bryan's number. He bolted back the way he had come, disappearing into the exhibition. Corvina heard the call disconnect. She passed Bryan's phone back to him.

"We have to catch him!" Corvina shouted, and ran for the stairs.

She looked around in every direction when she reached the lower level.

"Where did he go?" she asked when Bryan caught up with her.

"I don't know. Call Claude. We need help if we're going to find him in this place," Bryan said at her side.

Corvina called Claude and told him that she and Bryan had spotted Sergio and were in pursuit. She ended the call before he could tell her to stay put and leave the hunt to Interpol, as she suspected he would. She scanned the hall for Sergio and saw someone familiar approaching them.

"Is that—" Corvina began asking Bryan.

"Yes, the woman at the vertical tasting in Hong Kong and at the Champagne Academy tasting, Candy Turner," Bryan said.

"I think she saw you. She's coming over," Corvina said.

Candy strode right up to them.

"What a surprise to see you here. But what on earth are you still doing with her, Bryan?" Candy asked, looking at Corvina.

"Hello, Candy, nice to see you again as well," Bryan said. "Candy, this is—"

"Corvina," Corvina said. She didn't offer a hand. "Would love to stay and chat, but we're in a rush," she said, and turned to leave.

"Oh, Corvina, like the grape? How clever," Candy said, her voice dripping with sarcasm.

Corvina stopped and turned back to face Candy.

"Candy, is it? Like an exotic dancer?" Corvina asked.

"I see your taste in women has deteriorated significantly," Candy said to Bryan as her face turned red.

"Not as quickly as the women he's dated," Corvina responded with an appraising look.

Candy's jaw hung open and her entire body tensed. She glared at Corvina.

"Nice seeing you, Candy. We need to go," Bryan said. He took Corvina by the arm and led her away.

"*Meooowww,*" he said when they turned a corner.

"Okay, that was awkward," Corvina said. She was walking fast with Bryan in tow as they both looked for Sergio and tried to converse at the same time. "What on earth happened between the two of you, and why is she such a bitch?"

"We broke up after I was expelled from the Master of Wine program. She didn't take it too well," Bryan said.

"I see that. But was it not because of her that you were expelled?" Corvina pointed out.

"We're both to blame. We shouldn't have been dating when I was a Master of Wine candidate. I put her in an awkward position too. It's lucky that she wasn't expelled as well," Bryan said. "We're on better terms now, I think. She was helping me get another chance at taking the exam to become a Master of Wine."

"Was?"

"She read Malcolm's article and thinks we're accomplices."

"Oh no. In that case, sorry I was such a bitch," Corvina said.

"She deserved it," Bryan said. "But I'll need to make amends later."

"Why don't we split up? We can cover more ground that way and increase our chances of catching Sergio," Corvina suggested. "I'll send you Claude's number. Call him if you see Sergio." She forwarded Claude's contact details to Bryan's phone.

"Okay, got it. Keep in contact," Bryan said, and walked away.

Corvina watched him go and then waded through the crowds, allowing herself to be carried along in the swirling eddy of humanity through the middle of the expo. Keeping an eye out for Sergio, she overheard dozens of conversations. Philomena was featured in many of them.

"Someone in the States will figure out how to stop this Philomena bug. You know that it was American rootstock that saved the world's vineyards from phylloxera the first time," she overheard an American exhibitor boast.

"That's appropriate, given that the aphid originated in America," one of his colleagues laughed.

Corvina tried to avoid all unnecessary conversations and people who didn't match Sergio's physical appearance or wardrobe. She looked for anyone who was running or moving faster than the rest of the crowd, but then she came to the conclusion that Sergio did not have to run. He was in his element. He could blend in better than anyone. As a flying winemaker himself, he could stop at any wine stand and engage in tasting and conversation without raising suspicion or setting off alarms. It was what she would do—blend in and look for who was pursuing her. She moved to the side of the thoroughfare she was on and stopped moving herself. She looked from side to side, searching for anyone who was looking back at her or was not moving at all. Wherever he was, he would now be watching out for her and Bryan.

Then she saw him. He was standing with a group of men clustered around a crescent-shaped counter covered in tasting glasses and wine bottles. He had a glass of wine in his hand, but he was the only one not drinking. His absolute lack of motion had caught her attention. He was smiling but not talking with those around him. She could see he was trying hard to look around without moving.

Suddenly his eyes met hers.

Without acknowledging her or giving any indication he had noticed her at all, he set down his glass of wine with a preternatural calm, turned into the crowd around the stand, and then disappeared from view.

Corvina covered the distance between them in just a few seconds, but he was already gone. She looked around in every direction, but she had lost him. She called Claude.

"Claude, I just saw him. I'm in Hall One, Section C. Where are you?"

"I'm in section D, not far from you. Stay where you are! And stay on the phone. I'm coming to you."

Claude held the phone pressed to his ear and moved as fast as possible through the crowd to find Corvina. He hoped to catch Sergio running away from where Corvina had spotted him.

Claude searched every gait, garment, face, and head of hair that crossed his vision. With thousands of people to check, and so many on the move, it was an almost impossible task. He wished for gait and facial recognition software. He knew Alison was with the exhibition hall security team and would have access to their security camera feeds, but he didn't hold out much hope for her spotting Sergio, even with an eagle eye view. Experience had taught him that attention to detail was not her forte.

"I still don't see him. Could he have doubled back?" he asked Corvina as someone stumbled into him.

"I don't think so. He should be headed right for you."

He finished checking the Italian section of the exhibition, where all of the Italian winemakers and distributors were clustered together, and moved on to the next section, bringing him closer to Corvina's location. When he reached the area dedicated to German and Austrian wines, he stopped suddenly. Half of the attendees had blond hair and were wearing dark clothing. Finding Sergio among them would be an impossible task. He waded into the throng of blond, blue-eyed wine aficionados and tried nevertheless.

"Wait, I see you!" he said into the phone. He could see Corvina over dozens of heads separating them.

"I see you too," Corvina said. "There he is! Do you see him?" Corvina shouted, her voice almost piercing his eardrum.

"Where?" Claude stood as tall as he could and looked to the spot where he last saw Corvina. The moving mass of people passing between them made it difficult to see much of anything.

"I think he went right!"

"Your right or my right?" Claude yelled into the phone. His shouting and pushing past people was earning him a lot of pissed-off looks.

"My right, your left! Look, see him? He's there by the wall!" Claude spun around. He saw Sergio standing next to the wall less than twenty meters from where he stood. He was at the end of one of the main thoroughfares dividing sections A, B, and C from D, E, and F. He wasn't moving.

Something was wrong. Had Sergio turned left, he could have walked straight out of the building and Claude and Corvina would have lost him. Was there some reason he didn't want to go that way? Claude turned around to see what he was avoiding and saw only the exit through the main doors. Then it dawned on him.

Too late.

His realization and the sound of the fire alarm bells crashed into his head simultaneously. He saw Sergio remove his hand from a broken glass fire alarm panel. Seconds later, gallons of cold water poured down onto the crowds from hundreds of fire sprinklers.

"Go around the right, and I'll take the left!" Claude shouted into his phone. He tried to make eye contact with Corvina on the other side of the bolting crowd. "Let's try to cut him off! Don't let him get away! I'll see you at the exit. Don't let him out of your sight, Corvina! We have to catch him before . . . *merde.*" Claude watched helplessly as hundreds of people turned as one toward him and began running for the exit.

The exit only ten meters behind him.

And he was the only obstacle in their path. He braced himself for their impact.

Much of the crowd passed by him easily, but then a cluster of panicked people ran straight into him. Water streamed down their faces, blinding them, and as soon as one of them—tipsy from the wine tasting—fell, Claude felt himself dragged down by a tangled mess of arms and legs. His phone was knocked out of his hand, and someone fell on top of him.

Corvina lost sight of Claude in the crowd, and their call was disconnected.

Sergio disappeared into the throng of stampeding people trying to exit the exhibition hall. It wasn't clear if he had left the building with the crowd or just used their exit as cover to double back and escape another way. After another twenty minutes of fruitless searching, where she visited each level and checked every exit, Corvina returned to the Universal Wines stand. Getting there was easy, since most of the exhibition attendees were now outside. She found Bryan and Claude had arrived at the stand ahead of her. Claude was engrossed in conversation with Vicente, who was sitting down on a box of wine while the back of his head was examined by a paramedic. The sprinklers had been turned off, but everyone was soaking wet.

"What happened?" Corvina cried out, and rushed over to her ex-boss, her residual anger at him momentarily diminished.

"Sergio happened," he said, wincing as the paramedic probed the back of his head.

"Sergio came here?" Corvina asked.

"I was just as surprised to see him and relieved to see he was fine. I asked where he'd been all this time."

"I'm sorry, we should have told you he was here," she said, and cast Bryan a look.

"You knew he was here? Why didn't you tell me?" His wounded look pierced her heart. "I turned around to offer him a glass of wine, and the next thing I know I'm out cold on the floor and the exhibition hall is practically deserted. At first I thought the ringing was just in my head, but then I realized the fire alarms were going off as well. Thank God they've stopped. He hit me over the head with a bottle of wine."

"Why would he do that?" Bryan asked. Corvina could still hear the suspicion in his tone.

"I have no idea," Vicente said.

Corvina looked around the stand. "My case is gone!" she shrieked.

"It was right here." Bryan pointed to the pile of unopened Argentinean malbec where he had set the case down less than an hour ago. He moved several boxes, but the case was gone.

"I didn't see anyone come into this area except for Sergio," Vicente said.

Corvina's stomach lurched at the realization that Sergio must have stolen the case and with it the neurotoxin.

"What was so important in that case?" Claude asked.

"The only way to stop Philomena," Corvina answered.

CHAPTER 43

VINEXPO
PARC DES EXPOSITIONS EXHIBITION CENTER
BORDEAUX, FRANCE

"He's gone," Claude announced to Corvina and Bryan when he returned to the Universal Wines stand. He wanted to trust them, but he had to maintain his objectivity. Two hours had passed since Sergio pulled the fire alarm.

"I've got teams searching the perimeter," he said, "and event security and the local police searched the exhibition top to bottom, but he got out somehow. We did find his jacket and entry badge. He dropped them in a garbage bin on the way out."

"Have you checked the security cameras?" Bryan asked him.

"Alison Pittard is with the exhibition's security team now, reviewing their footage. She just called me to tell me that Sergio was recorded leaving through a side entrance. He was carrying a case as you described."

"How could he have known what was in the case?" Corvina asked. "There's no way he could have known Malcolm would send the neurotoxin to me or that I would have it with me in the case."

"You said he threw away his badge?" Bryan asked Claude.

"Yes. Why does that matter?" Claude asked.

"We can find out where he went during the expo," Bryan said, holding up a scanner. "Every exhibitor has one of these. When someone visits their stand, they get scanned." Bryan picked up a scanner and scanned Corvina's badge to demonstrate. "It allows exhibitors to track the number of visitors they received and also to contact them and send company literature through email after the event."

"I'll call Alison and tell her to get security to identify the stands Sergio visited."

"Do you think he would have let himself get scanned?" Corvina asked.

"He would if he had no reason to believe anyone was looking for him. Not allowing his badge to be scanned would draw attention to himself," Claude said.

Thirty minutes later, Alison Pittard and Secretary General Arsenault joined them at the Universal Wines stand.

"Did you find out which stands Sergio visited?" Corvina asked.

"You don't ask the questions," Alison said to Corvina. She looked to Claude and Arsenault. "Why is she still here?"

"What winery exhibits did he visit, Alison?" Claude asked, ignoring her question about Corvina's presence.

"Aside from Universal Wines, where I understand he stole the only means possible of stopping Philomena"—Alison looked at Corvina—"he visited only five stands." She held up her notepad. "Château Haut-Brion, Château Latour, Château Lafite, Château Mouton Rothschild, and Château Margaux."

"Oh no," Corvina said.

"Fuck me," Bryan said.

"What?" Alison asked.

"Don't you know?" Bryan asked.

"Know what?"

"In the original Classification of 1855 ordered by Napoleon, Bordeaux's châteaus were ranked in importance from first growths to fifth growths. Only five châteaus were ranked as first growths."

"And?"

"Those châteaus you just read out are Bordeaux's only first growths, the Premiers Grands Crus of Bordeaux—your country's top wineries."

"And you think the next target is one of the original five Premiers Grands Crus?" Claude surmised.

"It looks that way," Corvina agreed.

"But which one?" Arsenault asked.

"It could be one or all of them," Bryan said.

"But why would he go to the stands? Why wouldn't he just go to the vineyards and infest them if that's been his plan all along?" Claude asked.

"Maybe he's taunting us. Or maybe he came here to meet someone," Corvina said. "We should split up; each of us goes to one of the five châteaus."

"Absolutely not!" Alison erupted.

"And why not?" Claude asked.

"They," she said, waving toward Corvina and Bryan, "are not Interpol agents."

"Without them, we wouldn't know who was responsible and that he was here in our own backyard about to attack France's most treasured wineries," Claude retorted.

"Sure, sure. I'm still not convinced they're not responsible for this mess," Alison persisted.

"They also know what to look for," Claude addressed Arsenault. "They found Philomena in South Africa this same way, by splitting up and searching separate vineyards."

"I don't care. They're not authorized, and I don't trust them," Alison said.

"Stop! Enough, both of you," Arsenault said. "There are five Premiers Grands Crus vineyards, meaning five possible targets. There are five of us and not enough time to debate this all night."

"With Slater dead, the only way to stop Philomena is to catch Sergio and get that case. I'll go with Alison," Corvina said, surprising everyone. "We'll take Lafite."

"Sure, whatever." Arsenault pinched the bridge of his nose and closed his eyes. "Claude, you take Vicente with you to Château Margaux *and* Château Latour. Corvina goes to Château Lafite with Alison." He pointed at Bryan. "You take Château Haut-Brion, and I'll go to Château Mouton Rothschild. Understood?"

They all nodded.

"Then let's go. The helicopters are on the way," Arsenault said, pointing skyward.

Claude raced Alison up the stairs leading to the roof.

CHAPTER 44

CHÂTEAU LAFITE ROTHSCHILD, PAUILLAC
MÉDOC REGION
BORDEAUX, FRANCE

"Have you visited any vineyards in the last twelve months?"

"Do I look like a farmer to you?" Alison Pittard asked.

Corvina suppressed a laugh. She watched Alison fume and the man she was berating cower. She and Alison had just arrived at Château Lafite Rothschild.

"No, ma'am," the guardsman replied.

Corvina was standing with Alison in the middle of the asphalt road leading to the front gates of Château Lafite Rothschild. She was surrounded by vineyards, men in military fatigues, and armored vehicles. She observed a scrum of reporters and cameramen kept at bay on the side of the road, their vans broadcasting footage of the military positioned around the region's most famous vineyards. The helicopter she had arrived in continued to whip up the air around them as its rotors slowed. She held her bright-yellow scarf with a butterfly motif to her face to protect herself from swirling eddies of dust.

"Now I need you to walk through the chemical solution." The guardsman pointed at a series of gray plastic bins. They were the size used to transport carry-on luggage through x-ray machines at airports. A few centimeters of clear liquid covered the bottom of each bin.

"What on earth are those for? And why would I have to walk through them?" Alison asked in a raised voice. Corvina maintained a neutral gaze. She could feel the empty stare of the cameras on her.

"Madame, you have to walk through the solution to help prevent any potential contamination from the aphid. It's a precaution all vineyards have been instructed to take."

"Wet plastic bins won't stop this bug—I will," Alison said to the hapless guardsman. Corvina watched Alison walk past the bins to avoid getting her shoes wet and march to the gates of Château Lafite Rothschild.

"Miss Pittard?" A man in the uniform of the French military bearing three stripes on each shoulder approached her. He had closely cropped hair with no sideburns and a chubby face to match his tall, portly build. Alison looked up to address him.

"Who are you?" she snapped.

The man flinched. "Ma'am, I'm Sergeant Dupois. I'm in charge here."

"Not anymore. You and your men report to me."

The man looked at Corvina. She shrugged her shoulders in a small gesture. He looked back at Alison. "I'm afraid—"

"Yes, you should be. I represent the Interpol Central Command Centre in Lyon. I've been asked personally by our prime minister to root out and stop this vine-eating menace. He's given Interpol complete authority to bring any and all resources to bear against this threat to our national security."

"I'll have to check on that," Dupois said.

"Get someone else to check. Now show me your defenses," Alison demanded.

Alison marched toward the winery and a parked open-top Jeep. Dupois struggled to keep up. When they reached the Jeep, Alison climbed into the passenger seat without waiting for an invitation. Corvina followed her lead and climbed into the back seat.

"I'm not going to *walk* the entire perimeter," Alison said when the sergeant hesitated.

Sergeant Dupois jumped in and gunned the engine. He drove around the vineyards and pointed out the security measures the military was taking to ensure no one could bring Philomena in to infest the vines. An entire garrison of men was stationed in and around the winery.

"I can assure you they won't get through our defenses," Sergeant Dupois announced with conviction.

"I hope not, for your sake. And make sure the media don't get any closer." Alison pointed to the vans and the men and women from various news outlets.

Corvina turned to look for the source of a faint whirring sound she heard.

On the horizon, she saw a round black object making its way low in the sky for their position. As it neared she could see the circular craft was no more than a few centimeters thick and measured at least a meter in diameter.

"What's that? Is it some kind of surveillance drone? Is it ours?" Alison asked.

"No, ma'am, it's not," Sergeant Dupois answered. He stared at the mysterious approaching object.

The small, mechanized craft flew by a few meters overhead, powered by four horizontal propellers. Aside from the whirring sound it made, it was eerily elegant as it floated over the vineyards. Corvina noticed the media cameras followed its course.

Once over the vineyards, a small white cloud of tiny objects appeared to be emitted from within the drone's body. From this distance they couldn't see what had been released, but Corvina knew what had just happened; the most defended vineyards in France had just been attacked, and the world's most venerated vines were now infested with Philomena.

"Look, there are more!" someone shouted.

Corvina turned to look at the horizon.

More drones could be seen in the distance, approaching the vineyards from all directions. A small, well-spread-out fleet was approaching.

Corvina, Alison, Sergeant Dupois, the military, and a small cluster of the winery's team watched helplessly.

Alison was first to snap out of the shocked silence. She rounded on Sergeant Dupois.

"Stop them!" she screamed.

"How?"

"I don't care how! Just stop them! Blow them out of the sky!"

"You want us to shoot them?" Sergeant Dupois asked. He looked toward the media.

"Yes! I don't care if you have to drive the tanks into the goddamn vineyards. Shoot those drones down. They're almost above the vineyards!" Alison screamed.

Sergeant Dupois turned to his men and commanded them into action.

His men jumped into their tanks and Jeeps and bore down on the vineyards in pursuit of the drones.

"And get some flamethrowers into the infested areas. We'll burn the bugs out!" Alison shouted to a cluster of idle men.

Corvina watched on in horror as Alison Pittard waged a one-woman war on Philomena.

CHAPTER 45

CHÂTEAU LATOUR, PAUILLAC
MÉDOC REGION
BORDEAUX, FRANCE

Claude's stomach lurched as the Interpol helicopter deposited him and Vicente onto the grounds of Château Latour.

Following a shocked and hasty introduction with the winery owner and head winemaker, Claude took Vicente straight to the vineyards and asked him to inspect the health of the leaves on the vines and the rootstock in the ground. He watched as Vicente conducted a quick check up and down several trained rows, revealing nothing but healthy vines and grapes waiting to be converted into some of the world's most revered wine.

"Have you seen anything out of the ordinary lately?" Claude asked the winery owner, who followed at a wary distance.

"Do you mean like the military setting up camp around my vineyards or Interpol flying into my backyard?"

"No, I mean suspicious people around the vineyards perhaps?" Claude asked. He couldn't blame the winemaker for being defensive.

"Tourists and wine lovers are always coming up the drive to take pictures and touch the vines. No one stands out," he said, and shrugged.

"Do you know all these men?" Claude nodded toward the two dozen or so men milling about the property.

"I know them all. They're from town, and most have worked with the winery for years. They want to keep Philomena out as much as you do. I don't know any of the army men." He nodded toward the men in military fatigues positioned around the winery and vineyards. Just meters away, and all around the vineyards and winery, armored vehicles and dozens of men from the French army looked outward for visible signs of the enemy.

Finished with his questions, Claude paced up and down the rows of vines with Vicente. Claude noticed that neither of them was wearing appropriate footwear for being out in the dirt, but neither of them seemed to mind.

"You mobilized the army pretty quickly," Vicente observed.

"They were put into motion days ago. Our prime minister is a forward-thinking individual and understands the critical nature of what's happening. Interpol has the government's full support."

"That's good to hear," Vicente said. After a pause he said, "There seems to be some tension between you and your colleague Alison."

"My boss. Managing upward isn't easy."

"Or downward," Vicente said.

"Corvina seems to have her head on straight," Claude commented.

"For the most part, yes," Vicente said.

"And what about this man Sergio?" Claude asked.

"He was always a handful, but not unmanageable," Vicente said as he massaged the back of his head.

"Any indication he could do something like this?"

"No. He disappeared in Germany a week ago, and we were worried he'd been kidnapped or killed."

"We'll find him."

Vicente didn't reply.

They continued to pace between the rows of vines, their footsteps crunching loudly.

"You should call the others to get an update," Vicente said, breaking the spell of silence.

Claude called Alison at Château Lafite Rothschild.

"Hmm, no answer." He hung up.

"She must be busy checking their defenses," Vicente suggested.

"How do you defend against a bug?" Claude asked, looking around, not seeing the vines for the vineyard.

CHAPTER 46

CHÂTEAU LAFITE ROTHSCHILD, PAUILLAC
MÉDOC REGION
BORDEAUX, FRANCE

Corvina watched helplessly as armored tanks plowed into Château Lafite's vineyards, crushing forty-year-old vines in their path. The tanks tore down trellises as they dragged the vines behind them in their destructive wake. They carved out trails four and a half meters across the Premier Grand Cru terroir.

Soldiers on tanks fired their guns erratically at the drones as they whizzed by overhead. Others bearing flamethrowers torched the vines and the ground they grew in where the aphids had been scattered from above.

To add to the carnage, ominous dark clouds present throughout the evening began pouring fat drops of rain, rendering the scene even more hellacious.

During her destructive wake, Alison's phone rang. Corvina saw Alison look at the screen through the rain and ignore the call.

"Stop this madness! *Tu es fou!*" a man from the winery ran up to Alison screaming. Corvina couldn't agree with him more. Alison looked down on the man from her standing vantage point in the Jeep.

"Arrest this man!" Alison shouted at Sergeant Dupois.

"Miss Pittard," Sergeant Dupois implored, "he's Baron de Rothschild, the head of Château Lafite *Rothschild*."

"I don't care who he is. He's obstructing an Interpol operation, and I want him removed from my sight!"

Corvina kept her head low as the media recorded all of it—the drones, the tanks, the flamethrowers, the burning vines, the handcuffed winery owner screaming in fits of apoplectic rage, straining against his shackles.

Sergeant Dupois held out a satellite phone at arm's length to Alison.

"Can't you see I'm busy?" she shouted at the sergeant.

"He says his name is Secretary General Arsenault and that he's your boss."

Alison took the phone. This time she couldn't ignore the call. What Corvina overheard next was an extremely one-sided, monosyllabic conversation.

The look on Alison's face told Corvina that Alison's assignment to Operation Philomena was over . . . yet Philomena raged on.

CHAPTER 47

CHÂTEAU HAUT-BRION
PESSAC, GRAVES
BORDEAUX, FRANCE

"Corvina, all is quiet here," Bryan answered his phone when he saw her name come up on his screen. "How is Château Lafite?" he asked. He shielded his eyes from the sun and looked out onto the planted rows of vines stretching into the distance. It was eerily quiet, and he saw no signs of disturbance, Sergio, or Philomena.

"Unfortunately, Château Lafite was attacked," Corvina said.

"Oh no! How do you mean *attacked*? Did they catch Sergio?" Bryan asked.

"No. In fact, we didn't even see him."

"How are we going to find him now? He still has the neurotoxin," Bryan said.

"I honestly don't know."

"Are you and Alison okay?"

"Alison and I are fine. The vineyards are not. Sergio, or whoever's responsible, used mini-drones to drop the aphids onto the vineyards from the air," Corvina said.

"Drones? Wow, that explains how the aphids were spread without being detected. Was Alison not able to stop them?"

"No," Corvina said. She recounted the incident initiated by Alison Pittard.

"I knew she was unstable, but that's outrageous," Bryan said. He reeled at the thought of French tanks rolling through Pauillac's Premier Grand Crus vineyards. "Secretary General Arsenault should have kept better track of her, and on a short leash," Bryan said.

Corvina went silent.

"Corvina? I meant no offense. I don't propose we put a leash on her, or any other woman for that matter." Bryan stumbled over his words.

"Wait a second, Bryan . . . you're a genius!" Corvina exclaimed into the phone.

"Really? You think a leash is a good idea?" he asked, confused.

"No, of course not. I'm talking about a tracker," Corvina said.

"I don't think the secretary general would approve of putting a tracker on her either," Bryan said.

"I'm not talking about Alison. I know how we can find Sergio!" Bryan listened to Corvina's idea, and his excitement grew to match hers. It was a brilliant idea; he just wished he had thought of it.

CHAPTER 48

BATTERSEA
LONDON, ENGLAND

"Wine is like music," Max Perfetto said to the pretty blonde sommelier on the opposite side of the breakfast bar in his apartment.

Following the counterfeit wine incident at the auction house came the swift departure of his girlfriend, leaving him time to pursue women unfamiliar with his downfall.

Max kept glancing at his guest leaning on the counter separating his living room and kitchen. She wore a tight pink cotton top and a floral pattern skirt and had removed her high heels when she arrived. Her hair was tied back in a ponytail, and her face was only lightly made up. She was in her midtwenties and hung on his every word.

Max was cooking dinner for the two of them, trying hard not to stare at her cleavage.

"I bet you say that to all the girls," she said in an Eastern European accent. She smiled the same smile that had caught his attention in the boutique hotel, where she worked in a one Michelin star restaurant.

"You wound me," Max protested with mock indignation. To be fair, she was absolutely right; he did say the same thing to all the girls he invited over, precisely because it worked. Nine times out of ten, his scripted evening resulted in a hasty retreat to the bedroom following dessert or, as sometimes happened, complete removal of each other's clothing on the sofa during dessert. Something about a Niagara ice wine seemed to uncork a woman's inhibitions, he found.

"Allow me to continue. Like music, wine is infinite in its variety and manifestations. It plays a central role in history, is global, ubiquitous, and appeals to a myriad of tastes." Max opened the fridge. While his back was turned, he fished the woman's business card out of his front pocket to recall her name: Julie!

He fetched a well-chilled bottle of Bollinger 2002 R.D., a bottle saved for just such an occasion as the wanton seduction of a nubile sommelier. It was hardly an 1899 Château Lafite, but it would suffice for the purpose on hand. Where had Bryan taken the bottle of Lafite? And how did he know the beautiful woman from Universal Wines?

Max held the bottle up for Julie to see its label.

"Oooooh, nice! You know the way to a girl's heart," she said.

Yes, among other parts, he thought.

He peeled the foil and twisted the metal cage off the neck of the bottle.

"Short of a trained and experienced sommelier, such as yourself"—he winked at the blonde—"or a Master of Wine, such as yours truly, there are few individuals who can claim to be an expert on wine, just as there are few experts on all genres of music." Max twisted the cork and eased it out of the bottle. Its departure emitted a whispered *pssst.*

"Bravo!" Julie clapped.

"Like music," he continued as he poured the champagne into two Riedel champagne flutes, "wine should be discovered organically and through a process of vini-discovery."

Max slid a champagne glass over to her side of the counter. He held his glass up to the light.

"Beautiful color." Julie appraised her glass.

"Cheers to wine!" he exclaimed.

"Cheers to us!" Julie toasted back.

Much too easy. Where was the challenge? Max thought. He brought the glass up to his nose to inhale its freshly disgorged aromas. My God, that smells like sex!

"No longer is wine to be deified and made mysterious. Gone are the leather-bound tomes of Old World wine lists organized by unpronounceable regions and villages classified by centuries-old despots. Wine lists and labels, like their contemporary producers, are finally progressive and designed to educate and facilitate the ordering and enjoyment of wine. Long live the democratization of wine!"

"Cheers to that!" Julie giggled. She took her first drink of the vintage nectar.

"So whether you like jazz, classical, blues, or funky house music, I say enjoy what you like—and the same goes for wine," Max said with a flourish. He noted with satisfaction the gleam in the young woman's eyes.

"Dinner will be ready in just a few minutes," Max said. He glanced at the timer on the oven door. Inside was the salmon he'd prepared.

"Oooooh, I can't wait," Julie said.

"The best things are worth waiting for."

"I agree," Julie said. She straightened up, depriving Max of the sight of her cleavage.

Though he knew they were both alluding to the wine, they had entered the delightful realm of double entendres.

At that moment, someone banged on the front door.

Max looked up sharply.

"Expecting another sommelier?" Julie asked, and laughed.

"No, I'm not expecting anyone." Max looked at the door, confused. He came out of the kitchen and crossed the living room to open the door.

Standing on his doorstep were three of the biggest, scariest men Max had ever seen. He took an involuntary step back.

"We're with London's Interpol Incident Response Team, or IRT," the tallest of the three men said. "Are you Max Perfetto?" he asked in a heavy Yorkshire accent. Like his two counterparts, he was dressed in black from neck to toe.

"Yes," Max heard himself say, staring at the semiautomatic guns strapped across each man's chest.

"You work at Crosbie's Auction House here in London?"

"Well, I'm based out in Hounslow these days—"

"Answer the question!"

"Yes," Max said, swallowing.

"Did you recently give away a bottle of 1899 Château Lafite?"

Oh shit.

"Yes." Max felt his knees go weak.

"Good, come with us. Interpol requires your assistance in an investigation."

Before he could protest, the man took the glass of champagne out of Max's hand and passed it to Julie.

"Good evening, ma'am."

Max was led out his own front door surrounded by the three Interpol agents.

Julie was left standing in the middle of the living room holding the two glasses of exceptional champagne.

"How did you know about the bottle of wine?" Max asked as he was all but carried down the stairs and pushed into the waiting SUV outside.

"Your friend Bryan told us," the IRT leader said. He jumped in beside him and slammed the door shut. The smell of leather and after-shave overwhelmed Max's olfactory senses. He searched frantically for his seat belt in the dark interior of the SUV as it shot forward into the night.

CHAPTER 49

CORONATION CITY, CITY OF CHAMPAGNE
REIMS, CHAMPAGNE, FRANCE

Corvina leapt out of the TGV train as soon as it came to a complete stop and the doors opened. Her butterfly-covered scarf fluttered behind her, and Bryan jumped down beside her. Vicente stepped out and followed them along the platform. It was dark outside, and passenger traffic was light.

She was relieved that they had finally arrived in the city of Reims, Champagne, home to many of the world's most recognized and best Grande Marque Champagnes: Ruinart, Krug, Lanson, Veuve Clicquot, Taittinger, G.H. Mumm, Piper-Heidsieck, Charles Heidsieck, and Pommery.

Once Interpol in London had tracked the briefcase from Crosbie's to Champagne, Corvina was annoyed to hear that Claude and Arsenault agreed that it was getting too dangerous to allow the civilians to continue the pursuit with the Interpol teams. Corvina disagreed with their decision and took the fastest means at her disposal to get to Champagne—the TGV train, or *Train à Grande Vitesse,* one of the world's fastest trains.

"We have to find Claude and his team," Corvina said to the others on the platform. "They should have Sergio's exact location from the GPS tracker in the briefcase he stole. We have to assume he's come to Champagne to spread Philomena over the vineyards of Reims like he did in Bordeaux."

"We have to stop him," Bryan said.

"Not only stop him but also recover the only means to destroy Philomena from that briefcase," she said. She had shared what she knew with Vicente on the train ride to Reims.

They exited the train station onto Louis Roederer Boulevard.

"Now where?" Vicente asked. It was the first time he had spoken for some time. Corvina could only imagine what was going through his mind following Sergio's sudden reappearance and attack. It was a lot to process.

"There's a major intersection where the city's Champagne houses converge," Bryan said. "I suggest we go there."

She heard Bryan direct the driver to take them to place du Général Gouraud as they piled into a taxi outside the train station.

The taxi sped off.

A few minutes later, three police cars raced past them.

"It looks like we're going the right way," Vicente said.

"Follow those cars!" Bryan cried out in French to the taxi driver.

In the midst of the pursuit, Corvina's phone rang. The screen told her it was her father.

"Papà, we found a way to stop the phylloxera!" Corvina said when she answered.

"*Meno male*," her father said with evident relief in his voice.

"I'll get it to you as soon as I can. I've been tied up with work in France. The important thing is we won't have to pull all the vines."

"We'll still get a good harvest yet, but I told you it wouldn't be our best vintage. Not even close."

"What *was* your best vintage, Papà?" Corvina asked, unaware he compared them or had a favorite.

"The one I made two years after I met your mother."

"I didn't know you made a wine that year," Corvina said after a pause. She watched the unfamiliar city flash by outside.

"I didn't. That was the year you were born."

Corvina's vision blurred. She tried in vain to hold back her tears but failed miserably. She dabbed the corner of her eyes with her scarf.

"Dad, I have to go. *Ti amo*," she said, and hung up.

"Everything okay?" Bryan asked.

"*Sí*, great, thanks," Corvina said. She looked out the side window so Bryan couldn't see her tears.

Bryan asked the taxi to drop them off on Henry Vasnier Boulevard at the main gates of Pommery Champagne, where the police cars had stopped and set up a perimeter sealing off place du Général Gouraud. Beyond the gates up a long paved drive punctuated by tall white flagpoles sat the main brick building of Pommery. The outer façade of the three-storied building was flanked by two red-and-white brick turrets. She thought it looked like a fairy-tale castle.

At the entrance, the tall, black wrought iron gates were secured, and no one manned the guardhouse to the side.

"How will we get in?" Vicente asked.

Before Corvina could answer him, a convoy of military vehicles converged on the intersection of place du Général Gouraud, all aimed at the black wrought iron gates of Pommery.

She watched the lead vehicle, a military Humvee, drive at full speed through the gates, tearing them off their hinges and creating a fifteen-foot gap for the rest of the convoy to drive through. Mainly made up of personnel carriers, the fleet of trucks rumbled past. Corvina cringed at the dramatic entry and stared in awe at the massive amount of men and hardware thundering past.

"Claude wasn't kidding when he said the prime minister took the threat of Philomena seriously," Bryan said.

"Given that the vineyards in Bordeaux were so easily infested, I can see why they don't want to take any chances," Vicente said. "Don't forget that Champagne is also a UNESCO World Heritage site. It's not just French vineyards under attack but France's national identity and cultural heritage."

Corvina watched as several black sedans with tinted windows followed the convoy into the grounds of Pommery Champagne.

"Let's go," Corvina said. She jogged up the drive after the convoy.

"What the hell are you doing here?" Corvina heard Alison Pittard shout at her the moment she entered the massive hangar-like building that made up the reception hall of Pommery. It was currently being set up as the staging area for the military and Interpol Incident Response Teams. Corvina noticed the place was a hive of activity.

To add to the surreal nature of military personnel racing about the space, she saw that the reception hall also served as a gallery. On display was a giant cask, a mini BMW with a wicker basket affixed to the back, and a life-sized sculpture of an elephant balancing on its trunk.

"You wouldn't be here if it wasn't for us," Bryan said from Corvina's side.

"You really shouldn't be here," Claude said. He was busy donning a black flak jacket.

"I thought I made that clear," Alison added.

Corvina ignored Alison. "Where is Sergio now?"

"According to the tracking device in the case he stole from you, and our team's assessment in London, it seems like he went down there." Claude pointed to an opening at the far end of the room. It was a door leading onto a set of wide stone steps. Several men with weapons stood guard at the entrance. To the left, Corvina spotted a white cloth draped over what looked like a body.

"Is that . . . ?" she began to ask.

"Sergio's first human victim," Claude said. "It appears he killed an employee to gain access to the cellars. Intentional or not, this is now a manhunt for a killer."

"Oh no, Sergio, what have you done?" Corvina asked softly. What had driven him to such a desperate act?

"What's down there?" Vicente asked. Corvina saw him staring at the entrance to the cellar next to the body. He looked as pale as a pinot grigio.

"One hundred sixteen stone steps leading to a maze of chalk tunnels and cellars," Bryan said. Corvina was impressed at his apparent knowledge of the cellars.

"So the tracker is working?" Corvina asked Claude as she followed him across the reception hall to a bar and tasting area normally reserved for tourists and champagne aficionados. She wanted to put as much physical distance between herself and the dead Pommery employee as she could. The bar now served as Interpol's mobile central command station and staging area for Operation Philomena. Dozens of tables and chairs were occupied by Interpol agents poring over maps and hastily set up monitors. Everyone was focused and working to track and apprehend Sergio and put an end to the spread of Philomena.

"Yes, with the help of Bryan's contact, Max at Crosbie's Auction House, our team in London was able to pinpoint the signal the GPS tracker was emitting. Unfortunately, he had a sizable lead on us. Even with the helicopters and rapid on-site mobilization, he was able to get down into the cellars before we arrived."

"There must be another way out of the tunnels," Corvina commented as she looked at the large, crescent-shaped doorway leading deep down into Pommery's kilometers of chalk tunnels. She had never been down inside Pommery's cellars.

"There are, and they're all being placed under heavy guard, as are the skylights positioned over the top of each chalk pit."

"How many chalk pits are there?" Vicente asked.

"A lot." Claude pointed at a map of the surrounding area. Dozens of yellow *x*'s marked the locations of each of Pommery's chalk pits.

"And they're all connected?" Corvina asked, studying the yellow markers.

"Yes, each shaft is linked by a tunnel, creating an ancient network of stable, humid, and temperature-controlled cellars, ideal for storing champagne," Bryan said, again demonstrating his knowledge of the cellars.

An Interpol agent jogged up to the desk where Claude, Corvina, Bryan, and Vicente were examining the map.

"Sir, the outer perimeter is secure and local law enforcement has the roadblocks up, but you should know that there are a lot of civilians gathering outside."

"Who are they?" Claude asked.

"They appear to be mainly Pommery employees, residents of the area, winemakers, grape growers, champagne producers—all locals from what we can see," the soldier summarized.

"What's their mood?"

"Peaceful so far. Mainly curious. The media coverage is broadcasting our location and military presence, so their mood could change. We may attract troublemakers."

"We'll deal with them if and when they come. Update me every ten minutes."

"Yes, sir."

"Just keep them under control and outside. The last thing we want is another incident like we had at Lafite." Corvina saw Claude glance at Alison Pittard, who was sitting at a table studying a monitor.

At that moment, Secretary General Arsenault came over and Alison joined them.

"Claude, are you and your Incident Response Team ready to go down?" Arsenault asked. He glanced at Corvina in surprise and annoyance.

"Yes, sir," Claude answered.

"Good, then get going. Alison, you continue to liaise with the IRT in London to make sure we don't lose track of that case. Keep me updated on every move it makes. And don't, under any circumstance, deliver any operational instructions. All commands will come from Claude in the tunnels or from me in this staging area. The only reason you're still involved is that I need every resource I can use at my disposal. I'll deal with your actions in the vineyard when this is all over. Understood?"

"*Oui*, Secretary General," Alison said.

"I'm disappointed the three of you are here, but since you are, maybe you can help me understand what the terrorist's next move might be. You," he said, and pointed to Vicente, "come with me."

"What about us?" Corvina asked.

"Stay out of the way," Arsenault replied brusquely, and left with Alison and Vicente at his side.

"I have to go," Claude said to her.

"How can we help?" Corvina pleaded. Was this the end of their involvement, after all of the work she and Bryan had put in and after all of the discoveries they had made?

"Do as the secretary general instructed. Stay put and wait for us to catch Sergio," Claude said.

"And if you don't catch him?" Bryan asked.

"We can't risk Sergio getting away," Corvina added. "He has the only means to stop Philomena."

"Which you lost," Claude said.

"You know damn well what happened," Corvina bit back.

"Claude, if Sergio escapes, all is lost," Bryan interjected to defuse the mounting tension between her and Claude. "There won't be enough time to develop a new neurotoxin to save the infested vineyards."

"I understand that. That's why I have to go now." Claude turned to go but looked over his shoulder and called back to them, "Don't move."

"Come with me. I have an idea." Bryan grabbed her hand and led her out of Pommery's packed reception hall as soon as Claude reached the other side of the room to join his Incident Response Team.

"Where are we going? We need to get down into the cellars!" she protested.

"I know another way," Bryan said. She chased him down the drive back to the main gates and the intersection of place du Général Gouraud.

Bryan turned right, went past the gates, and ran a short distance up Rue des Crayéres while she struggled to keep up. Roadblocks were being set up around the intersection, and a small crowd of curious onlookers gathered around them. She could see other people converging on the intersection to see what was happening.

"Where are you taking me? We have to get into the cellars to find Sergio!" she shouted over the sound of all the vehicles and commotion.

"We can get in that way!" Bryan answered her. He pointed to a large dark-blue sign ahead and to their left that read Champagne Charles Heidsieck.

"But that's a different Champagne house. We won't be able to get to Pommery's cellars that way. They're not connected," Corvina shouted back at him.

"Of course they are," Bryan said as if she had suggested wine didn't come from grapes.

"What?" Corvina stopped dead in her tracks.

"All of the cellars are connected underground. The connections are never shown to the public, of course. They're kept hidden and locked. Remember, this whole area was occupied by Nazi forces during World War II. The French Resistance was active in Champagne. The extensive network of chalk cellars and tunnels running under the entire city enabled them to strike in one part of the city and disappear only to reemerge on the other side of the city."

"Okay, but how do you even propose to get inside in the first place?" Corvina asked. She inspected the formidable-looking door set in the even more formidable-looking stone wall. It looked impregnable.

"That's more complicated," Bryan said, and made a call on his phone. She heard him speaking French to whoever had answered his call.

No more than five minutes passed when Corvina saw someone approaching them on the sidewalk a block away. The woman was strikingly tall, had long, dark hair tied back in a ponytail, and despite wearing only a pair of narrow rectangular framed glasses, a light-blue nightgown, and pink running shoes, Corvina noticed she walked with poise and had an air of dignity about her.

"Is that a woman in a nightgown?" Corvina asked.

"Shhhh! That's who I just called," Bryan whispered.

"Who is she?" Corvina asked. She couldn't take her eyes off the apparition sashaying toward them. Corvina could see she was in her midfifties and beautiful.

"She's the brand ambassador for Charles Heidsieck. Her daughter flirted with me nonstop when I was on the Champagne Academy course."

"She must be twice your age," Corvina whispered from the side of her mouth since the woman in question was within earshot.

"I said her daughter, not her. That aside, we get on well and meet up whenever she's in London or I'm in Champagne," Bryan said, and shrugged his shoulders.

Corvina was stunned when Marie-Claire slapped Bryan in the face.

"Ow! What was that for?" Bryan asked.

"That was for breaking my daughter's heart." The woman spoke crisply with a French accent.

"Your daughter was seventeen when we met! And nothing happened," Bryan exclaimed.

"Her heart was no less broken. To this day she still pines over you. Now tell me again what you want?"

"We need to get into your cellars . . ."

"See"—Marie-Claire turned to Corvina—"that's how he talks to all the ladies of Champagne. No wonder my daughter fell for him."

"Marie-Claire, perhaps now is not the time. We really need to go. Can you help us?"

"Bryan, Bryan, Bryan. Only you would call me in the middle of the night to ask for a private tour of our cellars. Good thing I live just around the corner."

"Thank you, Marie-Claire," he said.

She smiled, and they hugged like two friends who hadn't seen each other for a long time.

"May I introduce you to Corvina?"

"You're lucky I heard the phone," Marie-Claire said to Bryan as she shook Corvina's hand. She used a key to open the blue wooden door they were standing next to and let them through. She followed them in and locked the door behind her.

"I'm sorry, were you sleeping?" Bryan asked.

"No, ha ha, more like passed out. Here, follow me," Marie-Claire said.

Corvina gave Bryan a surprised look. This was the woman they were relying on to get them into the Pommery cellars?

Marie-Claire led them along a paved walkway past a modern building with high glass windows. "I opened several vintage bottles for a visiting Canadian dignitary and his Brazilian mistress this morning, and we ended up drinking over a bottle each." Marie-Claire burst out laughing and stopped just as suddenly and raised a hand to her head. "Oh, killer headache."

"Are you alright?" Corvina asked with concern.

"Yes, yes, fine—just getting too old for that kind of nonsense," Marie-Claire said.

They stopped at another door, this one standing in the middle of a grassy area and backing onto a small structure set into the surrounding area made up of trees and tall grass. Marie-Claire used the same set of keys to unlock the door. She pushed the door inward and reached out for the doorjamb to steady herself as she lost her balance.

"Oopsy," Marie-Claire said, and laughed. Corvina reached out to steady her.

Beyond the open door, it was pitch black inside.

"Where are we going?" Corvina asked with concern in her voice.

"Down," Marie-Claire replied. She reached inside the doorway and flicked a switch, illuminating a narrow metal staircase spiraling deep into the ground.

"Marie-Claire, please be careful," Corvina said when she saw the spiral staircase; she fretted over the woman's ability to navigate the tight stairwell while inebriated and wearing a long nightgown.

"Don't be silly, dear. Follow me. Bryan, this one is adorable. And much more age appropriate," Marie-Claire said, and stepped through the doorway. Corvina went next, followed by Bryan.

On the way down, Bryan explained to Marie-Claire what was happening at Pommery and that their true purpose for calling her was to gain access to Pommery via Charles Heidsieck's cellars.

"*Et voilá,* this is all connected to Philomena. I must say, it sounds like something Alexandre Dumas would write about," Marie-Claire said.

Corvina counted over a hundred steps in their descent and shivered at the rapid drop in temperature. She adjusted her scarf to keep her neck warm. It was cold once they reached the bottom. Marie-Claire led them through a tunnel carved out of the chalk into a space that opened upward.

Corvina looked straight up.

They were standing at the bottom of a Roman chalk pit.

Looking up was like standing inside a small pyramid and looking out a skylight at the top. She could see the stars through the glass that covered the top of the pit at ground level, which prevented anyone from falling in.

"Wow, this is incredible," Corvina said, marveling at the space around her.

"And it's just one of hundreds in the area. The Romans were ambitious in their building works," Marie-Claire said.

"Bryan tells me that the Champagne house tunnels are interconnected," Corvina said.

"Yes," Marie-Claire said. "The most unique is the passage between Pommery and Veuve Clicquot. To pass from one to the other you have to find the staircase for the blind—the upside-down staircase."

"Upside-down?" Corvina asked. "Sounds like an Escher drawing," she said, referring to the famous Dutch artist of impossible architecture.

"The upside-down staircase is carved into the ceiling above a normal staircase. It was created by the monks who used the cellars. Because they had no natural or electric light back then and candle and torch light wasn't always sufficient, they carved a mirror-image staircase into the ceiling of the normal staircase so that they could count the steps with their hands above their heads before taking the next step. This made it easier to tell when the stairs ended and, in some cases, when they changed direction. Great for climbing in the dark."

"And the link between Charles Heidsieck, where we are now, to Pommery's cellars is similar?" Corvina asked.

"Same, but different."

Marie-Claire led them down another wide chalk tunnel. White fluorescent tube lights spaced every five meters lit the way. They walked for over five minutes in silence.

As they moved through the tunnels, Corvina noticed several faint red crosses painted on the tunnel walls.

"What's that?" she asked Marie-Claire, pointing at one of the crosses.

"The tunnels were used during both world wars to transport the wounded to hospitals. The routes were, and still are, marked by red crosses."

"So if someone needed help, they would just follow the red crosses?" Corvina asked.

"Exactly. Now enough with the history lesson. Keep moving. We're almost there."

Moments later, Marie-Claire stopped at the foot of a staircase. Unlike a regular staircase that began level with the ground, Corvina saw the peculiar staircase in front of them started one meter off the floor. The first step was substantial.

"This is the way into Pommery," Marie-Claire said.

Corvina peered up the staircase and was surprised to see a cage door shut across the staircase about ten meters up. The staircase continued beyond the cage door into darkness.

"Is the gate locked?" Corvina asked, looking up the dark staircase.

"Yes, but don't worry about the gate," Marie-Claire said. She reached out for Corvina's scarf and adjusted it, carefully patting it into place.

"Why? Do you have a key?" Corvina asked.

"Where you're going, you won't need a key."

CHAPTER 50

POMMERY CELLARS
REIMS, CHAMPAGNE, FRANCE

Claude led the eight members of the Interpol Incident Response Team—elite men and women trained in special weapons and tactics—down the 116 stone steps deep into the bowels of Pommery Champagne's chalk cellars.

The pounding of his team's feet as they descended the stairs echoed loudly off the walls and ceiling that curved around them and carried down the long tunnel ahead. Long fluorescent tube lights behind plastic covers, yellowed with age, lit the way down the staircase and into the tunnel beyond.

The temperature dropped as he descended. It was just ten degrees Celsius when he reached the bottom of the stairs. The humidity was 98 percent.

He heard French café songs playing in the background, piped through ceiling-mounted speakers for the benefit of tourists. He crinkled his nose as he smelled and tasted the humid air flavored by the scent of aging wine and stagnant tunnel air.

"Alison, where is he headed?" Claude spoke into his mic. His plan to capture Sergio was simple. Alison remained topside to monitor the movements of the tracker in the case Sergio carried, and she would relay the movements to Claude in the cellars. The only problem with the plan was it was *too* simple. There had not been enough time to properly map the cellar tunnels or gauge how many possible escape routes Sergio could use. That and Claude had to rely on Alison to guide him. He brought the IRT members with him in the hopes that they could split up and cover more ground. Now that he was in the cellars, he saw firsthand how impractical that would be. The members of his team could end up getting lost in the labyrinth underneath the Pommery Champagne House.

"He's due north of you and on the move," Alison's voice came through his earpiece.

"Copy that. If you can find someone to turn off the music down here, that would be helpful. I love Edith Piaf but . . ."

"Let me check." Her acquiescence surprised him.

He jogged the IRT past large bas-relief carvings of Bacchus in the chalk walls as well as offshoot tunnels where aging champagne was stored in magnums piled fifteen bottles high and forty bottles across. Thousands of dust-coated bottles stretched back into the side tunnels as far back as thirty meters.

As they raced north, the tunnels and cellars seemed endless. Claude masked his labored breathing and kept his communication with Alison to a minimum. Months of relative inactivity behind a desk and his passion for canelés were catching up to him.

He silently thanked the technology, both the tracker and the communication devices, that would lead them right to their target.

Even *with* the technology, tracking Sergio through 120 Roman-dug chalk pits connected by eighteen kilometers of cellars would be no easy feat. What concerned him more, though, was that they did not know what Sergio's endgame was.

The vines in Champagne's vineyards were all at ground level. If he was going to spread Philomena using drones again, why had he gone underground?

CHAPTER 51

CHARLES HEIDSIECK
REIMS, CHAMPAGNE, FRANCE

“Up you go!” Bryan allowed Corvina to use his clasped hands as a stirrup and lifted her leg onto the staircase. Corvina clambered onto the first step and entered the stairwell. She turned around when she was three steps up.

“Well, that was graceful,” she said from above him.

“Lucky for you, I work out,” he said. He placed his palms flat onto the first step and hoisted himself up behind her. Once his feet were off the ground, he brought his right leg up onto the step.

“What’s that supposed to mean?” Corvina asked.

“You’re not as light as you look.” He took Corvina’s extended hand until he could bring himself to a standing position beside her.

“Not as light as I—”

“Okay, good luck, you two,” Marie-Claire interrupted them. “The door we came through upstairs can be opened from the inside, and I’ll leave the lights on in case you decide to come back this way. Call me if you need me. I’m going back to bed. Try not to kill each other before saving the world.”

“Thanks, Marie-Claire,” Bryan said.

“She’s a strange woman,” Corvina turned to Bryan and said once Marie-Claire was out of sight. “Now let’s go find that case.”

Corvina went first. She climbed the staircase.

Bryan looked ahead at the gate and hoped it wasn’t locked.

"What do you think she meant when she said we wouldn't need a key?" Corvina asked.

"I don't know, but we'll find out soon enough."

Halfway between the start of the stairs and the gate, Corvina came to a sudden stop.

"What's wrong?" Bryan asked from a few steps behind.

"Wait there," Corvina said as she looked back at Bryan.

"Okay, want to tell me why?"

"Just watch," Corvina said. She turned back toward the gate and continued climbing the staircase.

Bryan watched as she climbed, wondering what he was meant to see. Suddenly Corvina began disappearing step-by-step as she walked farther away. Then she was gone, as though the stairs had swallowed her up.

"Corvina?" Bryan shouted after her. He ran up the steps and saw what she had discovered.

Halfway up the staircase, the steps went down, revealing another staircase, yet only a meter up and farther away. The staircase leading to the gate above continued upward.

From the entrance to the staircase, the hidden staircase was a masterful trompe l'oeil. Standing from below, it was impossible to see the descending staircase.

"This is genius," Bryan said when he saw the staircase within a staircase and Corvina walking down its steps.

"It's a clever way to hide the entrance to the connecting tunnel," Corvina said.

"Absolutely incredible."

"Let's just hope Sergio isn't familiar with it," Corvina said.

"That's what I'm worried about. Remember, Sergio was on the Champagne Academy course with me," Bryan said. He followed Corvina into the darkness, knowing that somewhere in the miles of chalk tunnels weaving deep underneath the country's twelfth largest city, Sergio and the only means of stopping Philomena were still on the loose.

CHAPTER 52

POMMERY CELLARS
REIMS, CHAMPAGNE, FRANCE

Claude jogged through a narrow tunnel connecting two larger tunnels in pursuit of Sergio. He felt like they were chasing a phantom. He could hear his team in lockstep behind him in the five-meter-wide tunnel as they followed his lead.

It quickly became apparent how difficult finding Sergio would be since Alison didn't have a map to the tunnels. She could tell him where Sergio was in relation to the IRT group, who was equally geotagged, but she couldn't see the maze of tunnels Claude was running through. At one point, Sergio was less than a hundred meters ahead; however, the space between them was made up of solid chalk, leaving Claude to find his way around the tunnels to Sergio's location. In their haste to pursue Sergio, no one realized just how deep and long the tunnel systems extended under Champagne.

Claude maintained constant communication with Alison as they tracked their quarry.

So far the signal from the case Sergio carried remained strong, though Claude worried how long it would last. After all, they were thirty meters underground surrounded by thick, damp chalk walls.

"Hold on a second," Alison said into Claude's ear.

A full minute passed while Claude held his team once they emerged into the next large tunnel. The café songs had receded into the distance long ago. Claude and his team were beyond where tourists and visitors were permitted to wander.

"Alison, what's going on?" Claude asked.

"Secretary General Arsenault just told me there's a mob of workers from the winery outside and it's getting bigger. They must have heard about our entrance."

"Are they causing any problems?"

"Not yet, but he wants us out of here as soon as possible before they do."

"Well, we're trying, aren't we!" he shouted into his mic, immediately regretting his outburst. He took a deep breath. "Can you see where Sergio is now?"

"Go straight, and hurry. The signal is getting weaker the deeper he goes into the tunnels."

Once Alison stopped talking, Claude heard the faint sound of running footsteps echo through the tunnel system.

Claude held up his hand in a fist. The Incident Response Team behind him stopped immediately.

Because of the sheer number and length of tunnels, it was almost impossible to tell where the footsteps were coming from.

A lone person came running out of a side tunnel ahead.

"Is it him? Is it Sergio?" one of the IRT members whispered as they all raised their weapons.

The figure turned left and ran right toward them.

"Hold your fire," Claude instructed. He could see the person wasn't their target. He wasn't armed or carrying a case. His team relaxed their grips but didn't lower their weapons. A man in his thirties wearing civilian clothes ran by, looking at them in surprise.

"Sir, shall we pursue?" the man next to Claude asked.

"No, our target is Sergio and that case. That was probably just a member of the Pommery staff."

As if to intentionally contradict him, dozens more people came running around the corner straight at them. Were these the winery workers Alison had told him about gathering outside? How did they get past the Interpol men and women upstairs?

The team tensed.

"Sir?" the man directly behind him asked.

"Hold your fire. I repeat, do not fire!" Claude instructed his team as over a dozen men ran past them. "Safeties on. Those were civilians, winery workers, I think. Be ready for anything." Claude resumed in the direction they were heading according to Alison's last transmission.

The manhunt had just become immeasurably more complex.

"Claude, can you hear me?" Alison's voice crackled in his ear.

"Yes."

"There's been another development up here."

"What happened now?"

"Vicente is gone," Alison said.

"What do you mean he's gone?" Claude asked over the radio.

"A group of the winery's workers rushed in, and now he's just disappeared," Alison said, her voice crackling.

"Find him. I can't have civilians messing up this operation," Claude said, wondering how the evening could get any worse yet confident that somehow it would.

CHAPTER 53

CHARLES HEIDSIECK
REIMS, CHAMPAGNE, FRANCE

"Whoever built this tunnel certainly didn't have comfort in mind," Corvina heard Bryan say from behind her. She searched ahead, but the tunnel appeared to have no end in sight.

"It was built by monks—what do you expect? The floor is uneven, and the ceiling is too low," Corvina said from her stooped position in front as she led the way through the hidden passage that connected Charles Heidsieck's chalk tunnels to Pommery's.

"How far do you think it goes?" Bryan asked.

"I have no idea. I can't see any light ahead. I guess we keep going." Corvina wrapped her scarf around her neck and used the flashlight on her cell phone to light the way. With her other hand, she felt the walls and ceiling around her to keep her balance and guide her.

"If the entrance into Pommery is similar to the stairs we took from Charles Heidsieck, then we won't see light until we're right on top of them. Watch out for that first step," Bryan said.

"I'm keeping a close eye on the ground. I don't want to step into a giant hole," she said. Her phone's screen went dark.

"Hey, turn the light back on," Bryan said from behind her in the darkness.

"Hold on," Corvina said. She tried a few more times to power up her phone.

"My battery died. Pass me your phone," Corvina said. She pocketed her own.

She reached behind her like a relay sprinter reaching for a baton. She felt Bryan place his phone into her palm.

"Here you go," Bryan said.

"Thanks," Corvina replied. Guided by the new light, she continued through the narrow tunnel.

"What will you do when we catch Sergio?" Bryan asked.

"Turn him over to Claude. But I have no problem with you interrogating him first if you want," she said bitterly. At this point, she knew she was being driven by anger and a desire for revenge against the man who had targeted her parents, damaged her career, and destroyed countless vineyards. At the same time, she didn't care; she just wanted this nightmare that had cost her so much to end.

"This next section is a bit tight," Corvina said as she squeezed through a narrow section of the passage. Her shoulders brushed roughly against the chalk walls.

If not for Bryan's glowing phone, she would have failed to see the descending steps right in front of her. A small staircase led downward.

"I think I found the steps into Pommery," she said.

"Great. Ten minutes in this claustrophobic tunnel is more than enough," Bryan said.

Corvina walked down twelve steps and found herself on a similarly arranged staircase as the one Marie-Claire had shown them at Charles Heidsieck. In another minute, she and Bryan emerged in a side tunnel of Pommery Champagne's chalk cellars.

"We need to be quiet," Bryan said. "If Claude and his team see us, they might shoot."

"Claude will kill us if he finds us down here," Corvina agreed. She gave Bryan his phone.

Corvina walked out of the side tunnel in silence and followed a larger tunnel branching off into three more. They were dimly lit by interspersed light bulbs hanging from the ceiling. The tunnels were wide and high enough to drive a bus through. Old Pommery-labeled champagne crates and wine-making equipment lined the walls. The place looked and felt like an abandoned mine to her.

"What do you think?" Corvina asked. She considered the three tunnels ahead.

"I don't know. I've never been in this part of Pommery's network. It doesn't appear to be a section for visitors," Bryan said.

She peered down each of the three tunnels in turn, looking for something to encourage her to take one over the other two.

"There's someone," Bryan whispered, pointing down the tunnel on their left where a figure had emerged from a side tunnel.

The figure was carrying something.

"It's Sergio!" Corvina said more loudly than she intended.

Sergio turned in their direction. He peered down the dark tunnel, turned, and fled, metal case in hand.

Corvina sprinted after him, not waiting for Bryan.

CHAPTER 54

POMMERY CELLARS
REIMS, CHAMPAGNE, FRANCE

"Do you see him?" Corvina shouted at Bryan. He had passed her and was running ahead.

They had been chasing Sergio for several minutes, but he was faster than expected. It reminded Corvina of the expression "the fox is only running for its dinner, but the rabbit is running for its life." Though she and Bryan were the fox in the current scenario, she had to remember that she was running for the lives of millions of vines, particularly those in vineyards above her head, her vineyards at home, and the livelihoods of thousands of people. Losing Sergio and the neurotoxin to stop Philomena wasn't an option for her.

"He's just ahead. He turned right. Come on!" Bryan shouted over his shoulder.

Corvina watched Bryan put on another burst of speed and picked up her own pace, thankful for all the hours she'd spent in her running shoes pounding the pavement.

She saw Bryan reach an intersection and begin turning right when all of a sudden a dozen or so people flew out of the intersecting tunnel, bowling Bryan to the ground. A few of them went sprawling themselves, while others kept on running across the tunnel she and Bryan were racing down.

"What the hell?" she cried out.

Corvina ran around the corner, careful not to be hit by anyone, and saw Bryan scrambling on the ground only meters away. Over his shoulder, she saw Sergio on his hands and knees. He had been knocked down too.

"Bryan, turn around!" Corvina shouted. Sergio was getting up and bearing down on him.

Bryan spun around, but Sergio was already on top of him and pushed him back to the ground.

Corvina gasped as she saw that the case was right at Bryan's feet! Bryan saw it, too, and snatched it by the handle. From his prostrate position on the ground, he slid it toward Corvina.

"Heads up!" he shouted as the case left his hand.

It hurtled across the floor, sliding between the few remaining runners who were helping each other up.

As the case slid toward her, she saw Sergio pick himself up.

Corvina stopped the case with her foot and lifted it by the handle. Sergio glared at her and then looked over his shoulder into the tunnels—and ran.

"Find Claude! Take the case upstairs to Interpol!" Bryan yelled.

"Where are you going?" she asked, clutching the case.

"To catch Sergio!" Bryan shouted.

Hesitating for only a second, Corvina took the case and ran in the opposite direction.

When she reached the third intersection in as many minutes, she stopped to try to get her bearings. She had no idea where she was or how to get back to the hidden passage to Charles Heidsieck. They had covered too much ground and taken too many turns.

With the exception of a few main tunnels and the tunnel sections reserved for visitors, the dimly lit tunnels separated by chalk pits, their shafts leading thirty meters back up to the surface, all looked the same.

Where was the main entrance to the tunnels?

Corvina looked around in panic and loosened her scarf, her breath coming in shallow gasps. She was completely lost.

CHAPTER 55

POMMERY CELLARS
REIMS, CHAMPAGNE, FRANCE

Bryan ran around the corner of the next tunnel and saw only empty space. He had lost Sergio. Bryan stopped and listened but heard nothing that indicated where Sergio had gone.

The collision with the other men hurt him more than he let on to Corvina. His left ankle throbbed, and his right knee felt like it had been smashed with a hammer. He wasn't as young as he liked to think he was, and his injuries slowed his pursuit of Sergio. Now the ecoterrorist was gone, and Bryan had no idea where to find him within the maze of Pommery's tunnels.

He checked his phone, but there was no reception this far under the earth. He couldn't even call for help. At least it still had battery left and could provide light if he needed it again.

He was on his own.

Though he looked down every offshoot and passage he came across, he didn't hold out much hope of finding Sergio. As his pace slowed and the numbing effects of the endorphins and adrenaline wore away, his thoughts turned to finding his own way out and hoping Corvina made it safely back topside to Claude with the case containing the neurotoxin.

Several tunnels later, he heard someone. He stopped to listen until he was positive he heard footsteps coming from the intersecting tunnel ahead.

Was it more of the men he and Sergio had run into? Or was it Claude and his IRT? He looked around for a place to hide, but there was none. There were crates of empty champagne bottles against one wall of the tunnel, not large enough to hide behind but full of bottles. He lifted one bottle and brandished it like a club.

He rounded the corner with the bottle of champagne raised high above his head, poised to bring it down in a vicious arc.

"What the—!" Vicente cried out in surprise when Bryan jumped out at him from the shadows. The man crouched in self-defense, arms raised above his head.

"Vicente?" Bryan stopped himself from bringing the bottle down on the man's head. Twice in one day would be cruel.

Bryan tossed the bottle aside. It hit the ground with a dull thud.

"What are you doing down here?" Bryan asked.

"I could ask you the same thing," Vicente replied, standing to his full height, regaining his composure. He looked around the tunnel and asked, "Where's Corvina?"

"She went to find Claude," Bryan said.

"She's not with you?"

"No, we ran into Sergio and managed to get the case back, but he escaped. I was chasing him but lost him. Did you see him on your way down?"

"No, you're the first person I've come across. I didn't realize how much of a maze it was down here."

"Tell me about it."

"How did you get down here?" Vicente asked.

"Through Charles Heidsieck's cellars next door. The tunnels are connected by a hidden passage," Bryan explained.

"No kidding. Well, now that we've found each other, let's try to find Corvina."

"And Sergio," Bryan said with resolve.

"Are you alright?" Vicente asked him.

Bryan walked with difficulty as he favored one leg at a time.

"I'll be fine. I banged up my right knee and twisted my left ankle something fierce."

"Right knee, left ankle—bad combination," Vicente said.

"It'll be worse for Sergio when I find him."

CHAPTER 56

POMMERY CELLARS
REIMS, CHAMPAGNE, FRANCE

Corvina dashed into a side tunnel and sprinted awkwardly with the case clutched to her chest.

She had to get the case to Interpol, but she was unsure how to find Pommery's main entrance or even return to Charles Heidsieck. She saw staggered groups and individual men running amok through the tunnels and kept out of their sight to avoid confrontation.

At the next turn, one of the men she saw far down the tunnel was Sergio.

And Sergio saw her.

She now found herself running not in search of him, but away from him.

She was halfway down another tunnel, looking for a place to hide, when she spotted a narrow opening set above ground level on her right. She slowed down to get a better look.

It was a staircase leading upward, a staircase with two sets of steps: one below and one above mirroring them. It was another passage, leading either back to Charles Heidsieck or to another Champagne house.

Without hesitation, she set the case on the ledge of the first step and pulled herself up.

She risked a look back into the tunnel; no sign of Sergio.

She took the steps as far upward as she could go.

As soon as the stairwell began descending—just as the staircase leading from Charles Heidsieck to Pommery had done—the light disappeared, and she found herself looking ahead into complete darkness.

She took out her phone to light the way and remembered that the battery had died and she had returned Bryan's.

Noting the steps in the ceiling and remembering Marie-Claire's instructions, she realized she would need her hands free to continue forward.

She returned a few steps into the light, where she could look back down into the tunnel she had climbed up from.

Sergio ran across the opening.

Corvina froze.

When Sergio didn't return, she set the case down on a step and opened it to retrieve the neurotoxin. She wrapped the box in her scarf and used it as a harness, tying it around her neck. She took one more item, leaving the case otherwise intact. She regretted leaving the bottle of wine, but she had no choice. Where she was going, she would need both hands free.

By leaving the case on the steps, Claude and the team at Interpol could track her as far as the stairwell and hopefully figure out where she went from there.

She jogged to the bottom of the steps and reached out to draw a thick red cross with her lipstick on the wall outside for Bryan to find.

She hoped he would recall the reference from when Marie-Claire explained what the red crosses signified when they were in the Charles Heidsieck cellars.

She climbed back up the steps and prepared to descend into the darkness, this time unencumbered by the bulky case. On the last ascending step, she stood on a stone the size of a half bottle of champagne.

The stone fell off the step, rolled down the stairs, and hit the case. She watched in horror as the case slid down the stairs and dropped loudly into the tunnel. It would be in plain sight for anyone to see—including Sergio.

She started running back down the steps to retrieve it, but then she realized she couldn't be sure Sergio wasn't in the tunnel or hadn't heard the case fall and was coming even now.

Committed to act, she moved back up the steps. Once at the top, she began descending the other side. The light from behind her receded until she was in complete darkness once again.

Corvina felt for the mirrored steps above her head. She took each blind step with extra caution until she began to get the hang of using the mirrored steps to guide her feet.

Just as she felt she was making progress and had convinced herself she would make it out the other side with the neurotoxin, Sergio's voice rose up the stairwell behind her.

"Corvinaaaaaaa . . ."

Corvina plunged ahead, taking the steps as fast as she could. She slapped each step above her head as she went.

She descended a long staircase that led her to a narrow, winding passage that went on for some time without steps until it ended in another descending staircase.

Corvina reached out to slap the next step but hit only empty space.

"Corvinaaaaaaa, are you there?" Sergio's voice called out from the dark behind her.

She stopped. Taking her time despite not knowing how close Sergio was, she felt the last step above her and followed it forward with her fingers. Corvina pressed upward and pushed her fingers forward until they reached empty space and pushed up into nothing.

The steps had stopped descending!

She lifted her right leg to take what should have been the first step leading upward and was rewarded with solid ground beneath her foot. Corvina was heading back up again.

She climbed the stairs as fast as she dared, feeling her way through the darkness, all too aware of Sergio's close pursuit.

As she climbed, she realized the perfect darkness was morphing into inky black and her eyesight was gradually returning. Looking up, she saw light at the end of the tunnel.

She ran up the last of the steps and found herself standing on a landing and looking out over thousands of dusty bottles at eye level. They were piled neck high and blocking her way out. She realized she was standing at the back of a storage cave with an arched ceiling.

In front of her was a room filled from side to side and one and a half meters high with thousands of aging champagne bottles. She looked over the top of the bottles to the other side of the storage cave and saw an empty tunnel ahead.

The familiar raised embossment on the bottles confirmed she had reached the cellars of Veuve Clicquot.

She looked back into the stairwell and could see a soft glow; it was Sergio using his phone to light his way. He would find her any second.

Without wasting any time, Corvina tucked her scarf with the neurotoxin into her blouse, scrambled onto the pile of champagne bottles, and started pulling herself across the dusty pile. The curved brick ceiling was only centimeters from her head, giving her less than half a meter's clearance—enough room to shimmy on her stomach, but not enough to crawl on hands and knees. The pile of bottles stretched five meters from side to side and at least four times the distance lengthwise. She was going to have to crawl fast.

The ancient brick ceiling was dripping with cobwebs. Her hands and face broke through them as she propelled herself forward.

She coughed as her movements raised swirls of dust motes.

"There you are!" Sergio's voice pierced the cave's empty space.

Corvina shrieked and made the mistake of stopping to look back.

Sergio was climbing onto the bottles and pulling himself toward her.

She doubled her efforts and pulled herself forward by moving from side to side using her elbows and knees. The smooth, uneven surface of the bottles made moving difficult but did offer handholds and footholds to pull and push from.

"You're a dead woman, Corvina. You have been since you started poking your nose into Philomena," Sergio shouted from behind her. "I bet you laughed when you heard I disappeared," he shouted. "Probably hoped I was dead!"

"*A fanabla!*" She cursed Sergio's scrambling figure behind her. Corvina looked straight ahead and pulled herself forward faster. She was halfway across the length of the pile of bottles.

"You could then be the golden girl of the company," Sergio taunted her. "No more Sergio to upset perfect little Corvina's life. And all of Vicente's attention to yourself."

She didn't respond; she was having a hard enough time just escaping. Corvina dug her hand into the bottom of a bottle and pulled with all her might, at the same time pushing with her feet.

"And where's daddy's girl now? Still feeling sorry for herself? Or feeling sorry for poor Sergio?"

Corvina reached the end of the pile of bottles and pulled herself into the empty space beyond.

She fell to the ground and immediately stood. Corvina turned and saw Sergio scrambling across the bottles toward her. He was much closer than she had thought.

Corvina grabbed one of the dusty bottles from the end of the pile. Sergio was less than a body's length away.

"Actually, I always thought you were an asshole!" Corvina yelled.

She launched the bottle at Sergio's sneering face. It hit him in the head but didn't seem to slow him.

"*Puttana!* You'll pay for that!" he screamed at her, his voice hideous with rage.

She grabbed another bottle and brought it down with all her might on his outstretched hand. The bottle remained intact, but she heard something break. Sergio screamed again. Corvina turned and ran down the cellar for all she was worth.

The tunnel curved to the left and led to a steel gate that spanned its width and height.

She ran to the gate and pushed the bars of the small barred door set in its frame.

The door wouldn't open. She pulled with all her might, but it was locked.

She spun around to run back the way she had come.

Sergio rounded the corner, holding his broken hand against his chest with blood pouring down his face.

She was trapped.

CHAPTER 57

POMMERY CELLARS
REIMS, CHAMPAGNE, FRANCE

"Claude. It's Henri. I'm here with Secretary General Arsenault."

Claude stopped in the middle of the wide chalk tunnel he was passing through and signaled for his team to do the same.

"Henri! Great to hear your voice! But what happened to Alison?"

"She's disappeared."

"What? Please repeat. It sounded like you said she disappeared." Claude tapped his earpiece to make sure it was working properly.

"That's what I said. But never mind that for now. We found tunnel maps for the five major Champagne houses in the area, so I can lead you through the tunnels."

"Good to hear. It's been a nightmare down here trying to find our way around." The look his team was giving him told him they felt the same way.

"I can only imagine," Henri said.

"Aside from Pommery, how many Champagne houses have chalk tunnels like this one?" Claude asked. He saw three men run through a tunnel ahead of him and without a word sent two members of his team to go and get them.

"Taittinger, Ruinart, Veuve Clicquot, and Charles Heidsieck," Henri answered.

"Do you still have tracking on me?" Claude asked.

"Yes, I can see your location," Henri said. Claude could hear the rustle of papers in the background.

"How far are we from Sergio and the case?" Claude asked.

"It appears that he's gone off grid," Henri said.

"What does that mean? *Off grid?*" Claude asked.

"He's no longer on the Pommery Cellar map."

"You lost him?"

"I think so. The tracker disappeared. Maybe there are unmapped tunnels."

"What Champagne house is next to Pommery?" Claude asked. Two of his team members returned with all three men bound at the wrists.

"Veuve Clicquot is closest to your current location, but you better hope he hasn't found a way in there," Henri said.

"Why?" Claude asked, and heard more rustling of papers. He could picture Henri spreading out a map of chalk tunnels.

"According to the map we have, Veuve Clicquot has over four hundred chalk pits connected by more than twenty-four kilometers of tunnels."

Claude looked down the tunnel he was in now and thought of all the distance he and his IRT had already covered. He tried to imagine an additional twenty-four kilometers of tunnels to search and began to doubt they would ever find Sergio. The fugitive had chosen his escape route well.

CHAPTER 58

POMMERY CELLARS
REIMS, CHAMPAGNE, FRANCE

"Any idea where we're going?" Vicente asked Bryan.

"No. I've visited all of the cellars here in Reims, but I don't know them well enough to navigate," Bryan replied. He grew frustrated at his limp. He knew he was slowing them down. "Did you hear that?" he asked. He'd heard a loud click.

"Yes," Vicente said. He picked up their pace to get to the next tunnel.

When they turned the corner, they saw no one.

"Hey, what's that?" Bryan asked, looking down the side tunnel.

"You found it!" Vicente exclaimed. "It's the case!"

Both men ran down the tunnel toward the case. Bryan winced with every step.

When they came to the case, Bryan was dismayed to see it had been opened. He lifted the lid and looked inside. Only the bottle of wine given to him and Corvina by Marielle remained. "The neurotoxin is gone, and it looks like the tracker has been disabled as well. There's an empty space where it looks like a battery may have gone."

"That means Interpol can no longer track the case," Vicente said.

"Without the battery, they won't even track it to this point. If the case is here and the tracker is gone, it means Sergio must have found Corvina and we have no way of knowing where they are," Bryan said. He closed the case and snapped it shut.

"Look here," Vicente said. He pointed at a bright-red cross written on the wall.

Bryan ran his finger over the cross, and it came away red with fresh lipstick. "This must have been left by Corvina," Bryan said. He recalled what Marie-Claire had told them earlier about the tunnels.

The fresh red cross was drawn next to a darkened opening in the wall. When he shined his phone's light into the opening, it revealed a narrow staircase.

A staircase with mirror-image steps carved into the ceiling.

"This way! I know where they went!" Bryan shouted to Vicente. He picked up the case and climbed into the opening.

CHAPTER 59

VEUVE CLICQUOT CELLARS
REIMS, CHAMPAGNE, FRANCE

"Give me the box!" Sergio shouted.

Corvina held the box containing the neurotoxin still wrapped in her scarf close to her chest, unwilling to give it up under any circumstances. It was the only way to stop Philomena; she had come too far to give it up now.

"I don't think so, *puto*," she said. "You're as trapped as I am, and I have reinforcements coming." Corvina had to stall him. She prayed that Bryan would spot the red cross she'd drawn on the wall and that he would lead Claude and his men to her and Sergio. It was her only hope.

"As do I," Sergio said. His smile gave her pause for concern. Was there someone down in the cellars helping him? Was this where they had planned to launch the next attacks on the vineyards above?

Footsteps drew their attention to the entrance of the cellar.

"Sorry to interrupt," Alison said as she came into view, pointing her gun at Corvina and Sergio beside her.

"Alison?" Corvina said with relief. "Where's Claude?"

"Claude's not coming," Alison replied. "Why don't you toss me the box?"

"You led her to us?" Sergio shouted, and pushed Corvina to the ground with his good hand. She held tight to the box as she fell and landed on her butt.

"Did you think you were going to get away?" Alison asked. Corvina noticed that she kept her gun trained on Sergio but her eyes on the small box wrapped in the scarf.

"Alison, what are you doing? It's Sergio! Arrest him!" Corvina shouted at her.

"Oh, I will. I'll be arresting both of you. Now toss me the box." She waved her free left hand.

"Both of us? What are you talking about?" Corvina asked. Did Alison really still think she was involved?

"I knew from the beginning that you were working with whoever was responsible for the stupid bug." Alison glared at Corvina. "You may have convinced Claude and the rest of the idiots at Interpol that you were only trying to stop the bug, but I suspected you all along. The stairs and hidden passages were an interesting find. That led me to believe that the two of you had been planning your escape for some time. It also dawned on me that with you"—she waved the gun at Corvina—"feeding Sergio information from inside the investigation, he was never at any real risk of getting caught."

"You're right," Sergio said. "We needed someone on the inside who could keep tabs on the investigation."

"What?" Corvina shouted. "Alison, he's lying! He's manipulating you."

"Sure, sure. I think you're the one who's been manipulated, and now you're being hung out to dry. I won't ask again." Alison held out her empty hand. "Give me the box."

"Claude will find us. The case has the tracking device inside," Corvina said.

"It won't transmit a signal or your location without this," Alison said, holding a small, round silver object aloft. "I removed the battery. And I sent Claude and the IRT in the opposite direction."

Corvina wanted to cry. With resignation, she threw the box at Alison, who caught it with her free left hand.

Sergio moved, but Alison aimed her gun back at him.

"Don't even think about it," Alison said. Sergio stopped and stayed still.

"Alison, you're making a big mistake. Think about this logically. Why would I want to destroy vineyards? My whole life revolves around wine," Corvina tried reasoning with her.

"So does his," Alison said, pointing at Sergio. "Besides, I don't really care." She set the box down on the ground and reached across her body for her radio, keeping her gun trained on Sergio. "In five minutes, this cave will be full of armed Interpol agents and you can tell them your sad life story."

Alison moved to unclip her radio and fumbled with the clip when it caught on her belt. The radio fell to the ground and bounced. She reached down to catch it.

"Alison! Behind you!" Corvina screamed.

Alison turned too late.

Corvina watched helplessly as Sergio swung a bottle toward Alison's head.

Alison swung her gun up to shoot.

She wasn't fast enough. The bottle crashed into the side of her head.

Corvina stared at Alison's crumpled body as it slumped to the chalk floor. She couldn't tell if she was still breathing.

She watched Sergio casually pick up the box with the neurotoxin inside and then prod Alison with his foot.

Alison didn't move or respond. She was out of commission, dead or alive.

Corvina saw Alison's gun on the ground a few meters away from the agent. When she'd been hit by the bottle, the gun must have flown out of her hand.

She was trying to scramble toward the gun when Sergio crossed the cellar and grabbed her by the hair, yanking her up. She cried out in pain.

"You want her gun? Why don't you go and get it?" Sergio spat in her face and ripped the handful of hair downward. She felt her head bounce off the ground. Corvina immediately saw stars and hoped she wouldn't pass out.

Sergio stepped away. He turned and kicked her in the stomach. Now she wished she would pass out. She gasped for air. Pain ripped through her body. She curled up defensively, alone and in agony.

Suddenly, out of the corner of her eye, she saw Bryan and Vicente run around the corner. She thought she was hallucinating.

"Vicente, get the gun," she heard Bryan yell.

Corvina wanted to cry with happiness when she saw her boss scooping the gun up and Bryan running toward Sergio.

She saw Bryan punch Sergio squarely in the jaw and Sergio fall to the ground.

The next thing she knew, she was looking at Bryan's face.

"We found your red crosses and the tunnel you climbed through. Are you okay?" He held her face in his hands.

"I'm so glad to see you both." She wrapped her arms around Bryan's neck.

Tears poured down her face as he brought her to her feet.

"Well, isn't that adorable," she heard Sergio say.

She let go of Bryan.

Sergio was getting to his feet. He was holding his jaw where Bryan had punched him.

Corvina looked around for Vicente. He was standing behind Sergio with Alison's gun in his hand, but he was looking at her and Bryan.

"Vicente?" she asked, confused. "Why are you pointing that gun at me?" Had everyone gone mad? First Alison, now Vicente.

"Sorry, Corvina," she heard her boss of many years say. "I recruited Sergio before you—not that I think you would have gone along with any of this." Vicente shrugged his massive shoulders.

He passed the gun to Sergio.

Bryan positioned himself protectively in front of her, shielding her from Sergio and the gun.

"That's why you were at Vinexpo," Corvina said to Sergio. "You knew I had the case with the neurotoxin."

"No, that was just dumb luck. I was at Vinexpo to update Vicente on our progress and make the final arrangements to infest France. Vicente found the neurotoxin in your case when you ran off to find me. Thank you for saving me the trip to California."

"But why?" Corvina asked. She turned to Vicente. How could the man she trusted most turn on her and on their shared passion of viticulture and wine making? She had to understand.

"Money," Vicente said, "and opportunity. By wiping out the world's best vineyards and our competition, we can reposition the entire company portfolio and rebuild the global wine industry—first by destroying it with phylloxera, and then by saving it with the neurotoxin."

"You'll never get away with it," Corvina said.

"Agent Duval and his Interpol team will be here any second," Bryan said, but his voice lacked conviction.

"I don't think so," Sergio said. "Agent Pittard disabled the tracker in the case," he told Vicente.

"That was helpful of her," Vicente said. He looked down at Alison and laughed. "Stupid, but helpful."

"So it was Universal Wines behind this all along?" Bryan asked Sergio. His hand clenched Corvina's tightly. She could tell he wanted to lash out at Sergio again, but the gun held him back.

"Sorry, but this isn't the part where the heroes get a full explanation of the evil plot." Sergio stepped forward and punched Bryan in the gut. Bryan doubled over.

Vicente rushed forward and side kicked him in the right knee and stomped on his left ankle when he fell.

Bryan screamed in pain.

"That was for Slater," Vicente said.

"What's going to happen now is we're going to set off our drones to spread Philomena throughout Reims, Ay, and Epernay to infest all of Champagne's best vineyards—just like we did in Bordeaux and over your father's vineyards." Sergio smiled and looked straight at Corvina. "The aphid will take care of the rest, and Champagne will be history."

"You bastard!" Corvina shouted at the man who had destroyed her father's livelihood.

"And the neurotoxin?" Bryan asked. He struggled back to his feet from his prone position on the ground.

"Mass-produced by Dusanti and sold to the world at a premium. Inside tip, you should buy stock," Sergio said, and laughed. "But by the time it is made available, it will be too late for anyone to stop or undo the damage done. Just think—it will level the playing field for wineries around the world."

"What about us?" Bryan asked, still holding Corvina's hand. She pressed something into his hand. She just hoped he realized what it was and what to do with it.

"Really? You have to ask?" Sergio asked. He raised the gun and pointed it at Bryan's face.

And it all ends in the cellar, Corvina thought. She closed her eyes, unable to watch.

Sergio pulled the trigger.

The gun clicked on an empty chamber.

"What the fuck?" Sergio cursed. He looked at the gun with disgust.

Bryan lunged at Sergio and plunged the corkscrew Corvina had passed to him into the back of Sergio's injured hand. It was the wine opener Marielle had given them that morning in Pomerol. Sergio cried out. The gun clattered to the ground.

Bryan punched Sergio in the face, and he fell to the ground and didn't move.

Corvina stood up slowly. Together, she and Bryan faced Vicente.

"You'll never catch me," Vicente yelled at them, and fled the chamber.

At that moment, there was a mighty roar. Vicente came flying back into the chamber like he'd been hit by a streetcar. His body slammed into the chalk wall, and he crumpled to the ground.

The room was filled with armed Interpol agents who secured every centimeter of the cellar chamber within seconds and bound Sergio and Vicente at the wrists.

"Corvina! Bryan! Are you okay?" Claude ran over to them.

"We will be alright. Check on Alison." Corvina nodded toward Alison's prone form.

"She's alive, sir. Strong pulse, but out like a light. We'll take her topside," one of Claude's men said from Alison's side. He had one hand on her neck and another checking for any injuries or signs of bleeding.

"How did you know where to find us?" Corvina asked Claude. "I had to leave the case with the tracker in Pommery's cellars, and Alison removed the battery."

"It turns out that Arsenault didn't think putting a tracker on Alison was such a bad idea after all," Claude said, and laughed. "He knew how likely she was to go rogue, so we planted a tracker in her walkie-talkie. As soon as she disappeared, we activated it. It kept me apprised of her location. We knew she never trusted you, so it was a good guess that wherever we would find Alison, we would find you." Claude placed a hand on her shoulder and gave it a firm squeeze.

"But what about her gun? How come it was empty?" Bryan asked.

"We emptied her gun, just in case. Good thing she's so predictable," Claude said.

"Yeah, good thing," Bryan said, and laughed nervously.

"Claude, wait. How did you know the Pommery and Veuve Clicquot Champagne house tunnels were interlinked?" Corvina asked.

"They're connected?" Claude asked. He looked at his team. "Oh hell."

"If you didn't come through the hidden passage, how *did* you get in?" Corvina asked.

"I'll show you," Claude said, leading her and Bryan out of the gallery, leaving the Incident Response Team to take out Sergio, Vicente, and Alison, who was still unconscious.

They walked for several minutes.

"So what happens next? Are the Lungs in Hong Kong involved or not?" Bryan asked.

"Hard to say. We don't have anything to connect them to Slater, Sergio, Vicente, Universal Wines, or Dusanti, aside from the purchase of one of Slater's patents. Hardly a smoking gun," Claude said.

"So if they are involved, there will be no further investigation and they get away?" Bryan asked.

"For now, yes, they get away. This is the real world. Sometimes the bad guys get away."

"Karma will catch up with them," Bryan said. Corvina sensed Bryan knew something that she didn't.

"If you believe in that kind of thing," Claude said. He smiled and turned to leave.

"What are we going to do about the Lungs?" Corvina whispered to Bryan.

"I have an idea about that," Bryan whispered back.

Before she could respond, Claude turned a corner ahead of her. When she did the same, she saw how Claude and his Incident Response Team had accessed Veuve Clicquot's cellars from Pommery's cellars; they'd blasted through a thick section of chalk wall.

Regrettably, she saw they had also blasted into several thousand stacked, aging champagne bottles and destroyed them all in the process.

She marveled at the wreckage. The ground of the cellar was covered in piles of broken glass and champagne. The tunnel reeked of vintage Veuve Clicquot. Frothy, bubbling champagne spread across the floor in small rivers.

Bryan picked up a cork and one of the broken bottles. Champagne dripped onto the floor. Its shattered pieces of dark-green glass were held together by the bottle's yellow label.

"Veuve Clicquot Grande Dame, 1996," Claude read the name and vintage off the label. "Was that a good year?"

EPILOGUE

ONE WEEK LATER
NAPA VALLEY, CA

"I think I heard something," Corvina whispered. She was crouching beside Bryan behind a stainless steel vat in the winery—the same winery where James Harvey's assistant was found dead and where Malcolm discovered the neurotoxin.

Soft morning sunlight illuminated the dozens of giant stainless steel vats standing in solemn rows like soldiers on parade. Dust motes floated languidly through the air, casting a magical twilight quality to the room.

Corvina inhaled deeply of the smell in the vast building. She always liked the combination of scents she knew was an accumulation of years of fermenting grape must in stainless steel tanks. It felt good to be out of Lyon and to have the intense week of writing statements, being interviewed, and rehashing all of the events leading to the incidents in Champagne well behind her. She wore jeans, a white top and jacket, and an orange paisley silk scarf from Etro. It was one of her favorites.

"Hey, Candy just sent me a text," Bryan said. "It says 'Nice work stopping Philomena. Your exam date has been approved. Good luck.' I owe you a big thank you, Corvina. If not for you, I wouldn't have stood a chance of getting back into the Master of Wine program. It's been good using my skills and experience to help the wine industry."

"Amazing. Can we celebrate later?" Corvina whispered. She was fumbling with a voice recorder they had purchased that morning.

"What have you got against celebrating?" Bryan asked.

"Get down—he's here!" She pressed the record button on the small device and tucked it into her jacket pocket. The man at the shop had shown her how it worked and assured her it would pick up any conversation.

The silhouette of a man appeared in the doorway of the winery. Once he stepped out of the sunlight, Corvina recognized the figure as Zhang Tao Lung. He was alone and looking down at his phone. Now all they had to do was get him to admit he was responsible for the spread of phylloxera and record his confession. She could then contact Claude and have Lung arrested.

"I see you received our message. Thank you for coming," Corvina said from behind the vat.

Lung startled. He stepped backward and peered around the winery, trying to make out who had spoken.

"It's you," he hissed when Corvina and Bryan stepped out of the shadows.

"Did you really think you and your brother had gotten away with it?" Bryan asked.

Corvina saw a perplexed look cross the industrialist's face before the dawning of comprehension.

"I see now what you've done," Lung said. "It was you who sent the message from that boy Sergio's phone. It said he left all of the research and information on Philomena here at the winery—information that supposedly linked me to the spread of the bug and the attacks on the vineyards."

"Sergio has been in Interpol custody for a week," Corvina said. The surprised look on Lung's face told her he had not been aware of this.

"We suspected you wouldn't trust anyone else to retrieve the information and would come yourself. That's why we set this trap," Bryan said.

Lung began laughing.

Corvina looked to Bryan, who shrugged his shoulders. A sense of dread began creeping over her. What had they missed?

"We can prove your involvement. We have Sergio's phone records," Corvina said.

"Circumstantial at best," Lung said.

"You came here to destroy evidence," Bryan said. "You and your brother are obviously working together. He purchased the patent on Philomena, but you've been the one manipulating the people at Universal Wines—Harvey, Vicente, and Sergio."

Lung laughed harder. "Yes, I've been working with my brother."

He stopped laughing and glared at Corvina with such unveiled hostility that she took an involuntary step backward.

"You think you have trapped me!" Lung roared. He reached into his jacket and pulled out the largest handgun Corvina had ever seen. He pointed the gun at the ground between her and Bryan and pulled the trigger. The sound of the gunshot inside the confines of the winery with all its hard surfaces was deafening. Corvina froze where she stood. She reached up for her scarf and held her arms protectively in front of her. She felt Bryan tense up beside her. They had not foreseen Lung bringing a weapon to the winery.

"Up onto the vat. Show me where you hid the information," Lung commanded her.

What he didn't know was that there was nothing in the tank except wine. Malcolm had removed the vials of neurotoxin and the USB memory stick following Harvey's assistant's death. Now, the hiding place and the fabricated evidence was their only leverage. As soon as Lung found out there was nothing in the vat and no evidence against him, there would be nothing stopping him from killing Corvina and Bryan.

Bryan went up first, and Corvina was forced up the spiral metal staircase at gunpoint behind him. Once they reached the catwalk running above the row of stainless steel fermentation tanks, Corvina led Lung to the tank next to the one Harvey's assistant had fallen into. He had the gun pressed firmly in her side. In less than a minute, Lung would know they had misled him and she and Bryan would be killed. She looked to Bryan for inspiration, but she saw only fear in his expression. With Bryan in the same precarious position as her, there was no escaping. They had totally misread and underestimated their adversary. At least their murder would be recorded on the device she carried, but that was little consolation.

"I hope we haven't come too late," a voice boomed out.

Corvina looked down from the vat toward the winery entrance. Relief swept through her when she saw Claude Duval march in with a full Interpol Incident Response Team. The team fanned out around the winery. Within seconds, the vat that she, Bryan, and Lung stood on was surrounded by armed men.

Lung spun Corvina around and wrapped his arm around her neck so quickly she had no time to defend herself or prevent it from happening. The knot of her scarf pressed painfully against her throat. Lung pressed the gun just as painfully into her side.

"I'll let her go as soon as she gives me the information hidden inside this vat," Lung shouted.

"Let her go, Lung. You're completely surrounded," Claude shouted up to him.

"What's on that disk is the only evidence we have against Lung!" Corvina bluffed, hoping Lung would fall for it and that Claude would know she was bluffing.

"If you don't tell me where it is," Lung whispered in her ear, "I'll shoot your boyfriend." She squirmed against his grip, but the gun pressing even harder in her side made her cease her struggles.

"Okay, okay, I'll get it. It's inside the vat, held to the top by a magnet," she said.

"No, I'll get it. You've already said this was part of your trap. I won't let you get whatever you've hidden in there and throw it to your friends from Interpol," Lung said. "For all I know you've hidden a weapon inside."

"No, I haven't, I promise. There's only wine inside," Corvina said.

"And the only evidence linking me to any of this mess," Lung said.

"Right," Corvina said.

"In another twenty minutes, I'll be sitting in my air-conditioned Rolls-Royce, heading to the airfield where my private jet is waiting to take me back to Hong Kong. Now open the hatch. I'll get the evidence myself."

Lung forced Corvina to her knees so she was crouched above the vat's sealed opening. Lung squatted next to her. One hand continued to press the gun into her side.

Corvina waved to Bryan with one hand behind her back. She hoped he understood she was waving to him to step back. She took a long, slow, deep breath and held it. She was grateful for all the running she did; she would need every bit of her lung capacity in the next few minutes.

With an unnecessary heave, Corvina twisted the hatch and pried the lid open on top of the tank. She swung the round hatch door upward, so it was vertical on its hinges.

"I hate California! Too much sunshine and everyone always so healthy looking," Lung said, and spat into the vat of wine.

She could have killed him for that alone.

Corvina shuffled back on her knees, still holding her breath. Lung looked down into the deep pool of dark-red wine below. Its fruity aromas pierced the air.

Lung looked at Corvina, and his eyes rolled grotesquely up into his head.

Corvina watched in fascination as Lung's body went limp. She reached out and caught him by the shoulders before he could fall into the wine. She was still holding her breath. She dragged Lung away from the opening and with her right foot brought the vat's hatch back down and pushed it all the way closed. Bryan came to her side, also holding his breath, and helped her lower Lung to the catwalk and twist the latch on top to seal the vat. He helped her over to the next vat along the catwalk. Only then did she exhale, take a deep breath of air, and collapse into his arms.

"Good thinking," Bryan said, looking down at her.

"We may have underestimated him, but he should have known better than to pick a fight with a winemaker in a winery," she said. She untied her scarf and let it hang over her shoulders.

Three IRT members rushed up and dragged Lung's unconscious body away while two more helped her and Bryan down from the vats.

"How did you know we would be here?" Corvina asked Claude once she and Bryan were outside in the fresh air and Lung was secured in a local police car. They were surprised to find Malcolm waiting for them outside.

"I neglected to turn off the Red Notice at Interpol asking all our National Central Bureaus around the world to keep tabs on you," Claude said.

"You're still tracking me?" Corvina asked.

"Unintentionally," Claude said, and held up his hands. "As soon as I received the alert that you were in California and I confirmed Bryan was with you, I called Malcolm. He told me your plan to entrap Zhang Tao Lung."

"I'm sorry, Corvina. I know you told me your plans so I could later write the story, but when Claude confirmed to me that Lung had come to California, I feared for your safety," Malcolm said.

"Well, I'm glad you told Claude," she said, and smiled. "But what about Lung? Will you have enough to send him and his brother to prison?" she asked Claude.

"Attempted murder should be enough; he did try to kill us," Bryan said. "Give Claude the voice recorder."

"There is that," Claude said. He took the recording device when Corvina offered it to him. "But thanks to you we also learned that he may be responsible for his brother's disappearance and possibly even his murder if a body is ever discovered."

"His brother's murder? Thanks to me?" Corvina asked.

"After you gave me Feng's keycard in London—the one he placed in your purse in Dubai—I ran the prints," Claude said.

"And?" Bryan asked.

"It turns out that the man you met in Dubai *was* Zhang Tao, not his brother as he led you to believe."

"Why would he want us to believe we were meeting his brother?" Corvina asked.

"Not just you—the world. And I don't know why yet, but rest assured Interpol will investigate Zhang Tao and the disappearance of his brother," Claude said.

"So was Zhang Tao involved in spreading Philomena or not?" Corvina asked.

"Possibly. A Chinese manufacturer in Guangzhou made the drones used in the Bordeaux attacks, but there's no clear link to connect them to Lung or his companies."

"What about the patent his brother, I mean he, purchased?"

"The Lungs made their dual fortunes in industry and agriculture," Claude replied. "They've also been heavily invested in the research and development of genetically modified crops. His purchase of the patent unfortunately proves nothing."

"I thought China was anti-GM?" Bryan asked.

"Generally they are, but what protesters say and do isn't always reflective of what's happening in the fields and markets. Chinese anti-GM activists claim they're being patriotic by preventing the US from controlling China's food supply through American-owned biotech companies like Dusanti and Monsanto. The irony is that China already uses plenty of genetically modified products. More than seventy percent of its cotton is GM. And most of the soybeans consumed in China are genetically modified imports, often from America."

"What does this have to do with Philomena?" Bryan asked.

"In 2009 China granted safety certificates for two GM varieties of rice and one of maize, putting it on track to become the first country in the world to use GM technology in the production of main staples. Lung and his subsidiaries stand to gain the most if these two varieties succeed."

"So a rich guy gets richer," Bryan said.

"It's more than just getting rich. It's about controlling the world by controlling its food production."

"Dusanti is one of Lung's subsidiaries, isn't it?" The connection suddenly dawned on Corvina.

"Yes. We believe Lung sponsored the development and spread of Philomena."

"But why target the wine industry?" Corvina asked. "Wouldn't it make more sense to attack rice or maize crops to take out the competition once he has his own GM crops to sell?"

"It's not the wine industry that he targeted per se, but the *grape crop*. The fact that grapes make wine as a by-product was inconsequential to Lung, or so Interpol believes."

"A by-product?" Bryan asked.

"How can you say that wine is inconsequential?" Corvina asked.

"To Lung, not to me." Claude held up his hands. "The industry has succumbed to phylloxera in the past, so for it to happen again in a globalized world wouldn't raise alarm to the same extent as if, say, wheat or corn crops were attacked."

"But it's not the same. This phylloxera was *created*," Corvina protested.

"To the outside observer it would be the same. As you know, many in the industry have long believed it was just a matter of time before phylloxera struck again. Destroying vineyards is newsworthy, but it's not a market stopper. Compared to crops such as wheat, rice, soybeans, and corn, wine isn't essential to global food security and human welfare. A shortage, indeed a drought, may impact winemakers and the wine industry, but no one will die of thirst without wine."

"What are you saying?" Corvina asked.

"Interpol believes that targeting grapes was just a trial run for Lung. He wanted to determine the best way to spread the aphid and watch how producers, industry players, and governments reacted and responded."

"A trial run? The destruction of the global wine industry was just a test?" Bryan asked.

"That's our current theory."

"So grapes were only the beginning?"

"Exactly. It was the first step in a global war on the food industry."

"But North American companies were involved."

"Yes, Lung played on their motivations and manipulated them. We believe they never knew what the endgame was. Slater was driven by idealism. Dusanti was driven by profits and the opportunity to patent and sell the only way to stop Philomena. Harvey, Vicente, and Sergio at Universal Wines were motivated to eliminate their competition and become the global powerhouse in wine production and distribution."

"That's a lot to process," Corvina said.

"Don't worry, I'll help," Malcolm said. "It's going to make a great story."

"I'll do what I can to help too," Bryan said. He took her hand in his and squeezed. She squeezed back.

"Is Alison out of the hospital yet?" Corvina asked Claude.

"She was discharged yesterday. She's taking leave for a couple of weeks. She'll recover from her concussion, but I don't think her career will."

"Will Secretary General Arsenault promote you into her position?" Corvina asked.

"He already has. Alison has been reassigned to take on my last assignment, Operation EuroHaz. She'll be handling garbage for the foreseeable future. I almost forgot to mention, Jacob sends his regards from Missouri, where he's been coordinating the distribution of the neurotoxin now being produced by Dusanti. He's been shipping and sharing the neurotoxin with anyone and everyone in true open-source spirit. He's becoming a bit of a legend."

"He probably feels guilty about inadvertently helping Slater. Any idea when Sergio will stand trial?" Corvina asked.

"Soon," Claude said. "The only question is where. A lot of countries want Sergio, Harvey, and Vicente on a spike. Universal Wines and Dusanti are also coming under heavy criticism. Since the two companies' involvement came to light, their stocks have plummeted and their employees are leaving in droves. It looks like Interpol will have to find a way to repay you two."

"I think your president giving us the reward money in Lyon for stopping Philomena was reward enough," Bryan said.

"True. *Now* we can celebrate. Too bad we don't have anything to make a toast with," Corvina said, and looked around.

"Are you sure about that?" Bryan jogged over to their rental car and returned with a bottle of wine in a plastic bottle carrier. It was the Château Petit-Village 1990 Marielle had given them in Pomerol. He cut off the foil and twisted out the cork with a wine opener he kept with the bottle.

"I'll grab some glasses from the winery," Malcolm said, and ran inside.

"I have to ask," Corvina said. "Why do you keep the cork each time a bottle of wine is opened?"

"You noticed that?" Bryan asked, embarrassed.

"I saw you do it in Santiago, DC, Hong Kong, and Veuve Clicquot's cellar."

Bryan held up the cork. "I like to believe there's a story in every bottle of wine, and every time a new bottle is opened it marks an occasion. For me, the cork is like a bookmark, marking the place in the story where the wine was opened and what was happening in my life, who I was with, and what I was doing. I have a cork for virtually every milestone in my life and career." He passed the cork with the château's name on it to Corvina. "Why don't you keep this one? It marks an important moment in your life."

"*Gracias*. And thank you for saving the wine," Corvina said. She studied the cork and admired the bottle's label.

"I wouldn't dream of leaving it. It was a gift to *us*," Bryan said, and poured wine into the four glasses Malcolm had returned with. "Unfortunately, the bottle opener Marielle gave us is still in an Interpol evidence locker."

Bryan raised his glass in a toast. "Cheers to a perfect finish."

"*Santé*," Claude said.

"*Cin Cin*," Corvina said.

"Bottom's up," Malcolm said.

"I've been meaning to thank you properly," Corvina said to Bryan after her first taste of the wine. She looked at Claude, who smiled warmly and walked back with Malcolm to the winery, leaving her and Bryan alone.

"Thank me for what?" Bryan asked.

"For helping me this past month. I'm usually the person other people call when they need help. I don't usually ask for it myself. I couldn't have stopped Philomena without you."

"We made a good team." He reached out and squeezed her shoulder.

"So, what's next?" Corvina asked. She looked hard into his eyes.

"I have the hardest exam in the world coming up, and I could use some help studying. How about you?"

"I have a winery to purchase and another to help rebuild with my father. And I could use some help too," she said, and smiled. She was thinking of how much she was looking forward to doing both. She took Bryan's hand and led him between a row of vines. It was time to let go of her past and focus on the endless possibility of her future. She looked out over the vineyard's bright-green leaves and basked in the sunshine's warmth.

It all begins in the vineyard.

Le Fin

ACKNOWLEDGEMENTS

Like a great vintage wine, it takes a dedicated team and a lot of support to bring a story like Root Cause to fruition. For this reason, I am eternally grateful to the following individuals for helping me along the way and in bringing Root Cause from nascent idea to full-fledged novel:

Tor Laine, my sister, for reading and commenting on every page I ever wrote and never once complaining.

Joel Peterson, head winemaker at Ravenswood Wines in Sonoma Valley, California, who led me to read *The Botanist and the Vintner: How Wine was Saved for the World,* which inspired me to write Root Cause. Cheers to the Godfather of Zin! No wimpy wines!

Steven Chudney, my literary agent at the Chudney Agency in New York, who saw the potential in Root Cause from the beginning and stuck with it even when all seemed lost.

David Groff, editor extraordinaire who was able to grok well with the original manuscript and helped improve the story immeasurably. No wimpy writing!

Stephanie Beard, Acquiring Editor at Turner Publishing for taking a chance on a thriller whose primary antagonist is a bug.

Heather Howell, Project Manager at Turner who shepherded the book through every stage of development and put up with all my tweaking and amendments.

Maddie Cothren, Creative Director at Turner who stabilized and clarified the cover and design to intrigue bibliophiles and oenophiles the world over.

Lindsey Johnson, Marketing Director at Turner who spearheaded my online presence and got the word out from an early stage.

Kelsey Butts, my publicist at Book Publicity Services in California for spreading the word about Root Cause further than even Phylloxera spread and driving awareness of the novel.

Alexandra Andrews at Tony Robbins for keeping me calm, energized, and in control though an incredibly busy time.

Wolfgang Bendl for having an unerring sense of what works in a story and who's reader advice I followed 99% of the time.

Emma Safavi, the first sommelier to read an early draft and provided great insight to enhance the story.

Oscar Wendel, a fellow aspiring writer, for reading and critiquing an early draft.

Jumi Lee who built her own business while I built castles in the sky yet supported me nonetheless and read the entire manuscript on the bus home each night on her mobile. Kudos!

Sandy Tan, fellow French Wine Scholar and wine lover, for offering great tips to tighten the wine references and never commenting when I brought the equivalent of a knife to a gunfight to her wine dinners.

Doug Harding for bringing Root Cause and I to life in video.

Edward Harvey, and Paul Beavis at Lanson Champagne for introducing me to the Champagne Academy.

Anthony Stewart-Moore, my GM in London, for indulging my passion for wines and ambitious career pursuits. I wouldn't be who or where I am today without him.

And to all the vignerons, winemakers, wine scholars, sellers, distributors, and wine lovers who make this the most passionate industry in the world and without whom the world would be a less cheerful place—cheers to a world full of wine!

Any notable flaws and imperfections are my own.

Cin Cin!

Steven Laine

Singapore, November 2018

ABOUT THE AUTHOR

Steven Laine is from Ontario, Canada and has dual Canadian and British citizenship. He has travelled the world working in luxury hotels for international brands including The Ritz, Hilton, Starwood, Marriott, Jumeirah and Pan Pacific. When he was Beverage Manager of a five star hotel in London, he learned all about wine and has since visited over one hundred vineyards and wineries in Napa, Sonoma, Burgundy, Bordeaux, Champagne, Spain, Portugal, Germany, Switzerland, Niagara, Lebanon, Chile, South Africa and Australia. As the only North American ever invited to be a Member of the Champagne Academy, he had the privilege to visit and learn all about Champagne at the major Champagne Houses in France. His circle of friends is made up of winemakers, Masters of Wine, Master Sommeliers, restaurant managers, and wine distributors from all over the globe. He is now working on his next novel and his Wine & Spirits Diploma.